AX & SPADE

A THRILLER

Kurt B. Dowdle

Black Feather Press
New Lebanon, New York

Kurt B. Dowdle/Black Feather Press
110 Darrow Road
New Lebanon, New York/12125

Cover Design 2014 Sarah Howard

Ax & Spade/Kurt B. Dowdle. -- 1st ed.
ISBN 978-0692297056

Author's Note

This work is fiction. Even though some of the incidents
portrayed in the story can be found in the history of
Bethlehem, Pennsylvania, they have been altered for the
purpose of telling the story. Despite a resemblance to
actual events and persons, the characters and incidents
in the story are creations of the author's imagination. As
such, the book should be read entirely as a work of fiction, not as an interpretation of history.

We will now discuss in a little more detail the struggle for existence.

—— Charles Darwin, *On the Origin of Species* (1859)

1

Kamp walked out of the slaughterhouse, wiping the blood from his hands and forearms with icy brine from the barrel and drying them on his apron. He surveyed the land downhill from his small farm. He focused on the tree line that stood between his property and the road. Kamp could only see the road here and there, and he made out the shapes of two people, one shouting and chasing the other.

The commotion pulled Kamp from a reverie in which he'd been musing on a fragment of a poem he heard as a boy, a particular line. He often went somewhere like that in order to stave off ruminating on whether madness had overtaken him or if it were merely approaching. But one distraction being just as salutary as another, he fixed his attention on what might have been a man's voice in the distance and coming closer. Kamp also thought it permissible to listen because he had just finished putting the last parts of the butchered pig in a barrel. If he'd heard the shouts even thirty seconds prior, he would not have paid attention, as doing so would have taken him from his butchery and thus spoiled not only so much hard labor on his part but also the supreme sacrifice of the pig. Kamp thought it best to finish all important matters, once started.

"Come back here!"

He could tell the man doing the shouting was also doing the chasing. Additionally, he determined that the man who was running away was not inclined to stop on the basis of the first man's entreaties. And yet, the shouting continued.

"Stop, you son of a bitch! STOP!"

He saw that the man in the lead made the turn up the path toward Kamp's farm, and he also noticed that the man behind him wore a uniform of some kind. The first man started to pull farther ahead, barreling straight for him, though Kamp realized that the man did not seem to notice him. He watched the man in the uniform slow his run and raise a pistol.

Kamp gently picked up a spade shovel leaning against the side of the slaughterhouse. The first man, still running full speed, head down, approached him. By this point, Kamp had cocked the spade back, and swung it hard, connecting squarely with the man's gut. The man doubled over and spun to the ground, gasping hard and clutching his stomach.

Kamp said, "Just stay there once."

The man grunted, "*Ach,* you didn't have to hit me," and he sat up.

By this point the second man reached them, also out of breath and gasping, gun back in the holster. He saw that the man indeed wore a uniform of brown wool, bearing the insignia of the Lehigh Valley Railroad, badge askew. The trio of figures regarded each other for a moment, the perpetrator gazing up at the railroad detective, the railroad detective staring back at him hard and Kamp looking at the detective and then at the man on the ground. The moment ended when the detective gave the man on the ground a sharp kick to the leg.

"Hey!"

"Hey, yourself."

With that, the detective straightened up, righted his badge and leveled his gaze at Kamp.

"He lit a fire on the train. On the train! You just wouldn't believe it!"

The man on the ground said, "It was cold this morning. And that boxcar was empty."

"You shut up!"

"It didn't hurt nobody. And I was cold!"

The train detective said, "It ain't cold in August!" As he said it, he kicked the man in the ribs.

Kamp set the shovel against the side of the building and turned to go back into the slaughterhouse.

The detective called after him, "Hey, Kamp."

"Yah."

"The train is stopped. They're waiting for me."

"Then go back."

"Ach, I will. But someone must take this, this fiend to the police."

Kamp turned back around. "John, I don't really know what this man did, or why."

The man on the ground said, "That's true! He don't!"

The detective persisted, "I'll see to it you get fair compensation from the railroad."

"That's not my point."

"Ach, I know. Just do this for me, and I'll settle it up with you later."

Kamp glanced up to a window on the second floor of his house, where he knew that by now, she'd be watching. And she was. He looked back to the men and took off his bloodstained apron.

"I'll walk him to the police station."

The train detective breathed a sigh and grabbed the man on the ground roughly under his arm and hauled him to his feet. He pulled handcuffs from his belt.

Kamp said, "He doesn't need those."

"Oh, yes, he does."

"Leave them *off*."

"Ach, you don't *know* this man."

"Then take him yourself."

"Christ! Well, at least take this." The train detective pushed his pistol toward Kamp, who shook his head.

"God*dammit*! He's a fiend. Ach, he is!"

Kamp looked at the man, now standing and said, "Maybe."

Since it was still morning, Kamp thought he could get the man to town and be back before sundown. He let the man walk slightly ahead of him, and they turned onto the road that ran past the farm. Having taken the man's measure, he felt certain that the man posed no threat. Kamp noticed the man's rough, dirty hands, plain clothing, black hair and sturdy boots. The man had broad shoulders and hollow cheeks. He reminded Kamp of a stray dog, tough but scared. The man turned out to be much more talkative than Kamp preferred. Immediately upon commencing their walk, the man began asking questions.

"If you wouldn't let him put the manacles on me, why not just let me go? How do you know I'm not just going to run away? How do you know the train detective? Who was that lady in the window? Was that your wife up there in the window?"

Kamp thought it best in these kinds of situations to allow the sounds to pass through his ears and let them not mean anything. He'd taught himself this ability a long time ago out of dire necessity and found that he could do it now almost without effort.

The man said, "You're not going to say *anything*?"

Kamp had already traveled a great distance in his mind from the conversation and from the situation. In an instant, he could snap back into the scene and take any action necessary, but the other man's words drifted into the background, miles away. Kamp preferred to slip into the rhythm of walking, to listen only at first to the sound of his footfalls. He let other sensations fill his consciousness, the greens and yellows of the leaves, the feel of the sun's rays on his face. He looked straight ahead as he walked, but as he allowed his senses to flood, his sight turned inward. Radiant pictures, scenes from the past and from imagination played behind his eyes. The separation between what he felt and saw and understood began to vanish.

"Hey, do you hear a word I'm saying? How come we're walking instead of taking a carriage? My feet are tired. Let's hitch a ride. Hey, are you listening at all?"

Kamp moved back into the scene.

"What?"

"I said, are you listening?"

Kamp took in a breath through his nostrils. "No."

The man stopped walking and blocked Kamp's way. He was the same height as Kamp, and now he stared straight at him. Kamp studied the man's face, which shifted from jocularity to agitation in a flicker. He saw the man's body tensing and his hands curling into fists. He stepped around him and began walking again.

"Hey! Hey! What's your name, anyway?" the man shouted after him. Kamp heard the man running up behind him and then in front of him, blocking his path.

He jabbed a finger in Kamp's chest. "What's to keep me from running away? Tell me. Tell me!"

Kamp said, "*Nix.*"

"All right then, I'm goin'. Just tell me one thing. One thing before I go."

Kamp waited for the question.

"What did you hit me for? I didn't do nussing to you. *Nussing*! And you walloped me with that *shpawd*. If you hadn'ta done that, neither of us would hafta be here right now."

"That's true."

"So then what did you hit me for?"

Kamp tilted his head back and looked at the clouds. "Well, John Heist isn't much of a runner, and he probably isn't much of a train detective, either. But he's a good shot."

"So?"

"If I hadn't knocked you down, you'd be dead." Kamp started walking again, and the man followed.

"Well, none of this is right. None of it. You know why I was on that train? You wanna know?"

Kamp kept walking ahead of the man.

"I was on the train, so I could go to the druggist in town and get medicine for my brother. My kid brother. Lawrence. He got hurt bad in the mines. Can't walk. Can't even think straight. The pain is terrible. Only thing he needs now is medicine."

He heard rage in the man's voice. "Where are your parents?"

"Nowhere."

Kamp said, "Tell them to get the medicine."

"They're dead, all right?"

"Where are you from?"

"Easton. Say, now that you know where I come from and where I was going and all this shit about me, how about you let me go? Forget about this."

"No."

"What do you want to do their work for? Ach, this ain't your problem. This ain't about you at all."

He heard the anger in the man's voice turning to exasperation. "What kind of medicine?"

"What?"

"For your brother. What kind of medicine?"

The man hung his head and spit on the ground. "Ach, it don't matter."

The town came into plain view under the thin afternoon sunlight as they crested the hill that overlooked Bethlehem. Kamp noticed the crisscrossing streets and the neat rows of buildings that lined them. He saw smoke rising from chimneys, drifty columns of black and grey that floated up and then diffused. It occurred to him that a man might consider the town's geometric patterns to be beautiful, as long as he could forget the rank brutalities, perversions and all the other new world syndromes that forced it into being.

Kamp walked into town with the man following. He called back over his shoulder, "What's your name?"

The man said, "What do you care?"

2

"His name is Knecht," the High Constable said. "Daniel Knecht. Oh, we know each other, don't we, Danny?"

Kamp and Daniel Knecht stood in front of the desk of the High Constable Samuel Druckenmiller, who sat comfortably, hands folded across his wide belly and looking up at the two men.

Knecht said, "I didn't do *nussing* wrong, constable."

"Of course you didn't, Daniel. Of course you didn't."

Kamp said, "Heist found him."

Druckenmiller said something in response, but Kamp wasn't listening. A war had erupted in his mind, a war between a million phantasms, ghouls and angels with sharp claws that meant to shred each other. He tilted his head back and let the grisly scene play out.

"...and anyway we don't want him here, Kamp. Kamp?"

Druckenmiller snapped his fingers twice, and he clicked back into the scene.

Kamp said, "That's between you and Heist." He tried to stand still as a demon soared in front of his mind's eye. On these occasions, he'd taught himself not to duck.

Druckenmiller shifted in his chair and pursed his lips. He studied Knecht for a moment, then stood up and took Knecht by the arm.

Knecht yelped, "Ach, *no*, constable!" Druckenmiller led him to a cell with iron bars at the back of the room. The war scene behind his eyes assumed the form of a great tornado, swirling upward and vanishing in an instant. Kamp put his hand on the corner of Druckenmiller's desk and let out a deep breath.

Druckenmiller walked back and sat down heavily. "You okay?"

"Yah, yah. Sure."

"Listen, we don't want this guy. He's trouble. He belongs in Easton."

"He doesn't seem all bad, Sam."

"He ain't all good, neither. Fighting, theft. What's he here for, anyhow?

"Heist said he started a fire on a train."

"Oh, for Pete's sake." Druckenmiller opened a desk drawer and pulled out a whiskey bottle and two shot glasses. He poured two shots and slid one across the desk to Kamp.

Druckenmiller held up the glass said, "To law and order," and they downed the whiskey. For the first time in months, Kamp felt his mind slow down. The last of the demons departed the battlefield. Druckenmiller immediately poured two more shots.

Kamp said, "I need to go."

"Ach, *where?*" The High Constable's face twisted in disgust.

"Druggist."

"What for?"

"Knecht told me he was on his way there to get medicine for his brother. He can't do that if he's locked up in here."

Druckenmiller cocked his head to the side and raised his eyebrows. "What kind of medicine?"

Knecht said, "Morphine."

Druckenmiller downed another shot and said, "You aim to buy morphine for a criminal? For a drug fiend?"

"I'll buy it and bring it back here. When he gets out, you can give it to him."

"You must be shittin' me. You can't tell me you believe he's gonna give that medicine to his poor, dying brother. Jesus Christ!"

Kamp turned and walked to the door.

Druckenmiller called after him, "You're still going with us to the hunting camp, say not?" He tossed back both shots.

"What?"

"The hunt. Saturday. You're going."

Kamp called over his shoulder, "Yah, yah. I'm going," and he closed the door behind him. He left the constable's office believing there was probably something wrong with him besides melancholia. He looked across the town to the stacks of Native Iron and was hit by a bolt of sadness so powerful he nearly crumpled to the ground, all torn down and broken. The drink must have triggered it, he thought, but from what height or, more likely, from what profound depth had it been loosed? And who had thrown it? He rubbed his left temple, took a breath, and walked to the storefront across the street.

The sign over the door read, "Pure Drugs & Chemicals, E. Wyles, Druggist," and when he entered the store, Kamp stepped into a box whose walls were lined with row upon row of transparent bottles, shop rounds with gilded labels and black lettering. Some bottles held powder, some liquid while others contained plant or animal matter. Square in the center of the room, behind a counter stood the druggist herself, E. Wyles. She wore a white dress, her long hair pulled back from her face. She

stood facing him directly, hands on the glass countertop.
He removed his hat.

"*Wie bischt*, Emma?"

"Good, good. How are you, Kamp?"

"Oh, you know."

Wyles said, "How's she doing?"

"She's good."

"How much longer?"

"Three months."

"You take good care of her."

"You too. Say, Emma. I need a favor once." Wyles
straightened up and pulled back her shoulders.

"Morphine."

Wyles studied his face. "No."

"Emma, it's not for me."

"Anything else I can help you with?"

Kamp felt a spark at the base of his skull, sensed the
kindling start to smolder and then the first tiny flames of
rage. He spoke slowly, "I said, it's not for me."

Wyles eyed Kamp. "Then who's it for?"

He fought back an eruption of anger that he knew
would derail the process. Prone as he'd become to fits of
pique, he preferred to interact with people he knew
well, people who understood his patterns, contours and
boundaries, who knew when to give way and when not
to give an inch. Such was the case with E. Wyles.

Kamp said, "It's for someone who needs it. I don't know the man, exactly. Story's already too long to tell."

Wyles stiffened. "No."

He gripped his hat in his right hand hard enough to squeeze the blood from his knuckles.

"You know you can't just saunter in here and ask for something like that."

"I told you twice already. It's not for me. It's to help someone else."

Wyles stared at him for another moment. "On one condition," she said.

"What's that?"

"You must go see the Judge. Today."

He slammed his fist on the edge of the counter. "Goddammit, Emma!"

"He said he needs to talk to you."

Wyles pulled a key from a drawer, turned and walked to the back of the room. He noticed that her hair was done in a single long braid that reached nearly to her waist. Her hair was black except for a few wavy, gray strands. A feather was affixed near the bottom of the braid. Wyles unlocked a cabinet, removed a few items and walked back to him. On the counter, she placed a syringe and a small vial.

"There you go."

Wyles put the vial and the syringe in a paper bag, folded the top and handed it to him.

"What do I owe you?"

"Nothing."

"Tell me what it costs."

"Since it's not for you, tell whoever it's for to come and pay for it."

Kamp shook his head. "Jesus Christ, Emma. You'll never change."

As he made his way from the drugstore to the town hall, it occurred to him that had he not just finished butchering a pig and stepped out of the slaughterhouse, he wouldn't have seen Daniel Knecht running up the road, nor would he have seen Detective John Heist raise his pistol. If he hadn't seen that, he wouldn't have cracked Knecht with a *shpawd*, wouldn't have had to walk to Bethlehem, to talk to the High Constable John Druckenmiller or to the Druggist, E. Wyles. Kamp saw a long iron chain of contingencies reaching straight from a butchered hog to the door of the Big Judge.

The door itself bore a brass sign at eye level that read "Strictly No Admittance." Kamp turned the doorknob and went straight in without knocking. The Judge sat where he'd been the last time Kamp saw him, sitting in the exact same position. Blended tobacco smoke twisted slowly from the Judge's pipe made of briar wood, held in the man's right hand. The Judge sat looking out the window through wooden blinds, the last orange rays of afternoon slanting down to the Persian rug, itself an explosion of geometric shapes and patterns working outward from a single triangle within a circle. His black court robes hung on the wall. The Judge spoke without changing his position or even looking at him.

"Wendell, Wendell. Good to see you. Close the door."

"What do you need, Judge?"

"Need? Nothing." The Judge took a long pull on his pipe and exhaled slowly. "The problem is that we already don't *need* anything. We're suffering from the need of need." Everything Tate Cain said sounded like a pronouncement and a last word, as if emanating from the void and then returning to it.

Kamp shifted impatiently. "You just wanted to say hello then?"

"Why the bad mood, Wendell? Long day?" The Judge turned to face him.

Tate Cain wore a Victorian dress the color of sapphire and a full gray beard that flowed over the ornate collar fashioned out of white lace. Atop the beard sat a wide, wide triangular nose and above that, two eyes that always seemed to him to be lit by blue flame. Beneath the dress, Kamp saw that the Judge was wearing black leather lace-up boots, also in the Victorian style.

Growing up, he'd often seen the Judge dressed in women's clothing, so while he knew it wasn't the norm and that it shouldn't be mentioned in public, he also accepted it without needing to analyze. Besides, Kamp had an aunt and uncle who were twins. No, the Judge's dress didn't faze him, although a number of other things about him did. For as long as he could remember, Tate Cain always held all the cards.

"There is only one need, Wendell."

Kamp sighed, realizing that he'd walked into yet another elliptical, obtuse, one-way dialogue with the Judge.

"What's that, Judge?"

"While you were at the university, did you study the writings of this man, Charles Darwin?"

"Yes, I did."

"What did you learn about him?"

"What do you want, Judge?"

"Wendell, what did you learn about Darwin?"

"When he was a child, he liked to collect beetles."

The Judge looked back out the window, refilled his pipe, struck a match, and lit it. "Yes, the child mind. I understand young Charles didn't want to be a physician, didn't care to be respectable. And if he wouldn't become a physician, his father wanted him to be a religious, an Anglican priest. And he tried, he tried. But it wasn't in Darwin's nature. When he sought, he found something he didn't need. He didn't need faith. In the process he found the secret, Wendell, he found what everyone, what every living thing needs. What you need."

"I need to leave."

The Judge took a deep pull on the pipe. Smoke cascaded from his mouth as he spoke.

"Your father wanted you to be a physician, too, as I recall. He wanted you to be respectable, wanted something more for you than a life spent with your lungs packed with coal dust or up to your elbows in pig guts. But you didn't want to be a physician, either. You wanted something different, always something different."

"What's that?"

"You wanted to see for yourself, naturally, to know, to understand. That's what you wanted. But that's not what you need. What you need is the same as what everyone else needs. You don't need what's in that bag, though at times, you think you do. No, what you need is simply to survive. To survive. And you need your child to survive."

"What's your point, Judge?" In these moments, Kamp always felt as if he were caught in a vortex, swirling down.

"You need to make a living. The world is evolving, Wendell. Look around. Look out the window. Everything is changing. You must change with it, in spite of the past, in spite of yourself. Your family will need more from you than you can provide butchering hogs or chopping firewood, especially with winter coming. You have a fine mind and a great strength within you, Wendell. I can put it to good use."

Kamp stared at the patterns in the rug.

"Now just listen, Wendell. The police need—"

"The police?"

"Well, the city needs someone like you, someone with your powers of observation not to mention your physical skills and your ability with a gun. They need a detective. Even better, a war hero detective. I'm seeing to it that they hire one."

"What do you think needs detecting?"

"See for yourself, Wendell. Wrongdoers. The criminal element. That roustabout you brought into the station isn't what I mean, either. I'm talking about serious malefactors, real villains. The parasites evolve right along with the beasts of the field. The more this town grows, the more of them there will be. I want you to investigate the crimes, collect the facts, make the connections and help bring the wrongdoers to justice. I want you to be a police detective, Wendell."

"Christ, no."

"You'll be paid a good wage, you won't need to wear any kind of uniform."

"Get someone else."

"You can do the job whatever way you please. You won't be chained to another man's timetable. You won't have to answer to anyone."

"Except you."

"You'll investigate crimes and report your findings to the prosecutor. I won't be involved until the prosecutor makes his case in my courtroom. You won't owe me anything for giving you the opportunity."

"Sure, sure."

The Judge placed his pipe in an ashtray and folded his hands across his belly. As usual, Kamp thought, the Judge knew all the details, all the angles and exactly where to apply the pressure. The Judge even held the deed to his farm.

He rubbed his right temple. The Judge opened a drawer, took out a sheet of paper and slid it across the desk toward Kamp.

"This is a contract. Sign it, and you can start working."

"No, thanks."

The Judge took the paper back, folded it neatly and placed it in an envelope. He stood up to his full height, six foot three, six five with the heels. He handed the envelope to Kamp.

"Think about it, and let me know if there's anything else you need."

Kamp put on his hat, picked up the envelope and walked out the door. He stepped out of the building into the fading light and heard the heavy click-clack of train wheels on their rails. Kamp saw the smoke billowing from the stacks of the ironworks. Indeed, he thought, there had already been great changes to the town, an evolution barely begun. He took the morphine back to the police station and made Druckenmiller promise that he'd give it to Knecht upon his release. He further instructed the High Constable to make sure that Knecht paid the Druggist, E. Wyles in full. After calling him a "damn fool" and a "nitwit," Druckenmiller shoved the morphine back in Kamp's hand. He walked out of town that day with a heavier burden but a clearer conscience.

And as for the Judge's comment that he was a war hero, he realized that although many people saw him that way, he himself had long since dispensed with the idea that anything he'd ever done rose to the level of heroism. He pondered the new complexities introduced into his life by his visit to town, then let it all go. He savored the fact that, for the moment, the warring factions in his mind had ceased hostilities. Kamp walked the miles back to his home and as the daylight gave out, he watched each star flicker into view, at first faintly, then brighter, and just before slipping footfall after footfall into bliss delirium, he wished that life meant more than bare survival.

He walked with the stars above and the dirt road under his feet, and his thoughts returned. He thought about how little he'd needed until now, how when he'd been in the war, he'd needed almost nothing. But now, Kamp knew he'd need more. He had no money in the bank and little stored away in barns. He still didn't believe he needed a job. He knew a job would be nothing more than a way to forestall something inevitable, though he could not imagine what. As he rounded the last bend toward home, he saw a candle burning in a downstairs window and another one upstairs. He thought she would have been asleep by now.

Bounding up the front steps, he noticed that the candle in the front window had melted down so far that the wick floated in a red puddle of wax, most of which had already dripped off the sill to the floor. He ran up the stairs and found her in bed with the blankets in a heap next to her. She thrashed from side to side. Kamp went to her and took her by the shoulders to calm her.

He said, "I'm sorry, I'm sorry I wasn't here." Her nightgown was soaked through with perspiration, her long, straight hair matted to her forehead and cheeks. She was gasping for breath, though the fever had broken.

"It was a nightmare." She gasped for air between the words. "I had a nightmare about you."

He cradled her the way he'd been held on the battle-field when they thought he was finished.

She twisted her head to look up at him and said, "Don't let them do it."

"I won't."

He felt her body go rigid. She said, "No, don't let them do it to *you!*"

It wasn't uncommon for her to suffer fevers as well as troubling dreams and visions. But they unnerved him all the same. And now that she was carrying their child, he feared for them both, and for himself. When he pulled her against him, he felt forces mustering in him and resolving into devotion. He cradled her for a long time, until he felt the tension drain from her body and saw the steady beats of her heart entrain with the lights of the last fireflies of summer.

Kamp didn't sleep. He sat in a chair by their bed, watching the rise and fall of her breathing and letting moments from the day float in his mind. The mass of sensory information in his memory swirled together and then straightened out in a sequence that he could sift through and examine in the quiet darkness, and on the basis of his examination determine how he felt about each matter and possibly make a decision or two about how to proceed. For instance, he retraced the chain of events that carried him from his farm to Bethlehem and back again. In the night calm, he questioned why he'd seized upon the notion of getting medicine for the brother of the dope fiend Knecht. He also questioned why he'd gone to see the Judge, why the Judge wanted him to be a detective and why he'd immediately rejected the notion. And beyond that, he wondered what force impelled him to keep asking these kinds of questions, night after night, instead of sleeping.

Kamp let the words of all the questions form a sphere before his mind's eye. The sphere spun faster and faster until the questions blurred together and produced lights of intense color. Eventually, the sphere began to slow down, the colors fading away and the black letters of the words coming back into plain view. By the time it stopped, he could clearly see that the questions had been replaced by answers, each one sufficient. He didn't re-member having to do this as a child but neither did he remember his life having been this complex.

3

He heard dawn in the murmuring of birds. She wasn't moving, apart from the easy rise and fall of her chest. Sound asleep. Kamp knew if he wanted to hop the train, he'd need to hurry. He hustled down the stairs and into the kitchen, where he pulled on his boots and sailed out the back door. He grabbed two eggs from the henhouse, cracking the first one, tilting his head back, and dropping the contents into his mouth. Still warm. He did the same with the second egg. He heard the train whistle wail in the far distance and figured he had roughly five minutes to cover the half mile down to the place he liked to catch out. By the time he hit the footpath to the tracks, he heard the click-clack and the screech of the wheels as the train began its curve that would bring it parallel to the road to his farm. In order to get to the tracks, he had to cross Shawnee Creek in

27

the dark. He knew where to step by heart, landing nimbly on each round rock in the creek and hopping to the next one, guided only by the memory stored in his body. Kamp clambered up the bank and onto the gravel by the tracks just as the headlight of the 2-8-0 locomotive came into view. The Black Diamond Unlimited was right on time.

The speed of the train varied depending on the weather, and when the tracks were wet, the train was slow enough that he could trot alongside and climb aboard without much effort. On a morning such as this, clear and dry, the train would surely be moving faster, maybe even eight to ten miles an hour. He let car after car pass, hoppers loaded with coal that glinted above him in the moonlight. The boxcars would follow the hoppers, and Kamp would need a head of steam if he had any chance of making it. The trick was to get into an even stride while making sure not to trip over the railroad ties, and to do that he ran two ties at a time, a feat that required nearly perfect balance and agility. At the same time, he needed to turn to look left at the passing cars. Boxcars began to pass him, and he started his run.

Kamp bounded along the ties, swiveling his head like a sideways metronome, lungs starting to burn. An open car pulled alongside him, and he readied himself. A mistake here would cost everything, though the train took no notice. He looked directly into the blackness in the boxcar and made his leap. In a single motion he caught the iron door latch with both hands and swung his right leg toward the open door in a kind of pirouette. He'd always heard that you're not supposed to let go of the latch until your body is completely inside the car, but he'd done it so many times that he knew precisely where he was and that he'd land on the hard boards inside the car. The momentum of his leap carried him all the way. Upon landing his fingers found cracks in the floor and held them tight so that if the car lurched he wouldn't be thrown out. Guys in the army told him that you're only supposed to hit a rolling boxcar as a last resort, but Kamp figured if you really know how to do something, you can do it as much as you want.

Jonas Bauer surveyed the landscape from where he stood, amid the tall trees in his front yard down to the road, across the creek to the railroad tracks and beyond to land newly cleared for cornfields and even farther than that to the mountains. Since the year before his first daughter was born, sixteen years already, Jonas Bauer had arisen each day to hack and scrape at the bottom of a hole, to chip coal from the earth and cart it to the surface so that it could be hauled away and burned up straightaway. For all those years, Bauer thought, he'd labored for the sake of a hope for a future for his family and for himself. In truth, though, in the stark, silent moments down the shaft, a whisper told him the single reason he mined coal was to survive. He and every man and boy alongside him fought to survive the cave-ins and the blowouts, the routine catastrophes that stole limbs from the miners, robbed wives of husbands and threatened to rob Jonas Bauer of his own present and future.

Even in the past week, six men had perished in an explosion with an unknown cause. All Jonas Bauer knew was that one moment he was shoveling loose coal from the floor, and the next he was laid out flat and looking into the blue eyes of his friend Roy Kunkle, already dead. Bauer couldn't see the rest of Kunkle's body and thought it must have been obscured by smoke and coal dust, but he noticed that in fact it was no longer attached to Kunkle's head. Bauer also realized that it wasn't just men killed in the explosion. A boy of twelve was found face-down in the shaft, covered by a thin coal dust shroud. Once Bauer returned fully to his senses, he and the other surviving miners placed the dead as carefully as they could in a coal cart. Bauer knew they'd lost their lives through no fault of their own, no fault of anyone's as far as he could tell. Jonas Bauer carried his friend Roy Kunkle's head out of the mine and handed it to the undertaker, already on the scene.

Bauer had worked back and forth over that moment a thousand times already, the moment immediately preceding the explosion. Bauer reviewed it in his mind again and again to discern whether he could have prevented the blast. And he wanted to memorize every detail so that if the same situation arose again, he would recognize it and clear everyone out before it blew. But Bauer knew there was nothing more to learn and that he'd never find the bottom of it or anything it might have meant. He knew that death's hand was invisible before it struck and that remembering it over and over amounted to nothing more than waves rippling out from the explosion itself.

But on this morning, Jacob Bauer pulled in as much clean cold morning air as his lungs could hold, and he thought not of survival, but of increase. He and his wife had been harvesting green beans, carrots, cabbage and potatoes from the garden beside the house, and his girls were picking apples from the orchard, piece-way up the hill. Not only wouldn't his family freeze this winter, but they'd be well-fed and warm. The firewood was already stacked high in the cellar. And Jonas Bauer had been able to save money, too, a little and a little more each year. Someday, even just a year or two from now, he'd be able to buy his house and the land around it outright. He dreamed of the day he'd go to the courthouse and pay his landlord, the Honorable Tate Cain, in full. And then the judge would hand over the deed and Bauer would be free of one burden, at least. Bauer and his wife Rachel agreed that there was one more way they could make extra money each month. They could take in a boarder. As always, on this particular Sunday morning Jonas Bauer was ready for church before Rachel and the girls. So he went to the shed behind the house and found a block of wood, a can of paint and a brush. Jonas Bauer painted "Room for Rent" on the wood and placed it on the sill of a window in the front of the house.

Kamp sat with his back against the wall of the boxcar with his knees bent, and he watched the countryside pass as the train swayed side to side. He felt awake now, and relaxed. Yesterday's events had floated to the far recesses of his mind, almost as if they'd never happened or had happened to someone else. He did, however, feel a distinct flicker of agitation above his right eye related to the events of the previous day. It bothered him that the train detective John Heist and then the High Constable Samuel Druckenmiller, then the Druggist E. Wyles and finally the Big Judge Tate Cain, all of them thought he was wrong about Daniel Knecht. Not just thought. They *knew* he was wrong. Heist knew Knecht was lying about starting a fire on the train to keep warm, and Druckenmiller knew Knecht was lying about his brother's suffering so that the court would go easy on him and so that he would buy him morphine. And so on. How could they be so sure? And why would they doubt him? If the Judge thought his logic and discernment were incorrect, why would he want him to become a police detective?

It angered Kamp that they knew without knowing, judged without any facts. So, in the tiny hours of the previous night, he'd determined that he would go to Knecht's house himself, find Knecht's brother, to verify the man's plight. He'd even administer the morphine if necessary. Having confirmed the rationale and the plan in his mind, he let the matter drop, and he spent the remainder of the ride to Easton watching grey morning light turn to purple, pink; then gold and listening to the song of the wheels on the tracks.

Easton proper was just as he remembered it, except that it had grown. More trains, canal boats, buildings and people. Relentlessly more. Kamp had last been to Easton on his trip home from the war, and hadn't thought about going there again until now. He already wanted to leave. If Knecht hadn't told him his street address, Kamp might have talked himself into hopping the next train back. But Knecht had said he lived on Ferry Street, a short walk from the train station where he got off. In fact, he could see Ferry Street from where he stood, and he headed off walking past drab, one-story houses and the occasional tenement building. The houses that were numbered counted down the closer he got to the river. Based on Knecht's description of his family's circumstances, he assumed that Knecht's house would reveal itself as the drabbest, the most run-down on the block. And he was wrong.

He found Daniel Knecht's house by a brass "2" affixed to the front door. The property had a low wooden fence around it, unpainted but in good repair. No detritus in the front yard. He walked up and knocked. A girl, eight or nine years old, opened the door. She wore a plain gray dress, and her hair was pulled straight back and tied with a pink ribbon.

Kamp said, "May I speak with your parents?"

The girl stared at him and said nothing.

"Is your brother here? Lawrence. Is he here? Can I see him?"

The girl furrowed her brow. "Who are you?"

"I need to speak with Lawrence. I have something for him."

"What is it? Show me."

"I'll show it to your brother."

"I'll give it to him."

Kamp pulled in a breath. "I need to give—"

She said, "Whatever you have, he doesn't need it."

"A minute or two, and then I'll leave."

He saw the color rising in the girl's face, and he saw her fists clench.

Kamp persisted, "I want to help your brother Lawrence. Where can I find him?"

"Try the cemetery!" As soon as she said it, the girl's head dropped, and her shoulders began shaking. Large tears splattered on the floorboards. He heard another voice at the back of the house.

"Mercy? Mercy? What's wrong? Is someone there?" A taller girl rushed down the hall. She looked at him, then at the little girl.

She said, "Who the hell are you? What did you do to my sister?" This girl wore the same kind of dress, though she was taller. She put her arm around the girl's shoulder.

"My name is Kamp. I spoke with your brother Daniel yesterday. He asked me to get some medicine for your brother Lawrence."

"Danny. Where is he?"

"I didn't mean to upset your sister. I'm just trying to help."

"Mr. Kamp, would you like to come in?"

He realized he'd walked into a scenario of great complexity compounded by a pattern of grief that stretched across more than a single generation. He followed the girls into the house and into a small sitting room. The younger sister Mercy's sobs had slowed and she sat beside her sister. He sat in a chair facing them.

The older sister started, "My name is Margaret Knecht. This is my sister, Mercy. You said you've already met Danny. And our brother Lawrence died last week. Yesterday was the funeral. Danny wasn't there. We didn't know where he went, but it seems like you do."

"He was on a train. He caused some trouble. The train detective asked me to take him to the police station."

Margaret said, "It's a good thing. No telling what he would have done."

"What do you mean?"

"Don't misunderstand, Mr. Kamp, more than anything he wants things to be good for us."

"How did your parents die?"

"Our father was a steamboat captain. One day the engine exploded. Our mother did what she could after that. She worked in a dress factory, but it wasn't enough." Margaret Knecht looked at her sister whose eyes were still downcast and then at him.

"Sometimes she had to do other things to make money. She died a few years after our father. And then it was up to Danny to take care of us. Once Lawrence was old enough, he went to work in the mines, too. That's how we have this house, from them working. A month ago, Lawrence got hurt. The doctors tried to help him, and we took care of him the best we could. But he just died. It was probably too much for Danny. He didn't go to our mother's funeral either. Was gone for a few weeks then."

Kamp rubbed his left temple. He realized that words could not address the magnitude of their suffering or their fortitude in the face of it.

"Well, girls, I'm very sorry for your loss, and I'm sorry to trouble you today."

Mercy Knecht, who had been silent and only stared up at the floor looked up and said, "At least you tried."

Margaret Knecht said, "Thank you, Mr. Kamp."

"Kamp."

"Thank you." She stood up and walked him to the door.

He trudged back to the train station, carrying the weight of the conversation and all its implications. He saw the faces of the girls in his mind's eye. He imagined the lifetime of trouble they'd already seen, though their lives had just begun. He remembered the desperation and the fury in Danny Knecht's eyes when they walked the road to Bethlehem. And now perhaps he'd glimpsed where the fire started. As he reached the train yard, he saw a passenger train pull in and disgorge its riders, a handful of railroad workers finishing their shift, a few soldiers in uniform. And businessmen. Dozens of businessmen, outfitted in tweed and watch chains, ready to do their part for the plunder.

He recognized new arrivals, too, weary and wide-eyed, clutching suitcases and boxes. A bundle of fresh souls, fodder for the mines and mills. All in all, on one train, he witnessed more than enough people to replace every doomed clan that preceded them.

Kamp knew that meditating on this kind of matter, as he'd started to do during the war and its aftermath, would engulf him soon enough and could bring on an unrelenting storm that could rage in his consciousness for weeks. In moments such as these, he'd learned to direct his thinking to the practical, the immediate and the corporeal. He noticed that he was hungry and bought a loaf of sourdough and a bottle of root beer from a street vendor outside the station. He caught another train out of the yard and headed back up the line. He settled in his empty boxcar for the ride home, unlacing his boots, slipping them off and letting out a long sigh. He tore off a piece of the sourdough and chewed it slowly in order to get all the flavor. He washed it down with a long pull of root beer. As the train swayed side to side, he fell into a rhythm of internal discourse, of clear logic and deduction, beginning, as usual, with questions. Why did Daniel Knecht lie about needing the medicine for his brother? What did Knecht think he'd do once he discovered the lie? How would Daniel Knecht's sisters survive if their brother went to jail? He surmised that all of Daniel Knecht's behavior pointed to a lack of forethought and an abundance of confusion. Knecht had been on the train that day because he was running away from his brother's funeral, only the most recent event in a sad string of occurrences. He made up the story about getting medicine for his brother to garner sympathy. He didn't think he'd be caught in the lie, because it would not have occurred to him that Kamp would go so far as to buy the morphine and then try to deliver it himself. He didn't know whether Knecht intended to buy the morphine and use it himself, though Kamp decided it didn't matter. He considered the mystery solved and his responsibility to Daniel Knecht and his family officially fulfilled.

The train neared the point where he would have to jump. Getting off a moving train could be even more harrowing than getting on. He directed his full attention to the process. The easiest way to bail was also the most painful. It consisted of simply taking a running leap out of the boxcar, making sure to clear the gravel and larger rocks beside the rails. Hitting the rocks meant heavy scratches and bruises, at best. Even if he were to clear the rocks, he could hit any number of hard things upon impact, usually fallen tree boughs. He wanted to avoid crash landings entirely, and over the years he'd devised a way.

The train crossed over Shawnee Creek at one point via an iron trestle. There was a bend in the creek directly beneath the trestle, and at the bend was a waterhole at least a few feet deep year round. When the creek ran higher, the water was easily six feet deep. So the water-hole was deep enough for what he wanted to do, but it wasn't very wide, measuring only a few feet across. Missing the hole even by inches to one side or the other would spell disaster. With the right speed and the right angle, however, Kamp could jump straight from the train and plunge into the waterhole.

Experience taught him that he didn't want to make the walk back from the train soaking wet, so he removed all his clothing first. He tied up everything, including his boots, in the blanket he brought for this purpose. Seconds before the jump, he hurled the bindle out of the car and onto the bank. He took two steps back, then blasted ahead, leaping from the car, clearing the trestle by inches, fully airborne, and sailing naked through the air, an instant of pure freedom. He let out a huge "YEEOWWW!" and then splashed down, hitting nothing but cold water and the bubbles that spun inside it. He bobbed to the surface and luxuriated in the water hole for a few minutes. He ducked back underwater, held his breath and then floated on his back, fully bare to the late summer sunshine. Kamp pushed his chest toward the sky and let all the hurt, misery and trouble wash away, at least for that moment. He hauled himself out of the water and up the bank of the creek. He collected his bindle from deep in the brambles, an exercise in moving with great caution. Kamp put on his clothes and pulled on his boots. He felt new.

He also felt like getting home. He wanted to see if she was feeling better and to tell her about the events of the day. As he turned from the road and onto the path to his farm, Kamp saw a horse tied up to the rail by the house. When he reached his porch, the front door swung open, and there stood the druggist, E. Wyles, who in addition to being an expert apothecary was known as the most capable midwife in the Lehigh Valley. He assumed that it was in this capacity that she visited his home, checking up on her to make certain that there were no problems. The look on E. Wyles' face and her body language, that imperious stance that had confronted him a hundred times since their youth, suggested otherwise. She was effectively barring Kamp from getting in.

E. Wyles said, "If an expectant mother is ill, you must never, ever leave her side until she's better or until there's someone who can provide assistance, such as me."

Oh, Jesus, he thought. Here we go.

She continued, "You don't understand the seriousness of the problem, I don't believe, no. Not if you just took off this morning without saying where you were going or when you'd be back."

Even during moments such as this, he marveled at her certitude and her willingness to share it. He considered it the price of their friendship.

Kamp said, "Well, is she all right, Emma?"

"That's not the point."

"I'd like to see her once and make sure for myself."

Wyles said, "I also got a message from the Judge, and he said—"

"The Judge?"

"Yes, the Judge was here earlier, and he found her on the floor. She had been ill. The Judge gave a message to your neighbor for me to come immediately, which I did."

"What neighbor?"

"Bauer, I believe. Jonas Bauer is the man's name. He did a good deed." Kamp knew of the neighbor, a miner, but he'd never met him.

He said, "Well, fine, but what was the Judge doing here in the first place?"

"She's been having fevers. You know that. Right?"

"Yes."

"And you know that she must rest, in bed, as much as possible. None of this is good for the baby, either. You realize that."

"Christ, Emma, yes! But what was the Judge doing here?"

He pushed past her and into the house.

"Shaw!"

E. Wyles grabbed him hard by the shoulder and hissed, "She's sleeping!"

He felt the fire starting to crackle at the base of his skull and the anger starting to thrum in his chest. He knew if he didn't check his temper immediately, he would lose control. He closed his eyes and watched the demons swoop in. The cosmic battle was joined again. Kamp tried to focus on his breath and counted silently and slowly. Moment by moment, he pushed back the anger until it began to recede on its own. He opened his eyes and looked at E. Wyles.

"Why was the Judge here in the first place?"

"I don't know. He only stayed a few minutes. I assume he was looking for you. He mentioned something about going hunting tomorrow. Believe it or not, he didn't invite me."

"Did he say anything else?"

"He said something about wanting to get a decision. I told him not to hold his breath."

"What else?"

E. Wyles pursed her lips and looked at the ceiling. "Nothing else I recall, though there was a man with him."

"What did he look like?"

"Oh, fairly tall. Your height, thin. Black hair, curly. Kind of scroungy, hungry-looking."

"That's the guy. Daniel Knecht. The guy I told you about who said he needed medicine for his brother."

"The *fiend*?" She cocked an eyebrow when she said it.

"That's him. But what in the hell was he doing here with the Judge?"

"I don't know, and it hardly matters. Shaw requires a few different medicines and remedies, some of which are not cheap. Most of all, she needs *you*. She needs you with her, to be there for her. Focus."

He reached into his pocket and pulled out the vial of morphine and the syringe. "Well, anyway, Knecht's brother won't be needing these. He's dead."

Wyles said, "Then keep the morphine. You never know when someone else might need it, god forbid."

Wyles packed up her medical gear in her satchel and headed for the door.

He said, "What do I owe you for the visit?"

Wyles called back over her shoulder, "Remember everything I told you, and take it to heart. I'll be back tomorrow. For now, she must sleep. Let her sleep."

E. Wyles untied her horse, got into the saddle and rode at a canter down the path. When she got to the road, she kicked with both feet, snapped the reins and galloped away full tilt. He watched her go and then headed up the stairs. He cracked the bedroom door to look in on Shaw, who appeared, in fact, to be asleep. He tiptoed into the room and sat down on the edge of the bed as carefully as he could. Kamp noticed there was a little color in her cheeks and no tension in her forehead. Her face was unblemished, save for the white scar in the shape of a crescent moon above her right eye. He brushed her straight, black hair from her face so that he could see her better and so that she would wake up. Shaw opened her eyes with her dreams still playing behind them.

Kamp said, "You were right. He was lying."

She said, "People lie."

He knew that with all that had happened during the day, he would not sleep. It would be hours before his mind had worked through all the questions he had.

Shaw said, "He was here, you know. That man Knecht. He's troubled. I could tell."

"Yes, I know. He's probably not all bad, though."

Shaw studied his face and said, "No one is."

4

Kamp was still awake when he heard the hunting party coming for him and breaking the sacred silence of the stretch between midnight and dawn. When he first heard them, he'd been thinking about the nature of men and how the way they think and move and interact is akin to a great machine whose parts are all unknown to each other in a conscious sense but magically make the machine move in unison. But whose hand sets men in motion, he wondered, in such a way that their machinations are known only to themselves yet work in concert with the others? Whose hand drives the machine?

The creak of carriage wheels, the yelp of a dog and the clatter of hooves told him that the party was on the road toward his farm. He'd pulled his gear together hours before and set his pack by the door. He checked on Shaw one last time and saw that she was sleeping soundly. He tiptoed back down the stairs, picked up his pack and walked to road, where the hunting party waited. Kamp couldn't see any of the faces of the men, let alone make out who they were. But he knew the voices, some anyway. He made a picture of the scene in his mind, based on a myriad of smells that flooded his nose. Animals, men and gunpowder. Liquor and tobacco. He fought for a moment to hold the picture of this morning, this present scenario, lest these sensations reel him back into the past long gone.

"*Ach*, if you're gonna make us come out all this way, you might as well be ready." That was the High Constable, Sam Druckenmiller. He held the reins of the first carriage.

"Missed you yesterday, Kamp. Didn't think you'd make it." The Big Judge's voice boomed in the dark and silenced the men and animals. "Everything good at home?"

Kamp said, "Morning, Judge."

Druckenmiller said, "If you're weary, we got a bed in the back." He could see the outline of a second team of horses pulling what appeared to be a small boat with a flat bottom. "You can sleep in the punt."

"Good enough." He threw his pack in the boat and climbed in. There was a wool blanket in the bottom of the boat, and he was able to lie down and look up at the dark sky. As soon as he was settled, the hunting party started rolling again.

Druckenmiller called out, "Did you remember to bring a gun this time, Kamp?" There was no reply. "Kamp?"

Nothing. He was already fast asleep.

By the time he roused, the sun blazed, and the party was close to their destination. Kamp sat up in the punt and saw a red cabin and heard the barking of hunting dogs. In addition to Druckenmiller and the Judge, Kamp realized that at least a half a dozen men were assembling at the front steps of the cabin. Kamp only recognized one of them, the Reverend A.R. Eberstark, who appeared to have left his vestments at home. The men were unloading the carriage and unpacking crates of supplies, mostly liquor bottles and bullets. Kamp joined in by grabbing two canvas bags, one filled with ammunition and the other with food. He dropped the bags inside the front room of the cabin, a spare, sturdy A-frame. The downstairs of the cabin was unfurnished except for a few twin beds and a gun rack on the floor that held several Sharps rifles and a few 1gauge shotguns. Everything looked new. When he went back outside, the Judge waved Kamp over to where he stood with a few of the men.

The Judge said, "Kamp, I want you to meet these gentlemen. This is Walker Gray." The man extended his hand.

Walker Gray said, "Pleased to meet you" and shook Kamp's hand.

"Likewise."

Kamp studied the man's features for a moment. Gray had an angular face, red cheeks and a cold stare.

The Judge said, "And this is Joseph Moore." Moore was at least six inches taller than Gray with black hair, a polite smile and a thick scar across his chin. He took Kamp's hand and gave it a good shake.

Moore said, "Good day, sir." He wore a tweed shooting jacket and high leather boots. Moore held a shotgun in one hand, action open, with the barrel resting on his shoulder. Two large dogs, both black in color, sat at either side of him. Kamp recognized them as Barbets, water dogs.

Kamp guessed that both men were forty years old and that both had worked hard to reach whatever station in life they now occupied. And both appeared to Kamp to be hungry for more.

The Judge said, "Gentlemen, this is Wendell Kamp."

Moore said, "The Judge tells me you have an interest in the natural world."

"That's true."

"I do as well."

The Judge said, "In addition to being a captain of industry, Mr. Moore is a world class scientist."

A shot rang out close by. The men swung around to see the Reverend A.R. Eberstark with a pistol in one hand and a whiskey bottle in the other. He pointed the gun in the air and shot it again.

Eberstark screamed, "It's now or never!"

A whoop went up from the men.

Druckenmiller yelled, "Ach, we better get him out in the field before the women get here!"

Walker Gray said, "What will we be hunting for?"

The Judge said, "Christ, anything that tries to get away."

Kamp and Druckenmiller stepped across a meadow of knee-high grass. Kamp hefted a Sharps rifle in both hands, and Druckenmiller nipped whiskey from a silver flask and cradled his rifle in his other arm. Druckenmiller offered the flask to Kamp, who refused. It had been years since he carried a gun and even longer than that since he'd gone hunting. He'd accepted the invitation to go on the trip without thinking it through. It was something he'd wondered about and wished to do as a boy. He'd watched his father and the other men embark on their quest, their wagon train laden with all they'd need. And he'd await their victorious return, wait to catch the first glimpse of his father dirty and tired but triumphant, bringing home the trophies from the hunt. As a boy, Kamp could only imagine the glory.

Now, he wondered why he'd accepted the invitation to go along, and why they'd invited him at all. Kamp surmised that the hunting trip, the ritual of the going there and the shooting and raising hell and all the rest of it, was one of Kamp's last connections to the world he'd inhabited before. To sever this tie would be to abandon a united fraternity. But for him the dreams of glory, the triumph and the trophies—the magic—was gone.

Kamp wondered what power kept it going for the rest of the men, who hit it all with gusto. Kamp heard crack after crack of rifles, an occasional shotgun blast and the delirious barking of hunting dogs.

Druckenmiller picked up on Kamp's mood. "Ach, what did you come for if you was just going to mope around?"

Kamp surveyed the small, clear lake a hundred yards or so ahead and beyond that a low mountain outfitted richly in every autumn color. He breathed a deep sigh. "Who were those men with the Judge? Gray and Moore. Who are they?"

Druckenmiller took another pull on the flask and laughed. "Friends of his, looks like."

"Right, but who are they?"

"Big shots. Money."

They heard a commotion near the edge of the pond, behind a duck blind. A few men carried the punt to the water's edge.

Kamp said, "Where are they from?"

"Oh, one of 'em is from the Iron, and I believe the other is from the railroad. High ups. Way up."

"What about the other men with them?"

The commotion by the lake grew louder. The punt was in the water, and another two men were carrying an extraordinarily large gun toward the boat.

"Druck, who are the guys with them? Do you know them?"

"No, never saw 'em before. Assholes who work for 'em, most likely."

Kamp and Druckenmiller made their way to the edge of the water where the gun had now been mounted on the punt. All the men, including the Judge, Walker Gray and Joseph Moore stood in a semi-circle and marveled at the weapon. The barrel of the massive shotgun measured at least eight feet, the bore more than two inches in diameter. Like a gleaming, sturdy cock, massive and new, Kamp thought.

The Judge said, "It's a vulgar thing, isn't it?" There was a reverent murmur of assent. "It's loaded and ready to go. Who wants the first shot?"

Apart from cannons used in the war, none of the men had ever seen an instrument with this kind of killing strength. To handle it first would be a thrill, to shoot it first an honor. The Big Judge Tate Cain surveyed the faces of the men slowly.

"Let me do it!" the Reverend A.R. Eberstark shouted. His eyes had gone wild from drink, and he surged forward toward the punt before Druckenmiller restrained him. A laugh went up among the men.

A pause followed, and then Joseph Moore said soberly, "I'll have the first shot."

The Judge said, "Hear, hear."

Joseph Moore climbed into the punt, and the Judge shoved the boat from the shore with his boot. Moore took up an oar and began to paddle calmly onto the lake. He headed for a part of the shoreline thick with reeds, while the rest of the men hunkered down behind the blind. Druckenmiller pulled a duck call from his pocket and started working it. Moore flattened himself in the punt and stopped moving. The men behind the blinds sat motionless as the minutes passed. The first duck wheeled across the sky and sailed in, gliding down to a graceful stop on the water. Then two more cruised in, then a half dozen. Soon, there were hundreds. Mallards, redheads, canvasbacks, ring-necked ducks carpeted the surface of the lake. Though the punt floated only a few feet away, the birds ignored it.

The men behind the blind could hardly contain their excitement.

The Reverend A.R. Eberstark blurted, "Praise God!" before the man next to him put his hand roughly over the reverend's mouth.

Joseph Moore raised his head so that he could sight the shot, the motion imperceptible to the ducks. If the punt were to drift to an unfavorable angle, Moore would not have been able to put himself back in position without scaring them off. But with the water so calm and the air so still, the boat sat in its place with the barrel pointed squarely at the mass of birds. Moore's finger curled around the trigger. Kamp thought he saw the man tense in anticipation of the recoil an instant before an extraordinary "*Boom!*"

All the uninjured ducks took flight in an enormous, cacophonous cloud, and a huge cheer went up from the men. The Barbets hit the water and retrieved the first of the slaughtered birds as the Reverend A.R. Eberstark passed the whiskey bottle to celebrate. Joseph Moore grabbed as many dead ducks as he could, then paddled back to shore where he was greeted as a hero. In all, thirty-three ducks were recovered, and everyone agreed that many, many more were obliterated in the blast or were so full of bird shot they sank to the bottom. The men gazed at the pile of dead birds on the shore.

The Reverend A.R. Eberstark said, "We really should bring back the ones we don't eat and give them to the poor" and then immediately forgot he said it.

The next man up, Walker Gray, took his place in the punt while the gun was reloaded, then headed out onto the water where the process repeated itself. For the remainder of the afternoon, the pile of dead birds grew on the shore of the lake as the men squealed with delight. Except for Kamp. The first blast of the punt gun had triggered a series of associations in his mind, each more unpleasant than the previous one. He left the group and found the creek that fed the pond. He followed a trail next to the pond for several miles, far enough so that he couldn't hear the sound of the gun. When darkness fell, Kamp turned around and followed the creek back to the lake and then back to the camp. Probably too late to get home, he thought.

Kamp heard loud laughter and shouting as he stepped onto the porch of the cabin. When he opened the door, he saw men and women in various states of undress. Cigar smoke filled the room, and the whiskey flowed. Druckenmiller sat in a chair in a far corner with a woman on his lap. Both were naked from the waist up.

"Kamp! Where the hell you been? We were worried!" Druckenmiller chased the woman off his lap, stood up and staggered across the room to Kamp. No one else paid attention.

"Kamp...Kamp." Druckenmiller threw his arm around Kamp's shoulders to steady himself.

"Judge tells me you an' me are gonna work together. Says you're gon' be a detective. We'll catch them malefactors an' scalawags. We'll catch 'em together. Jeezis Christ, I'm proud of you."

"The Judge got it wrong."

"Less have a drink an' celebrate."

Kamp said, "Where's the Judge?"

"Who?"

"You seen him? The Judge?"

"Oh, the *Judge!* Yeah, I saw 'im right over here." Druckenmiller led Kamp to a door off the main room of the cabin. He knocked gently, then put his ear to the door. Druckenmiller waited a moment, then turned the knob and slowly turned the knob and opened the door.

The only furniture in the room was a wooden chair and a four-post bed. The Reverend A. R. Eberstark was vigorously thrusting into a young woman bent over with her hands on the bed. The Reverend had a handful of the woman's hair in his left hand and a firm grip on her ass with his right. Both were moaning.

Druckenmiller said, "Pillar of the community," then closed the door. Kamp scanned the downstairs of the cabin and saw another room, the kitchen. Walking closer, he saw the Judge and two other men, Joseph Moore and Walker Gray sitting at a small table, talking. The conversation ended, and the three men stood up and shook hands. Then Moore and Walker left by the back door as Kamp walked into the kitchen.

Kamp said, "How was your meeting?"

The Judge eyed Kamp for a moment. "Excellent. Excellent. Not a meeting, though, as such."

"What was it about?"

"Oh, many things. We talked about the history and geography of the region, the flora and fauna. The origin of classifications. Taxonomies. Latin."

"All that, huh?"

"In addition to being a crack shot, Moore is a first-rate scientist. He knows a great many things as well, primarily regarding geology, ores, metallurgy. That sort of thing. They're both Quakers, too."

"Quakers."

The Judge said, "Was there something you wanted to speak with me about?"

"That's what I was going to ask you."

"Have a seat, Wendell."

Kamp sat down across the table from the Judge, who untied a tobacco pouch and slowly packed the bowl of his pipe. The Judge pulled a wooden match from his pocket and struck it on the rough surface of the table. He held the match to the bowl as he took a few pulls on the pipe, the flame leaping in rhythm with his breath.

The Judge motioned to the tobacco pouch. "Do you know where I got that? Never seen it before? I got this from your father, Wendell. He gave it to me as a gift."

"Do you expect me to care?"

"Not necessarily. A tobacco pouch isn't very interesting. But what's more interesting than the thing itself is how your father came into possession of it. Now, *that* is a story."

"Wyles told me you came to the house. Don't come to the house."

"Well, Wendell, it *is* my house."

"She also said you wanted a decision from me. The answer is no, Judge. I'm not interested."

"Wendell, Wendell, Wendell. It's really not a matter of interest." The Judge puffed the pipe and watched the smoke curl toward the ceiling. "It's simply a matter of accepting a gift. I'm giving you an important opportunity at precisely the right time. A gift freely given."

"Freely given."

"Exactly, just like the gift you gave that man Knecht. Daniel Knecht. He didn't ask you to buy that medicine for his brother, and yet you did it immediately, of your own volition. You wanted nothing in return. You simply wanted to give a gift. It wasn't your fault he was lying."

"Not doing it."

The Judge said, "By the way, I talked to your man Knecht at the courthouse after I learned you'd taken an interest in him. Difficult life. Lost his parents and brother, must take care of his sisters. All he really wants is to have a life for himself, just like you or me. He's been called a fiend. He's not a fiend. He's a human being. I believe every man deserves at least one chance in this world."

"Why was Knecht with you when you came to the house?"

"I wanted to help him."

"Help him how?"

"I find it so tiresome that when I'm on the bench, no one has the opportunity to ask me any questions. And so I can't provide any answers. I must simply listen to people blather on and on. But you, Wendell, you have so many questions. It's wonderful."

"What were you trying to do to help him?"

The Judge sat back in his chair and folded his hands on his belly. "You know, the philosopher Heraclitus had only two questions. What is the world like? And how can we understand it? Simple questions, enormous implications. Did you study him at the university? Heraclitus?"

"How were you trying to help Knecht?"

"Why, I wanted to give him a chance in life, starting with a place to live. He expressed a desire to leave his current conditions, to escape that hovel in Easton and get out on his own."

"Who'll take care of his sisters?"

"He will. Knecht will mine coal for a living, and he will support his sisters financially. They also have an aunt in Easton who will look in on them."

"How do you know those men, Moore and Gray? What were you meeting with them about?"

The Judge shifted in his chair, leaning forward. He sharpened his focus on Kamp.

"Terrible crimes have been committed, Wendell. Those men help to run the ironworks and the railroad. A criminal element has moved in. They were telling me about the wrongdoing that's been occurring. Theft, lawlessness. Violence. A scourge."

"That's too bad."

"It's awful, and they want it to stop. I want it to stop, too, but there's no one to investigate and bring these scoundrels to justice. You're the right man, Wendell, the perfect man. You're tenacious. You'll find the truth."

"Since when is the truth a concern of yours, Judge?"

"Oh, Wendell, you're too hard on people. And on yourself. You need to think about your family. Think about Shaw. Think about your child. What kind of world do you want for that child?"

Kamp stared down at the table.

The Judge went on, "Be practical. Raising a family costs money. Where will the money come from? It's different now. It's not just you. You need to provide for them for as long as you can. You need steady work, security, especially if you were to have another episode."

"Go to hell, Judge."

"Try it. Do it for one year. Give it everything you have. During that time, you'll be paid a good salary, and you'll do the detective work entirely as you see fit. You won't have to carry a badge or wear a uniform or any of that nonsense."

"I don't care."

"Perform the duties of the job for one year, and the house is yours. The farm is yours. I'll hand you the deed. You'll own it all. One year."

"That simple?"

"Not everything in life is as complicated as you make it out to be, Wendell. It's the right thing to do. And it's a gift. What do you think?"

"I think it looks bad."

"Well, thinking is a disease, and sight is deceptive. So said Heraclitus." After his pronouncement, the Judge took two deep pulls on the pipe, burning the last of the tobacco in the bowl.

Kamp had accepted long ago that the Judge would always have one more card to play, and another one after that. And he accepted that he would likely never even know what game the Judge was playing or how tall the odds were against the Judge's opponent, whoever that may have been. But Kamp knew he wouldn't see a better deal than this one.

Kamp said, "Put it all in writing."

The Judge banged the dead ashes from the pipe by rapping it on the table. "Consider it done."

Kamp walked out the kitchen door and into the night. A big moon in a clear sky lit the landscape, and he figured he'd have an easy enough walk home after all, in spite of the distance. Kamp needed the space outside to sort through the messages he'd received during the day, to find their meanings, if they had any. He needed to feel the cold air in his lungs and the life in his leg muscles if he were to have any chance of picking apart the Judge's "gibberish stuffed with horseshit," as Druckenmiller liked to call it. It would take a while to understand it, take a while to see the ramifications of the day's events, and take even longer to walk home in the dark. It would all take longer than he wanted. Everything does, Kamp thought.

By the time he made the turn from the road to his farm, purple light had begun to filter through the trees. Kamp imagined the sun rising on the hunting camp, on the mound of dead birds, considerably smaller than the day before, the raccoons and opossums having pilfered their hefty share in the dark. Footsore and dead tired, Kamp tumbled backward in his memory. He recalled the hours spent on the front steps of his house, awaiting his father's return from the hunting camp. He recalled the elaborate tales he told himself about the adventures his father must have undertaken, the battles he must have engaged with the ferocious beasts of the mountains. And when his father made the turn from the road, the young boy Kamp's heart leapt in love and exultation. But now, having seen it with new eyes, stripped of the protective delusions of childhood, Kamp reimagined his father for what he must have been and how he must have felt those mornings as he trudged the path back home from the hunting camp, just fucked-out, shot-out and hung over, a worn out cog in a *nix nootz* murderous machine.

5

Jonas Bauer never fretted that he didn't possess a fine education or a lofty position in life, nor did he begrudge those who did. Life had shown him "clear enough and day by day," as he reminded his wife, that hard work, a clear conscience and a right attitude are the foundations of a good life. Bauer often reminded himself, especially on mornings when he might otherwise have wanted to stay in bed that "he becometh poor that dealeth with a slack hand." He reflected, too, on the many ways the Lord had blessed him, beginning with his and Rachel's health, his three beautiful daughters and the rich bounty provided by the place where they lived. It surely wasn't paradise, but it gave them a full pantry and plenty stored up to last them through the winter.

Perhaps due to the many blessings the Lord bestowed upon him, Jonas Bauer was prone to worry now and again, worry about danger in mines, the pain he sometimes felt in his chest, the future of his daughters, and on and on. Bauer pictured the severed head of his friend Roy Kunkle and worried about the next explosion. He worried that the "Room for Rent" sign he placed in the window wasn't doing any good. It had been two weeks since he'd put it there. They didn't need a boarder's rent in order to survive, he reminded himself. But the extra money would help him breathe easier and give them something to put toward a better day tomorrow, even if he weren't there to see it. And so Bauer felt considerable relief and anticipation when he heard a knock on his door.

He opened the door and saw a young man, probably in his twenties, tall and lean. The man avoided Bauer's gaze.

The man said, "Good morning, sir. I come to see about the room."

Bauer studied the man and realized that he'd seen him once before. Then he heard a commotion in the hallway behind him. His girls must have heard the knock, and they wanted to see who it was.

Jonas Bauer said, "Good morning. Let's talk outside." He walked down the front steps and into the small front yard.

The man said, "I work for a living, and I'll pay my rent."

Bauer noticed his daughters in a second floor window, pressed against the glass and laughing. He said, "Weren't you here before?"

"Yes, sir, I was. I come here before when the Judge wanted me to ask you to go to town. To help that lady."

"I remember. What's your name?"

The man looked Bauer in the eye. "Daniel Knecht."

"I'm Jonas Bauer. Do you live close by, Daniel?"

"No, sir. Right now, I live in Easton, but I want to move out this way. When I was here before, I seen that sign in your window. I wasn't situated to be able to move right then."

"Where do you work?"

"Coal mine."

"Which one?"

"Up the line."

Bauer couldn't tell if this man Knecht was being evasive or simply terse. He said, "Up the line where?"

"Out of Mauch Chunk."

Bauer said, "You say you're a miner?"

"Yah."

Bauer saw Knecht glance up at the window where the girls were standing, then immediately look back down.

Bauer said, "I work there, too. How come I never seen you?"

"Well, it's dark down there."

Knecht waited to see how the joke went over. Bauer's expression had not changed. Knecht looked over Bauer's shoulder and smiled.

"Morning, ma'am." Knecht tipped his hat to Rachel Bauer who stood in the doorway.

She said, "*Guten tag, herr?*"

"Knecht. *Wie bischt, frau—*"

Bauer interrupted. "If you work in the same mine as I do, how come I haven't seen you down there? How come I don't know you?"

Knecht focused back on Bauer. "They just put me there. Before that, I was in Sla'dale."

"How long?"

"Ten years."

"*Ach*, how old are you now?"

"Twenty-three. Sir, I won't cause no trouble. That's all behind–I'll be a good boarder. Keep to myself. I need to save as much money as I can. Take care of my sisters."

"If you need to save money, why not work in the patch town?"

"I need a place where I can breathe, a good place like this. Besides, I like to keep myself busy around the farm, too. I can work extra for you."

The giggling and gawking continued in the upstairs window.

Bauer turned and said to his wife, "Tell them to settle *down!*"

"I can move in the first of the month."

"Why haven't you started a family, Daniel?"

Bauer saw Knecht's body stiffen, and he wished he hadn't asked the question.

"Mr. Bauer, how much is the rent?" Knecht let the question hang.

"Six dollars a month."

"Five. And I'll fix anything around here that needs fixed."

Bauer pulled in a deep breath. He imagined what the extra money would mean and what a pair of extra hands could do around the property. If Bauer saved enough money and made enough improvements, one day he'd own something permanent, something better. Taking in Knecht was a risk, and it would cause him worry, but Jonas Bauer decided it would be a good opportunity to grow in faith. He extended his hand.

"First of the month. Bring the rent. Five dollars."

Knecht gave Bauer's hand a vigorous shake and breathed a large sigh.

"Thank you, sir. Thank you."

Bauer said, "I'll see you on the first, and don't worry, I'll be here to help you move in."

"Very kind of you, sir. Say, can I see inside the house?"

"Why, sure."

Bauer led Knecht up the front stairs and opened the door and saw Rachel and their girls huddled there. Must've been trying to hear the conversation, Bauer thought.

Knecht said, "Well, well, this must be the welcoming party."

He took Rachel's hand gently. "*Frau* Bauer, it's a pleasure to meet you. My name is Daniel."

"Good to meet you as well, *Herr* Knecht. These are our daughters."

The youngest girl peeked at Knecht from behind the folds of Rachel's dress.

"This little one is Anna."

"How old are you, Anna?"

She said, "I'm seven" and began giggling before burying her face in her hands.

"And the middle one is Heidi. Heidi is ten." She had bright red cheeks, freckles and a red ribbon in her hair.

Knecht said, "Hello, Heidi."

Rachel motioned to the oldest and tallest girl who had long brown hair and fierce eyes.

The girl said, "My name is Nadine," and she extended her hand to Knecht, who took it. The other two girls burst into laughter.

Knecht said, "What's so funny?"

Heidi said, "Her name is Nadine, but no one calls her Nadine."

He said, "What do they call her?"

Anna answered, "She's Nyx. Everyone calls her Nyx."

Knecht said, "What would you like me to call you? Nadine. How about Nadine?"

"That will be fine."

This sent the younger two girls into a fit of hysterical laughter.

Rachel tried to get control of the situation and said, "*Girls!*" And then to Knecht, she said, "Nyx—Nadine, Nadine is sixteen."

The younger girls were laughing uncontrollably.

Bauer said, "Why don't I show you the room where you'll stay?" He started up the stairs and led Knecht to the hallway on the second floor. "Up here is where the girls' rooms are and where your room will be."

Knecht surveyed the hallway, and Bauer hoped he wouldn't notice that each door had a shiny, new brass lock.

"And this is where you'll stay." Bauer pointed to an open door. Inside the room was a small bed next to the window and beside the bed a wooden chair.

"This will do just fine. Much obliged." The two men headed back downstairs.

When he reached the bottom of the stairs, Knecht said, "Mrs. Bauer, you have a beautiful family and a beautiful home."

"Why, thank you, Daniel."

On the first of October, Kamp went to town. He'd received a letter from the Judge the day before instructing him to arrive at the county courthouse at nine in the morning, where someone would meet him. As he made the walk, he reflected on the fact that he'd never been employed, as such. The closest he'd come was being a soldier, and if having this job was like that, he knew he wouldn't last a week, let alone an entire year. When he told Shaw that he'd accepted the job, she'd been furious, because she didn't trust the Judge and hated the idea of him leaving every day. He sensed, though, that underneath her indignation, Shaw was relieved that he'd be making money and that he'd have something to get him out of his own head. Besides, he told her, if he kept at it, they'd have the deed to the farm before their baby's first birthday. On his way out the door that morning, she'd shaken her head in resignation and given him a kiss goodbye.

When he reached the foot of the courthouse steps, he saw a man at the door, outfitted in a top hat and a Chesterfield overcoat. The man had a thick black mustache, flecked with gray. He stood very straight with his chin tilted up and stared somberly as Kamp ascended the stairs.

"Pleased to meet you, Mr. Kamp," the man said, sounding displeased.

"Good to meet you too, Mister—"

"Crow. Philander Crow. District Attorney. We'll talk in my office."

Philander Crow led him into the building and up the stairs to an office on the fourth floor. Crow hung his coat on a brass hook and took his seat behind a large oak desk with a black leather top. The desktop was clear, except for two sheets of paper. Crow motioned for him to sit down.

"This is a letter I received from the Honorable Tate Cain." Crow held the first piece of paper away from his body between his thumb and forefinger, as if it were covered in excrement. Kamp raised his eyebrows.

"What's it say?"

"It says that you're the new police detective for the City of Bethlehem, effective today."

"So, what's the problem?"

Crow looked at him. "Where to begin."

Kamp looked around the room. Bare walls. No office supplies or curtains on the windows.

"New in town?"

Crow winced as if he'd been kicked in the shins.

"Mr. Kamp, I believe—"

"Kamp."

"I believe we can both agree that you're not prepared for this role. You have no training in the law, no police experience."

"How much experience did the last guy have?"

Crow said, "In order to become a detective, a man must study the application of criminal justice and attend a police academy to gain an educational foundation. He must learn about the basics of investigation, collecting evidence, writing reports and then pass a written test. If the man passes the test, he works in a probationary fashion under continuous supervision."

Kamp leaned back in his chair and said, "Is that right?"

He saw Crow's shoulders tense and the color begin to rise in his face. He felt himself slip out of his body and drift to the corner of the ceiling closest to the window. From there, he watched the conversation happening below, and he found that he was able to keep talking through his mouth.

Crow said, "In addition, the Judge superseded the authority of the county in awarding you the job."

"That's between you and the Judge."

Crow held up the second piece of paper, creased and yellowed with age. "I requested and received a record of your military service from Washington, D.C."

"Looks like you're quite the detective yourself."

"It says you were recognized for extraordinary gallantry in combat and that you suffered a serious injury. What was the injury?"

"I don't remember." At the same time that his body continued the conversation, Kamp drifted out of the window so that he could now look down on the street traffic, horses and carriages, people crossing the intersection diagonally.

"The letter states that you were discharged from military service on May 15, 1865 in spite of a very serious incident. A handwritten note states that had it not been for acts of heroism and bravery, you would not have been granted an honorable discharge."

"Uh-huh."

"What did you do in the years following the war?"

"I went to the college."

"What did you study?"

"Natural science."

"Anything else?"

"Philosophy."

Crow shook his head. "As far as real work is concerned, none of that will be of any use."

He shifted in his chair, set his papers aside and geared up for his closing argument. Sensing that the conversation would soon be over, Kamp willed himself back into his body and tensed his muscles to make sure.

"Kamp, your service to the Union is commendable, but you are unfit for this position. You lack the prerequisite skills and training, and you are very likely deficient in some way. It would be a grave disservice to the people of this city for you to be a police detective."

"*Mox nix.*"

"What's that?"

"*Mox. Nix.* Doesn't matter. None of it."

"If you'll please leave." Philander Crow opened a desk drawer and pulled out more papers to indicate that he was about to start working. Kamp felt the fire kindling at the back of his neck. He knew he only had a few seconds before the explosion went off.

Kamp said, "You don't know what experience the last guy had, because there was no last guy. I'm the first one. You're new in your job, so you don't know what you can do and what you can't do. I'm hired by the city, Judge or no Judge. And as for whether I'm fit for the job, stay out of my way and I'll show you."

"Officially, you report to the chief of police. But in reality, you work for me."

"Like hell I do."

"You don't understand how this works."

"Here's how it'll work. I'll investigate crimes. I'll assemble the facts, and I'll put it all in a nice report for you in writing and including all of the evidence, and you take it from there. That's how I understand it." Kamp stood up, tipped his hat and left.

6

"Settle down, Kamp. Settle down. Everybody knows he's a grade-A louse, a real son of a bitch, *and* a horse's ass. And he's only been here two weeks."

Kamp walked beside the High Constable as he made his patrol through town. He greeted each person they passed with a hello or a friendly nod. Druckenmiller carried a shepherd's crook, a stick made of hazel wood with a collar fashioned from a ram's horn.

Kamp said, "Where'd he come from?"

"Philadelphia."

"What's he doing here?"

"No one knows for certain. Rumor has it he got fired down there, and someone around here owed him a favor. He probably just feels out of place here, you know, among the unwashed. Don't let him get to you. Gives me shit all the time too. I don't pay it no mind."

"What kind of shit?"

"Don't matter."

"Tell me."

"Oh, take this for instance." Druckenmiller held up the crook. "He wants me to get rid of it. Says I should carry a gun instead. But I know the people here. There's nothing I can do with a gun that I can't do without it, except shoot someone. And so far I've come across no one that needs shot."

"Not everyone's walking the narrow path."

"More like no one is."

Kamp said, "Well, there are some things you have to put a stop to."

"Why, sure. You got your troublemakers and deviants. This one's *schtupping* that one's wife. This other one over here is stealing chickens. They all drink too much. People want to believe there are lowlifes we should be rid of. Lowlifes, lowlifes. *Ach*, look around. That's all of us. Life *is* low."

"Thanks for cheering me up."

Druckenmiller became animated. "They tell me everything's changing for the worse. But there's nothing different going on. Nothing different from five years ago. Probably nothing's ever changed. See? Right there, for instance."

Druckenmiller pointed his staff in the direction of a man with one arm propped against the side of a saloon, taking a piss.

"Every day in every city since the beginning of time, there's been a souse, *brunsing* against the side of a building."

They walked over to the man and Druckenmiller tapped him on the shoulder with his crook.

"Hey, Obie. Knock it off." No reply.

"Hey, Obie! Not here."

The man mumbled, "Lemme finish."

Druckenmiller pressed the crook against the man's neck, applying pressure evenly and pinning him to the side of the building.

"It's not a request, Obie."

"Christ almighty, Druck."

The man buttoned his pants and stumbled back into the saloon. Kamp and Druckenmiller started walking again side by side.

Druckenmiller said, "See, if I walk around here with a gun, it only makes things worse. Scares people. Makes them feel threatened. Makes me an enemy. Hostile. That's why I didn't want to wear no uniform. Reminds folks of the military. There's no need. Shooting begets shooting. War's over."

Kamp said, "What about these wrongdoers and malefactors I keep hearing about? The criminal element that's moving in?"

Druckenmiller shook his head with disgust. "*Ach,* what I see around every day here is the same. If there's a criminal element, it's these guys in gray wool suits. These iron and railroad guys. And them that run the coal fields. Those assholes want to kill everything and everyone, including each other and especially them that work for 'em. That's where the wrongdoing is."

"Well, there's laws to keep them and anyone else from doing that. Right?"

Druckenmiller held up and turned to face him. "Law hasn't caught up with 'em yet or more likely can't reach 'em. Ach, Kamp, I know you're just trying to get me worked up. Don't bother."

Kamp said, "I want to know why I was hired. Why would the Judge or anyone else want me to do this if all I'm supposed to do is help you catch drunks and chicken thieves? What is it I'm supposed to detect?"

"Fuck if I know."

"You must've thought about it."

Druckenmiller said, "The only thing I can figure is that they want you to make sure that you investigate crimes in such a way that you can prove that the laws don't apply to them. Make sure you detect that it's someone else's fault, or better yet you should detect that there wasn't no crime committed in the first place."

"Doesn't say much for me."

"Well, don't worry. You're just a lowlife. Same as me. Same as them. Cheers."

He pulled his silver flask from his pocket and took a sip, then strolled down the street away, laughing and whistling a happy tune.

Kamp used the walk home to sort out the bits and pieces of his trip to town and discern whether he'd actually learned anything new. He reflected on Druckenmiller's point about what his job would really entail, protecting the powerful from the law. He hoped it wasn't true but assumed it was. He wondered whether Druckenmiller was right about the fact that there weren't more criminals and more crimes now than in the past. It seemed impossible that human nature could have changed so that people could have become more nefarious somehow. And yet, maybe the conditions and circumstances had changed in such a way to make wrongdoing more necessary, or at least more profitable to some. No way to know. Kamp also thought back on his chat with Philander Crow. The Judge had told him he had the perfect qualifications for the job, and Crow told him the opposite. Based on his experience in the army, Kamp knew a man's actual skills were never the main reason he got the job, except in the case of snipers.

He didn't know how long he had to figure it all out. The visions and the voices, the nightmares and the headaches and the excursions outside his body. All of it had intensified and seemed to be getting its own head of steam. He wondered how long he had left. One year, he told himself. Just make it one year.

He hit the road for home, focusing on the sensation of the sole of each foot striking the ground and falling into the rhythm of a long walk. He felt the heat rising in his lungs and chest and noticed the way they pushed back against gathering autumn cold. Step by step Kamp allowed his nerves to calm. He crunched through the dry leaves on the side of the road and for an instant let the sound carry him back to the fragments of a thousand splendid days from his boyhood when escaping from turmoil and pain, alone or with his brothers, he'd surrender to the clean air and orange leaves, the cold water in the creek, the radiant sun.

When the moment passed, he brought himself back to the present and looked around. He breathed the same cool air, saw the same colors of the leaves, the same cold creek and the same sun. Nothing had changed from when he was a boy. Nothing was the same.

Kamp made it to the path to his house by late afternoon and saw a man on the front porch. The front door was open, too, and Shaw was talking to the man. As he got closer, he recognized the visitor. Even from behind, he could make out the black, wavy hair, the lean frame and the broad shoulders. It was unmistakably Daniel Knecht.

When Shaw saw Kamp, she called out, "Welcome back."

Knecht spun around, and it seemed to him as if Knecht had been surprised by his arrival.

Knecht smiled at him. "Afternoon."

"Good afternoon. What brings you out this way?" Kamp walked up the front steps and stood face to face with Knecht.

"*Ach*, we're neighbors!" Knecht was beaming.

Shaw said, "Mr. Knecht was just telling me that he's rented a room in the home of Jonas Bauer. You know Jonas Bauer."

"Not personally, no."

Knecht said, "And it's all thanks to you."

"How's that?"

"Well, if you hadn't taken me to the police in Bethlehem, I wouldn't have had to go before the Judge, and I wouldn't have been able to tell him my story. And if the Judge hadn't brought me out here to help me find a place to live, I wouldn't have seen that there was a room for rent at Mr. Bauer's house. So, it's all thanks to you. See?"

Shaw saw Kamp's face harden and said, "I need to check on supper." She turned and went back in the house, closing the front door.

"Anyway, I just wanted to come by and say thank you."

"You're welcome."

"I also wanted to see if Mrs. Kamp is all right. Seems like she is."

"Thank you for your concern."

Knecht said, "I mean, last time I was here, Judge was worried about her, an' you was away. That's how come he sent me over to Mr. Bauer to get help, to Mr. Bauer's house, where I seen the sign in the window."

"I understand." He felt the last few grains of his patience slipping away.

"Say, I hear you work for the Judge now. Or, no, no, the police. That's what I heard. I heard you work for the police now. City detective. Officially. Is that right?"

"Something like that. Who'd you hear it from?"

Knecht rolled his eyes. "*Pshoo*, well, I'll make *extra* certain not to cause no trouble then."

"Do that." He gestured politely for Knecht to step off the porch.

"Yah, well, I better get going now. You probably have a lot to do around here what with the baby on the way and this farm to take care of and your job in town. You're blessed, Mr. Kamp. You sure are."

"Thank you for stopping by, Mr. Knecht."

"Danny."

"Thank you, Danny."

Knecht stepped lightly down the stairs, and they watched him go. When he got halfway across the yard, Knecht turned around.

"My sister told me how you come by with the medicine and how you wanted to make sure they was okay. That was a kind thing to do. Real kind. Makes me kinda sorry I bullshitted you about the whole thing in the first place. Hope you don't hold nothing against me."

"I don't, Danny."

He watched him until he got to the road, then went back in the house to the kitchen, where Shaw was indeed making supper. She met him with raised eyebrows.

Kamp raised his hands. "Long day. Strange."

"Emma Wyles was here again today to check on me."

"Christ. What did I do wrong now?"

"She says everything is fine, says I'm doing much better. She also said congratulations on your new job."

"Yah."

Shaw said, "What about him? Knecht?"

"Our new neighbor? What *about* him? Jesus."

"Seems harmless to me."

"How could you tell?"

She said, "Weren't you the one who wanted to help him in the first place?"

"That doesn't mean I want him around here."

"He's just a lost soul, Kamp. Once he gets settled in, he'll be fine. Stop worrying."

"I'm not saying he's a fiend, Shaw, but he's *ab im kopp*. Know what I mean?"

"*Ab im kopp*? That's what you call it? Off in the head?" She was smiling now, teasing him.

Kamp said, "That's right."

"Well, so are you. Thank god."

She walked to him, put her arms around him and kissed him on the lips. He pulled her against him, and she kissed him harder.

He said, "What about supper?"

7

When Kamp was in the war, he often wandered into the forest during one of the countless lulls. This habit was strictly forbidden for a variety of reasons and, as he well knew, punishable by a number of exceedingly hash measures. But for him, not to perambulate of his own accord would have been far worse. His comrades in arms accepted his aberrant behavior, because they trusted him and because on some level, they realized that the machinery in his head had been assembled differently from theirs. They did worry that he never took a gun when he went on his nature walks. He never felt unsafe at these times, though, never considered that any harm could come to him. And none ever did. Alone in the woods, notions of the past and the future fell away so that all that was left and all that mattered was a blue sky, a puff white cloud, the scent of a pine tree, the sliver glimpse of a green valley. He didn't imagine that a war could be going on, or that he could participate in such a thing. He didn't yearn to go back to where he came from so that he could proceed with a life he had before. He never pictured a home or a beautiful woman waiting there for him or a family of his own. During these hours alone, he floated on the hum and buzz of the wilderness, lost to all but sensation.

And so Kamp found it strange that now he had returned to something like the life he had before. He did know the love of a beautiful woman, and they would soon have a child. Stranger still was the fact that he fell into a routine of going to work, a job with a kind of framework and structure that placed limits on his freedom. But as he walked back and forth to Bethlehem each day, he reflected on this curious turn of events. He recalled what he'd learned during his first months as a detective.

He thought about how everything that the Honorable Tate Cain, the High Constable Samuel Druckenmiller and the District Attorney Philander Crow had told him about himself and about the job had been mostly wrong. Kamp had learned, for example, that contrary to what Crow had said, he was able to handle the responsibilities of the role without having had any formal training. He quickly learned to conduct investigations, construct patterns of facts, draw sound conclusions and submit reports to Philander Crow, who prosecuted cases with strict efficiency. He had also learned that Druckenmiller's assessment that the rate of crime in any given place has remained static since the beginning of time was hugely inaccurate. In particular, in his routine investigations of reports of wrongdoing, Kamp found that Bethlehem was seething with criminal activity of all kinds, growing in scale along with the rise of industry. Murder plots predominated. People freely volunteered information with him regarding the homicidal intentions of any number of individuals and groups in Bethlehem. It seemed to Kamp that a majority of Bethlemites, a fraternity united only by their murderous impulses, wanted to kill each other at any given moment. But wanting to kill someone didn't constitute a crime. If it did, he thought every last soul would be guilty at some point, and often with sound and understandable reasons.

As he stared at the ceiling in the darkest hours night after night, Kamp reminded himself that his job wasn't to ponder the motivations of men or simply bring to light their evil inclinations. He had to prove a criminal had committed the crime. In this regard, Druckenmiller's words rang true. The easiest crimes to investigate were those that happened in the open and with no apparent forethought, such as fisticuffs in a saloon. Two men, three sheets to the wind, punch each other until one man gains the upper hand. If the fight stops there, most would argue that no crime has been committed. If the victor continues to pummel his opponent to the point of unconsciousness or worse, he has committed a crime. Someone in the saloon, one of the patrons or the proprietor himself will talk to the police, as long as the witnesses don't think the guy deserved it. In the end it was all personal, anyway, and none of the city's business. Whatever the case, Kamp realized, the so-called ironclad investigations, those that resulted in successful prosecutions were the ones with the simplest motives and the most eager witnesses. In his estimation that left a multitude of crimes undetectable.

Most crimes Kamp heard about couldn't be attributed to an identifiable human being. "Someone else" and "not me" were usually the prime suspects. Kamp noted as well that people's most common definition of criminal was simply a person in a group different from one's own. The Germans blamed the Hungarians for the increase in crime. The Hungarians blamed the Slovaks, and the Moravians blamed the Lutherans. The Lutherans blamed the devil, to their credit, though that fact didn't much help Kamp in his pursuit of justice.

If the criminal couldn't somehow be situated among the local varieties of European, it surely had to have been the work of an "injun," as in the Lenni Lenape. Their numbers were so small, owing to their near-extermination and expulsion during previous centuries, that they'd almost become useless as scapegoats and bogeymen. If neither evidence of Lenape could be found nor rumors of Lenape concocted, sometimes a freed slave could be drummed up to play the role of culprit. And if all else failed, the perpetrator was assumed to be a part of the most vague yet most reliable category–"outsiders."

He did his level best to cut through clannish prejudices, innuendos baseless and sinister, bald prevarications, and out and out bullshit that characterized nearly all of Kamp's conversations with the citizenry. In order to see his way through it, he focused primarily on motive, what he understood to be a person's need, that which the person had to do in order to survive. He tried to strip away the emotion and wear the light of reason as a head lamp. People wanted none of it. He detected a vein of malice and fear deeper and more powerful than rational thought process or any written law. He'd seen it his whole life and saw it ever more clearly now.

And yet, Kamp thought as he trudged into Bethlehem City Hall with really nothing to show for his first three months on the job, as autumn tumbled headlong toward winter, if he could make it nine more months, just make it to the next summer, he could relegate it all to the past. In the meantime if anyone could be helped by his work, if he could in fact right a wrong, so be it.

These were the thoughts that twirled in his mind as he turned the brass doorknob and stepped into Philander Crow's office.

As before, Crow now sat behind his desk, a tidy stack of papers in front of him. He didn't look up when Kamp entered the room, though he motioned for him to sit down.

Crow said, "I appreciate the work you've been doing. Your reports are highly informative and professional."

"You're welcome."

"It's a significant improvement over what Drucken-miller was doing by himself."

Kamp said, "He's doing the best he can."

"He's a drunkard and a fool. The fact that he's your friend is clouding your judgment."

"That's what you wanted to tell me?"

Kamp surveyed the office. Still nothing on the walls, no personal effects on the desk. Crow looked up at him. The district attorney's face showed a combination of hauteur and boredom.

"You've done better work than I thought you would, but that doesn't mean I was wrong about you."

"How's that?"

"Sweeping drunks and pugilists off street corners is worthwhile as far as it goes, but you haven't solved any substantive crimes."

"You mean I haven't done anything that's going to get you promoted back to Philadelphia or wherever the hell it is you're trying to get to."

Crow arched his eyebrows slightly without otherwise changing his expression of disdain.

"You were hired, against my wishes, to investigate significant crimes, the work of murderers and underground crime syndicates, actual detective work."

"If you don't want me for this job, how come I have it?"

Crow looked straight at Kamp. "The local cretins are always dug in deeper than one would prefer. But since I can't get rid of you for the time being, I'll use you as I see fit. You should also realize that the Judge is paying a heavy price politically for protecting you."

"That's on the Judge."

"My sense is that you're not interested in keeping your job any longer than I want to keep mine. What was the deal the Judge gave you? One year?"

Kamp rubbed his left temple and gazed absently out the window.

Crow said, "Yes, he told me about that. But why, why would he tell me?"

"Don't know."

"So, you're just going to hang on until when? August? September? And then you think the Judge is just going to hand you what you've always wanted and will never be able to afford?"

"A deal's a deal."

"Your injury must have made you naïve, detective."

Kamp turned his attention back to the district attorney.

Crow said, "You know, once the brain is injured, it never works the same way again, I'm told. Oftentimes a man can't think straight. Sad."

"Tread carefully, Mr. Crow."

"Is that why you won't carry a gun, detective? Afraid you might harm yourself? Someone else?"

The fire at the base of Kamp's skull erupted before he had time to check it. He slammed his fist on Crow's desk so hard that the floor shook and the windows rattled. Philander Crow's expression remained constant. He did not stand up, did not assume an aggressive posture.

Crow said, "Consider your next move very carefully, if you can. If you fail to control your words and actions, especially right now, you will be removed from your position. The Judge will not have the authority to prevent it."

Kamp clenched both fists and held on as the fire raged in his mind. He pictured Shaw. He pictured their home. Slowly, the fire began to recede.

"Stop goading me, Mr. Crow."

"Not goading you, detective. Just making a point. You have no comprehension of the power and scope of the forces arrayed against you, and even if you did, you are ill-prepared and ill-equipped to confront them."

Kamp stood up to leave.

Crow continued, "And you must have realized by now that the machine is in motion, and you are a part of it. If you simply let the machine run, it will grind you to nothing, certainly in less time than a year. And if you fight against it, they will kill you."

"Who's they?"

"You don't want to know. Not really. I suggest you resign immediately before you cause any real trouble and before you give them a reason to want to hurt you and your family. When they decide you're a threat or even that you have the potential to become one, they will remove you. Or, you can perform your duties in such a way that you're certain to accomplish nothing."

"Bullshit."

"You're too foolish to follow my advice, naturally. You believe you'll last a year and that the Judge will make good on his deal. If that's so, I suggest you start putting your affairs in order now. Your time is short."

8

Jonas Bauer pulled a spade from the shed behind the house and handed it to Daniel Knecht, then grabbed another one for himself. The men walked side by side toward the edge of the property, by the road.

Bauer said, "I had a dream last night, Danny. A kind of a vision."

"A vision?"

Knecht leaned on his shovel and peered at Bauer. In the days after he'd moved in, they'd felled a large chestnut tree in the forest behind the house. With a variety of saws Bauer borrowed from a neighbor, they sliced the trunk in half, then quarters, then the eighths they used for the rails of the fence. They took turns chopping the leftover wood with Bauer's own ax, more than enough to last the winter and repay the neighbor. Bauer and

97

Knecht performed the work, usually together and sometimes individually during the fall, digging the post holes and dragging the rails from the woods. For his effort Jonas Bauer reduced his rent by one dollar a month, though truth be told, Knecht benefitted a great deal more.

From the day of his arrival, he was invited to join the family each night at supper, and Knecht ate ravenously. Rachel cooked meals the likes of which Knecht had never tasted before. But more than all else, Knecht treasured the feeling of being there among the members of a real family each night, hearing about their trials and victories during the day, absorbing a kind of warmth he had also never known.

They reached the border between the road and the property, and the two men stopped at a point Bauer had marked with a stone the day before, the spot where they'd dig the last two post holes for the fence.

Bauer said, "Now, listen here once. It got me thinking, this vision, of something they taught us from the Bible, something I heard many times when I was a *junge*. I put it in my memory."

"What was the vision?"

"The verse is from the Gospel According to Luke. Something Jesus said."

Knecht made a wry face. "Is that right? Jesus?"

"Do you want to hear the verse?"

"Not exactly."

Bauer chuckled. "I suppose that's understandable."

Knecht tilted his head sideways. "What are you trying to say, Mr. Bauer?"

"Well, the idea behind what Jesus said is that if you find a home where there's peace, you should stay there. What you do to earn your keep is worthwhile, and you deserve to be there."

Knecht's expression darkened. "Ain't that what I'm doing already?"

"Yes, it's exactly what you're doing." Bauer tried not to sound defensive.

"Well, then why push the religion on me unless I done something wrong?"

Bauer said, "No, no. I meant you're doing exactly the right thing. That's what reminded me of it in the first place."

"No, you said what reminded you was a dream, a vision. What was it?"

Bauer proceeded as if he hadn't heard the question. He motioned for Knecht to begin digging the final hole, while he cut the earth with the shovel and settled into a working rhythm. In doing so, Bauer wanted to end the conversation and to dispel, if he could, the dread he felt from what in actuality was a nightmare he'd had. In the middle of the night, he'd seen what he took to be a fragment of a premonition, a glimpse of destruction and violence, a calamitous fire and its charred aftermath. And while Daniel Knecht himself didn't appear in the nightmare, Bauer felt he was in some way at the heart of it. He'd conjured the Bible verse to try to convince himself that Knecht did in fact belong in his home, that he hadn't made a disastrous decision in taking him in. And he'd mentioned it to Knecht in the hopes that Knecht would reassure him somehow. As such, Knecht's reaction rattled Bauer even further, as it revealed some kind of discontent on Knecht's part.

The only sounds were the scrapes of the shovel and the hard breathing of the men as they dug the holes to their requisite depths. With the comfort that exertion brings and with the passage of a few minutes, Bauer calmed his nerves and slotted the nightmare in its proper place in the background. He began to count his blessings. Bauer considered the choices he had made and the paths he had taken and concluded that, in spite of what seemed endless toil, the Lord had blessed him with hope and a future. For the first time, he could envision a future rolling out before him and flowing down through generations. His body was strong enough to bear every burden, his mind able to craft and follow a plan.

The fence meant something to him. His landlord, the Judge, hadn't asked him to build one, but Bauer took it upon himself to put it up once he realized Knecht could help him construct it during their time off from the coal mine. The fence would make the property and the house seem more like a homestead, at least to Bauer. Now that he was so close to finishing, he allowed himself to feel satisfied, and gracious. Bauer stood up and paused to let his breath slow and to wipe the sweat from his brow.

Bauer said, "I suppose what I was trying to say is that I appreciate the way you've done what you said you would. You come in and didn't cause no trouble. You're kind to my family, and you're a hard worker."

Head down, continuing to dig, Knecht said, "Ain't that what you thought I'd do?"

"Well, you done such a good job, consider next month's rent free."

"Don't want no charity."

Bauer knew he should stop talking, that he'd irritated Knecht, though he did not know how. But he wanted to reassure himself, and based on Knecht's reaction, he'd begun to wonder whether there wasn't something about Knecht that he'd missed, something he should worry about after all.

He said, "Danny, I just want you to know that you've been an excellent boarder."

"Thanks." Knecht said it with sarcasm.

Bauer said, "You're welcome."

"An excellent *boarder*." Knecht began digging with even greater intensity. He lifted the shovel in front of him as high as he could and brought it down powerfully, sinking the blade as deep as possible.

"What's wrong with that?"

"A boarder but never part of the family, right?"

"Well, you're—"

Knecht stopped digging, stood up straight and faced Bauer.

"Not really, not ever. You have a wife and beautiful children, a home, things to look forward to. Me? I'm a visitor. Five extra bucks a month. And a pair of hands."

A cold fear hit Bauer in the chest. It occurred to him that Knecht may have just had his own dark vision and even disagreeable intentions. He'd allowed Knecht to get far too close to his family. Reestablishing a boundary now would prove very difficult.

"Ach, Danny, I mean to–"

"The hell with all of you." Daniel Knecht threw down the spade and ran down the road.

The December chill had breached the barrier between Kamp's skin and the world. He stuffed his hands in the pockets of his thin work jacket and walked the road toward his house. He picked up the pace and found that the extra exertion did not warm him. He'd used the walk from Bethlehem thus far not to ruminate on Crow's warning hours earlier. To distract himself from feeling cold, Kamp had fixated on something the Judge had said during their conversation months before, namely when he asked whether he'd studied Heraclitus. The Judge mentioned that two of the philosopher's guiding questions were, what is the world like, and can it be understood? Kamp asked himself those questions now. He was nearing a conclusion about what the world Crow had described is like. It is like, he thought, the world described by another man, Darwin. It was exactly at the moment that he was about to answer for himself whether the world can be understood that the shriek of the Black Diamond Unlimited pierced his thoughts.

He looked up to see Daniel Knecht heading toward him at a dead run and was surprised to see that no one was chasing him.

As Knecht blew past him, Kamp said, "How goes it, Danny?"

Knecht grunted, "Not now, Kamp," and he kept running as the train glided past, oblivious to Kamp's philosophical meanderings and Knecht's personal distress. In the distance, Kamp saw a man standing next to a fence and holding a shovel.

He walked toward the man and said, "You must be Mr. Bauer."

"That's right, Jonas Bauer. And you must be Mr. Kamp."

"Kamp. I wanted to say thank you for getting the message to town when my wife was ill."

"Ach, don't mention it. How is she now?"

"Oh, good, good. Say, I noticed your man there, Knecht, hustling past me."

"Yah, yah."

Something wrong?"

Bauer raised his eyebrows, looked at the ground and shook his head. "He's been as good a boarder as you could ask for."

"What happened?"

"*Nix.* Got himself worked up, I guess. *Ferhoodled,* you know." A long silence followed, and neither man filled it. A raven called in the distance and got no response. Kamp knew he'd crossed a line with such a direct question and didn't expect an answer beyond Bauer's few words.

Bauer said, "The Judge tells me you know Danny."

"Not very well."

"I suppose he's a different sort. Well, good to meet you. *Machs gute.*"

"You as well, Mr. Bauer. I'll see you again."

He continued down the road, and Bauer picked up his shovel. He watched Kamp until he disappeared around the bend. He'd begun to rethink his decision to take in a boarder in the first place and decided that Knecht would have to go. Bauer finished digging his post hole, then finished Knecht's. He planted the last two poles in the ground, fitted the remaining rails in their slots. And the fence was complete.

Earlier that morning, Bauer had pictured completing the fence with Knecht and imagined how they'd feel. Relieved and happy. He'd imagined that Knecht would be grateful for having been forgiven the next month's rent and that they'd both be ready for a large supper. Instead, the dread surged back into him. Another saying of Jesus flitted through his mind, one where Jesus commented upon what's required to extract oneself from a difficult situation.

Bauer heaved a sigh, collected his shovel and Knecht's. The smell of pot roast filled his nostrils as soon as he turned to walk back to the house. It lifted his spirits, though not much, and Rachel recognized the trouble when he walked into the kitchen through the back door.

"Where's Danny?"

He heard the laughter of the girls coming from the front room.

"Not now."

"Did something happen?"

"He's going to have to move out. I'm going to tell him when he comes back." Just as he said it, Nyx strolled into the kitchen.

Nyx said, "What do you mean he's moving out? What did he do?"

"Nothing. He didn't do nothing, not that I know."

"Then why should he move out?"

Bauer pinched his temples with his thumb and fore-finger. "Something ain't right with him. I see it now. *Ach*, he might be planning to move out on his own. Save me the hassle." He looked at Nyx. "Anyway, don't say nothing to him. You understand? Nothing."

"All right!"

Rachel said, "Oh, Jonas, you can't put him out before Christmas."

"Daddy, you can't!"

Bauer's day had gone from bad to god awful, a spreading tangle of dreams and nightmares, words and misunderstandings with nothing to separate him from any of it.

He said, "Well, I'll ask for the Lord's guidance."

Bauer had forgotten the approaching holiday and hadn't factored it into his reasoning. He also hadn't taken into account the upset it would cause his family when he told Knecht to leave, though Nyx's reaction to the situation told him more than he wanted to know. Her feelings for Knecht might run deep, he worried. In terms of doing the right thing, he'd given Knecht the benefit of the doubt, but he no longer trusted the man. It seemed as if Knecht wanted more than any of them could give and much more than Bauer would allow. He didn't know where Knecht had gone for the time being or when he'd be back, but as far as Jonas Bauer was concerned, Knecht had no hope and no future. He'd already exiled himself.

That night, after everyone else had gone to sleep and silence had settled back on the house, Bauer went to the shed and retrieved a cigar box. Upon returning to the house, he locked all the doors and windows, and by the light of the lantern in the kitchen, he opened the box. Bauer removed a gun, a four-barrel pistol, and hefted it in his right hand. The barrels, fashioned from Damascus steel, glowed in the dim light. He placed it back in the cigar box and carried it with him upstairs. He set the box gently on the windowsill in the bedroom. Bauer thought, this will have to do.

In his wooden chair next to the bed and by the moon's light, Kamp watched the steady, even rise and fall of Shaw's chest. He imagined the baby curled inside her, asleep and floating. A memory from deep in his consciousness bubbled to the surface. He recalled himself standing, propped against a tree, Sharps rifle raised, focused on his target, a man in grey kneeling behind a low, stone wall. The enemy, some two hundred yards away, had his weapon raised as well and pointed back at him. Kamp sighted the man square down to a tiny point an inch above the man's eyes and dead center. In that instant of pure and primal focus, he perceived the silence before creation. He curled his first finger around the trigger.

Kamp squeezed off the round and saw the flash from the muzzle of the other man's rifle. He watched long enough to witness the halo of blood spray from the back of the man's head. He felt a bullet pass his left cheek before it whanged off the tree, scattering splinters. It was at that moment he felt a burning at his left temple then a thunderbolt of pain as the ricocheting Minié ball entered his skull. He fell toward the ground on his right side. In that moment, the instant before hitting the earth, he felt weightless and free of trouble, a complete absence of pain.

When he emerged from the memory, the moon was there, still shining slant through the windowpane. Shaw was there, chest rising and falling, breathing. He climbed into bed and lay down behind her. He put his arm around her and laid his fingers gently on her belly. He felt the baby move beneath his hand, knowing that he was there. The baby pressed part of its body, what part, an elbow or a foot, perhaps a hand, against Kamp's fingers.

Jonas Bauer awoke before dawn from a dream in which he'd heard a far-off gunshot to the first frigid morning of winter. The wind sang in the trees, and the birds could only hunker down and listen. He threw a few logs on the embers of last night's fire, working the bellows until it blazed anew, and the nightmarish gloom from the previous day burned up in it. Bauer saw that Rachel had been making preparations for Christmas, extra eggs, butter and a sack of flour on the kitchen counter. He knew by the time he returned home from work, the house would be filled with the scent of the holiday, the stench of yesterday gone. Through the kitchen window, Bauer saw the first sliver of purple morning light. Normally, Knecht would be up and about by now, eating his simple breakfast, joking with Bauer and prodding him to hurry up and go. For the past six months, they'd gone to the mine together and returned home each day, their simple routine ironclad. As Bauer pulled on his heavy boots and wool coat, he felt a pang of sadness.

Having readied himself, Bauer swung open the back door to the cold, pale dawn, and there stood Daniel Knecht, smiling.

Knecht said, "Admit it."

"*Ach*, Danny. You gave me such a start."

"You can admit it."

"Admit what, Danny? Christ!"

"Shh, don't wake the family. You missed me. You were worried about me."

"I could throttle you is what I could do."

The fear returned immediately to Bauer's chest, and he felt his windpipe constrict.

Knecht said, "Ach, you don't need to throttle me. I ought not have been upset yesterday. I'm sorry." As he said it, Knecht wrung his hat with both hands.

"It's in the past."

"I noticed you put up the last couple *fensariggles*. Looks good."

Bauer said, "Thank you."

"So you forgive me then?"

"Why, sure, sure."

"And you're not mad at me no more?"

Bauer realized that Knecht had instantly, effortlessly worked his way back in.

"No, Danny, I ain't. I wasn't mad at you to begin with."

Knecht heaved a dramatic sigh. "Well, that is a relief. Jesus, I thought I shit the bed for sure."

"Watch your mouth."

"Right, right." Knecht bounced from one foot to the other, then stamping his feet and rubbing his hands together. "I'm about to freeze. Let's go."

"Now wait, once." Bauer took two steps toward Knecht, inches from his face.

He spoke low in a grave tone. "Listen, Danny. No more monkey business." Knecht nodded soberly. "And mind your manners around the girls. 'Specially Nyx."

Knecht said, "Where'd *that* come from?!"

Candlelight appeared in an upstairs window.

"Give me your word, Danny."

The window opened above them. The two men looked up to see Nyx, bleary-eyed.

She said, "Is everything okay, daddy?"

"Yes, honey, I'm just out here talking. With Danny."

"Oh, hi Danny. Don't freeze. Bye." And she shut the window. The two men faced each other again.

"I have your word."

Knecht looked him in the eye. "Why sure, you got it. You have my word."

Kamp also had a dream that morning before sunrise, a dream about the Black Diamond Unlimited. In it he'd seen the sparkling engine constructed of a great framework of words, every seam, rivet and bolt. In the dream Kamp himself was the stoker, shoveling ever more words into the firebox, which had begun to blaze bright orange. Though the fire burned hot in the dream, he didn't feel its warmth. And all of the answers drifted out the smokestack, unseen and lost to the air. He awoke to an empty bed, toes cold with a frigid wind rattling through the cracks between the bedroom window and its frame. He accepted that he didn't have answers, not yet, though as he lay in bed, he sorted through what was what.

He reflected on his brief conversation with Jonas Bauer the previous day, and he felt relieved that a mile separated his house from Bauer's. Kamp had seen in Bauer's eyes and in his manner that the man had glimpsed the side of Knecht that some people detested and feared. And Kamp remembered Bauer had daughters. He'd also taken Jonas Bauer's measure during their talk. He'd struck Kamp as upright, wary and exact, traits that would serve him well in managing a character such as Knecht. Regardless, he resolved to pay his neighbor another visit or two to say hello and keep Knecht in line, if necessary.

As for his latest conversation with Philander Crow, he didn't know how the district attorney knew about his injury from the war, but it was clear to him that Crow hadn't simply guessed correctly. Someone had provided him with the information which meant that Crow had gone looking for it in the first place. That meant that Crow had been sufficiently curious, or sufficiently worried, enough to investigate him. As for the source of the information, that remained a mystery. Almost no one knew about Kamp's war record, or where to look for it.

And as for Crow's admonition regarding the "forces arrayed against" him, Kamp assumed this was not an exaggeration. During his first three months as the city's detective, he'd come across evidence of no fewer than twenty-seven secret societies in a town of fewer than five thousand people. He knew these organizations were typically nothing more than a reason for men to get together and drink beer. And in some cases secret societies contributed to the civic good, for instance, providing money to widows and orphans. The membership rolls, meeting times and objectives of most secret societies were also made public. Crow had hinted and Kamp had intuited that secret societies—whose membership and activities actually *were* a secret—existed. He understood that bringing justice might mean laying bare such an organization's secrets. He still believed that Crow may have been trying to taunt him into quitting, though Crow would have deduced by now, and the Judge would have confirmed, that Kamp wasn't one to quit.

That left the possibility that Crow had simply told him the truth. In other words, someone was or would be gunning for him. Maybe today, maybe tomorrow and for a reason that he had not yet discerned. But whatever the reason, a real threat existed. He resolved to meet it. Kamp smelled breakfast wafting from the kitchen and shook himself from the last of his stupor. Time to let that magnificent word train run its route, black clouds be damned. Time to move.

9

That Daniel Knecht had returned to his familiar role and returned to his former standing in the Bauer household could not be doubted. He sat in his same chair at each meal, told the same stories and drank from the same cup. Like a semi-feral house cat that leaves without explanation and seemingly for good only to return and immediately curl up on the preferred windowsill, Daniel Knecht was back. And yet, no one felt quite the same as before the argument with Jonas Bauer, before Knecht had run off down the road. Bauer felt a twinge of annoyance and suspicion whenever Knecht made a joke. In the months before, he'd appreciated Knecht's humor for the most part. Now, he saw it as ingratiating and manipulative. Bauer could tell that Rachel regarded him differently as well. She'd introduced a degree of distance and formality between herself and Knecht, unspoken but unmistakable.

Having had a lifetime of looking out for and interpreting other people's suspicion, anger and malice toward him, Knecht must have noticed the shift most of all. Bauer detected no overt change for the worse. He thought, if anything Knecht's doing an even better job as a boarder than before. But Bauer sensed that behind the jovial demeanor and the flashing smile, the wheels turned. Bauer knew that the fears and misgivings that led to their argument hadn't been resolved and that the conditions required for resolution couldn't be met. Knecht needed something he'd never get, and Bauer needed him gone.

Bauer had decided he'd wait until after the Christmas holiday, hoping that the girls would feel less anguish and that Knecht would be more amenable to moving on. Naturally, Knecht seemed to know it was coming and redoubled his efforts to play the part of family member. A week before Christmas, the family had hiked up the mountain to get the *weinachtsbaum,* cheering on Bauer with each swing of the ax. Knecht singlehandedly dragged the tree back down the mountain, stood it up in the front room in an iron stand he fashioned himself and helped the girls decorate it. When they finished trimming the tree, Knecht was the first one who ran out the front door so that he could look at it through the front window.

"Now *that's* a tree!" he'd said.

The day after that, Knecht had given Rachel a small bandbox adorned with a pattern of reindeer. When she opened it, Knecht said, "It's a bayberry candle, Mrs. Bauer. They say it gives you good luck if you burn it on Christmas Eve, but you have to let it burn all the way. Otherwise, it don't work."

As usual, Knecht had caught Rachel off-guard. She blushed and said, "Why, thank you, Danny. That's very thoughtful." She held up the candle. She said, *"Lieb, lieb,"* and then retrieved a candlestick. At the time Bauer had wondered where Knecht had gotten the candle and whether he'd paid for it.

With each kind word and gesture, Bauer's anxiety grew. He felt considerable relief when, the Sunday before Christmas, Knecht vanished early in the afternoon. Bauer hoped that he'd gone to Easton to celebrate with his own family. He felt relieved, too, that the girls made no mention of his absence and were content to recite rhymes and sing carols with each other. As he sat in his chair in the front room, he breathed in the aroma of the turkey cooking in the kitchen, listened to the sweetness and joy in his daughters' songs and watched the last orange rays of the afternoon slip behind the house. Jonas Bauer let the sensations overtake him and allowed himself to relax. *Gott ist gute, gott ist gute*, he thought and dropped off to sleep.

A moment later he snapped awake to the sound of loud banging on the front door. The girls' singing stopped abruptly, and they ran to the front door. The banging continued, and Bauer also heard what sounded like chains rattling on the front steps. The girls stood at the front window and craned their necks to get a glimpse. Rachel came running from the kitchen.

She said, "Father, *wer ist es?*"

"I don't rightly know who it is. Get back, girls, get *back!*"

"Let me in," a low voice growled from the other side of the door, and the girls shrieked in unison. Bauer's mind went to the four-barrel revolver on the windowsill in the bedroom. The banging continued, as did the rattling of the chains.

Heidi shouted, "Let him in, daddy!"

Anna echoed her. "Yes, let him in." Bauer realized that the scene had been rehearsed somehow, or at least mentioned to the girls in advance.

Bauer turned to Rachel. "What do you know about this?" She shook her head.

He swung the front door open to see a figure dressed in black wearing a fearsome, snarling mask with horns and an audacious, red wooden tongue. The figured was covered in an array of black furs and wore a black felt hat. In his right hand he carried a wooden broom. In his left, a coiled iron chain.

The girls screamed in unison, "It's Belsnickel!"

Rachel said, "*Oh, gott im himmel.*" Under the hat, the mask and the furs Bauer recognized the unmistakable form of Daniel Knecht.

"Let me in!"

The girls let out a peal of laughter and ran to the back of the room. Bauer stepped aside and let him pass. He noticed that Knecht also had a burlap sack slung over his shoulder.

Knecht said, "I have questions for you girls," and he walked across the room to Anna who hugged Nyx's leg.

"What's your name, little girl?"

Anna laughed and said, "You know my name."

He yelled, "What's your name!" All three girls shuddered and screamed.

"My name is Anna. What's your name? And what's that chain for?"

"Silence!" Knecht set the chain on the floor and opened the burlap sack. He removed a stack of paper dolls, girls holding hands, and offered it to Anna who snatched it from his fingers.

Knecht said, "They try to keep me in chains, but it don't work!"

He turned his attention to Heidi, who'd sat down in a chair. He bent down. "I have a question for you, girl."

"What is it?" Heidi said, stifling a giggle.

"Can you pray?"

"Can I pray? Why do *you* care?" She rolled her eyes.

"If you can pray, I'll give you a treat. If not, I'll beat you with this broom!" More shrieking, more laughter.

Heidi said, "Yes, yes, I can pray."

Knecht fished around theatrically in the burlap sack and produced a white porcelain figure of a ballet dancer. Heidi took it from him, amazed. Knecht turned to Nyx, and silence descended on the room. He leaned in toward her slowly, his mask inches from her face. She stood facing him, one eyebrow raised.

He said, "How old are you?"

Nyx said, "How old are *you?*"

"Me? Why, I'm three thousand years old!" He leaned in even closer so that the nose of the mask brushed Nyx's nose. "How old are you...Nadine?"

She said, "I'm old enough. Now what do I get?"

Knecht stood upright, arched his back and bellowed, "You...get...*nothing!*" At the same time, he tossed a handful of candies, each wrapped in brightly colored paper, into the air. He cackled as the candies clattered to the wood floor. He threw another handful, then another. Heidi and Anna scrambled on hands and knees to collect the treats. Rachel bent down discreetly to retrieve one for herself. In the corner Jonas Bauer fumed but kept his mouth shut.

Kamp knew the roads would be swept clean of carriages and people the day before Christmas. And in place of the typical muddy ruts was a new coat of snow, placid and untouched. He figured that not seeing anyone on his walk to town would lift his spirits. Kamp hadn't slept the night before, his mind crowded with the loud voices of unwelcome guests with whom he'd likely never make peace. Reminders of the season–a carol in the distance, a Christmas tree in a family's front window, the cookies Shaw made–any of them could set off an explosion of disturbing memories and associations. He walked the road to town, forcing himself at first to focus only on each step. Having established his walking rhythm, he lifted his gaze to the snowflakes spinning down and listened to the tiny sound they made when they landed on the brim of his hat. In this way he lulled the demons to sleep.

When he reached town, he discovered a great deal more commotion than he expected. In fact, he found the streets even busier than normal, despite the weather. He heard the Black Diamond Unlimited pulling out of the station, and he saw the stacks of Native Iron going full bore, blowing great plumes of black smoke as if light had never come into the world, and never would.

Kamp headed straight for the police station and found that it, too, was busier than normal. The jail cell, which normally held one or two wayward souls, was packed with men, some singing, some crying, none quiet, all drunk. He scanned the faces behind bars. Most of them he recognized, and a few called out to him.

"*Wie bischt,* Kamp?"

"Shouldn't you be at church?"

"Come down here to get a break from the old lady?"

Kamp could only make out part of what any of the men said due to the collective din they produced. And yet Druckenmiller sat at his desk, calmly reading a book. Kamp snapped fingers in front of Druckenmiller's eyes. Druckenmiller looked up, bemused.

"Sam, I need to talk to you. It's too loud in here. Let's talk outside."

"What!"

Kamp said, "Let's go outside. *I need to talk to you!*"

Druckenmiller pointed to his ears and said, "I can't hear you." He'd stuffed a large cotton ball in each ear. Kamp leaned over and gently removed them.

Druckenmiller said, "This book is fantastic." He held it up. "*Die Schwarze Spinne.* The Black Spider. You hafta read it when I'm done. Pure horror." The front cover showed an enormous black spider engulfed in flames. "Only problem is those goddamned noisy louses!" He jerked his thumb toward the holding cell. "It's too loud in here. Why don't we talk outside?"

As they headed for the door, the shouts of the men followed them.

"Was it something I said?"

"Don't forget about us!"

As soon as they got outside, Druckenmiller pulled the flask from his vest pocket, held it up and said, "Merry Christmas." He took a long swig and tried to hand the flask to Kamp, who looked at him with a blank expression. Druckenmiller stepped back and studied him. "*Ach*, what's the matter? You look a little *ferhoodled*."

"Sam, every guy in there is drunk, and you're standing on the steps of the police station, drinking."

"Yah, it's the holidays." Druckenmiller noticed Kamp's sour expression. "Jesus, what got up your ass?"

Druckenmiller took another pull from the flask, then put it back. When he did, Kamp saw a blaze of leather and metal inside his jacket.

"What's with the rig?"

"What rig?

"The holster, Sam. The pistol."

"Oh, yah."

"I thought you didn't carry a gun. Didn't you tell me the shepherd's crook was enough? What changed?"

Druckenmiller's expression darkened. "What did you want to talk to me about?"

"What do you know about secret societies? Crow told me–"

"Crow. That goddamn guy."

"Crow told me that there's real trouble coming, coming after me, and you."

Druckenmiller shifted back and forth and pursed his lips, looking very uncomfortable. He looked past Kamp's shoulder and then at the ground.

Kamp said, "Did I say something wrong?"

"No."

"I want to know what you know about that."

He saw the color rise in Druckenmiller's face. "It's just, it's just, you come down here..." He looked at Kamp and then at the ground. "You come down here, and I'm tryin' to be friendly, you know. Sociable. I'm tryin' to be sociable on account of Christmas and whatnot, and you're my friend, but you're being, you're being a, a..."

"A what?"

Druckenmiller's face went purple. "An ass, Kamp! You're being a horse's ass!"

The people streaming past the scene stared as they went by. A voice called out, "You tell 'em, Druck!"

Kamp watched the theatrics without flinching. He said, "I think you know what I'm talking about. You wanted to pretend it's not there, get soused, plug up your ears. This whole time you've been telling me nothing's really wrong, just drunks *brunsing* on the sides of buildings. Business as usual. But I think something scared you. Someone said something to you, or did something. You can't pretend. You can only go along with it, if they let you."

Druckenmiller stared at the ground and mumbled something.

"What did you say?"

"I said, what do you care?"

Druckenmiller looked up to meet Kamp's gaze, and Kamp saw shame and sorrow in the man's eyes. He'd meant to give him a shock, sharp and short, to jolt him. But he realized that instead he'd cut his friend to the bone. He'd overdone it.

"Even if you do care," Druckenmiller said, "what do you have to tear me down for? I'm the only one on your side. Christ." He hung his head and trudged back into the station.

10

In the moment before the explosion, that instant when every man and boy in the mine perceived at a level just below consciousness that doomsday had arrived, Jonas Bauer had been thinking about his friend, Roy Kunkle. They were working side by side that day, and Kunkle, a physically imposing creature, had been hitting it harder than usual, hacking full tilt. With every swing, he'd sent black diamonds flying from the seam. Kunkle had been working angry, though Bauer didn't know why and didn't wonder about it much. Kunkle was a stormy fellow after all, often at odds with others, though rarely with fellow workers. In that moment before the blast, Bauer had had a flicker of insight regarding his friend, and the cause of his anger. In the moment after the explosion, as he choked on the dust and wiggled his parts to see if everything was still attached, Bauer thought first of Roy Kunkle. He touched Kunkle's knee.

"Roy? Roy?"

Bauer had gotten no response. He laid his hand on Kunkle's chest and felt a heartbeat, then another, then nothing. Bauer held his hand over where Kunkle's mouth should have been and didn't feel a breath. When Bauer tried to touch Kunkle's brow to see if it felt warm, he realized the man's head wasn't there at all.

More memories, as well as new insights, had started to flow. Bauer realized he must have been knocked unconscious by the explosion, because now he remembered waking up on the floor of the shaft, coughing. Until now, he hadn't remembered anything about the moments prior to the explosion and barely anything after. He was starting to remember that Kunkle had been trying to tell him something and possibly had given him something right before it happened. Strain as he might, though, Bauer could not recall what it was or even what it might have been.

Jonas Bauer couldn't imagine why this particular chain of memories should have surfaced on Christmas Day, at the time of day, in fact, when Bauer felt most relaxed and satisfied. He'd eaten his fill of the feast Rachel had prepared, and Bauer had basked in the love of his daughters. Even better, Knecht had stayed away most of the morning, out of respect for the family, Bauer hoped. Knecht had returned just before lunch but went straight to the cellar to work on a project or repair one of the hand tools. Bauer was content to leave him alone, regardless. He settled back into his chair and felt the muscles in his hands and feet relax. He breathed a long, slow sigh. Fragments of memories from that day in the mine started drifting into his consciousness again. Bauer saw it now. Kunkle had stopped swinging his pick and had stood up straight to address Bauer.

He'd said, "Here, take this" and shoved something in Bauer's hand. Bauer remembered putting it in his pocket, though he couldn't remember what it was. Slowly, bit by bit, the memory continued to form, and as Bauer focused his full attention on the scene, he could just barely begin to make out what it was.

"Sorry to bother you." Knecht stood directly in front of Bauer.

The memory vanished. "Jesus Christ, Danny. *Was ist?*"

"Well, first, I wanted to say Merry Christmas, and second, I wanted to see if I could talk to you."

"Yah, sure, sure, sit down." Bauer could not hide his irritation. The peace and contentment he'd felt all day drained out of him. Knecht pulled up a wooden chair.

"Mr. Bauer, I know things ain't exactly been right since you and I had that falling out, if that's what it was.

And I know you have some questions about my intentions, 'specially regarding Nadine."

"Danny, it's just—"

"I understand, Mr. Bauer. I understand the situation you're in. You hafta do what's best and say the right things according to how to be a man and to raise your family. And I've learned a lot from being here. Learned a lot from you, sir. Thank you."

"You're welcome." Bauer felt his throat constrict when he said it and saw Knecht's fingers curl and tighten. "Anything else, Danny?"

"Well, I realized in this past week that I should probably be leaving soon. Find my own place. Get out on my own. Move out. That's what I need, seems like." A wave of relief washed over Bauer, and he prayed that the conversation would end right there.

"Mr. Bauer, there's one more thing." Knecht leaned forward in his chair, putting his forearms on his knees. "I want to start my own family someday. I want to live in a house like this one."

"That's good."

"I want to take Nadine with me when I go, sir. I want Nadine to be my wife."

The snow that had begun falling on Christmas Eve continued straight through Christmas morning, and Kamp figured there might even be a foot on the ground. He'd seen no travelers on the road that day, except for a sleigh drawn by a team of horses. He saw a family in the sleigh, probably headed for Jonas Bauer's house. He had no plans for leaving the house, no urge to go walking. He felt content to stay put, for a change. Shaw had already spent the better part of the day in bed, and he had no intention of waking her. E. Wyles had told him that the time was drawing near and that he should be ready to come get her if he thought labor had begun. Earlier, he'd chopped wood and stacked it next to the fireplace in the front room of the house. He threw a few logs on the fire, unlaced his boots and took them off. He let the warmth of the flames seep into his toes, and he felt a powerful relaxation overtake him. His mind drifted back to the moment he met Shaw, looked in her eyes, found his way. Kamp stretched out on the floor in front of the fireplace, and lying on his back, watched the snowflakes twirl and spin past the window. Soon, he drifted into a heavy slumber.

The Fogels arrived at the home of Jonas Bauer by sleigh in the middle of the afternoon on Christmas Day. The younger Bauer girls, Heidi and Anna, heard the bells, rushed to the front door and swung it open, oblivious to the conversation that had just ended between their father and Daniel Knecht. Rachel had planned an afternoon of games and singing, and the children immediately began playing with toys they got for Christmas. Jonas Bauer struck up a conversation with the father, John Fogel, about the ride over and about the snow. As he talked, he scanned the room and noticed neither Knecht nor Nyx was there. Bauer's heart started thudding in his chest. Rachel noticed Bauer's distress, and he motioned for her to meet him in the kitchen.

He said to John Fogel, "Excuse me."

"Why, sure."

When they got to the kitchen, Rachel put her hand on Bauer's arm. "What is it, Jonas?"

"*Ach*, it's Danny."

"What about him?"

"Says he wants to move out. And as far as I'm concerned, good riddance."

"Oh, Jonas."

"Yah, well, he wants to take Nyx with him. Wants to marry her. Wants to leave right away." Rachel held her hand to her mouth and laughed. "Oh, father."

"What's so funny?"

"Nyx isn't going anywhere with him."

"Why not?"

"Danny's just confused."

"About what?"

"She doesn't love him." Rachel put her arm around Bauer's shoulders.

"Well, *mebbe* she don't, but either he don't know that, or he don't care."

"He's harmless."

"Like hell he is. He's leaving tonight!"

"Keep your voice down. You can't put him out tonight. You can't just throw him out into the snow. Not on Christmas. Think about the strain it would put on everyone."

"Rachel, his intentions are wrong. I seen it in his eyes."

"Be firm with him. Tell him he must be out tomorrow."

"Ach, I don't even know where he *is*. Or Nyx."

Bauer left the kitchen and hurried up the stairs. He saw a light in Nyx's room through a crack in the door. "Nyx! Nyx!" No reply. Bauer burst through the door and found Nyx standing in front of her mirror, brushing her hair.

She looked at Bauer in the mirror. "Daddy, what is it?"

Jonas Bauer forced himself to breathe slower. "Nothing. It was just, I just—nothing. I'm sorry. How come you're up here and not with everyone else?"

"I needed quiet." She continued pulling the brush through her long hair.

"Where's Danny?" Bauer turned to leave.

"I haven't seen him. Is something wrong, Daddy? Did something happen to Danny?"

Bauer pulled the door hard behind him. He hustled down the steps to the first floor, then down again to the cellar. The cellar was dark, except for a small light in the back corner. Bauer stopped and quieted himself, listening, and heard nothing. He walked softly across the cellar floor around the corner and toward the dim light. Knecht was there, waiting.

Bauer said, "Danny, you're here."

"Where am I supposed to be?"

"Well, I don't know exactly, though I didn't figure you'd be down here in the dark."

"Then why come looking?"

"Well, I—how come you're here?"

"I'm getting my things together, some things I left down here. So I can leave tomorrow."

"Now, if you want to—"

"I heard."

"If you want to stay until–heard what?"

"What you said. What you talked about with Mrs. Bauer. I was down here. I heard it all through the hole in the kitchen floor."

"Danny, we can talk about—"

"Heard how you think I ought to leave right away, how you're certain I got wrong intentions. How Nadine don't love me." While he spoke, Knecht did not move but stayed crouched on the floor.

Bauer said, "Who's right or wrong…it don't matter. But what's best is for you to leave tomorrow morning."

"I know. I understand now. I won't cause no trouble, won't let on if that's what you're worried about. And if it's all right with you, I don't want to tell the girls till tomorrow. I don't wanna upset 'em…they're having too much fun."

"Well, that's kind of you, Danny. Let's go back upstairs."

For the rest of the evening, Bauer forced himself not to watch Knecht continuously. He told himself again and again that Rachel was right, that Knecht, no matter how confused or upset, was not dangerous. But he couldn't banish the worry. For his part Knecht displayed no distress at all. As soon as they emerged from the cellar, Knecht took up his typical role, playing games and joining in the singing. Most important, Bauer detected nothing unusual between Knecht and Nyx. He allowed himself to think, Knecht will keep his word. *Lord, make him keep his word.*

11

Daniel Knecht knew he'd crossed a threshold, knew that an overpowering darkness was threatening to invade, or already had. Still, he did not give himself over to it. He tried battling it one last time. The family had gone to bed at their normal hour that night, and so had Knecht. He hadn't slept much, and when he had, it was a brief and tormented. Knecht looked out the window to see a pristine world under starlight, bare branches blanketed with fresh snow and a cold, pure creek running by.

At two o'clock in the morning, Knecht went to the door of the bedroom where Nyx slept across the room from her sisters. He laid his hand on the cold brass knob. He heard wind in the trees outside and apart from that, silence. Knecht crept slowly into the room. By the moonlight, he easily discerned the form of Nyx in her bed. He got in beside her.

Nyx had known this moment would come, and she'd suspected it would be this very night. She'd seen it in his eyes before. Longing. It had been exciting to see the effect she had on this man, at first. She saw what it did to her father as well, how it made him angry. It thrilled her. It was a harmless game. She knew that nothing would come of it, and she believed Danny Knecht understood that too. At least he better. And if he didn't, her father would keep him in line. Then, Danny's interest began to scare her, too. She felt him watching her. Tonight it had been worse, though. Even if no one else could tell, she saw that he was desperate.

Roused from sleep, Nyx felt Danny's calloused hands on her hips and his breath on the back of her neck.

She gritted her teeth and hissed, "*Don't.*"

Under his breath, Knecht said, "Don't talk, Nadine." He started to lift her nightgown.

"No!" She said it loud enough to wake Heidi.

Knecht whispered, "Forgive me," and he pressed himself against her.

"I said, no!" Nyx swung a fist backward and caught Knecht across the jaw. Her second punch landed on his nose and brought tears to his eyes.

Knecht said, "I love you, Nadine."

She screamed, "Get away from me" and shoved him out of the bed. By now Nyx's sisters were both sitting up, trying to make sense of the grim drama playing out in their moonlit room.

Knecht stood up, rubbed his eyes and walked out of the room. He's gone, Nyx thought. Now he knows how I feel, and now he'll leave me alone for good. She felt relief as she watched him leave. He shut the door behind him, and the room became quiet. Safe from him.

Then Nyx heard a soft *click*. She knew the sound well. Daniel Knecht had locked the bedroom door from outside. She and her sisters were now locked in their room. If he'd wanted to get in there so bad in the first place, why would he leave and lock the door behind him?

"Kamp! Kamp! Open the door. Something awful has happened!"

He heard the man trying to open the locked front door. From where he'd been sleeping in front of the fireplace, Kamp scrambled to his feet and looked through the front window. He recognized the man's voice and outline in the moonlight. Daniel Knecht.

He lit a lantern and opened the front door. "What is it, Danny?"

"Robbers broke in. They hurt Mr. and Mrs. Bauer real bad."

"Are they still there?"

"Yah, they're in their bed."

"No, the robbers. Were they in the house when you left?" Kamp pulled on his boots and laced them up as he talked.

"*Ach*, I don't know. I doubt it. I ran here as soon as I seen what they done."

He put on his coat and hat and hustled out the door with Knecht following, making certain the door was locked behind him.

Kamp said, "We're going to Richter's first."

"What for?"

George Richter's was the one house in the mile between his place and Bauer's. Kamp and Knecht hurried up the road, then down the path to Richter's house where Kamp pounded on the front door. A bleary-eyed George Richter appeared in his nightclothes, holding a kerosene lamp. Kamp described the situation to him.

Richter said, "I'll get Hugh, and we'll go" and closed the door.

Kamp knew he was referring to Hugh Arndt, his hired man. A few minutes later the door opened and George Richter, now fully dressed stood in the doorway, pushing shells into a shiny double-barreled shotgun.

Kamp said, "Looks brand new."

"Christmas present."

Richter walked out the door, followed by Hugh Arndt who also carried a gun, a Sharps rifle. The four men broke into a jog once they reached the road.

Richter said to Knecht, "How bad are they hurt?"

"They aren't."

Kamp said, "You told me they're hurt real bad."

"Oh, I thought he meant the girls. They're not hurt at all...far as I know."

Richter said, "What about Jonas and Rachel?"

Knecht said, "Oh, yah, they're hurt real bad."

"Did you see them?"

"Who?"

"Them that done it. The robbers," Richter said.

Knecht said, "No, I did not."

"Not at all?"

"I must've been asleep until it was already over. When I looked in on them, it was already done."

Richter said, "Do you know whether they left or not?"

"It was just quiet in the house afterwards."

The men clutched their weapons, slowing down, stepping carefully as they reached the front of the house. The front door hung wide open, just as Knecht had left it. It gaped at them, the darkness inside much blacker than the night sky.

"George, go around that way," Kamp said. He motioned around the left side of the house. "Hugh, go around the other." The two men walked off, heads swiveling slowly.

Knecht started up the front steps ahead of Kamp and through the front door. They paused once inside, listening. They could hear crying, muffled through the walls.

Kamp called out, "Jonas Bauer! Are you there? Bauer!"

His voice boomed through the house. They listened again and heard nothing. Then, the children began to shriek. Knecht stole a glance at Kamp, and he touched the four-barrel revolver tucked into his waistband.

Kamp said, "Danny, get us a lantern." Knecht walked into the kitchen as George Richter and Hugh Arndt walked through the front door.

Richter whispered, "No one out there."

"Nope. No one," Arndt said.

Knecht returned with a burning lantern. Kamp turned to him and said, "Where are they?"

"That way." Knecht pointed into the darkness.

"All right. Show us."

Their boots thundered, *clop, clop* in the hallway. When the four men reached the bedroom door, George Richter raised the double-barrel and braced it against his shoulder as if to protect himself from what he was about to witness.

Large splatters of blood containing flesh and chunks of brain clung to the wall next to the bed. Jonas Bauer's head had been hacked nearly off, held on now only by a few cords of muscle. His face was split horizontally from ear to ear. Rachel's wounds were similar. Her skull was caved in above her eyes, and her face had been cleaved open at her mouth. The bodies lay side by side in the marital bed with the quilt pulled up to their chins. An ax lay crosswise on Rachel's chest.

George Richter lowered his shotgun, took off his hat and said, "Christ almighty. Jonas."

Kamp had seen a great deal of gore on the battlefield and never got used to it. At the same time, he'd come to understand that the ruination of human bodies was a requirement for war. This, however, was different. He immediately recognized the scene as personal, intimate, a paroxysm of violence unlike what he'd seen in battle. Some power wanted them to gaze at the bodies indefinitely, and he knew that having looked had already caused a great disturbance within him. He forced himself to focus on the other details in the room, the quilt pulled up to their chins, the way the ax had been placed, the open cigar box on the windowsill.

Kamp looked at the faces of the other men. George Richter appeared to be very angry, while Hugh Arndt stared at the floor. Knecht gaped at the bodies with a look of shock, disbelief and heartbreak.

Kamp said, "Let's find the children." Immediately Richter and Arndt were out the door and up the staircase. On his way out of the room, Kamp brushed past Knecht, who stood unmoving, fixed to the floor.

Richter shouted, "Nyx! Heidi!" When he burst into their bedroom, the girls shrieked again. Heidi and Anna held each other, wailing. Nyx sat on her bed, silent, head down.

Richter said, "Oh, thank God."

Nyx raised her head and screamed, "Where are they!"

"Settle down, child. Settle down." Richter moved to put his arms around Nyx, and she shoved him away forcefully.

Kamp walked into the room. Nyx looked straight at him. "What did he do? *Tell me!*"

Christ, Kamp thought. *Knecht.*

Nyx launched herself toward the door, but Richter blocked her path and held her fast. Kamp ran back downstairs to where he'd left Knecht standing next to the bodies. The corpses were still there. Knecht was gone.

By the time Nyx explained to the men what Knecht had tried to do to her and how he'd locked them all in her room, Knecht had broken into a dead run across the snow that covered George Richter's cornfield. The first rays of dawn slid through the trees at the border of the field. Sun up would bring the scene under the harshest light imaginable.

Richter stayed with the girls in their room, barring the door. He sent Hugh Arndt to get the word out. They would need help caring for the bodies, comforting the girls and finding Knecht. He walked out of the house into the grey morning light. He could only conclude that the fiend Knecht had finally appeared in full. That which everyone had sensed in him, and feared, had emerged. He wondered how Knecht's true nature could have remained so hidden, so deep, only to explode into view. And yet, he admitted to himself, it had. Perhaps the thousand tons of pressure it took for Knecht to keep it all underground had contributed to or even caused the explosion. Irrelevant now.

The goal was simple. He needed to find him, haul him back, bring him to justice. Kamp imagined that Knecht had shifted from murderer to fugitive. He'd want to get as far away as he could, but he'd know that at least a dozen determined men with horses and dogs would be hunting for him very soon. Knecht would know, too, that traveling in daylight would get him caught. He'll find a hiding place and lie low until dark, Kamp reasoned. And if anyone else but me finds Knecht first, they'll kill him on sight. And so Kamp went alone.

Following Knecht's footprints through the snow would have been the easiest way to track the man and certainly the most direct. Picking up his tracks would prove difficult, however. The front yard of the house was crisscrossed with many sets of footprints, making it impossible for Kamp to single out the right ones. He guessed Knecht would have wanted to run on the road as long as he could in order to avoid creating a single set of tracks into the woods. Eventually, though, and probably soon, he'd need to get off the road which would force him to cross the creek. And if he did that, he'd prefer to cross by bridge. Otherwise, his feet would freeze. Kamp headed off in the direction of the one place that, if his string of assumptions were correct, Knecht would be hiding.

Sainter's Mills was the name given to a collection of grinding mills adjacent to George Richter's property and powered by the Shawnee Creek. Next to each mill was a barn that housed the miller's tools, as well as the crop. None of the mills offered a hiding place, unlike the barns. Kamp guessed that he'd likely find Knecht in one of the barns, probably the one farthest from the Bauer house. Knecht would wait for the Black Diamond Unlimited, and he'd simply catch out the next time the train passed. If that happened, Daniel Knecht would vanish for certain.

He pieced together the logic while he jogged on the road. Just before he turned to cross the bridge, a horse-drawn sleigh carrying a man, woman and four children glided past going in the direction of Jonas Bauer's house.

A man's voice called from the sleigh. "Morning, Kamp."

People already know, he thought, and they want to go look. He kept his head down and trotted across the bridge and toward the mills. As he neared the first building, he slowed to a walk and stepped lightly to avoid crunching the snow. He scanned the ground for footprints and saw none, though it seemed certain Knecht would have erased his tracks by now. He recalled the empty cigar box he'd seen on the windowsill, and for the first time, Kamp felt acutely aware that he didn't have a gun.

He walked to the last barn and stopped to listen. A blue jay whirred in a tree. Kamp heard clumps of snow falling to the ground from the branches above, then nothing. He pulled back the barn door. Shards of morning sun slanted in behind him, and he let his eyes adjust to the semi-darkness. He saw a wagon in there, filled with horse tack and a kerosene lantern, painted green. He spotted two winnowing machines against the wall. Between them, he saw a wooden ax handle. No blade, just the handle.

Kamp stepped quietly across the floor and retrieved the handle. He took it in both hands and felt the heft of it. He strained to listen, to hear above the roar of blood at his temples. He stood motionless for several minutes, more hunter now than detective. He heard enough silence to convince him he was alone in the barn. He turned to leave.

Thump. Movement above. Then another bump. He's up there, Kamp thought. He walked silently to the ladder that led up to the second floor of the barn. He looked straight up into the darkness. He realized he wouldn't be able to climb the ladder and carry the ax handle at the same time. He set the ax handle aside and began to climb. The ladder creaked, sometimes loudly, as he ascended.

Kamp reached the top rung, shoulders hunched, ready to jump back down if necessary. He saw the shape of a man, sitting between two large piles of hay. The man sat cross-legged with his back to him, staring through a small window at the blue sky outside.

Kamp said calmly, "Danny."

Knecht gave no response. He stopped looking out the window and stared straight ahead.

"Danny, I need you to come with me."

"I knew you'd come and find me." He didn't move.

"I know what happened. I know something went wrong. I know it was a mistake."

"It wasn't no mistake. Say, remind me once. I need to give you something.

"What?"

"Don't let me forget."

"Give it to me later."

"And there's something else. Someone taught me something. Made me commit it to memory. That's what the person said. '*Commit these words to memory.*' Do you want to hear it?" Knecht turned his shoulders and neck to face him, and Kamp saw an expression of pure menace. It was Daniel Knecht, to be sure. But his face was contorted, a deeply furrowed brow and lips twisted into a snarl.

"Come on, Danny. Let's go."

Knecht said, "You hafta hear this."

"Get up."

"It goes, *Quia merito haec patior.*"

Kamp heard a hammer cock as Knecht lifted the four-barrel pistol to his own temple.

Knecht said, "How's that for a joke?"

Kamp lunged across the floor, reaching Knecht as the gun went off. The bullet grazed Knecht's scalp and lodged in the ceiling. He slammed into Knecht, knocking him sideways. He jammed his knee against Knecht's chest and pinned his head to the floor. He grabbed the wrist that held the gun and with his other hand, Kamp took the revolver. Knecht gave no resistance. Instead he rolled onto his side and stared blankly at the wall. The tension, the rage vanished. Kamp eased off slowly, the pistol trained on Knecht.

He said, "Danny, come with me."

It occurred to Kamp that considering the circumstances, most men would have let Knecht deliver himself to his maker. And some would've even enjoyed seeing him do it. Allowing Knecht to kill himself might have been an act of mercy, because by the time they emerged from the barn into full sunlight, Kamp could hear the shouts of the men and the barking of their dogs, all heading for Sainter's Mills. He saw that behind the dirt, blood smears and hard lines, Knecht's face had transformed again. He now looked like a broken child.

Knecht said, "Don't let 'em have me."

"Just walk." Kamp shoved Knecht in front of him.

With the pistol trained on Knecht, Kamp marched his prisoner back in the direction of Jonas Bauer's house. The first person to meet the pair was George Richter, and behind him his hired man, Hugh Arndt. Richter came running, losing his footing now and again in the snow.

Richter shouted, "He done it! It was him!" Richter slowed to a walk, breathing hard and trying to not to slip as he kept the muzzle pointed at Knecht. Hugh Arndt kept his gun raised as well.

"Step aside."

Kamp studied Richter's face, cheeks blazing bright red, eyes bulging from their sockets.

"We're going to take care of this right now. Me and Hugh. Step aside!"

Kamp stepped directly in front of Knecht and said, "No. This is not the appointed hour." Richter gently released the hammers on his shotgun, and Arndt lowered his rifle.

"Walk." As Knecht passed him, Kamp pressed the barrel of the pistol into the small of Knecht's back and followed him. When they passed Richter and Arndt, Kamp said, "Stay on either side of us when we get there. Hold your guns at your side, and keep your mouths shut."

"Jesus boom, you can't expect us to protect this filthy dog that done what—"

"Do it," Kamp said, and he kept marching Knecht down the road with Richter and Arndt in tow.

The closer they got to Jonas Bauer's house, the slower they had to move, owing to the swarm that had already amassed there. Sleighs and their horses lined the fence that ran alongside Shawnee Creek. Children chased each other through the snow on the lawn of Bauer's home. Women huddled at the side of the road, talking in hushed tones, barely beating back a feeling of collective hysteria. Men pounded on the front door, shouting, "Let us see it once! Now! Now!"

Kamp recognized the scene for what it was, a grisly carnival. So distracted were the carnival-goers by their apocalyptic fantasies that they didn't notice the villain in their midst, and he quietly guided Knecht to the door of the barn next to the house.

He said to George Richter, "Keep watch over him. You're my neighbor, George, but anything happens to him while I'm gone, you'll swing for it. That's certain."

Arndt snarled, "Figures someone like you would–"

Kamp said, "Protect him."

Richter seethed. He jammed the butt of the gun between Knecht's shoulder blades, knocking him into the barn. Then he and Arndt followed him in. Kamp walked around to the back of the house. A clump of men stood at the back door, pounding on it and shouting. No chance of getting in there. He went to the side of the house and spotted the bulkhead. He opened the door and scrambled down into the cellar. Kamp hurried up the cellar stairs and into the kitchen. He reasoned that he had a few minutes at most to assess the situation in the house before the mob found Knecht and ripped him to pieces.

Sam Druckenmiller stood guard at the door to the bedroom. He looked pale and scared and not likely to stem the tide of angry witnesses that might soon rush past him. He stepped aside as Kamp approached and entered the bedroom.

Having already seen the room, Kamp knew better than to try to take in the entire scene at once, particularly in the stark morning light. To do so would be to surrender his ability to analyze rationally and to be subject to the power of his visceral reactions. So unspeakable was the violence that shock, fear and revulsion could overwhelm him. He determined that he would process each sensory detail one at a time. He noticed first that almost nothing seemed out of place in the bedroom, including the bodies. Jonas and Rachel lay on their backs in repose, with their finely-sewn quilt pulled up to their chins. The only misplaced object was the empty cigar box, now on the floor below the windowsill and turned upside down. He looked at the blood on the wall next to the bed. He considered the force of each swing of the murder weapon it must have taken to create those patterns.

Kamp forced himself to inspect the ruined faces of Jonas and Rachel Bauer. They appeared identical in that each was an unrecognizable mask, not human. He wondered whether the killer's motive had been to obliterate these souls, to destroy them utterly with the most extreme and brutal force he could summon. He knew he was looking at an abomination, the likes of which no one should have to see, and certainly no man or woman should have to suffer. He looked upon a sight unnatural and perverse, evidence of an evil that should never have existed and always would.

Kamp put one hand on the forehead of the ruined Jonas Bauer and the other on the forehead of his wife Rachel. He allowed himself an instant to imagine them as children, running, laughing, picking raspberries. He felt a scream welling inside himself and stifled it.

He resumed the inspection, pulling back the quilt to look at the bodies, their bedclothes intact, bodies unharmed. He looked at the murder weapon, a common ax laid straight across Rachel Bauer's chest. Kamp pondered the placement of the ax and assumed it meant two things. First, the murderer may have intended to indicate the completion, the finality of the act. Second, the killer needed to demonstrate control, the imposition of order on total chaos. There could have been a rational process at work, a pattern he followed. Each swing of the weapon traced a predictable arc. The ax laid crosswise said, when I did it, I was not insane. I did precisely what needed to be done, what they deserved, and it is finished.

He tried to preserve his conclusions and wipe the entire scene from his mind, though he knew it had already left a permanent stain. Kamp opened the window to let in the frigid December air and to let out the intensifying stench. He heard anger and fear in the voices of the dozens, even hundreds of people outside, a rising wail. He heard the bedroom door open behind him, and he turned to see the coroner, A.J. Oehler walking in.

Oehler looked at the bodies and said in a low voice, "What's going on?"

Kamp said, "*Nix.*"

The two men stood side-by-side, staring at the corpses. Oehler was shorter than Kamp. He had thinning hair, a barrel chest and eyeglasses. He was unfazed by the carnage, which made sense to Kamp, given Oehler's line of work. Oehler produced a small tablet and pencil from his coat pocket and quietly began to take notes the way a botanist might note plant species in the field.

Oelher said, "Time of death, approximately."

"Three in the morning."

"Were the victims alive when you got here?"

"No."

"What time did you get here?"

"Probably four."

Oehler's manner brought a stillness to the proceedings. He continued taking notes and talking to himself. "Cause of death, by the looks of things, homicide." He looked up from his notepad and looked at the bodies, then the blood on the wall, then back at the bodies.

Oehler said, "Strange."

"What is?"

Another man stumbled into the room, the Reverend A.R. Ebertstark. The gruesome scene, the smell, all of it hit him full in the face. He said, "*Gott in himmel!*" and turned away, putting his hand over his nose and mouth.

Oehler asked Kamp, "Did you question him yet?"

"Who?"

"This man Knecht."

"No."

"Are you certain he done it?"

Kamp said, "Certain as I can be."

"Meaning what?"

"Meaning I wasn't here when it happened, so I didn't see him do it."

The Reverend A.R. Eberstark bent over and vomited on the floor.

Oehler said to Kamp, "They're going to hang him for sure."

Kamp said to Eberstark, "Reverend, Reverend." Eberstark struggled to steady himself. "I need you to talk to him, Daniel Knecht. He's in the barn."

The Reverend A.R. Eberstark stood up straight, and Oehler handed him a handkerchief.

Oehler said, "Go ahead. Keep it."

Eberstark wiped his mouth, and Oehler handed him a silver flask. The Reverend took a swig and handed back the flask. Oehler produced another handkerchief, wiped down the top and took a swig himself.

The shouting grew louder outside. Eberstark took off his glasses, rubbed his eyes and said, "The man is damned for certain. As well he should be."

Kamp said to him, "Talk to Knecht. Find out why he did it."

Eberstark gritted his teeth and said, "God will show this man no mercy."

Oehler said, "We will follow the law as best we can. We must follow a process to bring this man to justice."

Eberstark shot back, "You're a coroner, Arthur! You only handle 'em when they're cold. You're not a judge. And not an attorney."

Oehler boomed, "Christ, Reverend! The Judge isn't here. Attorney neither."

"The coroner is correct." The men in the room wheeled around to see Philander Crow standing in the doorway. "We will impanel a jury immediately. That's a killing rage outside. We must establish standard procedure if we're to keep those philistines at bay."

Kamp walked into the children's room, where Nyx was sitting on the edge of her bed, staring at the wall. She still wore her bedclothes. The color had drained from her face, and her hair was matted. He gently pulled a chair to the bedside and sat down. Nyx did not look at him.

He said, "My name is Kamp." No response. She continued staring. "Nyx, I know what happened. I'm sorry."

Without looking at him, she said, "I know who you are."

"What did you see, Nyx?"

"I looked through that stovepipe hole." She glanced over at the hole in the floor in the corner of the room.

"What did you see?"

"I saw him wiping off the blood. I saw him burning his clothes."

"Was there anyone else? Nyx, did you see anyone else besides Daniel Knecht?"

Nyx turned to face him and said, "Of course not." She turned back to stare at the wall, and he realized that Nyx had gone somewhere else.

What Kamp couldn't see was that she'd traveled six months back in her mind to a warm Sunday afternoon in June a few days after a stranger named Daniel Knecht had moved into their house. She saw herself on the railroad trestle next to Shawnee Creek.

Nyx's parents had taken her sisters to Bethlehem. Earlier in the day, their one day off from working in the coal mine, her father and Knecht had begun building a fence that would "line the whole road," as her father said. From her bedroom window, she'd watched them working together.

Before they left for Bethlehem, she heard her father tell her mother in the kitchen, "We done good, honest work today. Especially Daniel." Then he turned to look at Daniel Knecht and said, "Well done."

Nyx had stolen a glance at Knecht, who was looking down at the floor. To her, it appeared as if he felt embarrassed and proud. She'd heard her father say, "We didn't get as far as we wanted, but it was a decent start. We'll get back to it next Sunday. Fence won't go nowhere until then."

She'd also heard Knecht say that he'd be going back to Easton later in the day. So Nyx thought she was alone that Sunday afternoon. She listened to a breeze whispering to the branches overhead and farther away the songs of robins. Then Nyx picked up other sounds. Hammering and digging. She walked up the road and in the distance, she saw Daniel Knecht working on the fence, alone.

She went back to the house, made a sandwich and filled a cup with raspberries. She wrapped up the food and took it to Knecht. As she drew closer, Nyx watched him swing the sledgehammer, driving in a post. She could see that he'd perspired through his shirt. He worked with his back to her.

She said, "Daniel."

He didn't hear her. She tapped him on the shoulder, and he whirled around.

"I brought you this." Nyx handed him the food. Then, she turned and went back to the trestle. She lay down and listened to the breeze and the water as it burbled into the swimming hole under the bough of the chestnut tree and then back out again. She may have dozed on that warm afternoon, and she may have been sleeping when she became aware that Knecht was on the trestle. Nyx opened her eyes and saw him standing a few feet away. She felt no fear.

"Nadine, I just wanted to say thank you."

They looked at each other for a moment. Knecht wore work clothes, and he was covered with dirt and sweat. Nyx could tell he felt self-conscious.

"Wanna go for a swim?" she asked.

"Pardon?"

"A swim? Swimming. There's a deep spot."

In a graceful motion, Nyx stood up, threw off her dress and jumped in the water. Knecht turned to face in the opposite direction.

"Dammit, Nadine."

Nyx shouted, "Jump in the water!"

"*Shhh!*"

"Oh, come on!"

"Nadine, this ain't right. I hafta to go back to the house. I can't."

"Of course you can."

Knecht stood frozen in place for a full minute, then removed his boots and socks and then took off his shirt. He jumped off the trestle into the cold, green water. When he came to the surface, he called to Nyx, "You just stay over there!"

When they got out of the water, Nyx lay naked and prone on the warm concrete trestle. Knecht got fully dressed and sat close by but facing away from her.

He said, "Please put on your clothes. That's shameful."

"No, it isn't."

"Well, if anyone sees you like that, I'm done for."

"Probably." Nyx laughed, then laid her head down and closed her eyes again.

Knecht scanned the road and listened for carriages. He heard nothing.

"Nadine, why are you doing this?"

"Doing what?"

"The food. Now this. What do you want from me?"

There was another pause, total silence.

She asked, "Well, what do *you* want from *me*?"

Knecht swung his head around to look at Nyx who was now lying on her back, propped on her elbows and staring into the sky.

He looked away again and said, "Put your clothes on, girl. *Please.*"

"What's wrong?"

"You don't understand."

"Tell me," she said, "I want to."

Knecht saw all the locks falling from the box inside himself in which he'd buried the truth. He felt terror and shame. He said, "No." Nyx slid closer to him on the trestle. She gently ran the back of her fingertips across his shoulders.

"You can tell me."

Knecht took several deep breaths, and he let the box open. "Things happened to me, Nadine. Terrible things." He slumped forward, trying to hide his face from her.

"What kind of things?"

"Awful things. Shameful and wrong. All my fault."

"I can tell you're a good person. I can see it. Look at me, Daniel. I want you to know." He turned and let himself look into her eyes.

He said, "I'm broken, Nadine, no more than a wretch. You're too beautiful, far too beautiful for me." Nyx leaned forward and put her head to his chest, long enough to feel his heart pound out a few solitary beats.

They heard the clopping of hooves on the hard road, then the creaking of a wagon. Knecht scrambled to his feet as Nyx hurried to get dressed. Through the trees they could see Jonas, Rachel and the girls rounding the bend in the family's wagon. In a moment they'd have a clear view of the trestle. Knecht jumped down from the trestle and wound his way through the brush and back to finish the day's work on the fence. As she watched him go, Nyx knew that he was doomed.

She became aware of someone's hand on her shoulder, and eventually she could focus on the man sitting opposite her, that guy Kamp. She scanned the room and saw all the objects once familiar to her now utterly foreign.

"You're here, Nyx," he said. She looked straight in his eyes. "It's not your fault."

"What's not?"

"What he did to your parents. It's not your fault."

Her gaze hardened. She gnashed her teeth and said, "No shit."

"Why did he do it, Nyx?"

"Do what?"

Kamp said calmly, "Hurt your parents."

"He came in here. He wanted me. I said no."

"Are you saying he thought they were keeping you from him?"

She said, "No," and her expression went blank.

"Then why would he want to hurt them? Is he a monster?"

Nyx fixed her gaze on him again, and she said, "He isn't a monster. He's a sad little boy who believed a lie."

"But why did he hurt them?"

"Same reason anyone hurts another person. Because something went wrong."

Kamp rubbed his eyelids with his thumb and fore-finger, then glanced out the window and saw sleighs lining the road as far as he could see. In Jonas Bauer's yard alone he saw dozens, even a hundred people. He started devising a way to get Knecht to the jail.

12

The bedroom door flew open, and George Richter stomped in, holding the shotgun across his chest.

Richter said, "District Attorney needs her to talk to his jury in the next room."

He set his gun down in the corner and held out a hand to Nyx. She stood up and walked slowly out of the bedroom. As she left, Hugh Arndt walked in carrying a knife.

Richter stood directly in front of Kamp and said, "We don't want this thing to go Elijah Sample on us."

"It won't."

"Well, we're gonna make sure."

Arndt said, "Sample slaughtered his whole own god-damn family and they let him walk away. Insanity."

Kamp said, "This is different, George."

"This here Knecht is crazy as they come. We ain't taking no chances. Hugh, get going."

Arndt pulled aside the mattress, cut the rope and began to unstring the lattice. Kamp lunged for Arndt, but Richter caught him and pinned him hard against the wall by jamming his forearm into Kamp's throat.

Richter growled, "People want to see for themselves. See the truth."

Kamp heard more commotion downstairs and women screaming. Arndt coiled the bed rope, fifty feet or so, put it in the crook of his right arm and left the room. Richter eased the pressure on Kamp's neck enough to let him breathe.

He picked up his shotgun and said, "Kamp, you just make sure that girl is all right. We're gonna do what needs done. Do what's right. District attorney said so."

Kamp went to the next room, where Philander Crow's jury had assembled, eight men, most of whom Kamp knew by name. Nyx sat in a chair in front of them, and they listened, rapt.

She said, "I saw him burn his shirt. Then, he washed his hands and arms."

Kamp stood in the doorway and motioned to Crow, who walked over to him.

He whispered, "Has the jury decided?"

Crow said, "We've just started."

"Did you tell Richter to do anything?"

"Who?"

Kamp scrambled down the stairs and onto the front lawn. A group of men clumped at the door of the barn where he'd left Daniel Knecht.

The men shouted, "Bring him out! Let us see that devil!" The door opened, and Knecht emerged, head down. The crowd parted as Arndt slammed Knecht squarely between the shoulder blades with the butt of his rifle. Knecht stumbled forward and crashed to his hands and knees in the snow.

A man shouted, "He deserves worse!"

Across the yard, a woman screamed, "Lynch him!"

The mob surged around Knecht. Richter and Arndt guided him across the road and toward Shawnee Creek. People strained to tear at Knecht, slap his face and spit on him. Kamp tried to pick his way through the mob to get to Knecht, to restore order. But he was repulsed. The mob had already become a single living, swelling organism, a beast.

Kamp scanned the scene for Druckenmiller or other police officers who must have arrived by now. He saw none. They must be in the house, he thought, and they're not coming out. They're going to let it happen.

Richter and Arndt guided Knecht across the road toward the creek. They didn't drag him, because they didn't have to. Knecht offered no resistance and appeared to drift along with the deadly current toward the base of a spreading chestnut tree. Richter slammed Knecht against the trunk face first, producing a cheer from the mob.

Richter said, "Somebody hold him here once."

Immediately, two men Kamp didn't recognize stepped forward, grabbed the condemned man and yanked his arms behind his back. Knecht still did not protest at all. He stared at the ground. Arndt handed Richter the coiled rope. A noose had already been fashioned at one end.

Shrieks rang out all through the mob. "Hang him! Hang him!"

Richter looked up the trunk of the chestnut tree and at its branches. A large bough extended up and over the ground, fifteen feet overhead. Richter dropped the coils of rope on the ground and held the noose, gauging its heft. He swung it back and forth a couple times to gain momentum, then hoisted the noose skyward. It fell far short of clearing the bough. Richter tried once more. Same result. People began laughing and shouting suggestions.

"Tie a rock to the other end and throw that over!"

"*Ach*, why don'tcha just shoot the son of a bitch!"

As Richter and Arndt discussed their options, a boy, perhaps ten years old, stepped forward.

The boy said to Richter, "I can do it."

Richter hissed, "Step back, *junge.*"

"No, I can do it. I can climb it up there and throw it back down."

The mob weighed in. "Let him do it!"

"He can't do no worse than you, George!" A low chuckle rippled through the crowd. The boy reached for the noose, and Richter handed it to him. Another cheer rose.

Kamp knew that the only weapon capable of stopping the mob at this point would have been a punt gun. Apart from that, he wouldn't be able to keep this monster from finishing its grim business. He also had to consider the possibility that the mob would turn on him and that he'd end up hanging alongside Daniel Knecht.

All Kamp could think to do at that moment was to take Jonas Bauer's four-barreled revolver from his waistband, raise it above his head and pull the trigger. The sound, he hoped, would rouse the mob from its collective nightmare. He wanted to break the spell. And the sound did, in fact, stop the proceedings cold. Everyone ducked and then looked for the source of the noise. They saw Kamp holding the smoking pistol over his head. The gunshot's echoes died, followed by a moment of total quiet.

Kamp shouted, "You will release this man into my custody! You will hand over this man!"

The people stared at him, then turned to look at Daniel Knecht. The men who were holding him let him go. Knecht kicked idly at the snow on the ground, as if he weren't even aware of the events unfolding around him. He made no move to get free.

Kamp said, "Let him go under penalty of law."

The boy said something quietly to Richter, and Richter clapped the boy on the back.

Someone in the crowd yelled to Richter, "What'd he say?"

"The boy said, 'This *is* the law.'"

The mob erupted.

"Go home, Kamp! You're not needed here."

"This is our business. Leave it alone!"

"He's right! Look at that fiend. He knows what he done!"

The mob heaved forward again. Kamp felt hands grabbing him under his arms. Another hand closed over the pistol and yanked it from him. Three men dragged him backwards to the road and threw him to the ground. One man kicked him in the ribs. He lay there, breathing hard. The three men left him and rejoined the mob. Kamp rolled onto his belly, then climbed to his knees.

Richter placed the rope coils around the boy's shoulders so that the boy could use both hands as he went up the tree trunk. The people's eyes shifted from the boy to

Daniel Knecht and back to the boy. Knecht never looked up. He drew circles in the snow with his foot. No one paid attention to Kamp, who looked on from the perimeter of the mob. Kamp prayed the boy would fall out of the tree.

As the boy worked his way higher, women shouted up to him.

"Be careful once!"

"Well done, *junge!*"

The boy reached the bough and began to shinny out over the mob. When he got directly above Knecht, the boy clamped himself to the bough with both knees and gently lifted the rope off his shoulders. He dropped the noose to Richter who reached for it eagerly. The boy dropped the other end of the rope to the ground, and his mission was complete. Another cheer rose from the mob as the boy climbed back down. Hugh Arndt grabbed Daniel Knecht in a bear hug, and Richter fitted the noose around his neck. The mob pressed in even tighter. Men fought each other to lay hold of the rope, and women surged forward to get a better look.

Kamp felt an intense need to get as close as possible too. But instead of wanting to take part in or even to witness the execution, he was seized with a desperate urge to keep Daniel Knecht alive. He wanted to keep this mob, this group of quiet farmers, from becoming murderers themselves. He wanted to save the boy from the stain of having been their accomplice. But more than that, for reasons that he could not comprehend in that moment, Kamp believed that Knecht must not die this way.

He launched himself into the mob, crouching down and using his elbows to shove people aside. He reached the base of the chestnut tree before anyone else realized that he was coming, and he went straight for the noose, attempting to pull it off Knecht's neck. For his part, Knecht did nothing to help. He stood straight up and did not try to remove the rope himself. He and the mob had begun their death dance. In fact no one, including Knecht, even seemed to notice Kamp was there.

He shook Knecht by the shoulders. "Danny, Danny!"

"Oh, hello."

"Help me!"

Knecht said, "Do you know what it means? What I told you before?"

"What?"

"*Quia merito haec patior.* Do you know?"

Richter cinched the noose, and Knecht let out a gurgle. Kamp knew he wouldn't be able to remove the noose, and he was certain that he could not wrest the other end of the rope from the half dozen men who held it. He saw the slack coils of rope on the ground and he wrapped them around his own arm. In this way he placed himself directly between Knecht and the killing force of the mob.

George Richter shouted, "Now!" and the men yanked the rope in unison. Since Kamp had looped the rope around himself, he, not Knecht, jerked violently off the ground.

Richter said, "Again!"

The men dug their heels into the frozen earth as best they could, gritted their teeth and leaned back. Everyone wondered why Daniel Knecht had not been lifted from the ground yet. The rope cut hard into Kamp's arm. He could feel it going numb. He was now suspended at an odd angle six feet above the earth. With his free hand, he tried to right himself, to no avail.

Richter shouted, "Something's wrong! Something's wrong! Leave it go."

The men relaxed their grip, and Kamp slammed the ground. The force of the landing knocked the air from his lungs. For a moment he could not breathe at all. He found himself looking straight up at Knecht, who raised his eyebrows slightly, cocked his head and gave a little smile.

Knecht said, "I done it for them, Kamp. I done it for them."

Hugh Arndt unwrapped the rope from Kamp's arm.

Richter yelled, "OK. We're trying again. Go!"

When the rope went tight, the noose bit hard against Knecht's throat. This time nothing kept him from going airborne. He shot up a couple of feet, then glided slowly toward the blue sky. The mob let out a large, satisfied cheer.

"That's what you get, you son of a bitch!"

"Better than you deserve."

"Hang!"

The boy who had placed the rope turned away and buried his face in his mother's arms. Daniel Knecht's chest heaved, the tension left his limbs, and he went slack. The rage drained from the mob immediately, and they transformed back into people. George Richter looked at Kamp, lying on the ground, noticing him for the first time.

He said, "What are you doing there?"

Philander Crow emerged from the upstairs room where his jury had been deliberating. He walked quickly down the stairs and found Kamp waiting for him there. Crow noticed that the color had drained from his face and that he appeared battered.

Crow said, "The jury has just come to a verdict that Jonas and Rachel Bauer came to their death by blows and cuts inflicted on their heads and bodies with an ax in the hands of Daniel Knecht, this day, December twenty-seven, 1870."

Kamp said, "Look at this." Kamp stepped aside so that Crow could see across the road to Knecht's body, hanging slack and still. Crow hurried to the base of the tree. The mob had dispersed and only one man, an old farmer, stood by, eating a biscuit.

Crow asked him, "Who did this?"

"Why, the people did."

Crow shook his head and said, "This is all wrong. All wrong."

The old farmer said, "Is it?"

"It's murder."

The old man said, "You saw what this man did."

Crow said, "Did you have a hand in this?"

"No, sir. But it's just."

"Do you know who did?"

The old man stared at Crow and said, "No, and I don't care. Whoever did it did the right thing." He walked back to the road, whistling a tune.

13

Kamp and Crow stood side by side under the chestnut tree, staring at the corpse of Daniel Knecht, which swayed in the breeze.

Crow said, "If nothing else, I suppose you can say the troglodytes around here prefer their justice rough."

"It's a nightmare."

"You could say that, too."

"I saw the whole thing," Kamp said. "I know everyone who was involved. I can name them."

Crow gave him a long look. "We should get that body down."

"We'll arrest every man who took part."

"Your integrity is admirable, Kamp, but your thinking is colored by emotion."

"How so?"

Crow went to the trunk of the tree and began working at the knot that held the rope in place.

"No one's getting arrested. Nothing will come of this." Crow motioned to the body. "It's finished."

"Finished? What's the point of having any goddamned laws in the first place? And aren't you the one who told me I needed to investigate real crimes? How's this for a *real* crime?"

Crow continued working at the knot. "The jury reached a verdict. The man would have been executed anyway. And as for holding these vigilantes to account, you saw for yourself, half the town was here. The respectable and upstanding figures of Bethlehem just committed a murder."

"That's right."

"And they loved it."

"And no one's going to make them pay?"

"No one wants them to. Apart from you."

"Don't you?"

Crow said, "The crime was so egregious he granted them full freedom to kill him. If we were to prosecute them, we would be scorned, vilified, and in the end another jury of their peers—if we can find any jurors who weren't here—will say they did the right thing and let them go. It's pointless." Crow loosened the knot until it came free. "Help me with this."

Together, they eased the rope so that the body crumpled stiffly to the ground, face up. The two men looked at the face. Knecht's eyes bulged, and his purple tongue protruded.

Crow said, "Well, I suppose the coroner won't need to see the corpse."

"How's that?"

"The time and cause of death are fairly well established, I'd say. We'll need to notify the family, tell them what happened and have them come and retrieve the body."

"No one's coming for him," Kamp said.

"Why's that?"

"Trust me."

Crow said, "That leaves the burial. Someone will have to put him in the ground. And I'd suggest that whoever buries him makes sure not to mark the grave."

"Just get rid of it right away. Is that it? Throw dirt on it like it never happened."

Crow looked at Kamp with disdain. "It's going to rot."

They turned to walk back toward the house. Every last soul was gone along with the horses, sleighs and commotion.

When they reached the road, Crow said, "I need to return to the courthouse."

The men shook hands, and Crow started off down the road. Kamp went to the shed behind the house and retrieved a pickax and a spade shovel. He walked back to Knecht's body, selected a spot a few feet away and swung the pick. It bounced off the frozen ground the first few times before he was able to break through. He heard footsteps approaching behind him, and when he turned, he saw Philander Crow taking off his topcoat and rolling up his sleeves. Kamp handed him the shovel, and they soon fell into a rhythm. Kamp pierced the frozen soil, then Crow shoveled what was broken up. Together in the failing afternoon light, they dug the hole, and by nightfall the grave was finished. They dragged the body into position, and just before they rolled it into the hole, Kamp felt an object in the vest pocket of Knecht's wool coat.

Kamp said, "Hold on." He fished the contents out of the pocket. There was something that felt like a coin and also a folded piece of paper. Kamp put the items in his pocket.

Crow said, "What is it?"

"Nothing. I wanted to make sure he didn't have anything in his pockets. He didn't."

"All right then," Crow said, "one, two, three." They tipped the body into the hole where it landed with an impressive *whump*. The two men filled the hole with dirt and did their best to conceal the grave. When their work was complete, Kamp extended his hand to Crow. Instead of shaking Kamp's hand, Crow handed him the shovel and said, "Thank you." He politely tipped his hat and walked into the darkness.

Kamp lit a lantern and walked into Jonas Bauer's house one more time for the night to make certain all the doors were locked and that the house was empty. He knew tomorrow would bring another crush of spectators to the location which had gained instant and possibly permanent notoriety. People would want to see the place where not only the grisly murders had taken place but also where the murderer had been hanged on the same day.

He went through each room, starting with the front of the house where the Christmas tree now lay broken in the corner. The room was otherwise bare. People must have taken the furniture and other family possessions as souvenirs, he thought. He went up the stairs and looked in on the girls' room, which was empty, save for the bed frames and mattresses. He assumed that the girls had been taken in by a neighbor, and he resolved to check on them the following day. He then went to Knecht's room, where Crow had set up the makeshift courtroom. Here, too, everything but the chairs in which the jurors sat had been taken. He walked back down the stairs, each footfall echoing loudly. He walked to Jonas and Rachel's room and found that the bodies had been removed. Kamp knew that A.J. Oehler would have taken them to the morgue. Much of the blood remained on the wall, though someone, likely Oehler himself and his assistant, had begun scrubbing. He felt relieved that most of the gore was gone. He took a brief inventory of the room. Someone had put the cigar box back on the windowsill, but the ax and the quilt were both gone. He locked the bedroom door behind him, put out the lantern, left the house and stood on the front step.

Kamp forced himself not to contemplate the enormity of the tragedy, the way that three human beings had been utterly destroyed. He thought about the hardships Bauer's daughters would face, not to mention Knecht's sisters. He couldn't even begin to answer any of the questions large and small, immediate and long-range, that the catastrophe generated. Even though he decided he'd wait until tomorrow to analyze the day's events, Kamp's ruminations began right away. Images of the murder scene assailed him, fragments of memories that triggered other recollections much deeper down. He tried to explain to himself that the intensity of the storm in his mind was the result of everything he'd experienced during the day. No doubt the terrible power of what he'd seen and heard could drive any man to the brink of madness. He reminded himself that he had seen carnage before on the battlefield, and participated in it. Something was different here. The proximity of the catastrophe to his own home might have been part of it. He tried without success to banish the demons and then resigned himself to suffer. Kamp locked the front door of Jonas Bauer's house and walked home.

It was late, probably after midnight, and it occurred to him that he'd been gone nearly twenty-four hours. In that time Shaw had not come to see the goings-on at Bauer's house, at least not that he knew. And he felt glad she hadn't seen any of it. He saw a candle in the window as he reached the house and found the front door locked. The door opened, though, almost as soon as he tried it, and once again, he was met by the Druggist, E. Wyles.

Her hair was pulled back and matted to her forehead. The sleeves of her white blouse were rolled up to her elbows and spattered with blood. Her typical hawk-eyed expression had been replaced with what looked to him like a woozy smile. She let him in the front door and motioned for him to go upstairs.

"Quiet," she said.

He climbed the stairs and peered into his bedroom. A candle was burning on the table by the bed and by its light, Kamp saw Shaw cradling a sleeping baby.

Shaw looked up at him and said, "Ours."

"Is it a—"

"Girl."

He took Shaw's hand and knelt by the bed, marveling at the child. "I wasn't here. I'm sorry, I'm sorry. I know I should have been–"

"It's all right."

"I just got caught up. Everything that happened today. You wouldn't believe it."

"Everything is all right."

"What are we going to name her? We haven't even really, with everything that's been, we haven't—"

"Tomorrow."

"What kind of name is tomorrow?"

Shaw laughed. "No, love, I meant we won't worry about anything now. Tomorrow, we'll name her."

E. Wyles walked in the room and said, "They need to rest. You do, too."

"Right, right." He looked at Shaw and said, "I love you." He kissed her softly on the forehead.

"I love you."

Kamp and E. Wyles walked back down the stairs to the front room where a fire was burning. For the first time since he'd gone out the door the previous day, He noticed how cold he was. He also became aware that he was covered head to toe in grave dirt. The joints in his fingers thrummed with pain. He sat on the floor and unlaced his boots. Fatigue hit him like a sledge as he stretched out in front of the fire.

"Thank you, Emma, for everything."

E. Wyles stood over him and said, "It wasn't easy, for anyone. It was a difficult delivery for Shaw and for the baby."

"Tomorrow, Emma."

"Some men came to the door looking for you. I told them you were on official business."

"I want to hear about it all tomorrow."

14

He opened his eyes to a dead fire and a cold floor. He could smell breakfast, though, which enabled him to sit up and think about starting the day. He wasn't surprised to hear E. Wyles' heels clacking purposefully across the floor and to see her in her typical formal attire.

She said, "I've already checked in on Shaw and given her something to eat. She seems fine. I've also boiled some water for you. I want you to wash up. Get as clean as you can, and change your clothes before you go in to see them."

"Aye, aye, captain."

"This is serious, Kamp. She had a hard labor and a complicated delivery. She lost a considerable amount of blood, and she's weak. I need to return to the pharmacy.

It's up to you to take care of her. At least until others start arriving to help."

"I doubt anyone's coming."

"What about her family?"

"It's just her father. And I don't know where he is."

"Well, once they hear the baby's been born, the neighbor ladies will come and help."

"Not after what happened yesterday." He related to E. Wyles the events of the previous day and mentioned the likelihood that his actions on behalf of Daniel Knecht and his inclination to hold the lynch mob to account might dampen their neighbors' enthusiasm to assist them.

She said, "In that case I'll be back day after tomorrow. Until then, make sure she doesn't get out of bed. Give her everything she needs. Good luck." E. Wyles buckled her bag and headed for the door. As she left she looked back over her shoulder and said, "I made you some food, too. You should eat it."

He tiptoed up the stairs to take a look at Shaw and the baby, both asleep. He went back down to the kitchen and took off his jacket and shirt. The pot of water had cooled enough for him to be able to cup his hands and douse his face with the steaming water. He repeated the process until he felt clear-headed and clean and then toweled off. He wolfed down the scrambled eggs and hash browns E. Wyles had fixed for him. He saw that she'd even left him some coffee beans. He ground up the beans and made a cup. Sitting at the table, Kamp breathed a heavy sigh.

Immediately, thoughts about the previous day streamed into his consciousness. He remembered the things he found in Knecht's pocket. He picked up his jacket off the floor and fished them out. The first item was a piece of paper, which he now unfolded. It was a child's pencil drawing, showing a simple house with two smiling faces, one in each upstairs window. In one downstairs window was a candle, and through the other window, a Christmas tree could be seen. Across the top of the picture were the words "WEEL MISS YOU DANNY!" And across the bottom, it read, "LOVE MERCY." He wondered whether Knecht's little sisters had been notified yet, and if so, by whom.

The second object was an eight-sided silver coin. One side pictured a steaming locomotive engine. The other side depicted the bust of a smiling figure wearing a cap in the Phrygian style, superimposed on a crossed pickax and shovel and enclosed in a circle. Inside the edge of the circle were the words "*Ex Fratrum Ordine, Et in Corvo.*"

Kamp felt the coffee working in his system. These were the only things Knecht carried. No money, no food, no tobacco. Nothing he would have needed if he'd intended to get away. It's possible that before he committed the murders, Knecht had already stashed a bag somewhere, possibly in the barn where Kamp found him. Then again, the act itself was rash, an unplanned fit of rage. It seemed unlikely to him that Knecht would have made any preparation at all. Knecht would have had time after the murders, though, to think about and plan his next move. Kamp turned over the coin in his hand. He'd seen train coins before, particularly on his journey back from the war. But he'd never seen a coin such as this. He didn't know where it came from or what the motto meant, and he wondered how it came into Knecht's possession.

He stood up from the table and walked to the front room. Out the front window of the house, he saw a stream of sleighs and carriages all going in the direction of Jonas Bauer's house. He also saw Sam Druckenmiller riding a horse up the path. Kamp laced up his boots and walked onto the front porch.

Druckenmiller tied up his horse and called to Kamp, "One hell of a mess over there!"

"Hey, Sam. *Wie gehts?*"

"Oh, it goes, it goes." He walked up to the porch and shook hands with Kamp. Druckenmiller twitched with nervous energy. "We'll be lucky if they don't burn the house down. *Ach*, they're looking for the body so they can tear it apart. Do you know what happened to it?"

"It's taken care of."

"Where is it?"

"Don't worry," Kamp said. "We buried it."

"Yah, yah, but where?"

"In the ground."

"Say, have you been over there today, Kamp, to the Bauer house?"

"How come you went over, Sam?"

Druckenmiller cocked his head and furrowed his brow. "Why, to keep the peace."

"How'd that go?"

"*Ach*, why ya hafta be so, so disagreeable?"

"I'm asking what, in particular, you went there to do," Kamp said.

The color began to rise in Druckenmiller's face. "And I'm telling you, in particular, I went to keep the peace. Disperse the onlookers and so forth."

"Who sent you over there?"

"The Judge asked me to come over here and—"

"The Judge sent you?"

"No, I decided to go to Bauer's house on my own. But the Judge also asked me to come over and let you know he wants to talk to you."

"That's the message?" Kamp's left temple began to throb.

"That's the message. Christ, you're a piece a work. You really are."

"Sorry, Sam. Late night."

"Ach, yah well, don't worry about it. Say, did ya hear what they're sayin' about the murders? About why Knecht done it?"

"No."

"People are sayin' it was a hex murder. Someone put a hex on poor Danny. That's why he done it."

"Hex murder, huh. What do you say?"

"I told you from the first, Kamp, that guy was trouble, a no good goddamned *nix nootz*. Hex or no."

"Yes, you said that."

Druckenmiller studied him for a moment and said, "You know what else they're saying?"

"Tell me."

"They're saying maybe you had something to do with it. Maybe that hex is on you too."

Kamp said, "That so."

"Well, everybody seen the way you jumped in there and tried to help that bastard. People are just wondering why, I guess. Said they figured you'd want to uphold the law, not keep them from having to do it themselves. What made you wanna help that fool anyway?" Druckenmiller took off his hat and scratched the top of his head.

"Who specifically was saying this?"

"Just people in the crowd. Things I heard. Anyway, they're *fershmeering* your name over there. Don't worry, though. I stuck up for you. But I thought you'd want to know anyhow."

Kamp said, "You think maybe what people are saying has something to do with them not wanting to be arrested for murder?"

Druckenmiller stopped scratching his head and started pulling on his left ear. "I don't know what people want. Like I said, it's a real *mommick*. I gotta go. I gotta get back to the Bauer house, if it's still there." He chuckled and tipped his hat. "Say, are you goin' over there today? We could use the help."

"Tomorrow."

"Oh, well, see you then." Druckenmiller climbed on his horse and trotted back down the path.

Kamp had thought better of telling Druckenmiller that he couldn't go to Bauer's house because he had to stay home and look after Shaw and the baby. As a man alone, he'd guarded the myth of his invulnerability without realizing it. He believed he couldn't be hurt in spite of evidence to the contrary. But now that he had a family, the notion seemed ludicrous. He'd be vulnerable from now on. Druckenmiller had confirmed his assumption that with regard to his actions the previous day, at best, the citizenry wouldn't give him the benefit of the doubt. To do so would be to admit the lynching was wrong. At worst, the people would implicate him in the crime somehow and seek retribution. Whatever the case and for a variety of reasons, he thought it wise to stay at home.

Under normal circumstances the birth of a child would have brought all the mothers and grandmothers in the area to their doorstep. And by now, at least some of the neighbors would have heard about the baby's arrival. But no one besides Druckenmiller had visited that day. And what to make of Druckenmiller's visit? He never would have gone back to Jonas Bauer's house of his own volition. Someone had to have ordered him to do it, but Druckenmiller wouldn't say who. It also wasn't clear why he'd come to Kamp's house. Kamp realized he no longer trusted the man, if he ever did. And as for why the Judge would want to speak with him, he assumed it had to do with the fact that the Judge owned the house where the Bauers lived. The Judge would want him to give him the full story of what happened and to make sure that the buildings weren't destroyed. The Judge would have to wait.

He heard the baby crying upstairs, then the creaking of the floorboards. When he reached the room, Shaw was standing at the window, holding the baby in her arms and gently rocking back and forth.

Kamp said, "You can't be on your feet. Back in bed. Wyles said so."

She smiled at him. "Good morning to you, too. Do you want to hold someone?" She offered him the baby, and he took her in his arms for the first time. The girl had light brown skin, a full head of thick, black hair like Shaw's.

"She has my eyes."

Shaw lay back down in bed. "Wyles told me they might stay that blue, or they could get darker."

"I guess we'll have to wait and see." He rocked her slowly. "What are we going to call her anyway? We could name her after your mother, or your grandmother."

Shaw said, "Let's not call her anything right now. She can just be who she is."

He glided around the room, cradling the baby and singing to her. "Whoever you are...whoever you are."

The moment was lost when the first rock hit the side of the house. The second rock sailed through a first floor window. The sounds startled the baby who began to wail. He handed the baby to Shaw and said, "Stay up here, lock the door, don't go near the window."

Kamp ran down the stairs and looked out the window. A dozen men had assembled in the front yard thirty feet or so from the house. They passed around a bottle, each taking a swig, then fishing around on the ground for more rocks. He opened the front door and stepped onto the porch. A derisive cheer went up.

"Come on out here, you dog. We heard about what you done!"

"Coward, coward is what you are!" A rock sailed past Kamp's head and slammed into the doorframe.

"You think you can take up for a filthy murderer and not pay for it? Did you see what he done to them good people?"

Kamp walked down the steps toward the men. He scanned the faces of the group and didn't recognize any of them. A man in the center of the group stepped forward to meet him. He looked to be in his early twenties, taller than Kamp, and heavily muscled.

Kamp sized him up and said, "Leave."

The men erupted into laughter and jeering. When it died down, the man facing him said, "This is nothing."

"Oh, how's that?"

"They got plans for you."

Kamp studied the man's face. He had a heavy brow, a wispy beard and blue eyes. Kamp said, "Plans?"

"Everyone knows you was involved in them killings. Seems like folks know a lot of other shit about you, too. Shit they don't like at all."

"Where are you from?"

"Don't matter."

Kamp's body stiffened. "Where?"

The man leaned in until he was inches from Kamp's face and said, "I'm from right behind you. If you need to find me, that's where I'll be."

Kamp rolled his eyes. "I'll keep that in mind."

A man off to the side yelled, "You dirty son of a bitch!" and lunged at him. Kamp caught him with a straight right hand to the face that put the man on the ground.

Kamp looked back at the man in front of him. "What's your name?"

"We heard you got a family now. Congratulations." The man turned to leave, and the rest of the men followed. Kamp went back to the porch and picked up the rock that had hit the doorframe and tossed it back into the yard. He went back inside, locked the door and heard a sound at the back of the house, probably the kitchen.

He said, "Shaw?" No answer.

Kamp picked up the Sharps rifle next to the door and raised it to his shoulder. He stepped silently toward the kitchen. Blood pounded at his temples as he considered shooting his way into the room. Instead, he let his finger rest on the trigger. He peered into the kitchen and saw a man facing away from him. The man had broad shoulders and thick black hair woven into a single braid and streaked with grey.

Kamp said, "Joe."

The man turned to face him. He was smiling and eating the rest of the breakfast E. Wyles had prepared.

Joe said, "These biscuits are delicious. Where's the jelly?" Kamp relaxed his grip on the gun and set it on the table.

"Did you see that bullshit going on out there?"

"Yep"

"How come you didn't help me out?"

Joe laughed. "You know I never worry about you." Joe took him by the shoulders and pressed his forehead against Kamp's. "Besides, if they'd seen me, there'd have been blood on the ground for sure."

Kamp said, "All of it theirs."

Joe said, "How's she doing?"

"She's good, Joe, she's good. Tired, sore."

"The baby?"

"Let's go see."

Joe followed him up the stairs and into the bedroom.

When Shaw saw her father, she began to cry. She said, "*Nux.*"

Joe said, "*Nichan.*" He walked to the bedside and stroked Shaw's forehead. He gently rubbed his thumb across the crescent-shaped scar above her right eye. Shaw cradled the baby in one arm. In the other she held her father's hand to the side of her face.

"Do you want to hold her?" She offered the baby to Joe, who took her in his arms. He looked into the baby's eyes and began to cry as well.

Kamp said, "*Muxumsa.* Is that right?"

Joe laughed through his tears. "Yes, that's it. *Muxumsa.* Grandfather." He held the baby close and talked to her in a soothing voice in his original language.

Kamp said to Shaw, "What's he saying?"

"He's asking her what she thinks we should name her."

15

After Shaw fell asleep, Kamp and Joe sat in the front room of the house, each in a chair on either side of the fireplace. Joe produced a tobacco pouch and a pipe with a cherry stem. He filled the bowl with *kinnikinnick* and lit it. Joe took a long drag on the pipe and let the smoke billow up from his mouth. Kamp smelled the red willow and sumac. Even though it was dark, carriages and sleighs kept gliding to and from Jonas Bauer's house on the road. They saw the lights of lanterns and heard singing and the tinkling of bells going past. The wind whistled through the boards they'd hammered over the window that had been smashed earlier in the day.

Kamp said, "How did you know to come here? Did someone tell you?"

Joe handed the pipe to him and said, "Dreamt about it."

"Which part?" He took a pull and handed the pipe back to Joe.

"All of it. Last night. A man with two heads started a fire that grew and grew until it swallowed this entire mountain. And in the fire I saw you and my daughter and that little child. And other people, too. Dead, ruined."

"Those were our neighbors, Mr. and Mrs. Bauer."

"Yes, them and many more. In the dream this Doublehead's blaze burned down through four generations. One of his heads felt shame and regret. The other one felt great pride. Both heads had enormous, black, wide open mouths. Great hunger. Ravenous. He wanted to take everything into his mouths. And whatever he couldn't eat, he destroyed, burned it up."

"Well, he's dead now."

"You sure?"

"Put him in the ground myself," Kamp said. "Why?"

He looked at Joe's wide face and high cheekbones. He noticed the scars across the knuckles of both the man's hands. Joe puffed the pipe and stared out the window at the road.

Joe said, "Why do you suppose they're going to that house? What do they want to see?"

"Good question. I don't have an answer. How long can you stay, Joe?"

"Till tomorrow morning."

"Emma Wyles will be here to check on Shaw. Do you remember her?"

"Yes. We can be out before first light."

"We?"

Joe banged the ashes from his pipe. "They should come with me."

"I don't follow."

Joe motioned to the broken window. "This is how it starts."

Kamp felt a flicker of anger. "I thought you said you never worry about me."

Joe looked at him. "I don't. But this, whatever is happening here, has nothing to do with you. It's much larger, and you are simply caught up in it. You won't be able to protect them."

Kamp said, "They won't be any safer with you. Could be even more dangerous."

"Could be."

"And besides, Wyles said Shaw can't go anywhere yet. She's too weak. Tell you what. Stay here with us for another day or two. See for yourself. See if things settle down. After that, we'll decide."

Joe said, "Good enough."

Kamp was out the door before first light. He knew Joe would take care of things until E. Wyles showed up, and she could take over from there. He figured he had all day to work on finding answers to the questions that gnawed at him. He hustled to Bauer's house to see what condition it was in. By moonlight, he could see that all the windows had been broken and that the front door hung open. He walked down to the chestnut tree by the creek and found that, as he'd suspected, Daniel Knecht's body had been unearthed, and all the clothes had been removed. By the first rays of dawn, he saw mud caked in the eye sockets. He noticed, too, that the tongue had been cut out. He'd have to see to it that the body was buried again, but he couldn't do it now. He heard the whistle of the Black Diamond Unlimited in the distance, and by the time he made his way to the tracks, the train was almost there. He made his run alongside the train and then his jump, and he was on his way back to Easton.

Kamp rested his back against the slats of the boxcar and breathed a sigh. It felt good to be back on the train, and free. He let the snow-covered branches of the trees beside the tracks run together and blur by allowing his eyes to un-focus. He tipped his head back and let it loll back and forth with the rhythm of the wheels. He began to wonder. He wondered what the coin in Knecht's pocket meant, where it came from and who made it. He wondered about the Latin words Knecht spoke to him. Who'd told him that, and why? He reflected on Joe's arrival. Where had he come from? What made him want to take Shaw and the baby? And how long until someone came calling for Joe himself? He wondered where the souls of Jacob and Rachel Bauer had flown. Kamp received no whole answers, just half-formed ideas and speculation, fragments.

He opened his eyes and unfolded the sheet of paper with the pencil drawing of a house and two smiling faces. A simple gesture of love from a little sister to a big brother. And yet it too raised a new set of questions for him. Considering the condition of Daniel Knecht's corpse and the sorry state of the house where the Bauers used to live, he wondered, dreaded actually, what kind of shape Knecht's sisters would be in when he got to 2 Ferry Street in Easton.

And behind all of those questions, or maybe encompassing them all, was a much larger question. Who was writing the story, or to put it in Joe's terms, who was feeding the inferno which might engulf them all?

As he turned from First Street onto Ferry, Kamp braced himself for what he'd find when he got to Knecht's house. It seemed possible that the house would be empty, the girls having been taken to live with an aunt or uncle. More likely, once the news of the murders reached Easton, Knecht's sisters would have been put in an orphanage. He thought about what their lives would be like now that their parents and brothers were dead. When he reached 2 Ferry Street, however, he saw that the walk had been shoveled, and a wreath made of pine boughs hung on the front door. Everything looked normal.

He knocked on the door, and it opened almost right away. Margaret Knecht stood in the doorway. She wore a dress that appeared to be new and a bright red ribbon in her hair.

She said, "Hello, Kamp." He caught the smell of baking bread coming from the house.

"Hello, Margaret." The girl stared at him, motionless. "Margaret, I came to check on you and your sister. See how you're doing. Looks like you're doing fine."

"We're doing fine, yes. Thank you for coming. Have a good day." She tried to swing the door shut, but he stopped it with his hand.

"I was wondering if I might be able to come inside for a moment."

"No, I'm sorry. You can't."

Mercy Knecht called from the back of the house, "Who's that?" and then came running. She too was outfitted in what appeared to be a new dress and ribbons in a bow on each pigtail.

"Good morning, Mercy."

"Hi, Kamp."

"Mercy, he can't stay. Say goodbye to him."

He pulled the drawing from his pocket and showed it to the girls. "Mercy, do you remember making this?"

She stared at the picture for a few seconds. Her bottom lip began to quiver.

Margaret said, "Give that back," and she grabbed it from his hand.

"Do you remember drawing it, Mercy?"

"Uh-huh."

"Leave her alone, Kamp."

"Why did you write, we'll miss you? Why did you write that? Where did Danny say he was going?"

The little girl's eyes brimmed with tears. "He told us he was going away."

"When? When did he say—"

Margaret stepped in front of her sister. "It was last year before Christmas, okay? Danny had got in trouble, and he told us he had to go away for a while. He meant jail, all right?"

Kamp leaned down so that he was at eye level with Mercy. "Did you draw this last year? Or this year?"

Margaret screamed, "Leave us alone!"

He straightened to his full height and took a step back. "I'm just trying to understand. It's important."

"We heard the whole story about what happened to Danny." Now Margaret's lip started to quiver. "We heard about how you were the only one who tried to help our brother, even when they were...doing what they did."

Mercy stepped out from behind her sister and rushed to him. She hugged him hard around the waist and started wailing.

She said, "Why did they hurt him?"

He put his arm around the little girl's shoulders. "I'm sorry it happened, girls. I'm sorry."

Margaret Knecht gently peeled her sister away and guided her back into the house. She looked back over her shoulder and said, "You can't come back here, Kamp. Never."

Kamp ran to the station and barely caught the train headed for Bethlehem. He rode it past his normal jumping off point, all the way to the yard on the South Side. Kamp hurried into the courthouse and straight to the office of Philander Crow. The office door was locked, and he looked through the window. No one there. Kamp ran down the stairs, across the street, burst into the police station and found Druckenmiller at his desk.

Kamp said, "Seen Crow?"

"Jesus, where's the fire?"

"Sam, where's Crow?"

Druckenmiller leaned back in his chair. "Beats me. Hey, Judge wants to see you. Be careful not to piss him off."

Kamp wheeled around and headed for the door.

Druckenmiller called after him, "Come to think of it, I remember something about him going back to Philadelph-eye-ay."

He ran to the back of the courthouse building and saw Philander Crow taking off his hat climbing into a Brougham carriage.

Kamp said, "Hold up, hold up."

Crow stopped and turned to face him. "Not now, Kamp. Not now."

"Druckenmiller told me you're going to Philadelph-ia."

"Wrong."

"Why did he think that's where you're going?"

"He's probably shitfaced. Focus on doing your job. And let me focus on doing mine."

Crow stepped into the carriage. Before he could close the door, Kamp had climbed in as well. He sat down opposite the district attorney. Crow closed his eyes and shook his head indignantly. He said to the driver, "Let's go," and the carriage lurched forward.

Kamp said, "Hear about what they did to Knecht's body?"

"Yes."

"Pulled it out of the ground. Desecrated it. Still think nobody should be arrested?"

"What do you need?"

"It's about Knecht."

Crow took in a sharp breath. "I've arranged with the coroner to have the body removed and given a proper burial. They won't find it this time."

"No, not about that. About the murders."

"Why don't you go back to your little farm, take a rest, soak your head, commune with the rocks and trees? And then come back when you're feeling better, all righty?"

"You don't get it."

Crow said, "Settle. Down. For the last time, there's nothing you can do about—"

"He didn't do it."

"Didn't do what?"

"Daniel Knecht didn't murder Jonas and Rachel Bauer."

"Driver, please stop." The carriage slowed, then halted.

"I don't care if you don't believe me."

Crow said, "You should."

"It's been bothering me since Knecht showed up at my door right after the murders. That's not something he would do. It didn't make sense. Not right."

"With all due respect, get out." Crow swung the carriage door open, and Kamp slammed it shut.

"He was trying to tell me something, but for some reason he couldn't. He wanted me to know what really happened."

"What did he actually say to give you that impression?"

Kamp paused and looked up at the ceiling of the carriage, then settled his gaze back on Crow. "Nothing."

"Nothing. Hmm."

"He didn't say anything in particular. Or, he didn't say what you think a person would say under those circumstances."

Crow said, "How many other people have you talked to under those circumstances?"

Kamp felt the kindling at the base of his skull. He shut his eyes hard, trying to smother it.

"All right," Crow said, "I'll play along. If Knecht didn't commit the murders, who did?"

Kamp rubbed his left temple. "I don't know."

"How about this? Why would someone else, this mythical phantom about whom Knecht himself said nothing, why would that individual wish to kill an upright, law-abiding man and wife?"

"No idea. For some reason we haven't found yet."

"We?"

Kamp said, "Yah. My guess is you probably know more about this than I do."

"In the hours leading up to his execution, did Knecht himself ever protest his innocence?"

"No, he didn't."

Crow said, "So, you have no confession, no evidence, no other alleged murderer and no other motive for the killings."

"Correct."

"And yet you're certain that someone besides Knecht committed the killings?"

Kamp fished out the eight-sided coin and handed it to Crow. "I found this in Daniel Knecht's pocket. Mean anything to you?"

Philander Crow studied the coin. He said, "Driver, let's go."

Kamp said, "Where are we going?"

"Jonas and Rachel Bauer's funeral. And for the sake of Jesus Christ himself, keep your mouth shut."

16

In the two days following the murders, hundreds, perhaps thousands of people had descended upon the former home of Jonas Bauer. Kamp heard that the story had been reported in both the Philadelphia and New York City newspapers. The combination of a pair of grisly killings and "Pennsylvania's first lynching," as it was being called, generated massive, morbid interest. He expected the funeral might be yet another occasion for an onslaught of gawkers. Yet, when the cemetery where Jonas and Rachel Bauer were to be interred came into view, he saw only two other carriages and a small knot of people. He realized that the ceremony would be lightly attended due to the frigid weather but more likely, to the fear among the local folk that the power of the hex might somehow extend to the funeral. Drawing closer, he made out the figures of the Bauer girls and a woman standing next to them as well as the Reverend A.R. Eberstark. He saw another large man, wearing a black overcoat and stovepipe hat, the Judge. To his right stood another tall man, similarly dressed, except that he wore a bowler hat. Beside that man stood a man with a full mustache and sideburns flecked grey, wearing a black suit and Homburg hat. He recognized that man as the undertaker, Manfred Otis.

Kamp noticed for the first time that day that he was wearing the clothes he'd slept in, a rumpled red flannel shirt, brown wool pants and thin work jacket. Crow was nattily attired, as always, with a charcoal gray, three-piece suit, watch chain and black Chesterfield overcoat. The carriage pulled into the cemetery drive and stopped.

Crow looked him up and down and said, "You're welcome to wait here" and got out of the carriage. Kamp followed immediately after him.

The finely crafted hexagonal wooden boxes were arranged side by side and next to the open graves carved at neat angles and dug to a sufficient depth. Kamp stood away from the group, between two rows of headstones, and he took in the scene. The girls stood next to the coffins and beside them the woman he hadn't recognized before but now saw was the neighbor, Charlotte Fogel. The Judge, Crow, the undertaker and the other man took their places behind the girls, and before them all stood the Reverend A.R. Eberstark. The Reverend wore a heavy black gown with velvet panels around the neck and down both sides, and a white collar.

The Reverend surveyed his small audience, cleared his voice and began, "Sometimes the judgment comes sudden. Sometimes the trumpet blast sounds on a day and at an hour we don't expect. And we remember that the winnowing fork is ever in the hand, and He will purge his floor most thoroughly and gather his wheat into the garner. But the chaff..." The Reverend paused and raised his chin, "He will burn up the chaff with unquenchable fire! In this story on this day and at this time, know this, dear people of God."

He looked at the younger girls, Heidi and Anna as he spoke. Heidi stood with her arm around her little sister's shoulders, and both girls looked at the ground.

"Know, dear children, that when judgment came suddenly, God winnowed the wheat from the chaff. His own dear children, Jonas and Rachel, ever devout and stalwart in their faith, they were, they are, the wheat. They are like that lost silver coin that was found and over which there was great rejoicing. Yea, the wheat he kept, the coin he found, and even now in heaven there is great rejoicing." The Reverend held his right hand gently aloft as if setting the lost coin on a high altar.

"And know, too, that God most certainly did not withhold judgment from the evildoer, that vile reaper who delivered Jonas and Rachel unto the Lord." The Reverend turned his gaze to Nyx, who stood up straight, eyes forward. "Know that the chaff was swept from that threshing floor." From his vantage point, Kamp saw Nyx's body stiffen, her fists clench into tight balls and her chest begin to heave.

The Reverend continued, "Be assured that the chaff, that which he despises and must punish, the murderer, the most diabolical, he cast that foul fiend most expeditiously into the lake of fire, eternal torment, a fitting and well-deserved punishment!"

As he made the proclamation, the Reverend pointed his right index finger forcefully down. Spittle formed at the corners of the Reverend's mouth as he churned toward his crescendo.

"Dear people, know that God's judgment is perfect and just. I'm reminded of another para—"

Nyx launched herself at the Reverend A.R. Eberstark. She flew at him with both arms outstretched, and when she reached him, she clenched both hands around his throat.

She said, "Shut up! Shut up!"

The Reverend, having no time to brace himself for the attack, fell backward next to Jonas Bauer's coffin, the two of them nearly tumbling into his grave. Nyx held her grip which was tight enough to stop his breathing. Eberstark's face went purple, and he made gurgling noises.

"You don't know anything you miserable son of a bitch!" Nyx punctuated her words by slamming the Reverend's head against the ground. The undertaker Manfred Otis was the first to reach the entwined pair. He tried to hoist Nyx off the Reverend, to no avail. Her grip was too tight. The neighbor Charlotte Fogel knelt calmly beside Nyx and put her hands on Nyx's hands.

She said, "Sweetheart, let go. It's all right. Let go." Slowly, Nyx's grip slackened, and she slumped to the side. The Reverend clambered to his feet, gasping for breath and rubbing his throat. His gown was splotched with grave dirt, his collar askew.

He said, "This girl is unwell. The hex is on her too!"

Nyx threw her arms over Jonas Bauer's coffin and sobbed. "Daddy, daddy!"

Anna and Heidi ran to Nyx and hugged her. Charlotte Fogel put her hand on Nyx's head and said, "It's all right, dear. It's all right."

Nyx shrieked, "Of course, it's not all right!" The sound scattered the crows from the trees that ringed the graveyard. "They're gone, they're gone, they're gone."

Kamp saw the man whom he hadn't recognized walk over to Nyx. He held out his hand to her. She took it, and he guided Nyx to her feet. After saying a few words to her, he tipped his hat to Charlotte Fogel, walked back to his carriage, and left.

Kamp walked over to the undertaker and extended his hand. "Manfred."

The undertaker shook hands with him. "Hell of a thing, ain't it? Terrible shame."

"You better believe it. Did you know him? Bauer?"

The undertaker shook his head. "Can't say that I knew him. Good man, though, from what all everyone tells me. I know he cheated death once before, though."

"How's that?"

"Do you remember that explosion? Mine explosion a while back?"

"Which one?"

The undertaker took off his hat and scratched his head. "Oh, Christ. It was in the summer. Six, seven months ago. Anyway, Bauer was down there, right in the room where it happened."

"How'd he make it out?"

"Probably missed getting blown up by that much, by a hair, a blonde one, if you know what I mean."

"That close, huh?"

"Yah, well, his buddy wasn't as lucky. Head sheared clean off. It was Bauer himself who handed it to me when he come out of the shaft. Never forget it." The undertaker shook his head to banish the memory. "Stuff doesn't usually bother me."

"Do you remember that guy's name? The guy who got killed?"

Manfred Otis tilted his head back and opened his mouth. "Uhh...Kunkle. Roy Kunkle. Big bastard."

"Do you know anything about him?"

"Just stories. By the way, Kamp, Oehler had me bury Knecht. My guys went and got him early this morning, sewed him up in a linen sack and put him in a communal plot, unmarked. It's done."

"Much appreciated. Who was that man standing next to the Judge, the one who just left?"

The Judge walked up behind Kamp and joined the conversation. He shook hands with the undertaker and then with Kamp.

The Judge said, "That's Silas Ownby. He owns Confederated Coal."

"Owns it?"

"Correct."

Kamp said to the Judge, "Friend of yours?"

The Judge said, "Whenever one of his miners passes away, he tries to attend the service."

"He must go to a lot of funerals."

The Judge focused on Kamp. "I need to—"

"Yah, I know, you need to speak with me. Drucken-miller told me." He saw the Reverend walking into the church next to the cemetery. "How 'bout tomorrow?"

Kamp picked his way through the headstones until he reached the path to the church. He went in the same door where he'd seen Eberstark go. He smelled smoke and followed the scent to the back of the building, where he found Eberstark sitting next to a crackling fire in a potbellied stove. Atop the stove was a small frying pan, and in the pan was a little wire frame of a *tipi*.

The reverend said, "Oh, hello, Kamp. Come in, come in," as he placed a slice of bread on either side of the frame. Eberstark smiled. "I do like my bread *toastich*, especially on a cold day."

The Reverend had taken off his gown and wore a plain white shirt and wool pants. He'd also removed his shoes. He had a whiskey bottle at his side and poured a glass. He offered it to Kamp, who declined.

Kamp said, "I'll bet you never had a ceremony like that before."

Eberstark let out a laugh. "Well, no, but I'm sure Martin Luther himself suffered much worse. And more often." He raised his glass. "To Luther." The Reverend took a long sip, then tilted his head back, savoring it for a long moment.

"Reverend, do you mind if I ask you some questions? Reverend? A few questions?"

"Of course, of course." Eberstark gulped the glass of whiskey, then poured another. "Please, my son, have a seat." Kamp pulled a wooden chair from the corner of the room and sat a few feet away.

"Tell me about Jonas and Rachel Bauer."

Eberstark pulled in a breath through his nostrils and let out a deep sigh. "Well, as godly a man and wife as you'll ever find. *Salz der Erde*, you know? Salt of the earth. *Salz und Licht.* Here's to salt and light!"

He drained the glass. The bread on the stove had begun to turn brown. Eberstark carefully picked the slices of toast off the *tipi*, offering one to Kamp, which he accepted.

"Reverend, why do you think Daniel Knecht would want to hurt Jonas Bauer?"

Eberstark talked while he chewed his toast. "It couldn't be more obvious, could it?"

"Tell me."

"Lust. A deadly form of lust. More than once Jonas come to me, wondering what to do. I told him that gat-toothed fiend Knecht has lickerish eyes, like a wolf. And disagreeable intentions for the girl."

"Then why would he hurt Jonas? And why hurt Rachel?"

Eberstark shook his head and leaned toward him. "You wonder what such a man sees when he looks at himself in the *shpiggle*. You hafta wonder how he lives with himself, say not?"

"But why hurt them?"

"*Ach*, I told Jonas, told him again and again. That fiend has disagreeable intentions. He wouldn't listen."

"What I'm trying to understand, Reverend, is if Knecht wanted the girl, if it was a matter of lust, why would he kill her parents?"

Eberstark leaned back and savored the bread in his mouth. "Why did Eve eat the apple?"

"But does it make sense to you?"

"You mean, does evil make sense? Why, does it make sense to you? Evil, Kamp. Evil. We live in a fallen world. All have sinned. And all have fallen short." Eberstark refilled his glass. "Add to that the fact that someone put a hex on them all. That's the tragedy. They were all cursed. Doomed." The Reverend hung his head, and Kamp knew he'd soon lose his senses altogether.

"Reverend, did you know a man named Roy Kunkle?"

Eberstark lifted his head and sneered. "Oh, that guy."

"How did you know him?"

"Good friend of Jonas. Worked alongside Jonas in the mines. I couldn't stand him."

"Why not?"

At this question, Eberstark became much more animated. His cheeks, already red from the fire and from the drink, blazed red, and the color bloomed into his forehead.

"Wrong ideas! He started putting wrong ideas into Jonas's head."

"Ideas about what?"

"That goddamned guy was a *Scharfmacher*. Do you know what that is?"

"Yes."

"A real *Schnickelfritz*, you know. A rabble-rouser!"

"In what way?"

"Well, the things he was telling the men in the mines. He told them to disobey their supervisor. Told them outright! Disobey." Eberstark leaned close enough that Kamp could smell his breath. "Just imagine!"

"Do you know why?"

"*Ach*, does it matter why? It's a sin! Come to think of it, that might be the hex right there. Kunkle put that curse on Bauer and his whole family with them ideas. That's why Jonas couldn't see the truth about that fiend Knecht. Blinded by his horseshit!" Eberstark downed another glass. "Do you know what Jesus said about that? Render. Unto. Caesar. Do you know what that means? It means the peasants must do what they're told. Do you know what Martin Luther said about this?"

"No."

Eberstark sat up in his chair and cleared his throat. "Martin Luther himself said...I memorized this. He said, 'I think there is not a devil left in hell. They have all gone into the peasants. Their raving has gone beyond all measure! Therefore let everyone who can, smite, slay, and stab, secretly or openly, remembering that nothing can be more poisonous, hurtful, or devilish than a rebel!'"

"I appreciate your time, Reverend," and he stood up, catching Eberstark off guard.

"Did I say something wrong?" In an instant Eberstark's expression changed from indignation to hurt. Just as quickly, his expression changed again.

The Reverend squinted at him, "Say, what do you wanna know about all this for?" His words began to slur. "Why so many questions? They're dead, and now they're buried. What does it matter?"

"I don't know that it does."

"Now you're twisting words. Yah, well, you're not perfect neither. You're not, I'm not."

"I didn't—"

Eberstark boomed, "All have sinned and fallen short of the glory of god! And god will not be mocked! Sit back down."

"I'm sorry if I—"

"Do you know what Eberstark means?"

"Yes, I do."

"It means boar. Wild boar. We all have a sinful nature. Martin Luther himself knew worldly pleasures. He ate the food, he took the drink. And women, probably. Jesus, Jesus was wounded. He had a wound in his side. The little side wound! But that doesn't mean we can dishonor the Lord, Kamp. Doesn't mean we can just, just disobey!"

Kamp could still hear the Reverend raving as he left the building. He knew that Eberstark would forget most, if not all, of the conversation. The church was only a couple of miles from his house, and as soon as he started walking, he felt greatly relieved to be moving again out in the cold air. The conversation with Eberstark hadn't told him anything new about the inner-workings of the Bauer family or their relationship with Daniel Knecht. It simply added some color and texture. He reflected more on what Eberstark hadn't mentioned at all, namely that Nyx Bauer had tried to strangle him. If nothing else, perhaps the Reverend's need to get drunk could be explained by the trauma of having been attacked. What was new, however, was what he'd said about Kunkle's role in Jonas Bauer's life. Much more interesting to him than the information itself was the reaction it evoked from Eberstark. And the undertaker, when asked whether he knew Kunkle, alluded to "stories" about the man. Kamp resolved to look deeper.

As he walked, the sun dropped behind the mountains, and with it went the harsh wind that had been blowing all day. He listened to his breathing and to the soft creak of snow-heavy limbs. He felt his body warm and felt the first few beads of perspiration under the band of his hat. He watched the starry host appear, and he saw Saturn twinkle into view next to the crescent moon. When he reached his front door, he expected to see Joe, smoking his pipe by the fireplace, and he braced himself for yet another scolding by the druggist and midwife E. Wyles. Instead, he found the front door locked and the downstairs of the house empty. He unlocked the door and went inside. There was a fire smoldering in the fireplace and the smell of blended tobacco in the room.

Shaw called from the upstairs, "Kamp, is that you?"

He said, "Is your father here?"

"No."

"Wyles?"

"No." Shaw must be doing better, he thought, and he walked upstairs. When he reached the top of the stairs, he saw Shaw sitting in a chair and slowly rocking the baby by the bedroom window. A candle burned on the table next to her. He crossed the room and shut the open window.

Shaw said, "What are you doing?"

He fastened the shutters. "Closed. And doors locked. Front, back and cellar."

"Why?"

"From now on."

"Don't worry. My father was here, and then after that Emma came by. And then Emma left, and the Judge stopped in. He told me he saw you at the funeral and that you'd be home afterward."

"Right, but now it's dark, and you're alone."

"You're here."

He shook his head. "What did the Judge want?"

Shaw said, "And anyway what are we supposed to be afraid of? The Judge said no one's going to bother us."

"Why was he here?"

She smiled. "He came by because he wanted to see the baby."

His expression softened. "Ah, yes, the *boppli*. How is she doing this fine evening?" He reached for the baby who began to cry when he took her from Shaw's arms.

"Shh, it's just me, just me. Daddy." He turned to Shaw. "What are we going to call this girl?"

"Well, you know whatever we decide to call her, it's not her real name. It's just a nickname."

"Then what's her real name?"

"Just like my father's nickname is Joe. And my nickname is Shaw. It's not my real name."

"It's not?"

Shaw laughed. "No."

"How come you never told me?"

"My father said around the time I was born, for some reason people thought we were Shawnee. So my parents just started calling me Shaw. Just a nickname. Not real. And then everyone else started calling me that. My father is a name giver. He gave me my real name."

"What is it?"

Shaw took a breath, looked into his eyes and told him her real name and what it meant.

He said, "It's beautiful." He felt a stab of grief in his chest.

Shaw said, "Now that you know, don't say it to anyone but me," and she stood up and put her arms around him and the baby. My father will give her a real name too."

"When?"

"When it comes to him. The Creator must speak it to him first."

"When did he leave?"

"Who?"

"Your father."

"I don't know. I went to sleep before lunch, and when I woke up he was gone."

"Why'd he go? I thought he'd be here."

"Kamp, I don't know."

"What did Wyles have to say?"

"She was concerned about me, angry at you. The usual. She said I can start moving around more. Whatever I can do."

"What about the Judge? Anything interesting?"

"No, although he did leave a couple gifts. There's one with your name on it. He handed the baby back to Shaw and headed down the stairs. He went to the kitchen, fixed himself a sandwich and saw that, yet again, E. Wyles had left more food, this time several jars of dried beans and sliced apples and apricots. After that, he went into the front room to see what the Judge had left. One of the two bandboxes had already been opened. Inside, he found an embroidered white baptismal gown. The other box was wrapped in paper printed with a pattern of monkeys frolicking in trees. He hefted the box in his hand. Heavier than he expected. He unwrapped the band box and found another box inside it. The top of the box read, "5 CARTRIDGES MANUFACTURED EXPERT-LY for SHARPS RIFLES." A box of bullets. The box had a small label affixed to it that read, "Wendell, welcome to fatherhood."

17

None doubted that among the living, Nyx Bauer suffered most from the tragedy. That is, if they thought about it at all. Once the thrill and the shock of the murders of Jonas and Rachel Bauer had passed, a kind of amnesia, sudden and profound, settled in. Perhaps the destruction of those two godly souls was too much to bear in mind. And even more quickly than the people wanted to forget the killings of Jonas and Rachel, if not the precious souls themselves, they wanted to banish forever the fact of the hanging of the fiend Daniel Knecht. At least in public. To remember the events of that day and perhaps even to relive them in the collective memory of the community would lead to a kind of reflection and perhaps scrutiny that was grossly unap-

pealing. In private, in the woozy time between the out-
ing of the candle and the sweet release of sleep, those
who were there caught glimpses in their mind's eye of
blood on bedroom walls and taut noose coils. They
heard echoes of calls for execution, some from their own
mouths. But these fragments of memory were nothing
that couldn't be remedied with a few short glasses of
liquor or the recitation of Psalm Twenty-three.

But for Nyx Bauer, in the time since that day, the
torment had intensified so that she didn't know from
one moment to the next whether she was asleep or
awake, living or dead. The memories of that night, beginning with the realization that Danny Knecht was in
her bed and ending with seeing him through the stovepipe hole in the floor, burning the blood-soaked clothing, assailed her. Sometimes, the memories unspooled in
the order they happened, like a horror tale. More often,
pieces of memory flew at her like jagged shards of glass.
She remembered the sounds she heard through the
floor. She could not stop remembering that she never
heard her parents cry for help. Nyx didn't feel as if she
were recalling memories. She perceived that she had
crossed over into a nightmare existence where the murders were actually happening without end.

The fact that Danny Knecht had been killed in retribution brought Nyx Bauer no solace, either. The notion
that anyone else's death could put right her parents'

death sickened her. She'd always known Danny Knecht was doomed anyway. She just didn't know how, why, or what his end would be. And it was that thought that tormented Nyx the most. When the demons stopped plaguing her long enough for her to think, her first thought was invariably, *it was my fault*. And the first question she always asked herself was, *why couldn't I protect them?*

People knew that she and her sisters were suffering and would continue to suffer, and they tried to help. John and Charlotte Fogel, the people who took them in and in whose house they now lived, had begun trying to restore normal aspects of the girls' lives. And Nyx herself played that role of comforter as best she could whenever Anna woke up shrieking in the middle of the night or when Heidi began sobbing at the breakfast table. Nyx would put her arms around them, rock them gently, wipe away their tears. And yet, inside herself, she could not be consoled. The part of herself that knew love and trust, that could bask in joy and radiate it back out, that part was lost and gone. And Nyx could not fathom and would not allow herself to believe it could ever come back.

Kamp thought if he got to town early, he could get back home by noon. Stepping out the back door, he saw the moon was gone, but Saturn was there, shining out until the dawn washed it away. When he was a boy, this road had been a narrow dirt path, and all the cornfields had been untouched trees and brambles. Civilization had forced its way out from the city, plot by plot, one right angle at a time. He had dreamt the previous night of the time before the road, before the rails and the law.

Walking now and making good time, the final few fragments of his dreams from the night before slipped from his recollection. And by the time he reached the courthouse steps, Kamp was fully awake. The first person he saw there was the High Constable, Samuel Druckenmiller, toting his shepherd's crook and hustling in the opposite direction from him.

He yelled, "Hello, Sam!"

"Oh, Kamp, *wie bischt?*" He tried to act surprised.

"Good, good. *Wie bischt du?* A little early for you to be out, isn't it?" He walked to where Druckenmiller had stopped.

"It's that goddamned Crow. He's up to something."

"Now what?"

"Well, he's makin' me—oh, nothing, nothing." A silence followed, and he did not fill it. "Say, about the other day when I came by your house. I heard some guys went over there after I was there."

Kamp raised his eyebrows.

Druckenmiller said, "Yah, well, just so you know, I didn't have nothing to do with that. And when I found out they done it, I gave 'em hell. I told 'em—"

"Who were they?"

Druckenmiller waved his crook, reliving the moment. "I said, you goddamned louses. I should—"

"Who were they?"

"Some guys. I don't know."

"Were they the same guys that ripped Knecht's body out of the ground?"

"I don't know nothing about that."

"Where were they from?"

"Christ, I don't know. Easton? New Jersey, *mebbe*. Look, the point is, they shouldn'ta gone over to your house and hassled you, and when I found out, I done something about it."

"I appreciate that."

"*Ach*, you don't believe me."

"Seems a little strange."

Druckenmiller erupted, "Jesus Crackers, Kamp! I'm sticking up for you in all my *g'shwetzes* with the neighbors. You *daresn't* forget. I might be the only friend you got left!"

He watched Druckenmiller cross the street and disappear into the police station. When he turned to walk up the courthouse steps, he found Philander Crow standing directly in front of him.

Crow said, "Now, now, what were you little boys squabbling about?"

"Nice to see you, too."

"I could hear Druckenmiller, what's the word–*gretzing*–all the way up in my office. You must have hurt his feelings."

"I need to talk to you about Knecht, what I was saying yesterday."

"Yes, well, I need you to walk with me. There's something I have to show you."

The two men walked side-by-side down Fourth Street. Crow looked over each shoulder, and said, "All right, tell me."

"The first thing is, I spent enough time with Knecht before it happened to know he never killed anyone and didn't intend to."

"You know this how?"

Kamp said, "By the way he acted. The things he said."

"Irrelevant. What murderer ever says he's going to kill someone, particularly to a police detective?"

"After it happened, he came to me first."

"So what?"

"He wanted to tell me the truth. He wanted to give me that coin."

"Then why didn't he?"

"He was too scared."

"Of what? Of whom? He was already a dead man when he came to your front door. What reason could he have had to keep his mouth shut?"

"His sisters. Knecht said all along that all he wanted was to take care of his sisters."

"Seems he also wanted to take care of Nadine Bauer."

"The whole time he lived at Jonas Bauer's house, he was sending money to his sisters. What I'm saying is that he never would have done anything that would hurt them."

"I'm not convinced."

"The day after the hanging I went to their house in Easton. I was worried about them, what would happen to them. I thought for sure they'd already be in an orphanage, or worse. I thought they'd be distraught."

"And?"

"They were fine, probably better off than when I saw them the time before."

"So?"

"So, someone else is taking care of them now. Knecht made a deal."

"Traded his life for their security. Something like that?"

"I doubt they gave him a choice, but yes, something like that.

"Can you prove it?"

"Nope."

Crow said, "Then what else do you have?"

"The coin."

"What about it?"

"It got your attention when I showed it to you."

They reached the corner of Fourth and Iroquois. Crow stopped walking and faced him.

Crow said, "Do not, under any circumstances, show that coin to anyone. And don't talk about it."

"What is it?"

"*Ex Fratrum Ordine, Et in Corvo.* Fraternal Order of the Raven."

"What's that?"

"We don't know, but it's probably unrelated, in any case."

Kamp said, "Who's we?"

"We're not discussing it further out here. I've listened to your argument regarding your speculation that someone other than Daniel Knecht killed the Bauers, and I find it unconvincing.

"Unconvincing?"

"There's one glaring problem."

"What's that?"

"There's an eyewitness. Nyx Bauer."

Kamp said, "No. She never said she saw Knecht do it. She said she saw him burning the clothing. We don't know whose clothing it was. No one actually saw him do it. The girls were locked inside their room until I got there."

"Really, does any of this seem plausible, even to you?"

Kamp surveyed the intersection where they stood. Carriage wheels had cut deep ruts, now frozen, into the road. Buildings with storefronts below on bottom and apartments on top lined the thoroughfare. A street vendor hawked sausages in a wheeled cart.

Kamp said, "What are we doing here, anyway?"

"See that building? The brick one, halfway up the block. Doesn't look like much."

"I see it."

Crow said, "Whorehouse. Police are going to shut it down tonight."

"Good for them."

"Police, meaning you."

"I don't follow." A pushcart went rolling by, and Kamp gave it a long look. "*Ponnekuche.*"

"Beg your pardon?"

"Pancakes. Dutch babies. Want some?" Crow shook his head. Kamp held up two fingers to the vendor who wrapped the pancakes in paper and handed them to Kamp, who gave the man a nickel. Crow stared at Kamp, who'd begun eating. He chewed the pancake slowly, swallowed it, then said to Crow. "Not interested. Not doing it."

"I'm told by a reliable source that there will be significant activity there tonight."

"Well, that's what whorehouses are known for. I investigate crimes, Crow. I write reports. You prosecute. That's our deal. Sounds like this is work for the actual police. Have them do it."

"No one in the police department can know. In fact, no one else at all can know. If word gets out, it will go straight back to them. We'll miss our chance."

"Chance for what?"

"The Fraternal Order of the Raven. The coin. Some of their leaders will be there tonight. You will go in there, apprehend the wrongdoers and then interrogate them."

Kamp laughed. "You want me to march into a house of ill-repute, interrupt all the coitus, arrest the participants and then conduct interviews with the leaders of a murderous secret society. By myself. Mr. Crow, does this seem plausible, even to you?"

"You won't be by yourself. I'll be with you."

"The two of us?"

"You're convinced the coin is the key to your little mystery. If you want to find out whether that coin has anything to do with the murders of Jonas and Rachel Bauer, this is your opportunity. You won't get another one."

18

Kamp gave up on the notion of getting home by noon as soon as he realized what raiding a brothel would entail. He needed to know as much about the building as he could. He hadn't spent much time on the South Side, though he knew by looking at them that most of the structures were laid out the same, more or less. Some of the tenement houses had a slapped together look about them, though some, such as the building Crow pointed out to Kamp, appeared to be well-built. He wanted to get a detailed understanding of the place, and he knew he'd spend a good part of the day inspecting it from a number of vantage points, including the roof of a building across the street.

He also wanted to plan the exercise with Philander Crow, scripting and rehearsing as best they could how they wanted the scenario to play out. It had occurred to him that Crow had to be lying about some part of this mission: the rationale, the purpose of it, the people involved. He assumed that even if Crow weren't lying outright, he was surely withholding important details from him. Kamp endeavored to know more about Crow's intentions prior to the raid. Lastly, he needed a weapon. He would go home to retrieve his Sharps if he had to, but in this case a rifle wouldn't do.

Preparation would last all day, and the execution and the aftermath might well take most of the night. Shaw would be expecting him, and when he didn't show up, she would fear the worst. Besides that, she'd be unprotected. The outrage regarding Daniel Knecht in general and Kamp's attempt to save him in particular appeared to have died down. And the flow of gawkers to the Bauer house had slowed to a trickle. Nevertheless, he intuited that more trouble was coming their way. At the same time, he sensed that following the path he was on would be the only way to put an end to the trouble for good. He just needed to make sure that his family would be safe until he got home.

Kamp knew E. Wyles started work each morning before dawn and that the drugstore would be open by the time he got there. It was already after nine o'clock. He took a deep breath and marched in the door of her shop. She stood at her counter with her back to him.

"Emma."

She said, "Can't talk."

"I need a favor."

"That's the refrain, isn't it?"

"Just one more, and you won't need to worry about me anymore."

"It's not you I'm worried about. It's your wife."

"She's not my wife."

"You understand my point, Kamp."

"Yah, well, it's a favor for her then." He took off his hat and rubbed his temples with his thumb and index finger.

"I'm mixing a compound. I'm working."

"I need you to go to the house today. I can't get back there, and someone has to be with them. Emma, I need you to check on them."

She turned to face him and brushed a few strands of hair from her forehead with the back of her hand. "Believe it or not, there are people who need me besides you."

"Remember when we were kids, Emma? Remember what it was like? How we could go outside, go up to the woods, make up stories and adventures. That wall way up there we'd sit on. And how we'd go down and splash around in the creek and get freezing cold and then try to get warm in the sun. Remember that?"

"I do."

"It's been a long time since things were like that."

"Things change."

Kamp said, "That's what it felt like to be free."

"So what?"

"So, now it's different. I realize that. We all have people we have to look out for, not just ourselves. I understand."

"What do you need me to do?"

"Go to the house tonight, and let Shaw know I'll be back tomorrow morning. Find my rifle. It's in the kitchen. And make sure it's loaded."

By the time Kamp thought about getting a gun for himself, the sun had already begun its retreat behind the stacks of Native Iron. He didn't know whether Druckenmiller would still be at the police station, and Kamp hoped he wouldn't. When he walked in the station, though, there was the High Constable at his desk, feet up, smoking a cigar and reading a newspaper. He lowered the paper just enough to see that it was Kamp and then went back to reading.

"Sam, I need to borrow a gun." Druckenmiller ruffled the newspaper and said nothing. "Where do you keep the guns, Sam?"

Druckenmiller lowered the newspaper. "Oh, I'm sorry, beg your pardon?"

"Knock it off."

"I thought you didn't trust me. Unless you need something, I guess."

Kamp saw a locked cabinet against the far wall. "Where's the key?"

"Looks like you're *scheiss* outta *glück*. Go home and get your own."

"I don't have time. Believe me, Sam, this is just about the last—"

"You think you can just get people to do whatever you want, just by talking. Ain't that so?"

"This is serious," Kamp said.

"All right, well, in that case, what do you need it for?"

"Business. Official business."

"Police business? Oh, boy. Sounds exciting." Druckenmiller took a nip from the flask, his eyes shining.

"Sam, you can break my balls from dawn till dusk tomorrow, but right now, I just need a gun."

"Tell me what for."

"No."

"I'll make it simple. I'll give you what you want, and you don't have to tell me *nussing*."

"Good."

"You just have to take me with you."

"Forget it."

Druckenmiller let out a sigh and raised the newspaper again. Kamp looked out the window and saw that it was dark. Crow would be waiting for him, and soon they'd need to be set up.

"All right, all right, Sam. Come on, let's go."

Druckenmiller set the paper aside and smiled at him. "Well, why din'tcha say so?" He took off a necklace that had been hidden by his shirt. On it, there was a small brass key. He got up and went to the cabinet. "Whaddya need, pistol, shotgun?"

"Let me see what's there."

Druckenmiller swung open the doors of the cabinet to reveal a large assortment of firearms.

Kamp said, "Getting ready for war?" He scanned the two rows of weapons and quickly settled on a cut-down shotgun with a shoulder strap.

Druckenmiller said, "8-gauge. Make sure you know who it is you're shooting before you pull the trigger. You might not be able to tell afterward."

He took the gun from the cabinet, and Druckenmiller handed him a box of shells. On his way out the door, Druckenmiller reached for his shepherd's crook.

Kamp said, "Leave it."

The two men made their way down Fourth Street and stopped a few blocks short of the intersection with Iroquois Street, the appointed meeting place with Philander Crow. The district attorney stepped silently from between two buildings when he saw them approaching.

Under his breath, Crow said, "What is he doing here?"

"We'll need him."

"You're responsible for him, Kamp."

Druckenmiller cut in, "Listen, Crow, I'm the High Constable. You have no authority to do this. You shouldn't even be–say now, what *are* we doing here?"

Crow said, "You have a point. Our intention is to put a stop to a crime, and since you're the High Constable, you can be instrumental."

Druckenmiller raised his eyebrows and pursed his lips. He said, "What crime?"

Crow said soberly, "Prostitution."

Druckenmiller said, "Oh, Jesus Christ, Kamp, don't tell me you're going along with this!"

People passing by on foot had to sidestep the men, and some craned their necks to look.

Crow hissed, "Keep your voice *down*."

"You're telling me you want me to arrest people for, for *schtupping*?" Crow winced, as Druckenmiller continued, "I might as well arrest myself."

Kamp said, "It's more complicated than that."

"How so?"

"Trust me."

"You are a sworn officer of the law," Crow said. "It's your duty to uphold it. Failure to do so may result in your dismissal."

"Oh, go screw."

Kamp said, "He's coming with me. Sam, we're going up the fire escape, and in through a window. And, Crow, you're going through the front door."

Crow said, "Correct. We will get into position, and exactly one hour from now, we'll go in."

Kamp and Druckenmiller peered down the alley behind the building at 31 Iroquois Street. It was black, except for the intermittent glow of the cherry of a cigarette. They could smell the smoke.

Druckenmiller said, "Oh, well, there's someone down there. Let's turn back."

"Why do you think there'd be someone standing right there?"

"Guys smoke. Who cares? Let's go."

"You got handcuffs, right?"

Druckenmiller grabbed Kamp by the lapel of his coat. "Listen, up till now, you've asked a lot of questions, and you've made a lot of people angry. But you haven't...you haven't—"

"Haven't what?"

"Crossed the line."

"Sam, what do you know that I don't?"

"I'm saying, you do this, no one's gonna be looking out for you no more."

Kamp said, "We're walking side by side, like we're just strolling through. I'll talk."

They started down the alleyway, their footfalls echoing loud off the buildings. When they reached the man, Kamp noticed he was standing directly beneath the fire escape they intended to climb. The man threw his cigarette to the ground as they approached.

Kamp said, "Evening, friend."

The man grunted, "Ev'ning."

"Got any matches?"

"'Fraid not."

As he said it, Kamp raised the shotgun and pressed it to the man's forehead. With his free hand, he lifted a pistol from the man's holster.

"How about now?"

"Jacket pocket."

"Get 'em, Sam."

"Kamp, I don't—"

"Do it."

Druckenmiller pulled the matches from the man's pocket.

"Hold it up so we can see who we're talking to." Druckenmiller struck one on the wall and held it a few inches from the man's nose.

Kamp said, "I recognize you. You're that guy that came to my house and threatened me. You're the right-behind-you guy. And now you're here. What's your name?" The man stood motionless and said nothing. "And what are you doing back here?"

"Smoking a cigarette."

"Turn around. Face the wall."

"What for?"

Kamp hit the man in the jaw with the butt of the shotgun. The force of the blow knocked him against the wall of the building, and he crumpled to the ground.

"Sam, put the handcuffs on him. Lock him to the downpipe. Right there."

Druckenmiller snapped the cuffs into place. "Kamp, you *daresn't* hit a man for no—"

"What do you think he's doing here? We need to get up there. Now."

Druckenmiller said, "It's wrong. What you're doing is wrong."

Kamp wheeled around, eyes blazing, and faced Druckenmiller. "Why, Sam! Why is it wrong? Tell me!"

"You gotta calm down. You ain't seeing this right."

Kamp slung the 8-gauge over his shoulder, grabbed the fire escape ladder, pulled it down and began to climb. Without looking back, he said, "I'm going to need your help, Sam. Move."

Druckenmiller looked one way down the alley, then the other. He looked at the man on the ground, still not moving. He muttered, "Jesus boom," and he began going up the ladder himself. Kamp kept going until he reached the fourth floor, where he could see a dim light coming from one of the windows. The rest of the windows in the building were dark. Kamp took his watch from his pocket. 10:47. They'd agreed that Crow would knock on the apartment door at exactly eleven o'clock. Druckenmiller came up the ladder a few minutes after Kamp, cursing and trying to catch his breath.

When he reached the landing, Druckenmiller whispered, "Now tell me again what's so goddamned necessary about this."

Kamp leaned toward the window. The curtains were drawn, but he could see most of the room where they parted. He saw bodies, none of them clothed, all in motion. Most were on the floor, some standing, in a variety of sexual positions. He couldn't make out anyone's face.

Druckenmiller said, "Can you see anything? What's going on in there?"

"See for yourself." He moved so that Druckenmiller could peer in.

"Well, that settles it."

Kamp said, "How so?"

"It's just people having a good time."

"Just having a good time?"

"Yah, a party. We shouldn't bother them."

Kamp noticed that the window was also slightly open. He could feel warm air escaping, and he heard women moaning.

"Sam, for the last time—"

They heard a sharp knock on the apartment door. The orgy continued unabated, as the knocking grew louder. At the same time, they felt the fire escape move and heard it creaking.

Druckenmiller said, "He must've gotten out of the cuffs. He's coming up."

They heard a muffled voice, Crow's, "Open the door. Police!"

Kamp saw a man wearing what looked like a burlap sack over his head with cut-out eyeholes cross the room to the door. The man was fully clothed and carrying a shotgun.

Kamp threw open the window and shouted, "Crow!"

The man with the shotgun raised it and fired it into the door. Women screamed, and all the partygoers scrambled into other rooms. Kamp jumped through the window and reached for his gun. The man with the shotgun fired at the door again, extracted the spent shell and reloaded. Kamp pointed the 8-gauge at the man and fired. The man's arm splattered against the wall, shotgun clattering to the floor. The revelers, most still naked, some now half-clothed ran for the door, streaming past the man, who held the stump of his upper arm, groaning. Kamp trained the shotgun on the man and walked past him to where Philander Crow lay bleeding on the floor just outside the door.

Crow clutched his chest, which had been torn open. He took short breaths, and blood gurgled from his mouth. When he saw Kamp, he said, "Talk to Kunkle."

Kamp felt a sharp pain at the back of his head. In the instant before he lost consciousness, he saw himself and Philander Crow floating into Daniel Knecht's grave.

19

Emma Wyles had already been working for the better part of three hours when the bells above the door jingled and Kamp had appeared in the drugstore that morning. She'd started working early that day, in part due to him and the needs of his family. It wasn't unusual for her to spend significant time with a new mother in the days after the delivery, and given Shaw's fragile health during the pregnancy, Wyles considered it time well spent. It was also not in Wyles' nature to question or judge the character of the people whose needs she was committed to meeting. Nevertheless, his irresponsibility, which to Wyles bordered on neglect, meant that she'd had to jump in the breach at times when he should have been there. Wyles had even begun to won-

der whether he was intentionally disregarding her ad-
monitions.

She knew that when he walked in that morning, it
could only be to ask for another favor, and she assumed
correctly that it entailed her going, yet again, to look
after Shaw. Initially, she'd refused. She resolved to let
him handle his own matters regarding his work and his
family, and she hoped that his warning to find the rifle
was just anxiety, or manipulation. Still, the anxiety
worked its way into her, and by the time her normal
workday ended, she'd decided she'd have to ride out
there just as soon as she was finished. For Shaw, not for
Kamp. Wyles simply couldn't see why she should have
to suffer for his shortcomings. But the prescriptions had
piled up on her counter during the past two weeks, and
by the time she'd mixed the last compound, she'd lost
track of the time. When Wyles looked out the window,
the streets were empty, the last gaslight put out. She felt
a pang of remorse, then distress.

Wyles locked the front door of the drugstore, put on
her coat and went out the back door to where the horse
was tied. Once on the road, she said, "*Ya*," gave the horse
a sharp kick and took off across the New Street Bridge.
She couldn't locate the source of her unease, and panic
was a feeling unfamiliar to her. As she covered the miles
under the black sky, though, the worry magnified, and
by the time she turned the horse onto the path to

Kamp's house, Wyles' heart was pounding. She tied up her horse, bounded up the stairs to the front door and tried the knob. Locked. Wyles banged the door with her fist.

"Shaw! It's Emma Wyles. Open the door, please. Shaw!" She turned to look out over the property, and she tried to listen for whatever noises might have been out there. But darkness hid the night creatures, and the thumping of blood at her temples covered the sounds. Wyles turned back to the door.

"Shaw!"

The door swung open, and Shaw stood in the doorway, holding a candle and looking half-asleep. "Where is he?"

"Shaw, may I come in, please? Kamp asked me to come." Shaw stepped aside so that Wyles could enter. Wyles scanned the front room and found nothing unusual.

Shaw said, "What's the matter?"

"How are you? Is everything all right?"

"Yes, yes. I fell asleep. We were sleeping."

Wyles walked into the kitchen and lit a lantern. She called to Shaw, "Do you know where he keeps his rifle? Oh never mind, I found it." She walked back into the front room carrying the Sharps.

"What happened to him?"

"He's fine." She set down the rifle, grabbed the Judge's gift box of bullets from the mantle. As she took out a cartridge and loaded the Sharps, Wyles said, "I'm sure Kamp was just worrying about you."

The first shot came whistling through one of the front windows of the house and lodged in the wall over Wyles' head.

"Shaw, lie flat on the floor!" Before Wyles herself could get down, the next bullet slammed into her thigh. Another shot hit the side of the house, and the fourth one smashed the kerosene lantern. Shaw and Wyles lay down, listening. Silence outside. Wyles took the rifle and crawled toward the window. She pushed herself up just high enough to peer over the window sill, and she saw shapes advancing toward the house.

"They're coming."

Upstairs the baby began to wail, and Shaw jumped to her feet and ran for the stairs. Her motion brought a volley of gunfire, the bullets splintering the stairs a step behind Shaw. Wyles aimed and fired. She saw a body fall twenty feet from the front door. She scrambled back across the floor to get the box and reload. Bullets kept zinging through the window. Wyles waited for a lull, raised up, fired again and sat back down with her back to the wall. She could hear men's voices outside, talking to each other. She ran her fingers over the wound in her leg, assessing the damage.

Wyles called, "Shaw! Shaw! Are you there?" She heard nothing in reply, and there was silence in the house.

A loud voice boomed outside. "It's all right! We saw the guys who done it. Everything is under control. Just stay right where you are."

Wyles heaved a sigh. Then she smelled kerosene. She thought it may have come from the smashed lantern until she saw the glow of flames outside the kitchen window. She dropped the rifle and clambered up the stairs. Wyles burst into the upstairs bedroom and found Shaw crouched in the corner, holding the baby.

"Let's go."

By the time they reached the bottom of the stairs, fire had engulfed the kitchen, and flames poured through the windows.

Wyles retrieved the rifle and bullets and said, "The cellar."

Shaw went to the kitchen instead and picked up a large knife that she held in her free hand. She went down the stairs and into the darkness with Wyles following.

They breathed the cool air in gulps. Shaw had held the baby so that her mouth was pressed to Shaw's chest, and now she let the little girl breathe. The baby let out a loud wail.

Shaw said, "How bad are you hurt?"

"We need to wait."

"For what?"

"For them to think we're dead." Wyles loaded the rifle again.

The heat began to pulse in waves above them, and smoke started to seep through the ceiling. Wyles felt her way across the cellar to the bulkhead doors. She pressed against the doors with her shoulder.

"Something heavy up there. They must've blocked the doors."

Still holding the baby, Shaw got beside Wyles, and the two put their backs against the doors and pushed with all their strength. The ceiling of the cellar started creaking and sagging, and the women began choking on the smoke. Shaw and Wyles gave it one last surge, and the large stone that had been holding the doors shut tumbled to the ground. The bulkhead doors burst open. Wyles crawled out first, carrying the rifle and staying low to the ground. Clutching the kitchen knife, Shaw hauled herself and the baby out of the cellar.

Wyles grabbed Shaw under the arm and pulled her to her feet, as the baby began crying again. With Wyles in the lead, the two women hurried toward the tree line at the back of the property. The walls of the house collapsed with a massive *thwump* that sent out an intense ripple of heat.

Shaw said to the baby, "Shh, shh, a little farther." She heard footsteps coming fast behind her. Without looking, Shaw wheeled and in a single motion slashed the neck of her attacker, who grabbed her by the back of her dress. Wyles heard the commotion and spun around, rifle raised. She shot the man in the chest and reloaded. A second pursuer drew within a yard of Shaw.

Wyles yelled, "Get down!" Shaw dropped low, and Wyles shot the second man in the chest. He crumpled, as Shaw scrambled to her feet.

"There's more of them. Keep going."

Kamp woke up facedown, still clutching the sawed-off to his chest. There was blood caked in his nostrils, so he figured he'd been there for a while. He pushed up to his hands and knees, shook his head slowly and felt a bolt of pain at the back of his head where he'd been bludgeoned. When he was able to focus, he saw Philander Crow lying next to him. Crow's skin was blue, eyes open and expression serene. Apart from a few spatters of blood, there was nothing about Crow's face to suggest how he'd been killed. Crow's torso, however, had been shredded by the buckshot. He scanned the floor for the pistol Crow had been carrying and didn't see it. He checked under Crow's body. Not there. Kamp strained to hear over the loud buzzing in both ears. There seemed to be no sound coming from the apartment, or from outside. Where were the police? Where was Druckenmiller?

Kamp stood up and inspected the door of the apartment. It had large holes blown through it, consistent with the blasts he'd seen the man fire. The door also had a brass key sticking out of the lock, which Kamp pocketed. He walked back into the apartment. It was empty. Bare floors, no curtains. He left the building and walked into the cold, still night. He looked up the street toward South Mountain and back down at the glow from Native Iron and saw no one. He pulled out his watch and by the moonlight saw that it was two seventeen. He knew the police station would normally be locked up for the night but decided to check anyway. When he got to the front steps, there were no lights in the police station and none in the courthouse. No one reported what had happened, or if they did, the police weren't investigating it. He thought about Crow lying in the hallway. At a minimum, he thought he should tell the coroner A.J. Oehler to retrieve the body. More than anything, though, he wanted to make sure Shaw and the baby were all right. He wanted to get home.

Kamp smelled the fire long before he reached the house in the hours before dawn, and he broke into a run. In the last quarter mile, he saw a faint glow over the last small rise, and when the house finally came into view, he saw the brick chimney standing and everything else lost. The fire was still hot and sending up great black clouds of smoke, and he could make out the figures of people standing at a distance from what had been his home. As he approached, he saw George Richter and his hired man, Hugh Arndt, and ran to them.

Kamp said, "Where are they?"

Richter said, "I'm sorry, I'm sorry."

"Where are they!"

"Ach, we don't know."

"What do you mean?"

"When we got here, the house was all in flames, already *tzommag' folia*. No way in. We searched the property and didn't find anyone."

"How'd it start?"

"No way to know. Probably started around midnight."

"So they could've gotten out of the house."

Richter said, "Could have, though she didn't go to a neighbor. Not that we know."

"What about Emma Wyles? She was supposed to be here."

Richter took off his hat and rubbed his forehead. "Don't know about that, either. Though there's this." He pointed to the body of the horse on the ground. "All shot up."

The buzzing in Kamp's ears grew until he couldn't hear anything else. He felt his body go numb and began to lose his balance. He said, "I think I'll just wait here," and he sat down hard, cross-legged on the ground.

All the spectators who came to look at the aftermath of the fire once the sun came up that morning noticed Kamp sitting there, staring straight ahead, and some tried to rouse him. They soon realized, though, that what had happened couldn't be helped and that pulling him back from wherever he'd gone would make matters worse. By midmorning, the last of the curious had come and gone and, to a person, they wondered how a part of the world so small could have undergone yet another calamity. First the Bauers, now this. But then again, they thought, seems like maybe he brought it on himself. The way he tried to help that fiend Knecht, the questions he was asking after the hanging. The fact that he shacked up with that Indian in the first place. Come to think of it, he rubbed everybody wrong, one way or the other. The conversations took place mostly in people's own minds and sometimes out loud after a drink. Kamp is a good man. He is. It's just he come back different. Hell, he was different before he left. War just made it worse. Not his fault. And not that he deserved what he got. But still. And as Kamp and his misfortunes, the ones he suffered and the ones he created, slipped from their minds, the last thing they said to themselves was, I pray to god that the hex on him ain't on me, too.

Kamp didn't hear anything that went said or unsaid. He didn't feel the hand on his shoulder. He'd receded so far back that nothing reached him. He'd slipped down into a void he'd long suspected was there but that he'd never had to travel to before. He felt nothing and knew nothing. He could not have known how long he'd been on the ground, how much time had passed, until he heard a voice that pulled him slowly back out.

"Mr. Kamp, Mr. Kamp."

Kamp shut his eyes hard and opened them again.

"Wake up."

"Kamp."

"What?"

"Just Kamp." He still stared straight ahead, but the world was coming back into focus. The person talking to him wore a blue dress, and she bent down so she was at eye level with him.

"Okay then, Kamp, get up. You have to get up." He recognized her. The girl, Nyx Bauer.

He mumbled, "You shouldn't be here."

With both hands, Nyx grabbed him firmly under the arm.

She said, "You have to get up."

"You need to go home."

264 | KURT B. DOWDLE

"Move!" As she said it, Nyx pulled him to his feet. Pain shot through his body, bringing him further to his senses. He surveyed the scene anew. The house was smoldering, and the dead horse had been hauled away. Both the slaughterhouse and the hen house were standing, though the slaughterhouse looked a little charred.

Kamp said, "They're gone." He looked at Nyx. "They're gone."

"Well, yes, they're gone as in, they're not here. But some men went through what's left of the house."

"What men?"

"They went through as much as they could, and they didn't find anyone. Not Shaw, not the baby, not Emma Wyles."

"What about the cellar?"

Nyx said, "I don't think they could get there. But right now it looks like they got out is what I'm saying."

"Then where did they go?"

Nyx shrugged her shoulders.

"What are you doing here?"

"I came to talk to you. I have to talk to you."

He refocused back on Nyx. "It's not safe here."

"Tell me about it."

Kamp said, "No, I mean, you're not safe. Your sisters aren't safe. You need to go home."

"I can't stay with the Fogels anymore. I don't want to."

"What about your sisters?"

"They're fine there."

"Where are you going to go, Kamp?"

His gaze settled on the charred house. "Nowhere. I have to stay here."

"It's gone."

"Well, I still have to—"

Nyx said, "You're coming with me."

He walked to the hen house and opened the door. He held up two eggs and said, "Want one?" Nyx shook her head. He cracked one, then the other and ate them both. "Okay, let's go."

The two of them walked the road, and he expected they'd turn off on the path to the Fogels' house. When they got to it, though, Nyx kept walking.

He said, "I thought you were staying with them."

"I was before. I don't want to now."

"Why not?"

"No reason."

"So where are we headed?"

Nyx didn't answer until they'd rounded the curve that brought the house where the Bauer family had lived came into view.

"Back," she said.

The fence that Jonas Bauer and Daniel Knecht had completed only a few months before was gone. The posts and rails that hadn't been carted off lay broken on the frozen ground. Someone, possibly the police, had put boards where the front door used to be and painted "Keep Out" in black on the front of the house. All the downstairs windows had been boarded over as well.

Nyx said, "We can go in through the cellar." A rusted, heavy chain was looped around the handles of the bulkhead doors and fixed in place with a brass boxcar padlock bearing the insignia of the Lehigh Valley Railroad.

When he saw the padlock, Kamp said, "I'll get a sledgehammer."

"Never mind." Nyx pulled the charm bracelet off her wrist. One of the charms was a small brass key. She put it in the keyhole, and the padlock popped open. He swung open the doors and climbed down into the cellar with Nyx following. It seemed unlikely that anyone would be in the house, but they listened intently for noises upstairs all the same.

He turned to face Nyx. "We don't have to be here. There are other places to stay."

"Really? Like where?"

She walked past him, through the darkness and up the stairs. The first floor of the house had been ransacked. Most of the furniture was gone, including the dining room table and three chairs. Framed pictures either hung askew on their nails or lay broken on the floor. More than one liquor bottle had been smashed in the fireplace, and shards of bottle and window glass covered the floor along with a few old newspaper pages. In a corner on the floor by one of the front windows, there was a wood block that read in painted letters, "Room for Rent."

Kamp threw a broken chair and a picture frame into the fire. He crumpled the newspaper pages and stuffed them under the wood. Nyx struck a match on the mantle and set the paper on fire. He went out the back door and retrieved firewood from the stack behind the house, while Nyx went to the well with a pot from the kitchen. She came back in and set the full pot of water next to the fireplace. Soon, the fire was blazing, the room had been swept and the water neared a boil. Nyx took off her coat and wrapped it around the top of the pot so she wouldn't burn her hands.

Kamp said, "What's the water for?"

"First things first."

Nyx gently carried the pot down the hallway. When he found her, Nyx was in her parents' bedroom, cleaning the walls with a scrub brush and soap powder. Slowly, and with considerable effort, the bloodstains faded. He started another fire in the backyard and threw Jonas and Rachel's mattress on top of it. It went up in a flash, and by the time they were finished, the bedroom, the site of the horror, had been washed and swept as clean as it would ever be. And though the memory of the cataclysm had left its mark on them both, indelible and deep, the physical facts of the worst of it, at least, were gone. Nyx left the bedroom, locking the door behind her and sealing off that part of her memory as best she could.

It wasn't until after nightfall that Kamp realized that he was hungry, and immediately after that, he remembered he had no food. Nyx, however, remembered and pulled sandwiches from her bag, giving one to him.

She said, "I'll go back to the Fogels tomorrow and get more."

They sat cross-legged by the fire, and for a long time, neither of them talked. Out of the silence, Nyx said, "I have to talk to you about something."

"Tomorrow. We can talk about it all tomorrow."

Another long silence followed, and then Nyx spoke again without looking at him.

"This used to be our house. This used to be our room. We did everything here. Our family." Nyx shifted so that she could survey the room. She looked at the corner of the room where the Christmas tree had been and down where Belsnickel's candy had clattered to the wood floor. She stared out the front window, then said, "People are going to think there are ghosts living here."

He stared down at his boots and said, "There are."

20

T he Black Diamond Unlimited roused him from a dream set in the future in which his daughter, perhaps ten years old, played on the shore of a lake. She turned to look at Kamp, and she was smiling, holding out something she'd found at the water's edge. He thought it must have been a shell, but then he saw a radiant silver object with eight sides in the palm of her hand. It generated its own light. Before he could focus on the details of the object, the train whistle split the dream in half. He awoke staring at the wall just above the baseboard. He noticed that someone had carved the face of a small figure, wearing a cap in the Phrygian style and grinning. He sat up abruptly on the floor in front of the fireplace and then stood up and tried to shake off the cold and the hurt. He searched the house for Nyx and found her sleeping in her old bed. She must've brought blankets with her, or she'd found some in the cellar. Either way, she appeared to be sleeping fine.

He hit the road before sun up, walking his usual route to Bethlehem, passing the place that used to be his home. He had no anxiety about what might happen to it while he was gone, because there was nothing to protect. No possessions, no people. He wanted to go looking for his family, but there was no way to know even where to begin. And besides the kid Nyx, there was no one he trusted to help him look. He assumed that anyone else he talked to might, if armed with the knowledge of his family's whereabouts, seek to finish the work they'd started or tell someone who would. Kamp knew he needed to go back to Bethlehem to begin untangling the string of events, beginning with the failed raid. Under normal circumstances, he would have begun by hashing out the details with the district attorney Philander Crow. Since that was no longer an option, he might have checked in with Druckenmiller. But he wasn't giving his old friend the benefit of the doubt and would seek to learn more on his own first. That left the Judge.

Kamp didn't want to see anyone he knew on his way into the courthouse, and he hurried up the steps. He knocked on the door to the Judge's chambers.

He called through the door, "It's Kamp."

"Enter."

He walked into the room to find the Big Judge Tate Cain sitting in his usual place, facing the window, pipe smoke curling toward the ceiling. At first, he thought the Judge was wearing his court robes, but when he looked closer, he saw that it was a black Victorian dress.

Without turning to face him, the Judge said, "Pure silk, if you're wondering."

"What's the occasion?

The Judge turned in his chair to look at him and said, "Isn't it obvious?" The Judge studied him. He said, "I've seen you looking rough before, but Christ almighty, Wendell, you look awful."

"*So gehts.*"

"You know I've been wanting to talk to you. I'm sure someone must've told you. Emma or Druckenmiller or somebody."

"Things have been happening."

"Indeed, a veritable Hericlitean fire, don't you think?"

"Fire?"

"Change upon change upon change. Unceasing."

"Not sure today's the day, Judge."

"Not that any of us has a choice, Wendell. 'This world,' Heraclitus was said to have said, 'always was and will be an ever-living fire, with measures of it kindling, and measures going out.'"

"A philosophy lesson."

"Philosophy has its limits. Then again, so does science. Alas, now we see through a glass, darkly. Someday, we shall know even as we are known. But when is that day?"

The Judge opened a drawer, pulled out a sheet of paper and placed it on the desk in front of Kamp.

"The contract."

The Judge said, "Yes, Wendell, and in light of the circumstances, *force majeure* and so on, I'm changing the terms. I'm giving you the deed to the property. Now. You can quit your job as detective, if you'd like. You don't have to finish the year."

"Why did you want to talk to me in the first place?"

The Judge hammered the ashes from his pipe and refilled the bowl with tobacco from his leather pouch. He lit the pipe and took two large puffs. "It's irrelevant now." With a pen the Judge wrote on the contract and affixed his signature to the changes. He tried to hand the pen to Kamp.

The Judge said, "Here, Wendell, make it official." Kamp didn't move. "I thought you'd be relieved."

Kamp took the eight-sided silver coin from his pocket and placed it on the contract. The Judge picked it up carefully between his thumb and forefinger. He inspected both sides of the coin as well as the edge.

The Judge said, "What about it?"

"Where's it from? Who made it?"

The Judge looked directly at him. "I don't know."

"Bullshit."

"All right, then you'd like me to speculate. Well, judging by the locomotive, it appears to be a railroad coin. No actual railroad insignia, though." He looked up, eyebrows raised. "You deduced that already, I'm sure." The Judge went back to scrutinizing the coin. "Here we have the crossed pickax and shovel, signifying, what, coal mining? Industry?"

"Seems like."

"And then this little familiar fellow, smiling, as always. We've all seen him." The Judge pointed to the face on the coin. "You know where he comes from, right?"

Kamp gave the Judge a dead stare.

The Judge said, "Well, what I've heard is that he's a trickster, a symbol of allegiance to revolution. When the British were in charge, for example, the local gunsmiths crafted weapons for the militia, but they typically didn't sign them, since doing so would put them in danger. So instead of signing their guns, they'd engrave this chap in the brass on the stock, a symbol of the revolution."

"What about the Latin? Fraternal Order of the Raven?"

"Well, that's the mystery, isn't it? One would presume that it's an organization of some sort."

"A secret society."

The Judge laughed. He spread his arms and gestured toward his dress. "Everyone has secrets, Wendell. Even you, I'm sure. And with respect to any particular secret, some are in on it. And some are not."

"Fair enough. But this coin was in Daniel Knecht's pocket when he was hanged. I think he wanted me to find it so that I'd know—"

The Judge bristled, "Yes, well, I heard about your, uh, theories regarding Knecht. That *is* what I wanted to talk to you about."

"Not theories. Facts. There's no way–"

"Let it go, Wendell."

"Judge, it's wrong. What happened is wrong."

"You can't prove it, and it doesn't matter. Look at the price you've paid already. And you are no closer to finding out what you think are secrets than when you started."

Kamp looked down at the floor and rubbed his left temple. "All right, what about Crow? What do you know about that whole thing?"

"What...*whole thing?*"

"He was killed. Someone shot him."

The Judge stood up and went to the window. He parted the curtains and looked down on the street below. "Yes, well, I'll grant you that that's being kept quiet."

"Why?" Kamp felt the fire starting at the base of his skull.

"Out of respect for his family, and out of respect for the office he occupied. After all, it's shameful."

"What is?"

"Well, we don't know what the coroner's final ruling will be," the Judge said, "but it seems certain that Crow's death will be ruled a suicide."

"Suicide? The man was gunned down!"

"Indeed. By his own hand. His body was discovered in a bed with a whore, also shot, also dead. He probably killed her and then turned the gun on himself."

Kamp said, "I saw it happen. We were there to shut down a brothel on Iroquois Street."

"Ooh, a brothel."

"Ever been there?"

"Afraid not."

"Well, Crow knocked on the door, and a man came out and shot him through the door. When I came to, he was lying in the hallway next to me."

The Judge said, "If they killed him, why didn't they kill you?"

"Are you telling me that's not what really happened?"

The Judge turned to look at him. "Not at all. I'm sure your recollection is very clear. As I said, Wendell, everything changes. Memories, stories, facts. Especially facts." And then he went back to staring out the window.

"Then what are you saying?"

The Judge said, "The version of events I told you is the truth as far as the police are concerned, as far as the city is concerned."

"But you're the judge."

"That's right. I adjudicate the cases that come before me. Cases that have a plaintiff and a defendant. This case has neither. In fact, it's not even a case. It's unfortunate, and it's tragic. But it's not a case. It's more like a dirty secret."

"Holy shit. You're with them. You're on their side."

"Hardly."

Kamp said, "Then why not do something about it? You have the authority. Demand answers."

There was a knock at the door and a man's voice. "Your honor, there's a message for you. Your honor?"

The Judge said, "Yes, thank you." He leveled his gaze and spoke in a low voice. "I heard that your father-in-law—"

"I'm not married."

"Right. I heard he paid you a visit. Joe? Is that what he told you to call him?"

"What's your point, Judge?"

"What do you know about *his* past, his secrets? Do you know his real name? Do you know where he is?"

"All I know is you told me to become a police detective, because you wanted to help me. You told Jonas

Bauer to rent a room to Daniel Knecht because you wanted to help them. And yet now you seem to have no interest in doing what's right."

The knock came at the door again. "Your honor! Your honor!"

The Judge walked to his desk and calmly picked up the contract, put it back into the drawer and said, "My offer stands. I realize that since the house has burned down–and mind you, that's a total loss for me–since the house has burned down and your wife and daughter are missing, the property is less appealing at the moment. But houses can be rebuilt. Everything changes. Everything evolves. The Heraclitean fire burns."

"I'll keep that in mind." Kamp walked to the door.

The Judge put on his court robes over the dress. "*Quo vadis, Wendell? Quo vadis?*"

Kamp left the courthouse and walked to the building at 31 Iroquois Street. A sandwich board had been placed on the sidewalk in front of the building. It read, "Luxury Apartments for Lease," and it appeared to be new. Kamp jogged up the front steps. As he reached for the door, it opened and a man stood in the doorway. He had a thin build and a grey three-piece suit. He wore a neat beard in the Van Dyke style and no hat.

The man said, "Good day to you, sir!" Kamp attempted to walk past the man, but the man stepped in his path. "How may I help you, sir?"

He grumbled, "Who are you?"

"Why, I'm the manager of the Monocacy. And may I inquire as to with whom I'm speaking."

"I need to see a room."

"Oh, well, I'm delighted in your interest in the Monocacy. I think you'll find all of our apartments charming and well-appoin—"

Kamp said, "Move." He shoved the manager aside and went into the lobby of the building.

"Sir, I'm afraid you may not enter the premises without first scheduling a visit. Once you do, however, I think you'll find all the apartments at the Monocacy charming and well-appointed."

While the man talked, Kamp went to the door to the stairs and found it locked. "Open this door."

"Sir, if you need a place to sleep, I suggest you take a room at the Christian Mission. It's just two blocks down Fourth Street. There's an angel on the sign." As he spoke, the manager tried to wedge himself between Kamp and the door.

"Open it."

"Sir, I'm afraid if you continue, I'll be required to inform...the police."

Kamp surveyed the lobby and saw a fire ax hanging on the wall. He took it off its hooks and walked back to the door.

"Step aside."

"Good heavens. Sir!"

The first swing of the ax barely missed the manager's head, and he jumped out of the way. The ax sank deep into the wooden door.

"All right, all right! Please stop, sir. Please." The manager produced a ring of keys from his pocket and found the one he wanted. "Here, look."

Kamp eased up and let the manager open the door. He said, "Fourth floor. Go."

Still carrying the ax, he followed the manager up the stairs until they reached the fourth floor landing. He passed the manager and went to the apartment where the shootings had taken place. The apartment door that had been destroyed by the shotgun blasts that killed Philander Crow was gone. In its place was a brand new door. Kamp looked at the floor, which had been bare. It was now covered by a large rug. He pulled back the corner of the rug, looking for the bloodstains. They were gone as well.

"Sir, if I may inquire as to the nature—"

He tried the doorknob to the apartment. Locked.

"Open it."

"Sir, I'm afraid that under the circumstances it's entirely inappropriate to disturb the residents."

Kamp heard a noise in the apartment and started pounding with his fist. "Open the door. Open the door!"

He heard footfalls approaching, and he stepped to the side of the doorframe, leaving the manager standing directly in front of the door.

From inside the apartment came a woman's voice. "Who's there?"

"Open this door."

"Sir! I demand you leave this instant!"

"Open the door. Police!"

The manager said, "Madame, may I strongly suggest that you not comply with this demand."

A baby started crying in the apartment.

Kamp said, "Please, ma'am, open the door. I just need to look around."

"Madame, under no circumstances should you–"

The door cracked open, and from behind the door, he saw a woman with long, curly red hair and a pink dress. The manager inserted himself between Kamp and the door.

"I'm terribly sorry, madame. Please know that this type of disturbance is completely out of the ordinary at the Monocacy." The wailing of the baby grew louder.

The woman said, "Excuse me," and she walked back into the apartment. She called over her shoulder, "Please come in. Make yourself comfortable."

The manager stared at him and then stepped aside. Kamp set down the ax outside the door and walked into the apartment, which was no longer empty. It was filled with finely crafted furniture, a dining room table and chairs, and an immense Highboy. On the floor was a luxurious Persian rug and on the windows what appeared to be velvet curtains. The woman walked back into the room with a baby in each arm, each of whom was wrapped in a pink blanket, neither of whom was now crying.

She said, "Please excuse the commotion" and gestured sweetly to the infants. "Twins."

The manager piped up, "Madame, I'm so terribly sorry this is happening."

"It's all right. This man must have an important reason for being here. Otherwise, he wouldn't have gone to the trouble. Isn't that right, mister—"

"Kamp."

The manager said, "Yes, well, I trust now that he's seen what he needed to see, he'll be leaving.

He looked at the woman. "What's your name?"

"I'm El–"

The manager erupted, "Sir, you've caused quite enough trouble today. Leave this woman alone!"

The woman said, "My name is Elise."

"Pleased to meet you. I apologize for being rude. You have a lovely home."

She laughed and said, "Why, thank you. It's only temporary. And as for being rude, I'm sure it was a misunderstanding." The tone of her voice, the way her hair spilled down over her shoulders, the scent of her perfume perhaps, some part of the woman, or perhaps the totality of her, struck a deep well in him.

He said, "It wasn't my fault."

She raised one eyebrow. "These things happen. Now if you'll excuse me, I must tend these beautiful children."

As she said it, he caught a flash of gold at her neck, a pendant. Engraved on the pendant was a smiling face that appeared to be wearing a cap in the Phrygian style.

He pointed to it and said, "Where did you get that?"

"Why, it was a gift from—"

The manager jammed himself between Kamp and the woman and said, "That's quite enough! Here at the Monocacy, we value the comfort, not to mention the security, of all our residents. Madame, I'm terribly sorry for this most unwanted intrusion." As he spoke, he guided Kamp toward the door.

The woman laughed. "Oh, it's all right." She turned and walked toward the back room of the apartment.

As the manager shoved him out into the hallway, Kamp got a good look at the doorjamb and noticed a few pellets of lead shot still embedded there. The manager made a point of shutting the door firmly and making sure it was locked. By the time he turned around, Kamp was gone.

He hustled back down the crowded streets of Bethlehem, picking his way among the pedestrians and pushcarts and back to the police station. Time to talk to Druckenmiller. Kamp went there with the intention of wringing the truth out of his old friend, but when he burst through the door, he didn't see the disheveled and decidedly lowbrow High Constable in his typical seat with his feet upon the desk. In Druckenmiller's place was a different fellow, a man sitting upright, writing notes with a pencil that had a very sharp point. When he saw Kamp coming, the man stood up, chest out, shoulders back.

He said, "Detective." The man stood several inches taller than Kamp. He had a long, straight nose and under it a thick, broad mustache, trimmed with precision.

"Where's Sam?"

Without emotion, the man said, "High Constable Druckenmiller is indisposed, detective."

"Kamp."

"The High Constable is indisposed, detective."

"Fine, but where is he?"

"Indisposed."

"Who are you?" He glanced at Druckenmiller's desk. The messy pile of newspapers and novels was gone, as was the rest of the clutter. There was a neat stack of police reports and a glass of water. "What's your name?"

"I'm Markus Lenz, acting High Constable." He extended his hand, and Kamp shook it.

"Lenz?"

"Right."

"Acting High Constable?"

Lenz nodded.

"And you're not going to tell me where Druckenmiller is." Lenz shook his head slowly. "Except to say that he's—"

"Indisposed." The two men said it in unison.

Kamp said, "May I have the key to the cabinet?"

"I'm sorry, the what?"

"The cabinet. The gun cabinet." He saw Lenz's body stiffen.

"No, you may not."

It occurred to Kamp to ask all the people he spoke to that day in Bethlehem whether they knew the whereabouts of his wife and daughter. He wanted to ask each person, because he felt certain that all of them, directly or more likely indirectly, had a hand in the series of events that led to their disappearance. He knew that the Judge, the manager of the Monocacy, Elise, and the Acting High Constable Lenz had information he needed. But Kamp also knew that none had sufficient reason to tell him, and perhaps more importantly, the crucial details had been withheld from them. Except the Judge. It seemed plausible that the Judge himself was orchestrating the entire production, but he couldn't conceive how or why he might.

On his way back to Jonas Bauer's house, Kamp visited Druckenmiller's farm and found, as he'd expected, that Druckenmiller wasn't there. He asked the few neighbors he saw whether they'd seen the man for the past two days, and all said they hadn't. Kamp also stopped at the site of the house where he'd lived. Snow had begun falling, and the fire was dead out now. He walked in the remains and saw shards of their former lives, all ruined, but he did not find skeletons. He even climbed down into the cellar to see if perhaps his wife and daughter had perished there. When he was satisfied that they hadn't, he climbed back out. The fire had melted all the snow within a hundred feet or so of the house. He walked to where the snow began again so that he could wash his hands in it. When he bent down to scoop up the snow, he noticed footprints heading into the woods.

He realized that Shaw and E. Wyles had escaped this way, and he felt a jolt of anger for not having checked before. He hurried into the woods as far as he could follow the tracks. The trail led him a mile to the creek. But from there, he couldn't pick up the tracks again, and now it was snowing harder. He scrambled up and down the creek bed, searching for footprints and finding nothing. The afternoon light began to fail, and snow soon hid the answer to his most important question. When he realized that his feet had begun to freeze, he felt a stab of anguish, knowing that Shaw and his daughter must have suffered when they fled the fire. As darkness fell, he could do nothing but retreat to the former home of Jonas and Rachel Bauer.

The fire burned in the fireplace when he came through the door, and Nyx was sitting on the floor in front of it, holding his Sharps rifle in her lap. He sat down next to her, unlaced his boots, peeled off his wool socks and inspected his toes, which had turned blue. He massaged one foot, then the other. He leaned back on his elbows and wiggled his toes in front of the flames.

He motioned to the rifle and said, "It's not loaded, is it?"

"How would I know?"

Kamp sat up and held out his hands, and Nyx handed him the Sharps. He checked the breech and handed it back to her. "Did you get any food?"

"Plenty. Aren't you wondering how I got it?"

"The food?"

"The gun. Aren't you wondering where it came from?"

"I'm taking a break from wondering about anything."

"Well, I want you to teach me how to shoot it. And just so you know, I was walking around in the woods when I found it. I also found this." Nyx held up a lace handkerchief that he recognized as Shaw's. Kamp gestured for her to give it to him, and when she did, he held it to his nose and mouth and took a deep breath.

Nyx said, "Still don't know where they are, huh?" He stared at the handkerchief. "Can I talk to you about what I wanted to talk to you about?"

Kamp said, "Can I eat something first?"

Nyx handed him a satchel that contained a length of ring bologna, a wedge of cheese and a slice of shoo-fly pie. He devoured the food. In between bites he said, "Where'd you get this stuff?"

Nyx leaned forward toward Kamp. "All right, here's what I wanted to talk to you about."

"Do the Fogels know you're here?"

"Listen."

"You need to tell them. Tell Charlotte Fogel you're here."

"Kamp, listen! The other day I was thinking about everything that happened with my parents and Danny Knecht. And I just couldn't figure out how he could've done that. I mean I knew him. I know the way he was with our family. He just would never have done such a terrible thing."

"What's your point?"

"My point is that, well, I guess I don't think he killed them, and I want to hear what you think."

"Did you see him do it?"

"No. All I saw was him burning clothes."

"What clothes was he wearing when you saw that?"

"I don't remember."

"Think."

Nyx closed her eyes and took a few breaths. "He was wearing the same clothes I saw him wearing earlier in the day."

"Seems unlikely that he would have changed clothes, carried out the killings, then changed again, especially if he was enraged. Possible, but unlikely. Did you hear anyone else in the house? Any other voices?"

"No."

"If Danny Knecht didn't kill them, he had to have been working somehow with the person who did. That means that someone else wanted to hurt your parents, and they needed Danny's help for some reason."

"I understand."

"Do you know of anyone who was angry at your parents? Your father?"

"No one. They didn't have quarrels with anyone. I mean no one."

Kamp said, "Do you remember your father acting strangely in the days or weeks before the murders? Anything different about him?"

"Just that he was angry at Danny."

"For what?"

"Oh, just the way he was around me. And, no, Danny never did, we never—if that's what you're going to ask next."

"Can you think of any person who came to your house, someone you didn't recognize, who may have talked to your father or to Danny?"

Nyx bit her lip and looked up at the ceiling. "Nope."

"Go back to last summer. Around the time he moved in, or just before. Can you remember anyone coming to your house?"

Nyx's eyebrows popped up. "Yes, I remember, there was a man. A fine carriage pulled up in front of the house. My sisters and I were at the creek. We saw him get out and talk to my father at the front door. Probably a few minutes. Then he left."

"Was it an argument? Could you tell?"

"It didn't look like an argument. He shook my father's hand right before he left."

"Did you ever see the man again?"

"Yes. He was that man at the funeral." Nyx stared into the fire.

"The one who spoke to you at the funeral? Silas Ownby. The owner of the coal mine?"

"Uh-huh. The man who came up and talked to me after I throttled the reverend."

"What did he say to you at the funeral?"

She turned to face Kamp. "He said, here's exactly what he said...he said, 'My child, it wasn't your fault.'"

"What did you say to him?"

"I said, 'Of course it wasn't my fucking fault.' But I said it in a nice way."

"What do you think he meant?"

"He probably meant that he knows that the reverend is a pervert."

"A what?"

"A pervert. A *dreckich wutz*. He touches children, when they're alone. Lots of people know. It's not exactly a secret. But no one does anything about it."

"Did your parents know?"

Nyx looked out the window. "I don't know whether they did or not. I think they had to have known something. But I'm sure they didn't want to believe it. They would have tried to protect us. I don't know."

"Did the reverend ever do anything to you?"

"He'll get his."

Kamp said, "What did he do?"

"I should've thrown him down in that hole."

"Did he ever do anything to your sisters?"

She leveled her gaze. "No."

"How do you know?"

"He never had the chance. I made certain he was never alone with them."

"So, that's why you went after him at the funeral, because of what he did to you."

Nyx's lips curled in disgust. "No, that's not *why*."

"Then why?"

Nyx erupted. "All that garbage about how Danny is burning in hell, how he deserves to burn in hell. And how my parents are just floating up there in heaven and how pleased god must be with them and how if you think about it, they're lucky they got hacked to pieces because now they get to be with god forever and ever. And how they all got what they deserved. Which means I guess my sisters got what they deserved. I guess I got what I deserved."

Nyx's eyes brimmed with tears as she focused on him and said, "Danny is dead. My parents are dead. No one got what they *deserved*. I couldn't listen to one more word from the mouth of that filthy liar. That's why I choked him."

She dissolved into tears. Between the sobs she said, "I don't want to cry about it." And then she began crying even harder. He felt the sadness welling in himself, and he let himself feel it for a moment.

When her tears subsided, she said, "My father didn't like guns. He hated fighting. He just wanted to take care of us."

"He was a good man."

Nyx wiped the tears from her cheeks with the back of her hand and said, "Is your father alive?"

"No."

"What was he like?"

Kamp stood up and shook the stiffness out of his legs. He said, "I'm going to get more firewood. Tomorrow, you need to go back to the Fogels. You have to tell them you're staying here. If they strongly disapprove, you have to go back with them. Promise me you'll do that."

Nyx said, "On one condition. You teach me how to shoot this gun."

"Deal."

Long after Nyx had gone upstairs, Kamp lit a lantern and went down to the cellar. He found what he was looking for, a large metal bathtub. He hauled it back up the stairs and set it next to the fireplace. He retrieved a pail from the kitchen and filled it with water from the well in the backyard. He poured the water into the tub and repeated the process until the bathtub was nearly full. The fire heated the water until it steamed, and then he peeled off his clothing. His pants were shredded and muddy, as was his jacket. Even his shirt was tattered at the collar and had holes in the elbows. He rolled his clothes in a ball and threw them in the corner.

Kamp put one foot and then the other into the bath. He held the sides of the tub and lowered his body in. He tilted his head back and let his face submerge. He lifted his head from the water and leaned it against the back of the tub. Kamp felt the living hum come back into his bones, and he listened for all the voices in the house, the ghosts who lived there. He heard Jonas and Rachel, all the things they talked about, what they wanted for their girls. He heard Danny Knecht, his dark confusion and his desperate hope for a future. He heard the voices of ghosts from farther back, before the house was built, voices of original people, Lenape driven from the longhouse that had stood on the same site. He could hear their songs and their trailing cries.

Kamp lay in the tub long enough so that the sweat began pouring from him and mingling with the well water in the tub. He waited until the heat nearly overtook him and then he went out the back door with the pail. He drew one more bucket of water and poured it over his head. A great cloud of steam rose from his body, and he felt clean. He let his body dry by the fire, and then Kamp went back into the cellar and found a wooden chest, secured with a padlock. By the light of the lantern, he picked up a sledgehammer and removed the lock. He opened the lid and found the personal effects of Jonas and Rachel Bauer, a Meerschaum pipe, a worn Bible, and a silver locket. Beneath the items were their clothes, neatly folded. He removed a pair of Jonas Bauer's pants, a cotton shirt, wool socks and a coat. He tried on the clothes, and they all fit. He folded Shaw's handkerchief and put it in his pocket.

21

At first light he went to the clearing in the woods where Nyx said she'd found the gun and the handkerchief. Rain had washed away all but the last bits of snow. He could see that there had been footprints, but he couldn't discern which way they pointed. From there, he walked the railroad tracks to Bethlehem, instead of the road. He wanted the solitude, and in light of the circumstances, he thought it best to stay as far out of the public eye as possible. He knew that he was still functioning officially in the role of detective, but given what appeared to be a significant rupture in the town's criminal justice system, Kamp wasn't sure what it meant to be a part of it. Still, Kamp felt compelled to mine for the truth in the hope that it would lead him to his family.

When he reached the outskirts of Bethlehem, Kamp pulled the brim of his hat low and headed for the morgue. Once inside the main doors of the building, he walked to a row of tall windows and at the far left, the door to the morgue itself. He didn't knock but simply turned the knob and walked in. The coroner A.J. Oehler stood hunched over a cadaver, scribbling notes in a book. He didn't look up when Kamp entered the room.

Oehler said, "Unless you're dead, you shouldn't be here, whoever you are."

"It's Kamp."

Oehler stood up to his full height, adjusted his glasses and looked at him. "You *really* shouldn't be here."

"Tell me about what happened with Crow."

The coroner turned back to focus on the cadaver. "Someone's always shuffling off the mortal coil. I'm especially aware of that on a day such as today." Oehler gestured dismissively to the eight tables in the room, each of which had a corpse on it, covered with a sheet. "Accidents, disease, trauma. I have work to do, and no time to talk."

"The Judge told me you said it was a suicide."

"*Ach*, please leave." Oehler continued inspecting the cadaver and taking notes.

"A suicide? Christ, Abner, you think Crow would've done that? You knew the man."

Oehler stood up straight again. "I don't concern myself with what might have led anyone to do anything. I focus on what actually happened, the facts."

"The facts? You mean your investigation led you to believe that Philander Crow murdered a prostitute and then made his quietus with a shotgun to his own chest?"

"You do your work, and I'll do mine."

Kamp said, "You noticed he was shot more than once. Tell me how he managed that. And where's she?" Kamp scanned the rows of corpses.

"Who?"

"The prostitute. Where's the body?"

"*Fergonga.*"

One by one, Kamp pulled the sheets off the corpses.

The coroner said, "Have some respect!"

"Just tell me one thing. Did you see this for yourself, the room, the bed where it happened? Did you actually see for yourself where all of this was supposed to have taken place? Did you see any of it?"

"I saw the bodies, yes. I saw them both. I conducted both autopsies."

"But were you *there*?"

Oehler said, "The bodies were brought here."

"Brought here."

"Yes, they were left outside on the front steps. I don't know by whom."

"You don't know how they got here?"

"You're the goddamned detective. Aren't you supposed to be figuring all this out?"

Kamp said, "I *was* there. I saw Crow, and I saw everything that happened. Whatever you wrote was a lie."

"What I wrote was consistent with the outcome of my investigation. It's tragic, and it's over."

"Where's Crow's body now?"

"Gone to the undiscovered country." Oehler began putting the sheets back over the bodies.

"Tell me."

Oehler said, "It's not here."

"Who took it?"

"It was retrieved and buried. By his family. It's gone. There's nothing more to say. For the sake of Christ, leave."

"Does Druckenmiller know what you said? Did he see your report?"

"Druckenmiller can't see anything at the moment."

"Where is he?"

"Hospital."

Like most people, Kamp avoided hospitals. As he walked the miles to the new hospital in Bethlehem, fragments of memories of the months he passed in army hospitals began trickling through his mind, the doctors' low murmurs, the shrieking of the man at the end of the ward, the endless procession of the dying, the darkness, the smell. By the time he reached the front lawn of the hospital, he found he had to force himself to enter the building. The trickle of his memories had become a torrent of loud voices and bodily sensations. In an instant Kamp felt as if he were the patient again, as if the years between his time in the hospital and now had evaporated. But having begun the process of discerning the truth, he continued on through the doors of the hospital, not so much dispelling his demons as ignoring them.

Kamp disregarded the people working in the hospital, even those who inquired regarding the purpose of his visit. He quickly established that the hospital was divided into two main wards, one for women and one for men. He glanced into the women's ward and saw that most of the beds were empty, while the men's ward was overfilled. He scanned the large room and saw that the beds were laid out neatly, if somewhat close together, and in each bed was a man or in a few cases, a boy. Kamp didn't see Druckenmiller and nearly turned to leave. But he noticed that the back corner of the room had been cordoned off with a curtain.

He pulled back the curtain to find Druckenmiller in a bed with heavy bandages wrapped around his eyes. He wasn't moving.

"Sam? Sam?"

"Kamp?"

"Yah, it's me."

Druckenmiller said, "There's something I need you to get. It's in the pocket of my coat. It's important. Do you see my coat?"

"I see it." He grabbed the coat which had been slung over a chair. He reached into the vest pocket and felt a metal object. "The flask?"

He whispered, "Oh, Jesus, yes. Goddamned nurses won't give me a drop." Kamp handed him the flask, and Druckenmiller carefully unscrewed the cap and took a long pull. "Thank you, thank you." He took another sip, screwed the cap on and handed the flask back to Kamp. "You gotta leave. You gotta get outta here now. As soon as they hear you're here, they'll come for you."

"Who?"

"Same guys that got us at that cathouse."

"Sam, what happened to you that night?" He sat down in the chair next to the bed. He noticed Druckenmiller was still wearing the necklace with the brass key on it.

Druckenmiller said, "I went in the window after you. I saw you get bopped on the head by a different guy."

You saw him?"

"Yah, well, no, he come in right after you pulled the trigger."

"What did you do?"

"What did *I* do?" Druckenmiller shifted his weight in the bed.

"You were on the fire escape, at the window, right?"

"That's right."

He leaned closer to Druckemiller. "Sam, what did you do then?"

"Well, I jumped in the window. There were people running, you know. Mayhem. Titties everywhere. And I raised my pistol to shoot the guy coming after you. And that's all I remember."

"That's it, huh?"

"Yah, musta been the guy that come up the fire escape after us."

Kamp said, "The guy you handcuffed to the building? That guy?"

Druckenmiller became still in the bed and said flatly, "Yah, that guy."

"Maybe you didn't cuff him at all. Or maybe you cuffed him and gave him the key."

"Here we go again. You think I was helping them? Do you know what they did to me? Do you want to know? When they were done with me, they left me out on the street in front of the morgue alongside Crow. You want to see what they did? You don't trust me. See for yourself. Here!"

Druckenmiller unwrapped the bandages from his face. Both eyes were swollen shut, his eyelids bright purple. "They don't know whether I'll ever be able to see again. Are you happy now?"

Kamp leaned back in his chair. "Why do you suppose they didn't kill you? And why didn't they kill me?"

"All I know is, I'm telling you, they—"

"Who are *they*, Sam? They didn't give you a choice. I know. Tell me who they are."

"It's not that simple."

The curtain jerked back, and a nurse stood glaring at Kamp. She said, "My goodness, this can't be. Sir, you must leave right away. This patient is not to be disturbed under any circumstances."

Kamp said, "I apologize, ma'am. This is official business. Police business." He focused back on Druckenmiller. "Sam, the last thing Crow said to me was, 'Talk to Kunkle.' What does that mean to you? What does Roy Kunkle have to do with this?"

"*Ach*, I don't *know* no Roy Kunkle!"

"Sir! You must stop bothering the patient."

Druckenmiller said, "It's okay, Sue. He really is sorry. You just can't always tell."

The nurse interposed herself between the two men and began removing the bandages. She talked under her breath. "I don't know what in the world makes a person think he can just—"

Kamp said, "Who are they, Sam? What's the Fraternal Order of the Raven?"

The nurse wheeled on him and said, "You will leave *now*, sir!" The commotion drew the attention of other people, and within moments, another nurse and three orderlies appeared.

The other nurse said, "The police have been notified."

Druckenmiller said, "It wasn't about you. None of it."

Kamp leaned over Druckenmiller and removed the necklace with the key on it. "See you when you're back on the job."

The nurse said, "Show this man the exit," and the orderlies began moving him, politely but forcefully, away from the bed and hustling him toward the back door.

One man opened the door, and the other two shoved him out. Kamp scrambled to his feet and ran for the police station, hoping he could get there ahead of the news of his visit to the hospital. As he rounded the last corner and the station came into view, he saw the acting High Constable Markus Lenz burst out the door and climb into a carriage. The carriage driver snapped the reins and the horses started off, heading in his direction. He pulled the brim of his hat low and looked at the ground. When the carriage had passed, he bounded up the front steps and in through the front door. Once inside, he went straight to the gun cabinet and opened it with Druckenmiller's key. He found a canvas bag and filled it with all the boxes of rifle cartridges it could hold. He slung the bag over his back and was out the door before anyone could ask him what he was doing there.

Kamp hoofed it back out of town the way he'd come, via the railroad tracks. The wind had picked up, and he buttoned the top button of Jonas Bauer's coat. He imagined how Bauer must have done this same thing many times, buttoning the coat, tilting into the gales, marching to the coal mine and back again. Soldiering on. Kamp let his mind-wheels start to turn in time with his footsteps on the train tracks. He allowed himself to wonder where his family was. He pictured Shaw and their daughter. He ticked off the places they could be as well as the likelihood they might be in any given place. He even allowed himself to imagine they were dead and gone, their corpses tossed into a creek or buried shallow, like bodies from the war, zigzagged out in ditches, as hopeless and lorn as a trampled down split-rail fence. Unbearable as the image was, he considered the reality unlikely. If they had been killed, he surmised, it would have happened close to where they lived. By this time, someone, a hunter or a hired hand, would have found the bodies and told him.

He also considered that perhaps they'd been kidnapped and that they were being held somewhere. This possibility seemed even less likely, as no demands had been communicated to him. At least not yet. He speculated further that if there had been a kidnapping, it was possible that Shaw, or more likely E. Wyles, would have resisted and in the ensuing struggle, they would've all been killed. This seemed implausible, if for no other reason than that he could not envision E. Wyles losing a fight. It seemed more likely that the three of them were out there, hiding but probably not lost. Kamp had waited this long to see them again. He could wait longer.

He switched tracks in his thinking and tried to discern whether he'd learned anything of value during the day. The fact that the murderers left Crow's corpse outside the door of the morgue meant nothing, perhaps. If they needed to get it out of the Monocacy, and apparently they did, they could have thrown the body anywhere. As for the prostitute, he'd learned nothing. He didn't know her identity, or if she'd even existed. If she had, she'd either been shot mistakenly or murdered. Regardless, her death had been conveniently inserted into the official narrative about Crow's demise. That the killers took the trouble to take them to the morgue was meant to indicate their level of control and the absence of fear. Why they took Druckenmiller there as well, if they did, was yet another mystery. Why not just leave him there at the Monocacy, he wondered. The conversation with Druckenmiller at the hospital yielded no new information, save the confirmation that he was working for the murderers, or was at least complicit in what they were doing. He'd discerned the rough outlines of what they demanded from Druckenmiller as well as what he got in return. The beating he took was likely punishment for him having botched some detail of the plan to kill Philander Crow. Or by going to town on him, they wanted Druckenmiller's story to seem more credible. Maybe both.

Kamp's gut started to growl, and it occurred to him that there might not be any food when he got back. He veered off the tracks and took a trail to Druckenmiller's house. He broke in the back door and headed to the cellar, where he found onions, potatoes, winter squash, a jar of apple butter and a ringwurst. He loaded the food into the canvas bag, closed the door behind him and headed for the trail.

The canvas bag was now nearly full, and the strap cut into his neck. But Kamp kept walking the tracks, stepping from tie to tie and listening for noises in the woods. Far off, he heard the Black Diamond Unlimited. He looked back over his shoulder and saw the engine's headlight sparkling at least a half mile away. He was close to Jonas Bauer's former house, so he had no need to catch out. And even if he'd wanted to, the bullets weighed him down. The train caught up with him just before the bend by the trestle, and he paused while it passed. He waved to the engineer and felt the cold *whoosh* as it went by. He picked his way through brambles and across the ditch to the road. He saw a thin trail of smoke curling up from the chimney, but all the windows in the house were dark.

Kamp went in the back door and listened to the silence in the house. "Hello? Anyone here? *Hello?*"

He heard nothing but the wind whipping the trees. In the fading twilight he saw the Sharps rifle leaned against the doorjamb, where he'd left it. He set down the canvas bag and took out a box of cartridges. He slid one into the Sharps, and tiptoed to the front room. The bathtub had been propped against the wall, but otherwise the room looked the same. He heard a bump on the other side of the house and he raised the rifle to his shoulder and pointed in the direction of the sound. He stepped silently, staring down the barrel of the gun. He saw that the door to the bedroom where Jonas and Rachel had slept was cracked open. He shoved the door open with his foot and entered the room.

Nyx was lying face down on the floor with her arms by her sides. Kamp kept the gun raised. He scanned the room, moving the gun barrel along with his gaze. There was no one else in the room.

"Nyx? Nyx?" The girl didn't move.

He lowered the gun, opened the breech and removed the cartridge. He crouched down and rested his hand on her back. He could feel her inhaling and exhaling.

"Nyx, are you awake?"

"No."

"What's wrong?"

"Ridiculous question." She rolled over and leaned on her elbows. Her hair was matted to her forehead, and her dress was dirty.

"Let's go. I'll make supper."

She sat up and looked at him. "I understood for the first time today. I think I did."

"Understood what?"

"You want to know what I did today?"

"Yes."

"Nothing! I did nothing all day but sit in this room. That's what Nyx means, right? Nothing. I'm nothing."

"Come on, girl. Stand up."

"What about you, Kamp? What did you do today?"

He looked out the window and reflected on the day's events. "Nothing."

Nyx put her hands in her hair and hung her head. "You can't love them so much that they come back. You can't think about them enough for them to be alive."

"No, you can't."

"This is what it feels like from now on."

"No, it isn't."

Nyx craned her neck to look at him. "You opened that chest in the cellar. You're wearing my father's clothing." He nodded. "And everyone else goes on. My parents don't need any of their things anymore, but I still need my parents."

"You're hungry."

He held out his hand to her, and she took it. He helped her to her feet, guided her out of the room and locked the door. He lit a fire in the stove and cooked up the vegetables he nicked from Druckenmiller's in a stew. Kamp and Nyx sat at the kitchen table and the famished pair downed all the food. When her spoon scraped the bottom of the soup bowl, she set it down, raised the bowl to her lips and gulped the rest.

She looked at him and said, "My mother would not have approved."

"Mine either. Not that we gave her a choice."

"Do you have brothers and sisters?"

"I did. Three brothers."

"Where are they now?"

"Gone. War."

Nyx studied him. "You were in the war, too, right? What did you do?"

He stared down at his food. "Marched around. Slept in the dirt. Same as everyone else."

"You know what I mean. What did you do? Didn't they give you a little job?"

"*Heckenschütze.*"

"What?"

"I was a sniper. Your father didn't like guns. My father loved them. I don't even remember how old I was when he taught me to shoot. I just remember always knowing how to do it."

"Like walking."

"Yah, like that. So, when they tested us in the army, I was the best at it."

"It's good you'll be teaching me, though."

"I'm probably not as good at it now as I used to be."

"How come?"

"Well, for one thing, I got shot in the head myself."

"Ouch."

"And my balance isn't as good as it was. That's why I have trouble riding in wagons. I get dizzy. And besides that, I hardly ever shoot anymore."

"So, you got shot in the head, and then you couldn't fight?"

"I thought *I* asked a lot of questions."

"That's how it was, though, right?"

"Not exactly. After I got hurt, I was in the hospital for a long time, and by the time I got better, they were running low on guys, especially good shots. So they sent me back. But then I got in trouble, so they put me back in the hospital again." He sliced a length off the ringwurst, slathered apple butter on it and popped it in his mouth.

"Put you in the hospital for getting in trouble?"

Between bites, he said, "Yah. There wasn't anything wrong with me, though."

"What did they say was wrong with you?"

He finished chewing the ringwurst and swallowed. "Madness."

Nyx paused and then said, "Oh, well, as long as you can teach me, I don't really care if you're the best at it. Or if you're mad."

"Thank you for your candor."

She got up from her chair. "All right, show me now." She picked up the Sharps and set it on the table. Kamp turned up the flame on the lantern and pulled a box of cartridges from the canvas bag. She looked inside the bag and saw how many boxes there were.

She said, "*Pshoo*, looks like you're going to war again."

"You have to shoot a lot to get good at it. These are for you. For learning. And one more condition, Nyx." He leveled his gaze at her, and she met it. "No revenge. I'm not teaching you so that you can go kill Eberstark or get revenge on whoever killed your parents, if we ever figure out who it was."

"Why take the fun out of it?"

"That's the deal."

Nyx took a few breaths and didn't speak. She drummed her fingertips on the table and then said, "Fine. I promise, no revenge. Now, how do you load this goddamned thing?"

22

Kamp tried not to think about his brothers. They only came back to him in fragments of memory sparked by a sensory impression. The scent of a pine bough might trigger an image of his oldest brother at the very top of the tree, laughing at Kamp's fear that he'd fall. Or the sight of wet autumn leaves brought to mind all four brothers sleeping out on the top of the mountain, before it got too cold. He let these memories pass through him, trying not to hold on to them. But that night, after having mentioned them to Nyx, he dreamt of his brothers, dreamt of them all as boys, but without the overhang of sorrow. In the dream it was spring. The daffodils were blooming along with the lilacs, and the grass in the meadow was still green. They

314 | KURT B. DOWDLE

were heading off together somewhere. He woke from the dream to a new moon, pitch dark. No sound, save for the rustling of night creatures. It occurred to Kamp in that waking instant that Roy Kunkle might have had a brother and if Kunkle's brother were living, he should find him and talk to him.

The next morning just after sun up, Kamp went to Nyx's room and said, "Let's go."

She was slow to rouse, and when she did, she said, "Where?"

"Target practice. Hurry up."

When she found Kamp in the backyard, he was setting up old bottles at a distance of fifty feet or so from the house.

She said, "Doesn't that seem a little too close?"

He set up the last bottle and walked back to her. He picked up the Sharps, which was leaning against the side of the house.

"First thing," he said. "Listen carefully. Make sure the gun is unloaded, and never point it at anyone."

"Got it."

He held up the rifle and said, "Put it in half *gacock*, like this. Then, open the breech using the lever. Watch." He went through each step slowly.

"I see."

He held up a cartridge and slid it into the chamber. "Make sure the end with the bullet is pointed down the barrel."

"Ha ha."

"Then you just close the breech, and it's ready." Kamp raised the rifle, aimed at one of the plates and fired. The shot hit the plate dead center, shattering it. He opened the breech and removed the spent cartridge. "Here, you try." He handed the rifle to her.

He said, "Remember, hold it steady. And squeeze the trigger. Don't yank it."

"I got it, I got it." She raised the rifle to her shoulder and looked down the barrel. She jerked the trigger back, and the gun went off. The butt of the rifle slammed back into her shoulder, and the shot sailed into the trees. She lowered the gun, dazed. "Ow." Nyx held the rifle in her right hand and soothed her bruised shoulder with her left.

Kamp said, "Okay, we'll do it the right way now."

He reloaded the Sharps and adjusted Nyx's stance. "Lift the rifle, and make sure it's firm against your shoulder. And press the stock to your cheek. Hold it there, firm." She followed the instructions. "Now, focus on your breathing. Notice how when you breathe in, the barrel moves up a little, and when you breathe out, it goes back down."

"So?"

"So, everything you do or don't do affects where the bullet goes. Be very calm, stay still, keep breathing. See the target. Fire."

Nyx pulled the trigger, and the shot kicked up dirt next to one of the plates.

He said, "This time you do it all."

Nyx removed the spent cartridge and loaded another one. She calmly raised the rifle again and fired. One of the plates shattered. Nyx lowered the rifle and blew away the smoke curling out of the barrel.

Kamp said, "End of the lesson."

"That's *it?*"

"I have to go. Besides, I'm sure we woke up all the *nuchbars.* They're going to wonder about the commotion. We can shoot more when I get back. No shooting until then, okay? None."

The whistle of the Black Diamond Unlimited shrieked through the forest. Kamp put on his coat, picked up the canvas bag, went running across the road and down to the tracks. The Unlimited was headed back from Easton to Bethlehem, and it would get him there before most of the town was awake and before the courthouse started work. He jogged alongside the train, waiting to see the open boxcar door that was the signal to make his run and leap. Locked car after locked car passed him until it was only empty coal cars. He preferred not to ride suicide, but he had to make time. He zoomed up alongside one of the coal buckets and made his jump, catching the rail and landing his right foot in the iron stirrup. He swung gracefully onto the small platform at the back of the car. There was just enough room to stand on both feet.

The side-to-side swaying of the train and the rhythmic click-clack of the wheels made Kamp drowsy right away. But falling asleep here would spell death as he'd tumble straight under the wheels. He wound the shoulder strap of the canvas bag around his wrist and then lashed it to a rung of the iron ladder that went up the side of the car, a trick that had saved him in the past. He calculated that he'd be at the Third Street Station in half an hour, and he figured he could fight sleep that long. His eyelids soon grew so heavy, however, that his chin dropped to his chest, and he began dreaming. He dreamt of a day in the war when he was set up on a ridge, sighting grey uniforms one by one, awaiting the order to start shooting. Just before he nodded off completely, a bullet whanged off the rung of the ladder just above his head and splintered the wooden side of the coal hopper on the ricochet. He snapped awake and saw a wagon drawn by two horses on the road that ran parallel to the train. The wagon kept pace with the train, and both the driver and the shooter were wearing burlap sacks on their heads. As the shooter reloaded, Kamp scrambled to untie the strap from his wrist. When he got free, he reached for the handle on the far side of the car with his right hand. He felt the bullet in his left arm an instant before he heard the shot. He managed to swing himself around the corner so that the shooter could no longer see him.

He held fast to the side of the hopper until he was certain that the tracks had veered from the road. Kamp moved back to his original position and inspected the wound. The bullet had passed through the flesh of his upper arm, but other than the pain, he felt all right. He knew the wagon couldn't travel fast enough to meet him at the train yard, and even if it could, the men wouldn't be brazen enough to come after him there. Once the train came to a halt, he climbed down and hustled across the yard, picking his way across the tracks, out of the yard and onto the street. In the condition he was in, he knew he'd attract attention, and at this point, he couldn't even guess how many people might be looking for him. He cut down the alley behind the building that housed E. Wyles' drugstore. He found the back door to the shop and broke in.

Once inside, Kamp took off his coat and shirt. He felt dizzy from losing blood and from the pain, which appeared first as a dull thud and now throbbed. He washed the wound in E. Wyles' sink and dried it with clean towels. Kamp remembered that Wyles had a carbolic acid spray device. He'd once seen such a machine in the war, and he knew it might be the difference in whether or not he kept his arm. He found the device and set it up. He lit the fire which produced the steam that delivered carbolic acid. He held his arm in front of the spray and tried not to breathe any of it, lest he vomit. Kamp put out the fire and wrapped his arm in sterile bandages. He searched the drugstore until he found a jar of willow bark extract, two vials of morphine and a syringe. By now, the pain was clouding his thinking, and he thought it best to take some of the morphine. He tied off his left arm and injected the needle. He depressed the plunger half-way, knowing that if he took the full dose, he wouldn't care to carry out his work and would probably just pass out on the floor.

Kamp felt warmth spreading through his body, beginning at the base of his skull and then moving outward. The sensation easily overtook the pain in his arm and transported him back before the battlefield, before any realization. He sat down and allowed himself to rest in it for a minute and then willed himself back to his feet, fighting the languor. Kamp gathered up the medical supplies, including additional bandages and dressings, and he left the way he came. He didn't bother pulling the brim of his hat low on his face, because the morning sun felt good and because he felt like enjoying it. He told himself he should worry whether he was discovered, especially so close to the courthouse, but found himself incapable of taking care. The town was waking up, and it felt glorious to let it do whatever it wanted. And yet, he continued on his mission. He broke a window in the side door of the courthouse, opened the lock and proceeded straight to the records section. The clerk had not yet materialized, and until he did, Kamp had free rein. The records room was stacked high and full with shelves, boxes and slots that held all the official information amassed on paper since the founding of the county.

Normally, he would have conducted a careful and precise search with the aid of the clerk. He would have assiduously written down the relevant information, leaving the records complete and intact. Now, he rummaged for all of the records that might have had any value. Loose sheets of paper, entire books of county information, anything that might be useful he dumped into the canvas bag. He pilfered as many records as the bag could hold, and then he picked up a couple more books and carried them under his good arm. He headed out of the records room just as the clerk appeared.

The clerk said, "What in god's name?"

Kamp said, "I'll be right back," knowing he'd probably never return.

He left the building via the side door and hustled into the street, mixing with the morning mass of souls. He made a beeline for the train yard. It had already been more than an hour since the shot of morphine, and he wanted to be certain that he'd be in a safe place when the agony returned. He lugged himself and his canvas bag across the train yard once again to the Unlimited, which was being prepared for its return trip to Easton. As such, it was unladen. Kamp situated himself inside an open boxcar, as far inside as he could get. It occurred to him that the man who shot him might be waiting for him again, though it seemed unlikely. He reasoned that they knew he was on the morning train, because they'd watched him leave the house. They would not, however, have known when he'd return, or how. He also reflected on the likelihood that the men had gone after Nyx. He wanted to think they hadn't, though he knew he had no basis for the assumption.

The train lurched forward and started to roll. Kamp's thoughts shifted to how he'd get off once he reached his destination. The injury to his arm made the thought of hurling himself out of the car unpleasant. Then again, he still felt no pain and figured it wouldn't matter one way or the other. The creek had frozen over in places, particularly around the waterhole he typically aimed for, so that wasn't an option. There was deep snow, however, even under most of the trees. If he cleared the rocks beside the tracks, depending on what was under the snow, there was a chance for a soft landing. As the train rounded the last curve before Jonas Bauer's former house, he tied the canvas bag closed and flung it into a patch of brambles. He moved to the opposite side of the boxcar and readied himself for the leap. Kamp saw what looked like a snowdrift a few feet from the tracks. He ran across the floor of the boxcar and jumped, sailing over the rocks and hitting the spot exactly. But what he thought was the top of the snowdrift turned out to be a discarded railroad tie sticking out of the ground and buried under a few inches of snow. He took most of the impact with his right hip and then came down hard on his elbow.

He tumbled into a deadfall and came to rest upside down with a mouthful of ice and leaves. He waited for a surge of pain that didn't come. He breathed a few times, trying to tell if he had any broken ribs. He wiggled his fingers and toes. Slowly, he got right side up and extracted himself from the deadfall. The Unlimited's caboose rolled out of sight, and the only sound he heard was a mockingbird. Kamp stood up and inspected his body. A ragged hole had been ripped in his pants where he made contact with the tie. Other than that, no visible problems. Since he'd landed on his right side, he knew he hadn't injured his left arm further. He felt a renewed urgency to get to a safe place. He couldn't know the full extent of the injuries until the morphine wore off, but when it did, the pain would be unbearable. And if he'd broken bones, he might soon be incapacitated.

Kamp staggered through the snow and the underbrush and found the canvas bag which had burst open on impact. He retrieved the files and stuffed them back in the bag. He picked up the trail back to the road, passing the tree from which Daniel Knecht had swung and the open grave that briefly held his corpse. Kamp shuffled through the snowy underbrush until he reached the road in front of the house. He paused to listen and observe for a moment. There was no light in any windows, no smoke from the chimney. He saw that a sheet of paper had been affixed to one of the planks covering the doorway, at eye level. Kamp scanned the landscape for movement and saw none. He walked as quickly as he could across the road, though he noticed a hitch in his gait, meaning that his hip had begun to swell.

He made his way to the front door and read the notice: "By order of the Honorable Tate Cain, this house is CONDEMNED. Under penalty of law, KEEP OUT." He went to the bulkhead doors. A heavy chain had been looped under the door handles and secured with a large iron padlock. The back door had been sealed shut as well. He could think of a number of reasons why the Judge would want to keep people out. The house did, after all, belong to the Judge, and so perhaps he was protecting his investment from squatters and vagrants, categories into which Kamp himself had begun to fit. At some point the Judge would want to rent out the house again, or sell it. He might have thought it too soon to do either. Most likely, though, he reasoned, the Judge caught wind that he and Nyx were there, and he wanted them out. And whether that was for his own good was the question.

He considered breaking back into the house, because there remained the possibility that the Judge wanted to keep him from finding something that, as yet, no one had been able to locate. More important, Kamp needed a roof over his head. Snow, then sleet and now a cold rain had begun to fall. He tested one of the planks on the back door by pulling on it with his right hand. He felt a twinge of pain in his elbow. He tried it with his left hand and felt an even stronger jolt in his arm. Kamp went to the tool shed, looking for an implement to pry off the boards, but the shed had been picked clean. He checked all the windows on the ground floor, searching for a loose board, a way in. But whoever had hammered the planks had been thorough, and the house was bound up tight. His thoughts turned to Nyx's whereabouts. He walked to the spot where he'd given her the shooting lesson. The ground was covered with cartridge boxes, now disintegrating in the rain. She'd predictably ignored his instruction not to fire the gun in his absence. Kamp counted the boxes on the ground. There were nine. He knew that he'd taken ten boxes from the police station and that he'd left all of them with Nyx. Either she'd been interrupted before she finished shooting, or she'd saved one box. Either way, he didn't know where she was. She may have been taken into custody by the police, in which case they'd have the Sharps. Or she may have gone back to the Fogels. A fear skittered through his mind. She might have been left in the house. Apart from seeing her himself or getting the definitive word, for now, Nyx was missing.

The rain came harder. Kamp took off his coat and wrapped it around the canvas bag. He walked out of the yard and onto the road, head down. No one else was out and so he took no care. The idea of bedding down at a neighbor's house would have been appealing but for the fact that he didn't trust any of them. Not that they weren't good people, as far as that went. But they were the same people who, when given with the opportunity to execute Daniel Knecht, didn't hesitate. And considering the attempts on his life as well as the general hostility of the populace toward him, Kamp thought it wise to keep to himself. He trudged up the path to where his house had stood. Water ran down through icy ruts. He stifled the memories of the many times he'd walked this path before, happy and relieved to see the lantern in the window and smell wood smoke on the breeze. He didn't even glance at the scorched foundation. Instead, he went for the slaughterhouse. The wide front door was singed but intact, as was the rest of the stone building. Someone had removed all the tools, and so it was empty except for the large table he used for butchering. A few sizable leaks in the roof let in enough water to soak most of the floor.

Kamp found a dry place next to the door, sat down and opened the canvas bag. Some of the records had gotten wet and were now unreadable, but most had stayed dry. He stacked the books and papers next to him. Underneath the records, he found the medical supplies from E. Wyles' office. They too were nearly dry. He took the gauze off his left arm and surveyed the damage, an all-around ugly, red and purple mess. He splashed ethyl alcohol on his wounds. The pain, which had been gathering force like a far-off storm, now thundered in. Kamp pressed a large dressing against his arm and wrapped it as tightly as he could with gauze. The pain in his left arm now came in sturdy waves. His right hip and elbow, the parts of his body that took the brunt of the fall from the train, also began to throb. For a moment, he thought he might lose consciousness.

At the very bottom of the bag, he found the vials of morphine and the syringe. Both vials were broken, their contents drained. The bottle containing the tincture of willow extract was unbroken, and he drank the bitter liquid. He knew it couldn't erase the pain, as the morphine had, but it would help. He tried lying down and found it impossible to get into a position that didn't cause extreme discomfort. He sat back up, leaning his back against the door with his legs stretched out in front of him. In similar situations in the past, Kamp had learned to focus on pain in one part of his body, as opposed to letting it all pour over him or trying to escape it. He pictured the place on his hip that had struck the railroad tie. He narrowed his attention to the smallest point imaginable and observed every sensation, until only the pain existed. Within minutes, he slipped deep within himself, and moments after that, he lost consciousness, head slumped forward.

What followed was a series of nightmares, each more ferocious than the last, as the retreat of the morphine gave way to the full effect of the trauma. He awoke in total darkness. The rain had stopped, and he heard nothing but howling wind. He discovered that he couldn't raise his left arm or bend his right elbow, which he assumed was broken. And though his left leg moved easily, the pain radiating from his right hip made moving his right leg impossible. Kamp tilted his head back against the door and listened to the wind. He brought Shaw's face to mind. He pictured the few strands of straight black hair falling across her forehead, the three freckles across the bridge of her nose, the crescent scar above her eye. He imagined himself cradling his daughter in his arms and rocking back and forth. He held these images in his mind until he saw the grey morning light through the cracks in the slaughterhouse roof. He'd grown so cold that his body shook uncontrollably. And even though he didn't have an appetite, Kamp knew he needed to eat in order to survive. He wanted to stand up to try to shake off the cold and scrounge for food but found his injured limbs wouldn't work. He also noticed he'd pissed his pants. He considered screaming for help. The worst that could happen would be for his attackers to discover him and finish him off, which didn't seem so bad, all in all.

But given the hour–he estimated that it was six or so in the morning–no one would be on the road. And even if they were, his voice wouldn't carry far enough. He concluded that if he waited long enough for the pain in his hip to subside, even a little, he could try to get to the road. He waited throughout the day, to no avail. Late in the afternoon, he tried to put his hand on his right hip. He immediately became dizzy, lost his balance and toppled sideways so that the right side of his head lay flat on the ground. He could not right himself. He lay on the floor and watched his breath, puffing out in rasps. He'd stopped shaking and noticed while his breath slowed that he'd begun to feel warm. Kamp had a vague recollection that this change signaled extreme danger, but he couldn't remember why and certainly could do nothing about it. He felt a strong urge to crawl into the corner but decided instead to try to get outside one last time.

He rolled over so that he was facing the slaughter-house door. He used the muscles in his torso to angle himself out of the door's path. Then he curled his fingers around the edge of the door and opened it enough to be able to see outside. The orange sun slid over the horizon, and he tilted his head to see the first stars dotting the eastern sky. He wiggled like an earthworm out of the slaughterhouse so he could feel the wind on his body. He rolled onto his back in order to stare straight into the sky, and when he did, he saw Joe, standing above him and looking down.

Kamp said, "Where'd you come from?"

"You look like you could use a little help."

"How so?"

Joe hooked his hands under Kamp's arms and started dragging him. He said, "I'm not that far ahead of them. They're on their way."

"There's a bag. In there."

"We can't take it now. I'll come back for it."

"No, they'll find it." He stiffened his body in order to make it harder for Joe to drag him. "Get it." In the distance they heard the sound of a carriage and men's voices. Joe let go of him and went into the slaughterhouse.

He came out with the canvas bag slung over his shoulder.

Joe said, "You have to get on my back. You have to get up."

Kamp barely moved. Without hesitation, Joe rolled him onto his belly, pulled him to his knees, then raised him to his feet. Joe put one of Kamp's arms over his head and hoisted his body across his shoulders in a fireman's carry. Joe made for the tree line, hauling both Kamp and the canvas bag. The sound of the carriage grew louder, though they heard no voices. In a moment the carriage would make the turn that would bring them into view. Joe couldn't turn around to see whether they'd been discovered. He had to move forward. Kamp heard Joe's breath growing louder, but the man did not slow his pace or falter. They heard shouting behind them.

Joe carried him into the woods, and in one motion, he set Kamp and the canvas bag on the ground and wheeled around to see three men pursuing them. One of the men was raising a gun at a distance of a hundred yards. The other two sprinted toward them. Joe picked up a rifle and dropped to one knee as the man fired the shot. The bullet whistled through the trees just above Joe's head. Joe fired and dropped the man. The second man running toward them was bearing down. Joe dropped the rifle and pulled a pistol from a vest rig. He stood up and shot. The man tumbled to the ground a few feet from Kamp. The last man turned and ran back toward the road. Joe trained the pistol on the retreating man. He held it there until the man reached the road, and then Joe put the gun back in the holster. He picked up the bag, then Kamp and finally the rifle.

Kamp said, "Where are we going?"

"Over."

As Joe started trudging up the trail, they heard another pair of approaching footsteps. Heavy laden as he was, Joe was essentially defenseless. He swung around with Kamp still draped over his back and saw Nyx Bauer standing in front of him. She was carrying the Sharps.

She said, "I'm coming with you."

"No, you're not," Joe said, and he turned around and started walking.

Nyx reached for the canvas bag, took it off Joe's shoulder and slung it over her own.

"Don't touch that."

She said, "Let me carry that rifle too."

"Get out of here. Go."

Kamp mumbled, "Don't bother, Joe. She won't listen. Trust me."

Nyx took the rifle from Joe and walked the trail ahead of them. "I'll make sure no one's up there waiting for us."

Joe adjusted Kamp's weight on his shoulders and began walking again. Kamp drifted in and out of consciousness, each time waking to the sound of Joe's feet
on the trail and fresh pain in his body. When they
reached the far side of the mountain, the sky was dark
except for the light of the sliver of moon. Joe pointed
the way to the wagon he'd left on the road on the far
side of the mountain. The horse nickered and stamped
her hoof when she saw Nyx, who climbed in the wagon.
Joe loaded Kamp next to her and then calmed the horse
by rubbing the spot in the middle of her forehead and
whispering a song. Once the horse had settled down, Joe
clambered onto the seat, took the reins and instructed
the horse to run.

Kamp heard ravens calling to each other in the chestnut
tree outside the window. He scanned the room and saw
that he lay in a bed in a clean, spare room of a wooden
building, probably a cabin. Apart from the bed and a
chair, the only other piece of furniture in the room was
a dresser. On the dresser was a large bowl of steaming
water and a silver tray containing metal implements, a
syringe and a green, ribbed bottle. Kamp felt excruciat-
ing pain in his hip and elbow, as well as in his head. He
focused on the warm yellow sunlight slanting in the
window and the blue sky outside. He also heard voices
through the bedroom door and assumed they belonged

to Joe and Nyx. A moment later, however, the door opened and E. Wyles entered the room.

"Good morning."

"You're here."

"Indeed, I am." She smiled at him.

She looked exactly as she always did, with one exception. She wore a starched, white cotton blouse with the sleeves rolled up and a long, grey skirt and boots. But her hair, which was normally pulled back and tied up, was now loose and fell past her shoulders.

He said, "Where are they?"

"They're not here. But they're fine. They're safe."

"Where are they!"

Wyles crossed the room and stood facing him. "Settle down. I'll explain everything later. Right now, I have to take care of you."

"Take care of me?"

Wyles looked Kamp straight in the eye. "Your injuries are severe, life-threatening. I'm going to try to save your left arm, if that's possible, by performing surgery. And I'm going to reset your right arm so that it can heal properly."

"Reset it how?"

"By breaking it."

"I thought you were a midwife."

"I'm a lot of things." Wyles walked to the dresser. "And lucky for you, I'm also a druggist." She inserted the tip of the syringe in the green bottle and filled the barrel. "Make a fist."

23

S ilas Ownby stood at the head of the table and took
his wife's hand with his left and his oldest daughter's hand with his right. He surveyed the other faces at
the table, his mother and father, the two younger girls.
All bowed their heads, and Silas Ownby used the moment to listen for the Inward Voice, and as he often did,
heard silence. In times past Ownby took the silence to
mean that all was well with him and that he was walking
in the light. But he'd begun to doubt the meaning of this
quiet, if not the purity of his walk. The moment passed
quickly enough, and the family sat down to their typical
Sunday feast, served on ornate dishes and from silver
bowls. Silas had never been one to worry, placing all his
faith in the divine grace and providence that guaranteed
the rightness of his purpose. One had to look no further

than the warmth of his home, the bounty on the table and the happiness of the people gathered around it, he assured himself, to be certain that his path was true.

And yet he did not feel certain. In fact, Silas Ownby felt greatly troubled. Beads of perspiration formed on his brow and upper lip. His heart began to thud in his chest, and he stood up abruptly from the table.

His wife said, "Silas, what is it?"

"Nothing. I just remembered something. Excuse me."

Silas Ownby exited through the back door of his large home and stepped out onto the stone patio. He looked back in through the dining room window and watched his youngest daughter, Jennie, talking to her sister and laughing. Ownby felt an overwhelming sadness in his chest and struggled to push down a sob. Earlier that morning, the girl had come to him and said she'd found something mysterious.

She'd held it up to him and said, "Look, papa, it's a beautiful, shiny treasure." The object was an eight-sided silver coin, newly-minted. On the coin Ownby saw the face of a smiling figure wearing a cap.

"I love him. I think he's funny. And there's a picture on the other side, too." She flipped the coin over to reveal a picture of a locomotive inside a circle. Around the circle were the words "*Ex Fratrum Ordine, Et in Corvo.*"

Jennie said, "Where do you think it came from?"

"Where did you find this?"

"I wonder who wanted me to have such a beautiful thing. Was it you, papa?"

Ownby snapped, "Where did you find it?"

Jennie looked at him, puzzled. "Where?"

"Yes, where did you find the coin?"

"I didn't find it. It was under my pillow when I woke up this morning."

"Give it to me." Ownby reached for the coin, and Jennie pulled back.

"No, papa. It's mine. I think *he* wanted me to have it."

"Who?"

"The little man on the coin."

Ownby had grabbed his daughter by the arm and pried the coin from her fingers. She'd begun sobbing, but he'd kept the coin. He took it out of his pocket now and turned it over in his trembling hand. That someone had entered his home and gone in his daughters' room terrified him. Ownby also felt certain that the person intentionally put it under Jennie's pillow, because she was the youngest and most vulnerable. The message was not subtle. Ownby had heard stories, especially in recent weeks, regarding the actions of this alleged group, the Order of the Raven. In particular, any crime whose perpetrator was unknown was assumed to have been committed by a member of this organization. Ownby knew that dozens of secret societies operated in Bethlehem, nearly all of them in plain view. However, he'd also heard of genuinely clandestine groups whose membership rolls were known only to their own leadership and whose members were, in fact, sworn to secrecy.

In particular, it was Ownby's understanding that this shadowy cabal worked to undermine the authority of the management structure in industrial settings, such as coal mines. He'd heard a rumor–darkly fantastical it seemed to him at the time–that the group orchestrated an explosion in one of his own mines. Another tale made this Order of the Raven responsible for the recent death of the former district attorney, Philander Crow. Ownby had dismissed these rumors out of hand. It never occurred to him that he'd have reason to fear such a group. He never felt threatened, because his walk was upright. The labor practices in his collieries were considered to be, by a wide margin, the safest and most humane in the region, if not the world. He paid his workers the highest wages. The anger and violence between management and labor that plagued other operations in the area did not exist in his. So Silas Ownby had no real reason to fear any secret society, especially one that might not even be real.

Nevertheless, he'd heard that when the Order of the Raven intended to exact punishment, they invariably delivered a silver coin, without explanation. It was said that if the victim tried to get help, in particular, if the person told anyone or showed anyone the coin, their wrath was swift and terrible. Upon completion, the Order retrieved the coin. It was this detail that initially had made Silas Ownby most skeptical, for it seemed that the lack of physical proof, the lack of the mythical coin, somehow proved to the gullible that the Order was behind the crime. But now the coin had appeared, and he held it in his own hand. It could be a fake, a joke at his expense. But judging by the quality of the coin, the design, execution and overall craftsmanship, it would have had to be an extraordinarily elaborate ruse. Someone had taken considerable time and great expense to mint the coin. And someone had actually broken into his home to deliver it. Silas Ownby wanted to believe that the threat wasn't real or that it was meant for someone else. The fear in his chest told him otherwise.

Kamp didn't feel better when morning came. Though his body was numb, he knew that the pain was there underneath it and ready to storm back when the drug wore off. But he felt as if he had rested, and perhaps best of all, he wasn't cold. Judging by the stillness outside, he knew it was the middle of the night. By the moonlight coming through the window, he looked at his arms, both heavily bandaged. The first twinge of feeling came in the form of an itch in his left ear. He tried to scratch it, first with his left hand and then with his right. The efforts were futile, as Wyles had immobilized both arms.

He lay in bed and waited for the itch to depart of its own accord, and when it did, he fell back asleep.

When the morning came, he awoke to the raw pain of his convalescence and also to the smell of breakfast. His stomach growled loudly, announcing the return of his appetite. The bedroom door opened and Nyx Bauer came in carrying a tray of food that included scrambled eggs, bacon and a large mug of hot coffee.

She said, "*Guten tag, herr detektiv.*" Nyx carried the mug of coffee to the bedside. As soon as he tried to reach for it, Kamp realized he had no way of getting the mug to his lips. He couldn't bend either elbow.

"Morning, Nyx. Do me a favor and take the splint off my left arm."

"Sorry, can't do it."

Kamp felt the blood rising in his face. "I have to eat."

Nyx shook her head. "Nope. Wyles said so."

He let the fury wash over him, looked out the window, took a few deep breaths and then looked back at Nyx.

Nyx said, "Finished?"

He gave her a hard stare and then focused on the coffee mug. Nyx guided the mug toward his lips. He inhaled the steam, as she tipped the mug gently so that the liquid trickled into his mouth. Kamp closed his eyes and savored a moment of bliss.

"Too hot?"

"More."

Nyx poured the coffee down his throat, and he felt warmth spreading in his chest. Soon, the caffeine started working, too. The fog receded, and his mind began to engage.

"Where's Wyles?"

"In the other room."

Nyx got the tray of food from the dresser and set it on his chest. He breathed in the smell of the food as deeply as his lungs would allow. She fed him a strip of bacon and some of the eggs.

Between bites, he said, "What about Joe? Where's he?"

"Don't know. Not here."

"Where's here?"

She shook her head. "Don't know that, either. Joe said something about a hunting camp. That we're close to where that is. He said you'd know what hunting camp." She continued feeding him while she talked. "I like it here. Emma and Joe are teaching me more about shooting. Different stances. How to hit a moving target. A lot more than *you* taught me."

"Good for them."

"I'm a good shot, too. You should see me."

"What about your sisters? Do they know you're here?"

"Before I came and found you and Joe, I told them I'd be going for a while anyway. They're fine. They're at the Fogels." Nyx finished feeding him. "Let me guess, you want more."

He nodded. "And tell Emma to come here, and bring me that canvas bag."

Nyx said, "*Yawohl, herr detektiv*" and got up to leave.

As she reached the door, Kamp said, "Oh, and Nyx, thank you."

She turned back and raised an eyebrow. "*Gern gshehne*, Kamp."

A moment after Nyx had gone, E. Wyles strode into the room, purposeful as ever.

She walked to the bedside, studied his face and put her hand on his forehead. "Feeling better?"

"A little."

"You look better. No fever, which probably means no infection."

He looked at his arms. "How'd it go?"

Wyles said, "Very well. We took proper care of the wounds to your left arm and reset the bone in your right."

"We?"

"Yes, Nyx assisted me throughout both procedures. She's remarkable."

Kamp said, "What about my hip?"

"It's severely bruised but probably not broken. No way to know for certain, except to wait and see how it heals."

"Where's my family, Emma?"

Wyles inhaled deeply. "They're not here, and they're not close. Shaw and the baby went with Joe to stay with their people."

"You didn't go?"

"I stayed here and waited for Joe to get back. And as soon as he did, he went looking for you." Wyles unwrapped the bandages on his left arm. "This is healing properly. I'm going to keep it immobilized for the time being so that you can't disturb it."

"I need to use it."

"Tough." Wyles applied clean bandages to the wounds. "The dressings will need to be changed. I'm leaving. Now that you're on the mend, I need to get back to work."

"Do you think that's a good idea, considering?"

"People are depending on me. I need to be there."

"Tell me about the night the house burned."

"Another time. The only thing that matters is that we made it out." Wyles packed up her medicine and moved toward the door. "Shaw wanted me to tell you she started calling your daughter by a name. She wanted me to be certain to tell you it's not her real name, but that's what she's calling her."

344 | KURT B. DOWDLE

"What's the name?"

"Autumn."

Kamp said, "Works for me."

Silas Ownby paced back and forth on the patio, breathing the cold air in gulps, waiting for the panic to subside so that he could begin to assess the situation and to plot a course of action. He never imagined the world to be a peaceable kingdom, but neither did he envision that evil would be unleashed on him for no earthly reason. He searched his memories of the recent past for some turn of events or perhaps a comment or decision of his that could have given offense or otherwise run him afoul of a member of the Order of the Raven. He recalled nothing. Ownby then brought to mind all the individuals he could remember with whom he'd interacted in the previous year. Since he was the owner of a significant enterprise, that list of people ran to the hundreds. Ownby flashed each of them before his mind's eye, and once again, he recalled no ill feelings and certainly no conflict, apart from the expected friction generated by business dealings.

The fact that he couldn't identify enemies led Silas Ownby to the conclusion that an individual or, it appeared, group intended to do great harm to him for reasons unbeknownst to him. As such, he concluded, any person, known to him or unknown, might be a malefactor. Still, Ownby knew that he had to trust someone or else simply suffer the consequences of his fate. He assembled a new list in his mind, men he felt certain would not wish to harm him, because they didn't know him personally and, more importantly, would gain nothing from his demise. In addition, Ownby knew he needed someone who had information regarding the Order of the Raven and would have a motive for helping him. Under normal circumstances, Silas Ownby viewed police officers as agents of coercion. But intuition told him that the police detective he'd seen at the funeral of Jonas and Rachel Bauer, was the man in whom he should confide. He'd heard this man Kamp had become an irritant to his peers and superiors. Ownby also recalled hearing a story that, against overwhelming public sentiment and at the risk of his own life, he'd attempted to intervene to prevent the speedy and ultimate punishment of the alleged fiend, Daniel Knecht. Silas Ownby now saw himself as the condemned, doomed to a swift execution, and as such, Kamp was his man.

Two thoughts trailed Silas Ownby as he stepped from the stone patio and back into the warm house. The first was that he hadn't a clue as to the whereabouts of the detective. The second, more troubling, was that despite Kamp's best efforts, Daniel Knecht had gone straight to his grave.

As soon as E. Wyles left the room, Kamp began removing the splint from his left arm. An hour later, and as the sun went down over Blue Mountain, he managed to wiggle nearly all the way out of it. With a final twist, it dropped to the floor with a thud. He breathed a deep sigh as he slowly bent his elbow back and forth. The splint on his right arm remained, and he was happy to leave that one in place. If he tried to hurry the recovery, or if he reinjured it, he knew the arm would never work the right way again. He allowed himself to fall back onto the mattress and relax for the first time that day and fell asleep immediately. When he awoke, Joe was sitting in the wooden chair next to the bed, smoking his pipe. A single candle on the table next to the bed lit the room.

"Evening, Joe."

Joe puffed his pipe and exhaled. "*Anixit gulaqueen.*" He handed the pipe to Kamp, who took a puff and handed it back.

"Me too."

Joe noticed the splint lying on the floor. He let a long moment pass and said, "These things can't be rushed."

"Emma worries too much."

"Does she?"

He sat upright in bed. "Where are they, Joe? I need to see them." Joe looked at the candle flame and said nothing. "They're my family."

Joe settled his gaze on Kamp. "They're up the line. Close to Mauch Chunk."

"I'm going."

"They're my family as well. Our people."

"You don't trust me."

Joe inhaled a long breath. "When I visited you, I told you about a dream. And I told you to leave so that my daughter, my granddaughter and you would not be harmed."

"And I didn't listen."

"You decided to stay in your home and to protect your family there. But what was foretold in the dream came to pass, and is coming to pass."

"I won't make the same mistake again, Joe. Just tell me where they are."

Joe shook his head gently. "Even now you don't see."

"See what?"

"If I tell you where they are, you'll go there. And you'll take this trouble with you. Everyone there will be killed. If you're not followed there, soon you will try to return to your home, and then you will all be killed."

Kamp said, "How do you know? Did you have another dream?"

"Common sense. This is how it is, and there is only one—"

"You don't know that. I almost have it figured out. I'm close."

Joe looked at him with a flat expression.

"Joe, I've almost got it. And once I do, we'll be out of danger. They'll be safe."

"You'll never be safe."

"Why not?"

Joe said, "You think you're fighting against a man. Or a group of men. You're not. You're fighting against a way. Their way. As long as you fight alongside them, you can't see their way. You've been inside their room the whole time, and you didn't know it. Once you're outside, they punish you. You leave, or you're exterminated. You're outside their room now. That's how it is."

"I disagree."

Joe banged the dead ashes from his pipe on the bedside table. He opened his tobacco pouch and packed the bowl. "Has the Judge ever shown you his tobacco pouch?"

"I don't see how—"

"Next time you see him, ask him where he got it."

Kamp said, "What did you do to make the Judge so angry?"

Joe struck a match on the table and lit the pipe. "You have one choice. If you decide that you must see your family now, I will take you there. But from there, you must all leave. Move away and never return."

"What's the other option?"

"Return and finish your business."

"Meaning what?"

"Fulfill the responsibilities of your job. Earn the deed to your property, and make peace with your enemies. And then you may see your family again."

"But you're saying you don't think it's possible."

"I'm saying that's your choice, and I'm leaving to-night. Go with me, or ride back with that girl. Think about it and decide."

Kamp counted the costs of each course of action, while he lay in bed that night. The throbbing in his arms and hip made it difficult to think, but little by little, he worked his way to a conclusion. It must have been around midnight when he swung his legs over the side of the bed and planted his bare feet on the wood floor. He tested the strength in his muscles before standing and felt a powerful, agonizing surge in his injured hip. Kamp stood up and let the pain have its say. He took a couple of halting steps and found that he could walk. He stepped out of the bedroom into the front of the cabin. He expected to see Joe resting by the fire, but instead there was Nyx sitting in a chair. The Sharps was lying on the table in front of her.

He said, "Where's Joe?"

"Gone. He left a long time ago."

"He did?"

"He said he knew what your decision would be."

Nyx watched him absorb the information. She said, "I heard your whole conversation with him through the door. I knew what you'd do too."

The Sharps had been disassembled, and she was cleaning the parts while she talked. "Don't worry, Joe taught me how to do it. I'm going to need more ammunition, too. Joe said you could teach me how to make the cartridges myself and that you knew somewhere around here to get all the stuff."

He walked to the front window and looked outside. "What's your plan, Nyx, apart from learning to make your own ammunition?"

"Every day I'm getting better at shooting. You should see me."

"When are you going back to Bethlehem?"

Nyx began reassembling the Sharps. "Whenever you're ready."

Kamp awoke the next morning to find he wasn't ready. His left arm, though free of the splint, didn't want to move, and neither did his hip. He hauled himself out of bed and fixed a cup of coffee, which helped. He lit a fire in the fireplace and set the canvas bag on the table. Kamp removed each record book and file, making stacks on the floor. He began grouping individual records according to their purpose and relevance: birth and death certificates, real estate and business transactions, and criminal records. He searched for records associated with the property on which his former house was situated. Kamp learned that the parcel of land was originally included in a much larger area that had been divvied up in the mid-1700s. Records showed that the land was originally held by a Lenape tribe called the Munsee, of whom Joe and Shaw were members. According to the records, the Munsee sold the land as part of the "Walking Purchase," the deal in which the Lenape were said to have agreed to sell as much land as a man could walk in a day to the heirs of William Penn. That the brothers Penn hired three men, not one, to do the walking and that the men ran instead of walked and that the original treaty on which the deal was based was unsigned and unratified and, at worst, an outright forgery did not appear in the official records. Kamp knew this to be true from his own study. The document included a clause that "upon completion of the transaction, it will be necessary for all indigenous persons to vacate the entirety of the acquired area posthaste."

According to the records, the land passed to the Penn brothers via the Walking Purchase. They granted several hundred acres to one of the runners, a certain Felix Rauch, who divided the land into a number of parcels. One of the parcels was purchased from them by another man named Walter Gottschalk. Kamp recognized this name as the ancestor whom Joe sometimes mentioned.

According to Joe, Walter Gottschalk took this name in order to assimilate into what had become a foreign land. In the records Kamp saw that the deed for Walter Gottschalk's parcel had been passed to Gottschalk's son, then grandson, and finally to his great-grandson, Abraham Gottschalk in 1799. Kamp could find no further transactions related to the deed, and it did not appear to have been transferred to anyone else. He did, however, find another deed for the same property, dated 1845. The new deed made no mention of the previous deed, and it stated that the property belonged to one Abraham Cain. Kamp also recognized this name. The man was Tate Cain's father. He concluded, though he didn't have all the details, that he'd found the source of the animosity between Joe and the Judge.

From there, Kamp worked his way through books of records for persons with the last name beginning with the letter "K, focusing on two names in particular. He looked for the name "Knecht, Daniel" in the book of criminal records. He knew that Knecht had been arrested and jailed for at least a dozen offenses including disturbing the peace, criminal mischief, petty theft and vagrancy. But there was no record of any of Knecht's crimes. Kamp found Knecht's birth and death certificates. He scanned the death certificate and saw that it read:

"Knecht, Daniel: Cause of Death: Accident (neck trauma)."

The certificate was signed, "Abner Johannes Oehler, Northampton County Coroner." He then looked up the property records for the house where Knecht had lived in Easton and found that the records were incomplete. Specifically, the document detailing the transaction for the house was missing the portion that indicated to whom the house belonged. Someone had cut that part off.

Kamp looked for records for Roy Kunkle. He found document after document detailing Kunkle's misdeeds. Kunkle had been arrested a total of seventeen times for offenses ranging from destruction of property to fighting and resisting arrest. Most of the incidents appeared to have taken place in or around the mine where Kunkle worked as an employee of Confederated Coal. In most cases the arresting officer was a member of the company's police force. Kamp found Kunkle's death certificate, which read:

"Kunkle, Roy: Cause of Death: Accident (neck trauma)."

It too was signed by the coroner A.J. Oehler. He continued searching the Kunkle family's records and learned that Roy Kunkle's father had died but that he had a twin brother, Anton Kunkle, who lived in Bethlehem.

Kamp also researched the history of 31 Iroquois, address of The Monocacy, and found documents indicating that the building had been sold in December of the previous year. No individual name appeared as an owner of the building. The official new owner was a business entity called "Black Feather Consolidated." Kamp scoured the records for real estate transactions that had taken place in South Bethlehem during the previous year and found that in most cases the buyer was Black Feather Consolidated. Prior to the previous year, however, the name Black Feather Consolidated did not appear in any real estate records.

Lastly, Kamp searched the new business filings for the last two years and found a document indicating that three persons filed for a business license to create Black Feather Consolidated. The three men, the principals of the company, affixed their names: Joseph Moore, Walker Gray, and a third man named James Shelter, the owner of a shipping company. According to the document, Black Feather Consolidated intended to do business in the areas of "manufacturing, transportation and energy," and the filing had been signed and sealed by the Honorable Tate Cain. In the documents he researched, Kamp saw the outlines of the creation of a cartel, formed privately by three men and linked, albeit legally, to the Judge. He also saw that work had been done at a number of levels to hide, obfuscate or otherwise wipe clean inconvenient details. What Kamp knew he lacked, though, was proof of wrongdoing. For instance, there was nothing connecting Moore and Gray to Roy Kunkle or to the deaths of Daniel Knecht and Jonas Bauer. Knecht, Bauer and Kunkle had all worked in coal mines, an industry in which neither Gray nor Moore had any involvement, as far as Kamp knew.

"How goes?" Nyx walked into the room and saw the files covering the table and a good part of the floor. "What's this?"

"Part of a story." He began cleaning up the documents, and she helped him.

"How much of it?"

"Not enough. Nyx, did your father ever talk about a man named Joseph Moore?"

"Not that I can remember."

"What about a Walker Gray?"

"Nope."

"What about James Shelter? Did he ever mention him?"

She shook her head. "No, but I was thinking about what you said about how there must have been something hidden in the house that people were looking for."

"Right."

"Well, on that night, before it happened, probably a few hours before everyone went to bed, I remember Danny was in the cellar. He was down there for a long time. He must've been looking for whatever it was. Do you think he found it?"

"Maybe." Kamp pulled the silver coin from his pocket. "Did he ever show you this?"

"Who, Danny?"

"Your father."

"No. Let me look at it." He handed the coin to her. She turned it over slowly in her palm. "Hey, that little guy. That face. That looks like the face someone carved into the wall at our house. Was it the same person?"

Kamp said, "I don't know."

"Well, it has to mean something." She looked at him. "Doesn't it?" They finished picking up the files from the floor, making a single stack of records on the table.

He looked at the files and exhaled. "It's a long story. I'll tell you on the way. Bring the Sharps."

Kamp climbed into the wagon and covered himself with a wool blanket, and Nyx took the reins.

She said, "Where are we going, and how come you can't drive?"

"Once you get to the road, turn left and go for a few miles or so. I'll keep an eye out and tell you when to turn."

Nyx got the horse moving to a trot and called back over her shoulder. "Do you want to tell me where we're going?"

"No."

"Well, then do you want to tell me your long story?"

As they made their way down the road, Kamp told her what he'd learned regarding the coin, the Fraternal Order of the Raven, the Monocacy, Black Feather Consolidated and anything else that seemed relevant to the situation.

When he finished, Nyx said, "Oh, shit."

He popped his head out from under the blanket and said, "The turn is coming up. Right after this bend."

She guided the horse down a dirt road just wide enough for the wagon. They continued for another mile, and he instructed her to turn off the road, go through a meadow and finally into a grove of trees. He climbed out of the wagon and tied up the horse.

Nyx said, "Now what?"

"Now we walk."

Kamp limped off into the woods, barely pulling his right leg behind him. After the first few minutes the stiffness in his hip began to ease, and he found he could almost walk with a normal gait. They followed a footpath through the forest for half an hour, crossing a small stream, picking their way over dry rocks to the other side, where a wood cabin came into view. A trail of smoke issued from the chimney. Before they reached the front steps, the door of the cabin swung open, and a man stood in the doorway. Kamp kept walking toward the cabin with Nyx following.

The man said, "Normally I shoot on sight, but in your case, I guess I'll make an exception."

Kamp said, "Nyx Bauer, this is my cousin Angus Schmidt."

Nyx said, "Nice to meet you." Nyx studied the man, who bore a subtle resemblance to Kamp. Angus appeared to be a few years younger than Kamp with oiled hair, combed straight back, and finer features.

Angus said, "Pleased to meet you too. Come in once, come in." They followed Angus into the cabin, which was part living quarters and part workshop. The back wall of the main room was taken up by work benches and long gun racks, filled with rifles.

Kamp sat down stiffly in a chair. Angus noticed his discomfort. "You doesn't look so good, cousin. I heard you was in trouble down there."

"Angus, we need cartridges for the Sharps."

"Ach, I don't have none ready."

"I was hoping you had the materials."

"Yah, that I do have. Lemme see that rifle." Nyx handed Angus the Sharps.

Angus said, "Jesus, but this one's been through the wringer." He inspected the gun from every angle. "I need to go to work." Angus immediately disassembled the

Sharps, laying out all the parts on a table. He cleaned and oiled each part and put the rifle back together.

Angus pointed to the muzzle. "There's a burr there, a small one. That's going to cause problems with accuracy."

Nyx said, "It's accurate enough."

Angus took out a set of tools, including a file, and he re-crowned the muzzle. "See, good as new." He handed the Sharps back to Nyx and went to one of the cabinets against the wall. Angus removed a number of items and placed them on the table. "There's your bullets, your nitrated papers, and the dowel."

He went back in the cabinet and pulled out a metal canister. A label on the canister had a picture of two small children, a boy and a girl, playing next to a brook. The label read "Shawnee Mission Soap Flakes." Angus removed the lid and showed them that it was filled to the top with black powder.

"Pour seventy grains." Angus looked at Kamp, then Nyx. "Seventy grains. Every time. Got it?" He turned to Nyx. "And remember, with this powder and that paper, any spark will set it off. This mix is very *naerfich*."

Kamp said, "One more thing." He held up the silver coin. "Have you ever seen one of these?"

Angus took the coin and studied it. "Heard about them. Never seen one."

"What did you hear?"

"I heard that if you see one, the next thing you know, yer *dode*."

"Anything else?"

"Well, back when they was making Bethlehem long rifles, they used to carve that face into the stock."

"Why?"

"You know the story. If a soldier asked them what the picture meant, they could say, 'Oh, that's nothing. Just a little Indian.' But to them, it was a symbol."

"Of what?"

"Don't know. Secret, probably. People have secrets."

"Why do you think it's on this coin?"

Angus looked at it again. "You got an engine on one side there. And you got the little Indian on the other with that pickax and shovel behind him. And there are some words there. Different language. Coin has eight sides. Don't know what any of it means. They know what they're doing, though."

"How so?"

"It's not easy to make coins this good. You need a special machine."

"What kind?"

"A special screw press. Steam-driven. Gives you these nice, clean edges. Perfect shape. No flaws."

"Do you know anyone who has one?"

"I don't. But a guy come through a few months back. Told me he helped deliver one."

"Where?"

"Oh, Lemme think. Saucon, I believe."

"What else do you remember?"

"Nix. Nussing."

Kamp stood up to leave. "Angus, I owe you one."

Angus laughed. "Yah, at least one." He gave Angus a hug.

Angus said, "Give 'em hell."

"Thanks, Angus."

They headed out the door and back onto the trail with Kamp leading the way. Nyx looked over her shoulder as they made their way back to the stream. Angus stood in the doorway, waving goodbye.

After they'd crossed the stream, Nyx said, "He's a good man." She snapped him out of a reverie.

"What?"

"Your cousin. I said he's a good man."

"He sure is."

"How come he lives all the way out here, where there's no one else?"

"He used to be a girl."

"What?"

He said, "Angus used to be a girl. Agnes. He always wanted to be a boy, though. When people found out, they wanted to kill her. Even her own family. Especially them. So, he moved out here."

"Does that bother you, that she's like that?"

"No."

"Why not?"

Nyx kept asking questions until she realized that the conversation had ended for Kamp. He'd slipped back into his reverie, reliving the days he'd spent with Agnes and his other cousins when they were children. Rolling down the hill behind their house, catching frogs by a pond. He remembered the beautiful child Agnes had been. That day, he saw the same beauty in his cousin's face, though so much had been stolen.

24

Kamp filled the next three days with research of the records. He scrutinized each page of every document, thousands of records in all, including a search for any information related to the delivery or use of a steam-powered screw press in Saucon. He found nothing related to it. But he continued to work through the documents until he'd pieced together enough fragments to assemble a clear picture for himself. At night, he rested and let his bones heal. Nyx spent the better part of her time making cartridges the way Angus had instructed her and then putting the Sharps to good use. She went hunting every day for squonk and brought back something even better, a strange bird newly introduced to the region, called a pheasant. Kamp had heard that it made good eating, and they feasted on it.

On the third night, he removed the splint from his right arm and found that the arm could bend. It felt exceedingly weak at first, and he didn't attempt to lift anything. But he practiced moving it back and forth until he was exhausted. E. Wyles had done an expert job on the surgery, and he could tell the wounds were healing correctly. Nyx changed the dressing on his left arm at regular intervals. The angry purple bruise that covered his left hip had turned greenish-yellow, a good sign. More important, it felt better, and it felt good to walk. He slept as much as his body and mind would allow, which is to say that his sleep was always troubled. Each night, when Nyx heard shouting, crying and bumping in his bedroom, she lit a candle and investigated. And each night, she found Kamp asleep but thrashing in bed. The shouts and cries were all his.

On the seventh morning, Kamp awoke hours before dawn. He lay in bed testing his arms and legs. Everything hurt but seemed to be in good working order. He walked into the front room, lit a candle and fixed a cup of coffee. He walked onto the front porch and looked at the stars blazing out in a black sky. The crescent moon, a narrow white shard, hung high. When he turned to go back in the cabin, Nyx met him at the door.

He said, "Time to go." She nodded.

They loaded their few possessions into the wagon and locked the cabin doors. As he prepared to load himself into the wagon as well, Nyx stopped him.

She said, "There's one more thing." She lit a lantern and went around the side of the cabin. Nyx pulled back the corner of a tarred canvas pall to reveal the punt gun. "Joe found it at the hunting camp and stole it. He said you'd probably need it at some point."

"Is that what he said?"

"Yah, and he even threw in a couple pounds of powder and shot. Right there."

Together they managed to lift the weapon into the wagon. He lay down on his back, parallel to the barbarous instrument. Nyx covered them both with the tarred pall, leaving only his head exposed. He stared up at the stars and breathed the cold, still air. Almost as soon as the wagon started to roll, he got very drowsy and soon slipped into a lucid dream, where each star became a twinkling, silver coin. Kamp found he could travel to each star and read every one of its grooves and letters, decipher all its fire-born mysteries and see all the way back to its birth.

Nyx reached the path that led to the house where Jonas and Rachel Bauer had lived. When she brought the horse to a stop, he awoke. Kamp sat up slowly in the bed of the wagon and scanned the surroundings. Together they pried the boards off the bulkhead doors and unloaded the contents of the wagon into the cellar, save the Sharps.

Kamp said, "I want you to ride to the Fogels. Go see your sisters and show them you're all right."

"What do I tell everyone about where I was?"

"Whatever you want."

"Okay, but what should I tell them about you?"

"Nothing. But if they want to know where I am, just tell them I'll be at the police station this afternoon. Save them the trouble of having to look for me."

Nyx held out the Sharps to Kamp, who shook his head and said, "Keep it."

"No. It belongs to you."

He said, "I won't be able to shoot it. Not for a while. You're probably already a better shot than I ever was anyway."

And he walked down the path toward the road. Normally, he hated walking on an empty stomach, but now that the pain had begun to subside, Kamp forgot his hunger and savored the feeling of putting one foot in front of the other. He took the main road to Bethlehem instead of the tracks, because he knew no one would be looking for him. While he walked, he allowed his arms to swing as freely as he could bear. His thoughts soon shifted to what he'd learned during his convalescence with respect to the county records. In particular, he'd come across the name of a certain Otto Vorde-mgentschenfelde, who, according to records, was a chemical engineer and an employee of Native Iron. It also appeared Otto was a numismatist. Kamp knew this because the man had filed for a business license to deal in coins. The address listed for the business was 127 East Broad Street in Bethlehem. From tax records, Kamp had also learned that Vordemgentschenfelde owned a property in Saucon.

When he got to Bethlehem, Kamp bought pierogies from a street vendor. He stood on the corner, ate two of them and pocketed the other two for later. He then made his way down East Broad Street, expecting that when he reached the business at 127, he would find the storefront empty. And he was right. Kamp cupped his hands around his eyes and pressed his face to the front window. He saw that the place had recently been occupied, though only a few old chairs and a display case attested to the fact. He went down the alley behind the building and found the back door, which he kicked open. A thin layer of dust had settled on the floor in the back room. He noticed nail holes in the walls where pictures or perhaps a tool rack had hung. But nothing remained. He went to the front room, looked in the abandoned display case and found it had been stripped bare. He turned on his heel and surveyed the room. On the far wall, at eye level, a countenance had been carved rather delicately into the wall. The face was smiling and wore a cap in the Phrygian style.

Kamp left through the front door and headed down East Broad. He wondered as he walked whether the records related to Vordemgentschenfelde, perhaps the man himself, had been made from whole cloth. He decided they may have been. This possibility called into question the accuracy of all the records he'd studied. If someone had gone to the trouble of fabricating one set of documents, could the entire batch be fake? And if all the county records had been falsified, Kamp worried he'd have nothing in black and white, no facts, upon which to base his assertions. Having ruminated at length, though, on the nature of the forces arrayed against him, he concluded that the official county records, like the records of any county, contained mostly fragments of verifiable facts in addition to outright lies. The remainder of the documents consisted of expeditious half-truths that could never be proved or disproved. For example, he recalled that according to the documents, Roy Kunkle's brother Anton lived at 283 Goepp Street. Since Anton Kunkle's known address didn't include an apartment number, he assumed it was a house.

283 Goepp Street turned out to be a tenement building, and a monstrous one at that. Kamp went in the front door, through a small lobby and into what appeared much more like an aboveground rabbit warren

than an apartment building. People streamed through dark, narrow hallways and up staircases that appeared in unexpected places and at odd angles. Due to the low light, the cramped conditions and the haphazard layout, he found it impossible to discern where one apartment ended and the next one began. He followed the main hallways as best he could, calling the name "Anton Kunkle" in the hope that he would stumble upon the man himself or that the residents would point the way to him. Neither happened.

He attempted to find a manager or any person in charge or at least in possession of an address book. No such person existed. Eventually, Kamp resorted to traversing each hallway, knocking on each door, and if anyone answered, asking the inhabitant whether he was Anton Kunkle or where the man could be found. Most people answered with a blank stare or a stream of invective delivered in German or Hungarian, sometimes both. A few people responded with a simple "no." By the time he'd knocked on the last door, Kamp had begun to suspect that Anton Kunkle, too, was a fictitious person.

He left the tenement building at 283 Goepp Street through the back door, and when he did, he noticed a small light in a cellar window. He got on his hands and knees and pressed his face to the glass and saw a burning candle on a table. He circled the building, looking for a way into the cellar. Kamp found the wooden bulkhead doors, secured with a heavy iron chain but no lock. With some difficulty, Kamp eased the chain away and gently swung open the doors. He stared down into the cellar.

"Hello? Anyone there?" No reply.

He stepped down slowly into the darkness, working in the direction of where he'd seen the candle. Though he'd left the bulkhead doors open, Kamp soon found himself in pitch black darkness. He shuffled his feet along the floor and ran his hand along the wall. Kamp turned a corner and saw a sliver of yellow light coming from the crack beneath a door. He moved toward the door, and as he reached for the doorknob, he heard a loud *click* and felt two cold barrels against his left temple.

Kamp said, "Anton Kunkle?"

"Everyone calls me Duny."

Kamp sat with his back against the wall in the cellar room Anton "Duny" Kunkle had fashioned into his living quarters. A straw mattress and a wool blanket lay in the far corner on the dirt floor. The candle burned atop a produce crate in the center of the room. There was a long, clay pipe on the crate next to the candle. Duny sat on the other side of the room cross-legged, a Pepperbox pistol at his side. It was a boot pistol, a double-barreled breech loader. Kamp knew it held four cartridges. And he also noticed that Duny Kunkle was short, not even five feet tall, and wiry. He had hollow cheeks, deep-set eyes and long, stringy brown hair matted to the sides of his head.

In a flat tone Duny said, "You know you's a stupid shit. You know that."

"We need to talk."

"That so?"

"And since I figured you wouldn't come looking for me, I thought I'd look for you."

Duny said, "No, I don't mean you're an idiot for this, not for coming here, though you gotta be a stone fool to come to this shithole without a piece. Either that or bat fuck insane." Duny watched him for a long moment. "I heard about you."

Kamp said, "Who from?"

"Don't matter."

"What did you hear?"

Another long pause. Duny cocked his head and kept staring at him as if he were a magnificent curiosity. He tilted his head back and scratched the wisps of hair on his chin.

Duny said, "What kind of a man puts hisself between a killing mob and a criminal?" Duny shook his head. "Shit, ain't nobody that goddamned dumb."

"I came to talk about your brother."

Duny cocked his head to the other side, parted his lips and let out a sharp breath. "He ain't here no more."

"I know. Part of what I'm trying to understand is why he was killed and who's responsible."

"I heard you went to college," Duny said.

"I did."

"That must be what made you stupid. I'm guessin' before you went up there you had common sense."

Kamp said, "I don't think it was an accident, Duny. I think someone murdered your brother, and I want to know who it was. I think you can help me."

Duny considered the comment and said, "More like not."

"Daniel Knecht knew who was responsible for killing Jonas and Rachel Bauer. They wanted it to look like Knecht did it so that the mob would go after him."

Duny Kunkle looked at him with a flat expression and said, "Ho-lee shit."

"What?

"They got you turned six ways from Sunday, boy. I mean, they got you upside down and backwards with this."

"Who does?"

Duny Kunkle leaned forward slowly and picked up the pipe. He laid it in his lap and pulled a tobacco pouch. He packed the bowl, struck a match against a stone in the wall and lit the pipe. The flame bounced up and down as he pulled in a few breaths. He held the last one and then exhaled a great cloud. Kamp smelled tobacco mixed with another ingredient with a pungent smell that he recognized as marijuana.

Duny handed the pipe to Kamp. "This stuff will cure anything. I mean *anything*. I got it off an Indian." Kamp took a long pull and let the smoke spread in his lungs before exhaling and handing back the pipe.

Duny said, "Okay, here it is. First off, the reason my brother died is that his head got blowed clean off. City asshole showed it to me at the morgue when I hadda go down there and tell 'em it was him. God *damn*, how did they know to tell *me* to come down there if they din't already know it was him!" He looked up, resting his back against the wall and letting out a deep sigh. "So that's the first thing. There's explosions in a mine, and men get killed. Boys, too. As far as for why it happened, what kinda one thing led to another, hell if I care."

"I don't believe that."

"Well, it wasn't your brother died in that mine, neither."

"No, all my brothers were killed in the war."

Duny said, "Yah, I also heard that, heard you was in the war. That's another thing seems goddamned foolish to me, how a man can go off to war and shoot another man, a man he don't even know, kill him at some other asshole's behest." He shook his head angrily. "But that's what you did, right? You went and killed some other poor bastard's brothers, folks you didn't even have no quarrel with, not really."

"Sometimes."

"Sometimes. Christ, you probably did it every goddamned day, killed someone every chance you got. *Hero.*" He struck another match and lit up the bowl again. "And now you're here. You come down here, because you want to know who killed my brother. You want to help *me* out. Talk about bullshit!"

"Duny, I can understand if—"

"Understand? Mister, the shit you understand wouldn't fill a thimble. Daniel Knecht? Danny Knecht? I knew him. He's exactly the kinda sonuvabitch you'd expect to see swinging from a branch, but he wouldn't know nothing about no murderous intrigues, believe me."

"Maybe he had different sides to him."

"Different sides? That idiot?"

"Yah."

"More like one side. For shit."

Kamp reached for the pipe, and Duny handed it to him. He took a pull and gave it back.

"Did you know me and Roy was twins? You didn't know that either, didja?"

"No."

"That's all right. You wouldn't know it to look at us, me and him. Big Roy. Big and strong. What, six-five? Two-fifty. An' look at me. Five-one, buck-o-seven. Little runty bastard. We was twins, though. That's a fact. Born five minutes apart. Me first. Fraternal. An' five minutes after that, our mother died."

Kamp felt himself starting to drift out of his body, and he steadied his gaze on the candle flame so that he could stay put.

Duny said, "He was big, and I'm small. He's dead, and I'm still alive. We killed our mother just by being born. How's that for a story? That's real."

"Well, it is and it isn't."

Duny stood up and tucked the revolver in his waistband. He straightened one leg and shook it, then the other.

Kamp said, "Where're you going?"

"Let's get this over with."

Kamp moved from his sitting position and very stiffly and slowly balanced on his left knee and put his right foot on the floor. He winced and let out a groan as he moved.

Duny said, "Jesus, boy, howdja hurt yourself?"

"Say, Duny, I need to show you something. I'm going to reach in my pocket once."

"Go right ahead."

He pulled out the silver coin and held it up. Duny squinted to look at it. He leaned closer to the candle, and Duny leaned in as well.

Duny said, "Oh, yah, I'll be taking that—"

Kamp lunged for the pistol and got his hand on it a split second before Duny, who wrapped his hands around Kamp's. They tussled briefly in the middle of the room with Duny trying to wrest the pistol from him.

Through gritted teeth Kamp said, "Listen, Duny, I'm pretty sure the barrel of this gun is touching your balls. And I'm certain my finger is on the trigger. So, if you keep fighting with me, I know the gun isn't loaded. Otherwise, there's going to be one helluva mess. Duny eased his grip and took a step back from Kamp, who trained the pistol on Duny's chest.

Duny said, "We was just having a conversation. Whaddya wanna go and do that for?"

"You and your brother are twins. I did know that. And your mother is Irene Kunkle. But she didn't die giving birth. Matter of fact, she lives down the street."

Duny nodded.

Kamp went on, "You know everything I said before is true. That's why you lied about your mother. You don't want me to go looking for her to ask her questions. You're afraid they'll go after her, too. It's also why you're living down here in the dark. You're afraid they'll come after you."

"They already did. Already sent someone. I took care of that. But there'll be more. That's sure."

"Not if they're stopped."

Duny let his arms hang at his sides and shook his head. "You can't get to 'em."

"Why did they go after your brother?"

Duny heaved a long sigh. "See, it was like me and him was born into different worlds. Roy always seen things as right. Me, I always seen things as wrong, right from the first. But if Roy thought something wasn't right, he said, well, it should be. Like how he didn't like the way they run things in the mines. He thought men should be protected more and get paid better, shit like that. He wanted 'em to be fair."

"And he wasn't afraid to say it."

"That's right. That's why churchgoers like that Jonas Bauer looked up to him. They didn't like that he was a rabble-rouser, but they liked what he said, 'specially if it might make things better for them. Guys like Bauer figured it was okay for someone like Roy to speak up and take the grief for it, you know. Roy didn't have no wife or children. But Jacob and Mrs. Bauer caught it anyway, didn't they? Caught it something terrible."

"For what?"

"Hell if I know. Just for being friends with Roy, seems like. You know, I told him to shut up. Million times I told him. But Roy just got more an' more worked up about it. Kept shootin' off his mouth, rilin' men up. So, one day, in his lunch pail at work, he finds a coin. Just like that one there. Well, he takes it as some kind of threat, which most likely it was. I thought it was really more like a suggestion to shut the fuck up. But Roy got so goddamned mad about it, he couldn't see straight. Naturally, instead of shutting up, Roy tells the guys down there in the mine about it. Including Jonas Bauer. Scares the shit outta all of 'em, and rightly so. But what Roy really wants to know is who's behind it. He wants to know where the coin came from, who's responsible, you know. Now, there's this squirrelly little fucker down there in their outfit. Roy hated this guy, because he knew the guy was an *elfetrich*, ya know? A rat. Roy called him the rat squirrel."

"What was that guy's name, the rat squirrel?"

Duny scratched the top of his head. "Dunno. You got anything to eat?"

Kamp fished the bag of pierogies out of his pocket and tossed it to him.

Duny wolfed down the first pierogi, then continued, "Roy told me all this the same day it happened, when he come home from work. Anyway, Roy figures it hadda be the rat squirrel who put the coin there. Couldn't be no one else, he said. So the same afternoon he lights into the rat squirrel, slaps his face a few times, tells him he wants names. Rat squirrel says he don't know *nussing*.

Roy blacks his eye and whatnot. Eventually, the guy gives up the names. Also something about birds, crows, something like that."

"Ravens."

"Ravens. That's it. A group of 'em. Roy said he made sure to write down the names."

"Then what?"

"Well, he come home all *strubbly* an' *ferhoodled*, showed me that coin, told me what I just told you."

"And what did you say?"

Duny scowled. "What did I say? Christ, I told him to run. Run and never go back."

"And?"

"And next morning Roy fills up his lunch pail and goes to work. Says he's gonna put things right. That very day, *kaboom*. Roy's head on a platter. You can bet they didn't think none of 'em down there would survive, and none did, not even that rat squirrel. None 'cept Bauer. And they told me that's because he was standing next to Roy. Roy shielded him when it went off. Roy was six-five."

"Where's the list?"

"What?"

"The list of names. Where is it?"

"Never saw it. Roy never showed me. After it happened, after the funeral and everything, they sent a guy looking for it. I took care of that, like I said. Since then, I been down here mostly. And, yah, I do worry they're goin' after our mother. So far, they haven't. They will. I mean, just you coming here, they'll prob'ly know I'm down here. You fucked me good."

"Since we're both in the same predicament, you're welcome to come with me."

Duny Kunkle shook his head. "For a smart guy, I can't believe you're so goddamned dumb. Going with you just means I'll be dead that much sooner."

"I'm sorry for everything that's happened. I'm sorry about your brother."

"Sorry for me? Don't worry. I'll settle up with them fuckers soon enough." He cleared his throat and spit on the ground. "Besides, same shit really is happening to you. I used to do hard work. Honest work. They saw to it I can't get no job no more. Do you know what I do now? What I have to do for money just to eat? I go out at night. I go over to the South Side, and I suck cocks in the graveyard. When you get down that far, brother, if you make it that long, let's see who you're sorry for."

25

K amp walked without looking over his shoulder and pulled the brim of his hat low. He took the shortest route he knew in the direction of the police station. As he made his way, he wondered what Duny Kunkle's information added to his understanding. Duny had confirmed that his brother and the rest of the miners who died in the explosion were murdered. He'd also made the connection between Roy Kunkle and Jonas Bauer clearer. Roy Kunkle had been certain his life was in danger, and he may have confided in Bauer. If so, he might also have given the coin to Bauer. But even more important, Bauer may also have known about the list of names Roy Kunkle had written down. On the day Roy Kunkle discovered the coin in his lunch pail and then

382 | KURT B. DOWDLE

beat the names of the members of the Fraternal Order of the Raven out of his co-worker, the rat squirrel, someone in the Order would have heard about it. The rat squirrel would have had to tell them something. They would have known Kunkle had a list of names in his possession and that he may have given it to Jonas Bauer.

Kamp approached the toll booth in front of the New Street Bridge. The collector stood at the window in his wooden shed. A sign affixed high on the framework of the truss bridge read, "Pedestrians 1 cent." Kamp hunted in all his pockets and came up empty. He stepped up to the window.

"I don't have a penny."

"Then swim." The toll collector's tone was matter-of-fact.

"I'll pay you on my way back."

"It don't work that way."

Kamp felt the kindling at the base of his skull. He looked back and saw a black carriage pulled by two white horses approaching. He didn't recognize the toll collector, and he wondered why the man was holding him up. He stifled an urge to punch the man in the face, and he walked past the toll booth and onto the bridge.

The toll collector's voice trailed after him, "You ain't special, Kamp."

Kamp glanced back over his shoulder and saw that the carriage had gone through the toll and was gaining on him. When the carriage reached him, he stiffened his shoulders, bracing for whatever would happen next. But the carriage, a hearse bearing a casket, simply cruised alongside him.

The undertaker Manfred Otis was driving and called out to him, "Evening, Kamp."

"Evening, Manfred."

"*Wie gehts?*"

"It goes."

The carriage glided past him, and he watched as it reached the end of the bridge and turned left. Headed for the cemetery, Kamp thought. He looked at the rafters and posts of the truss, up through the triangles and into the twilight sky. Kamp remembered a fragment of the poem he'd been thinking about at the moment he first caught sight of Daniel Knecht running up the path to his home.

"I am set to light the ground,
While the beetle goes his round"

He remembered the verse from childhood, and the rest began flowing back to him. He walked with his head tilted back, seeing all the way into the moon and then the Lodestar. Soon, novel insights and previously misunderstood associations came roaring through, and by the time Kamp stepped off the New Street Bridge, his train constructed of questions had returned with nearly all the answers he needed.

384 | KURT B. DOWDLE

He strolled up the steps and into the police station as night fell. Kamp took a deep breath of the early spring air and walked through the door. Druckenmiller sat at his desk, feet up and reading a book. He looked up, eyebrows raised.

"Well, Jiminy Christmas, if it ain't Detective Kamp."

"Evening, Sam."

"We heard you was coming this afternoon."

"Long day."

Druckenmiller set the book on his desk and put his feet on the floor. Kamp noticed that the swelling was gone from his face. A thin, black crescent under each eye was the only remaining evidence of his injuries.

Druckenmiller said, "*Ach,* but you look a little rough around the edges."

"I haven't looked in a mirror lately."

"Well, sit down, sit down." Druckenmiller stood up and offered his chair. "Relax, lemme get you a cup of coffee."

As Druckenmiller turned to go to the back of the office, the door opened.

A voice behind Kamp said, "Put your arms out at your sides. Do not turn around."

Kamp said, "I don't have a weapon."

Druckenmiller crossed the room to where Kamp stood. He gave Kamp a cursory pat down and shook his head. "Nothing."

The man behind him said, "Walk to the cell. Slowly."

Kamp complied, and Druckenmiller went ahead of him and opened the cell door. Once Kamp was inside, he closed the door and locked it. Kamp turned around and saw that the voice belonged to the former acting High Constable, Markus Lenz. Lenz wore the same formidable moustache and dour expression he had on when Kamp met him.

Druckenmiller said, "Kamp, what do you want in it?"

"Come again?"

"Your coffee. Remind me what you take in your coffee."

"*Nix*."

"Comin' right up." Druckenmiller disappeared into the back room, and Kamp heard the coffee grinder. He sat down on the wooden bench in the cell, eased off his boots and rested his back against the wall.

Lenz said, "Detective, you're under arrest."

"I see that."

Druckenmiller returned with a steaming mug. "Here you go."

He handed the mug between the bars of the cell. Kamp stood up, took it from him and sat back down. He set the coffee mug on the floor next to him without taking a sip.

Lenz said, "People have been looking for you. You understand that. Looking for you and that girl."

Druckenmiller cut in, "Oh, yah, but they found her today. Or she showed up over at the Fogels. She's fine now. You probably knew that, though. Helluva story all the way around, ain't it?"

"Kidnapping," Lenz said. "That's what it's called. And that's only one of the charges."

Kamp shifted his gaze back and forth between Lenz, who looked stern and resolute, and Druckenmiller, who didn't.

Druckenmiller stammered, "We got an arrest warrant for you. That's why we had to put you in there. Just business. Procedure. We don't actually know what they want you for. Say, is there something wrong with your coffee?"

"I don't know. Is there?"

"*Ach*, Kamp, I know this is a tough spot for you. I wish it weren't so."

Kamp said, "I've never seen this cell empty before. Where're the rest of the criminals?"

Lenz cleared his throat. "Your arraignment is tomorrow morning at eight."

Druckenmiller said, "I'm sure once you explain everything to the Judge, he'll understand. Send you someplace besides jail, maybe."

"Like where?"

"Oh, I don't know. Somewhere you might be more comfortable, you know, down around Philadelphia.

They got what they call 'moral treatments' down there. I read about it. It's new."

"I don't follow, Sam."

Lenz stepped forward and said, "The Pennsylvania Hospital for the Insane."

Kamp cocked an eyebrow.

Druckenmiller said, "Yah, might be the trouble you're having is, you know—"

Lenz cut in, "There are some who believe, Detective, that your crime spree is the result of the madness, not malice, per se."

Kamp said, "What do you think, *per se*?"

"Don't matter what I think. At your arraignment tomorrow, the Judge will determine the course of action." When he finished talking, Lenz hooked the key ring onto his belt and folded his arms across his chest.

Kamp sat up on the bench in the cell. "I'm looking forward to it. I'm looking forward to setting everything straight. I'll tell the Judge how I kidnapped Nyx Bauer and took her to the mountains with me and how I broke into the county office and stole as many records as I could. Hell, I even broke into Sam's house and nicked a ringwurst."

Druckenmiller said, "*Ach*, save it for the—"

"And I'll tell the Judge how I read all the records, and from that, I figured out who's in the Fraternal Order of the Raven and why they're killing people. The story's in

388 | KURT B. DOWDLE

the records. It's all there. And then I'll tell the Judge the names of the men in the Order. I have a list. I'll read it for everyone. You said it's a helluva story, right Sam? Just wait."

Druckenmiller said, "*Ach*, shut up!"

Kamp said, "I'm sure there'll be newspaper reporters there. They get to hear my story, too. So, after that, the Judge can decide a course of action. For everyone. Sound good?"

Lenz said, "Eight o'clock."

"Say, can I have a blanket?"

"No."

Markus Lenz left the station an hour later without saying anything. Half an hour or so after that, he returned. He took off his coat, sat down at his desk and began filling out paperwork. A minute later Druckenmiller put the book he was reading in a desk drawer and closed it softly. He stood up, shoulders hunched and head down. He said, "*Gut nacht,* Kamp. See you tomorrow."

"*Gut nacht*, Sam."

As he reached the door, he said, "G'night, Markus."

Lenz said, "Good night, High Constable" and locked the door. He returned to his desk, turned up the flame on the kerosene lantern on his desk and went back to filling out the paperwork. The only sound in the station was the pencil scratching the paper.

Kamp said, "How're you guys gonna do it, Markus? March me outta here and toss me off the New Street Bridge? Or hang me by my belt from the rafter?"

Lenz didn't look up.

Kamp went on, "Either way you'll say I did it to myself, right? We tried to help him, but the raving lunatic escaped and went running out of the station and hucked himself straight off the bridge. Didn't even stop to pay the toll. He just couldn't take it, the way he fell apart and humiliated himself. The shame of it all. Heartbreaking but understandable, you know, considering."

Lenz looked at the pocket watch on his desk and kept writing.

Kamp continued, "I realize you're not much of a talker, Lenz, but seeing as how this is my last earthly conversation, think you can make an exception?"

Lenz didn't move. Kamp stood up and walked to the front of the cell and said, "When did they get to you, Lenz? It had to be before you got here. Or maybe not. You thought it was all on the up and up at first, maybe. They told you that you were doing a good deed by filling in for Druckenmiller. Maybe you even believed the story that Philander Crow committed suicide and that covering it up was for the sake of the greater good. It's possible, though you don't strike me as being that naïve. Hell, I bet you're the guy that shot him. Where's that sack you wore on your head? Plan to wear it again tonight?"

Lenz looked up for a moment and paused as if he were going to say something, then glanced at his watch again and looked back down.

Kamp said, "Well, I know I got one thing right. You're not going to do it alone. You got other guys coming, too. Soon, I bet. It's too complicated to do what you need to do by yourself. I mean, even if you just wanted to shoot me right here, you'd still need help dragging out the body and getting rid of it. So, who else is coming? Anyone I know? Not Druckenmiller. Did he tell them he didn't want to participate, or did they just give him the night off out of the goodness of their hearts? Either way, he doesn't have the stomach for it. But you do. You even convinced yourself you're doing the right thing. Upholding the law. Probably get a nice promotion too, say not."

Lenz cleared his throat softly and said, "Detective, I admire your diligence with respect to what you believe is your investigation. But I suggest you rest now."

"You mean go quietly."

"And I suggest that tomorrow you speak only when the Judge orders you to speak and only to answer the questions you're asked."

"Markus, you do realize your name is on the list, don't you? And, no, I don't have the list on me. No telling who has it. Killing me doesn't solve your problem. Sooner or later, someone will come and find you."

Lenz said, "Process must run its course."

"I respect that, Markus. Say, will ya let me use the men's room once?"

"No."

"Markus, I need to do my business. And besides, if I go now, there'll be less for you to clean up later."

Lenz stopped writing and closed the record book. He stood up and went to the back corner of the room. He picked up a pail and walked toward the cell.

Lenz said, "Piss between the bars."

They heard men's voices at the station door and then banging. "Markus! Open up! Markus!"

As Lenz set the pail on the floor, Kamp pulled Duny Kunkle's Pepperbox revolver from his boot.

Kamp said, "Let me out."

Lenz, who was still looking down said, "Time's up, detective."

"Markus! Let us in!" The pounding on the door grew louder.

Kamp said, "Markus, unlock the door. Move slowly. And don't speak."

Lenz looked up to face Kamp and saw the pistol staring back. Lenz spun on his heel and tried to lunge away. At the same moment Lenz yelled, "*Ach*, he has a gun!"

Kamp put the first bullet through Lenz's right temple and the second one into the base of his skull. Lenz fell straight to the floor, but he lay a few feet from the cell, his key ring out of reach. Kamp reached for Lenz's foot and barely caught hold of one of the legs of his pants.

The men outside bellowed, "Markus! What the hell!"

A moment later a shotgun blast splintered the door. The men outside tried the door, but the lock held. Kamp managed to get a handful of fabric on Lenz's pants. He pulled one leg close enough so that he could get both hands around one ankle.

Boom. The second shot put a hole through the door, and Kamp could see the brass lock was damaged. The men tried the door again, and again it held. One of the men threw his weight against the door. It shook in its frame but did not open. Kamp tried to drag Lenz's body close enough to reach the key ring on Lenz's waist, but he didn't have the strength in his arms. He sat on the floor of the cell with his knees bent. He braced his feet against the bars of the cell and held Lenz's foot as tightly as he could. By straightening his legs and pushing himself backward, he was able to pull the body closer. He dove for the key ring and pulled it off Lenz's belt.

As Kamp turned the key in the lock and clicked it open, the shotgun went off again. This time the brass lock on the station door blew clean off. Kamp jumped out of the cell and trained the pistol on the station doorway. He shot the first man in the chest as soon as he appeared. He grabbed the record book from Lenz's desk and ran for the back door. The next shotgun blast ripped a hole in the doorframe next to his head as he tumbled out into the night. Kamp got up running, gripping the pistol in his shooting hand and the record book in the other.

26

The Big Judge Tate Cain arrived at the county courthouse at the normal time and found the door to his chambers locked, as usual. He noticed, however, some scratches on the brass that he hadn't seen before. The Big Judge opened the door and went in, locking it behind him. He crossed the room and sat down heavily in his chair by the window and began packing the bowl of his pipe with blended tobacco. He looked across the room and the figure of Kamp stretched out on the leather divan in the corner of the room, barefoot and fast asleep. When the Judge struck the match, Kamp's eyes popped open.

"Wendell, my boy, good morning."

"Morning."

"I didn't expect to see you until eight."

"Yah."

"Heard about the commotion, though. Sounds an awful mess. And what happened to your shoes?"

Kamp rubbed his eyes with his thumb and forefinger. "Where'd you get that tobacco pouch?"

"Wendell, I need to get ready for work."

"Tell me."

The Judge said, "We don't have time."

"Where'd you get it?"

"I told you before. Your father gave it to me as a gift."

"Okay, where'd my father get it?"

The Judge set down his pipe, took his robes off the wall and put them on. "You need to get ready, too, Wendell. You have an appointment."

"Where!"

The Judge sat down and sighed. "At one point, your father earned enough money to buy the parcel of land from my father. This was before you were born."

"I heard that, but I didn't see a record of it."

"That's right. Because not long afterwards, I won it back from your father in a card game. So, the property never changed hands according to the official record. But that's immaterial to the story, more or less. Around that same time, a man showed up, an Indian. He said that he had the legal rights to the land, that it had been stolen from his ancestors. Really, he was just an inter-loper. Well, this same fellow–I don't know his real name. Everyone called him the same thing, not just the Indians. Everyone called him Six Killer. So, this Six Kill-er sets about making a commotion about how the land was stolen and how he wants it back."

"And?"

"Wendell, there's no time to—"

"Keep going."

"No one paid attention to this man. So what does Six Killer do? He packs up his belongings, packs up his fami-ly—wife, mother and children—and moves the whole kit n' caboodle onto the land, without any permission. Just up and squats."

"Get to the point."

The Judge sat back in his chair and faced Kamp di-rectly. "Long story short, your father, having earned the money to buy the land and then having lost it just like that, he took the whole thing personally. And he took out his anger on Six Killer and his family. Killed them all one night whilst they were sleeping."

"My father?"

"Yes indeed, Wendell. Murdered the whole family, except for one child, a boy who had been sleeping out in the woods that night."

"Bullshit."

"Hardly, Wendell. I have proof." The Judge held up the tobacco pouch. "That's where this comes from. Made out of old Six Killer himself. And you can ask around. There are plenty of people who remember. Not that anyone wants to bring it up. If something's two weeks old around here, it's ancient history, at least in polite company."

Kamp sensed that the Judge's anger was rising and said, "Who should I ask?"

"Ask your father-in-law. He's the child who survived."

"Joe?"

"Yes, Joe, or whatever the hell his real name is."

"So, if it was my father who did it, why does Joe hate you?"

"I suppose he thinks I had something to do with it, too."

"Did you?"

"At the time I was a boy myself."

"That wasn't the question."

"Time passes, Wendell. Everything changes. World keeps spinning." The Judge stood up again, signaling the end of the conversation.

Kamp persisted, "If you weren't involved, why do you have the tobacco pouch?"

"Well, you have to admit it's a finely crafted pouch. And it was a gift. Now, Wendell, I insist that you come with—"

"Sit down." Kamp pointed the pistol at the Judge.

"Put that away."

"Why Knecht?"

"Settle down, Wendell."

"Why did you send Knecht to live with Jonas Bauer? Why not just kill Bauer straight away? Why drag it out and make it so elaborate?"

"Convenience and simplicity. Is that what you want to hear? Knecht was a loser. I saw him in my courtroom half a dozen times before that day you brought him in. And I would've seen him half a dozen times more. Eventually, I'd have sent him away for good. Or worse."

"In other words he deserved what he got."

The Judge said, "*Quia merito haec patior.*"

"What's that?"

"It means, 'I deserve to suffer for this.' Very Dark Ages."

"Is that how you sold it to Knecht?"

"Sold what?"

"You gave him a deal. Allow him to take the fall for the murders and in return, you make sure his sisters are taken care of. He already thought he deserved to suffer. You convinced him he had it coming and gave him a way to make it seem like it meant something."

"Ridiculous."

"You told him to go live in that house."

"No, I didn't. I guided him in the direction of Jonas Bauer. But I didn't give him a deal."

"Someone did. They told him to retrieve the coin and find the list of names, and they'd take care of his sisters."

"Well, in that case Knecht failed."

"How do you know?"

The Judge inhaled deeply and tilted his chin up. "You showed me the coin, which means Knecht never got it back to *them*. If that's so, Knecht didn't keep his end of the deal. Correct? And as far as a list of names is concerned, I haven't seen or heard of one, and I can't imagine such a thing would be valuable, in any case."

"That's not what Anton Knecht said. Roy Kunkle's brother. He said Roy Kunkle was murdered for speaking out against the management of the mine."

The Judge shook his head dismissively.

Kamp continued, "Five other men were murdered along with him. They made it look like an accident. But Kunkle got the list of names, the members of the Fraternal Order of the Raven. He knew."

The Judge said, "Anton Kunkle? Duny? A worthless, dirty flea. A ghost. And the word on Roy Kunkle was that, yes, he was an agitator. But he angered everyone. It's just as likely that the miners themselves killed him. Don't trust Duny."

"You've disagreed with or dismissed every idea, every bit of evidence I've told you about. Why would you pull me into all of this in the first place if you think I'm always wrong?"

The Judge relaxed in his chair. "Oh, that one's easy, Wendell. The state attorney in Philadelphia has been pressuring us for the past year. Wanted us to clean up our act, as it were. That's why they sent that nasty son of a bitch Crow. They wanted their own detective, too. I forwarded your name to keep that from happening. Even though you didn't have any police experience, they went for it."

"Why?"

"People love war heroes. Listen, Wendell, I'll admit it hasn't worked out precisely as I'd envisioned. You've turned out to be more compromised than I thought you would be."

"Compromised?"

"Indeed. Wild fantasies, erratic behavior, wrong-headed theories. I didn't expect that, and I'm sorry for having encouraged you to do something you weren't fit to do. You need help."

Kamp slowed his breathing. "When we were at the hunting lodge, just before I talked to you, you had a meeting with two men, one in charge of the ironworks and the other in charge of the railroad."

"It wasn't a meeting, Wendell."

"What did you discuss? What was the purpose?"

"Wendell, this has to stop. You shot and killed a police officer last night, and you will be held to account. You're not well. No matter how the trial proceeds, I will rule that you're not guilty by reason of insanity. I'll see to it that you go to a hospital, not to prison."

Kamp picked up the record book from the police station and handed it to the Judge. "This is the last entry in the official police record."

The Judge read, "At midnight, the prisoner, Wendell W. Kamp, began speaking incoherently in his cell. He appeared distraught at first and then withdrawn. At one thirty-five a.m. the prisoner complained of hunger and thirst. I went to the kitchen, and when I returned, the prisoner was hanging by the neck in the cell. He had affixed his own belt to the rafter. I freed the prisoner from the makeshift noose and laid him on the floor. Efforts to revive the prisoner were unsuccessful. Wendell W. Kamp perished at one forty-three a.m. Signed, Markus Lenz, Deputy Chief of Police, Bethlehem."

The Judge looked up from the book and said, "I guess that settles it. As far as the law is concerned, you're already dead."

"Talk about compromised."

The Judge set the book down on his desk, and Kamp picked it back up. "Wendell, we'll sort it all out."

"You guys sorted it all out already, didn't you? The night Crow was killed. I went in there, too, and all they did was hit me over the head."

"Wendell, so many of the things you've done lately, including that debacle, appear suicidal."

"If these guys can kill anyone they want, whenever they want, why didn't they kill me that night?"

"I had nothing to—"

"It's because you told them not to. At first, you thought you could keep me in line, so you told them they could hurt me but not kill me. And then you realized I wasn't going to cooperate, and that was that. Or maybe they just stopped listening to you."

"Wendell, I can arrange for you to leave today. Give you everything you need to get somewhere else, Wendell. With your family."

"We made a deal. Year's almost up. See you soon."

Kamp bolted from the office, while the Judge yelled, "Police! Police!"

He ran down the courthouse steps, hoping to get out of town without being noticed. Before he reached the bottom of the steps, a voice called, "Detective! Detective!" Kamp saw a man twenty feet ahead of him on the sidewalk. The man wore a black overcoat and bowler hat and stood next to a Brougham carriage.

He yelled, "May I have a word with you?"

Kamp ran to him and said, "Keep your voice down."

"I'm Silas Own—"

"Yah, I know who you are. You probably don't want to be talking to me right now."

"Quite the contrary. I must."

"This yours?" Kamp gestured to the carriage.

"Yes, but—"

"Get in. And hurry up."

Kamp put the Pepperbox revolver in his belt, tossed the record book in the carriage and climbed in after it. Then Silas Ownby stepped in after him. The driver snapped the reins, and the horse bolted. Kamp looked through the back window. No one followed. The carriage departed the South Side of Bethlehem and made its way up the road over South Mountain. Kamp noticed the first buds of spring on the trees as the carriage wheels sloshed through the thaw and slipped in and out of the ruts. He sat beside Ownby, fighting the dizziness that began as soon as the carriage started rolling.

Ownby began, "I found this. Or, rather, my daughter found it under her pillow three days ago." He showed Kamp the silver coin. "I don't know who put it there, or why."

"Why do you want to talk to me?"

"Well, you're the police."

"If you want to speak to the real police, you should probably turn around and go back to the station. Let me out first, though."

"But you're the detective."

"I'm *persona non grata*." He closed his eyes and put his head down to keep the carriage from spinning.

Ownby said, "That's probably a good thing. I don't believe I can trust them."

Kamp teetered to one side.

"What's the matter, Mr. Kamp?"

"It's Kamp. I get dizzy when I ride sitting up. Vertigo. I'm fine."

Ownby studied him for a few moments. Both elbows of Kamp's shirt were torn, his bare feet scraped up. The little toe on his left foot was purple.

"Kamp, do you know why I've been targeted?"

He opened his eyes and looked at Ownby. "You have enemies."

Ownby sat back in his seat. "No, I don't. I've given it considerable thought and—"

"If someone wants to kill you, trust me, you do. You just haven't figured it out yet."

The color rose in Ownby's face. "I treat my colleagues and competitors with the utmost respect. My workers enjoy the best conditions and the highest wages in the nation. I take care of the workers. You have no idea of the care I take. I'm an honest man."

Kamp put his head back down. "I don't know you, Mr. Ownby, but that's probably the beginning of your problem."

"How so?"

"Are you aware of a business concern called Black Feather Consolidated?"

"No."

"Do you know anything about a property called the Monocacy, a high rent building, used to be a brothel?"

"No."

"How about Castor and Pollux Shipping?"

"Yes, they're the outfit that transports coal and iron via water."

"They intend to take over your business, Mr. Ownby. Walker Gray, Joseph Moore, and the guy that runs Castor & Pollux. What's that guy's name?"

"Shelter."

"Who?"

"James Shelter."

"New to the area?"

"That's right."

Kamp said, "Well, the three of them are forming a single conglomerate. They'll own all the mining, manufacturing and transportation business in this half of the state. I'm sure their ambitions are even bigger than that, though. They know you won't suspect them. Once you're gone, they'll snap up your business. And they'll say they're doing it as an act of charity, for the sake of your family and the community."

Ownby shook his head dismissively. "I've known Gray and Moore for years. They're not above reproach, but I hardly think they're planning what you say. We've had no conversations regarding the sale of the collieries I own. It's never come up."

Kamp rubbed his left temple. "It never will."

Ownby became more agitated. "If they're behind this, why the coin? Why try to scare me first? Why not simply offer to buy my business?"

Kamp pressed his palms against either side of the carriage to steady himself, and he stifled the urge to vomit. "The coin really isn't intended to scare you. You're already dead."

"Then why?"

"To scare everyone else. People hear you found the coin. One way or the other, word gets out. And then a few days or a few weeks later, you die. It will appear to be an accident, but people will know it was them. No one will be able to prove it, and no one will even try. But everyone will know who's behind it."

"Who?"

"The Fraternal Order of the Raven."

"Nonsense. You're saying Walker Gray and Joseph Moore have formed a secret society?"

"I don't think they formed it. But they're part of it. They joined it. From what I can tell, it's been around for a long time. You're a good person, Mr. Ownby. I understand why you wouldn't—" Kamp paused and held up his hand. He lurched forward and threw up on Ownby's shoes and then wiped his mouth with the back of his hand. "Sorry, sorry about that."

Silas Ownby shook his head. "Quite all right, although I must say, I was wrong about you. You're not well."

The carriage turned onto the gravel drive and stopped in front of Ownby's stone mansion. Kamp leaned heavily against the side of the carriage. There was no light or sound coming from the house.

Kamp said, "Kind of quiet."

"I sent everyone away to someplace safe. Even the servants."

"Very thoughtful of you."

The driver climbed down from the carriage and went to the front door. He jiggled the key in the lock, but it didn't open.

Ownby said, "Yes, well, actually I sent them to their respective homes. They're likely not in any danger, as such. It's my family I'm worried about. After all, they went in my daughter's room."

Ownby got out of the carriage as another wave of dizziness and nausea washed over Kamp. The feelings forced him to kneel on the floor of the carriage. Ownby saw the driver struggling to open the front door and walked in that direction.

He called back over his shoulder. "It just occurred to me that one of the servants may have put the coin there as a prank."

Ownby took the keys from the driver and said, "Let me have a go." He worked the key in the lock and finally got it to turn. "That's strange. This feels warm."

He turned the knob, and the house exploded.

27

The blast charred the carriage and turned it over several times before it came to rest on its roof. Kamp lay in the carriage, looking through the side window at what was left of the mansion. He saw the remains of Silas Ownby and his driver scattered among the bricks and broken glass. Kamp assumed that whoever had rigged the explosion would want to inspect the damage firsthand in order to be certain Ownby was dead. So he waited. Moments later, he heard footsteps crunching softly on the gravel drive. He also heard men talking to each other in calm, low voices. Kamp curled his fingers around the Pepperbox pistol and gently pulled it from his belt. It held just one cartridge, so even if he came out firing, he'd only be able to put one of them down. The footsteps grew louder, and the men's feet appeared next to the carriage. They were looking at the horse, which lay dead on the ground, a shard of glass protruding from its neck.

One of the men said, "Shame."

The pair started walking toward the house, and when they came into view, Kamp saw them from behind, one taller than the other. The taller man wore a laborer's clothes and carried a shotgun, while the shorter man wore a suit and a bowler. He carried a pistol. The smaller man found Ownby's legs and torso and searched the pockets until he found the coin and put it in his own pocket. The taller man disappeared into the wreckage of the house, and the smaller man went around the back.

Kamp waited a few minutes before crawling out of the carriage. He made his way around the house in time to see the men disappearing into the tree line. Kamp knew that at any moment neighbors would appear and after that the fire brigade. He wanted to be gone before anyone arrived. To step into the rubble of the house would be to shred his already injured feet, but he found that although the explosion had obliterated the front of the house, the back, including the kitchen, was partly intact. Better still, Kamp found a pair of work boots by the back door that fit. He pulled on the boots, went in and grabbed a potato sack lying by the cellar door. All the glass in the kitchen was shattered, covering the wood floor and countertops. He discovered a tin bread-box on the floor and inside it a fresh loaf of sourdough. He put the bread in the sack with ring bologna and jar of apple jelly. He also found a butter knife among the utensils scattered on the kitchen floor. Kamp dusted off the knife and threw it in the sack.

He picked his way through what was left of the downstairs, looking for the room Ownby would have used as an office. He didn't find such a room, though under a pile of debris he noticed a cylinder roll top desk tipped over on the floor. He removed the cylinder and gathered all the loose papers and a ledger he found inside. He stuffed it all in the potato sack and made his way back out of the ruined mansion. By the time he reached the stone patio, Kamp heard shouting and the clatter of carriages in the distance. He took the same path he'd seen the two men take minutes before.

The trail took him through a stand of birch trees and then a meadow. He moved quickly, staying low to the ground. The path itself was narrow but easy to follow, winding across the clearing and then parallel to a small creek. Where the trail crossed the water, he stepped on dry stones and made it to the far side. He saw fresh foot-prints on the muddy bank. Kamp hadn't noticed any pain since the explosion, and it hadn't occurred to him that he may have been injured in the blast. But now his head began to throb at both temples, and his arms start-

414 | KURT B. DOWDLE

ed to ache. He sat down at the base of a chestnut tree and opened the potato sack. He tore the loaf of sourdough in two and put one half back in the bag. The other half he slathered with apple jelly and ate, along with most of the ring bologna. When he finished the food, Kamp went to the creek, cupped his hands and gulped the cold, pure water.

He sat down again with his back against the tree and removed the ledger from the potato sack. He remembered Silas Ownby's last words to him, that one of his servants may have put the coin under his daughter's pillow. The timing of the explosion—after Ownby had sent the servants away—made the likelihood even greater, and now he scanned the ledger for names of the people working in the home. By the looks of it, records of the family's day-to-day business had been meticulously kept by Ownby's wife, in ink and in a very neat hand. He leafed through the records of the weeks leading up to the day Ownby's daughter found the coin and noticed that Ownby's wife had created a daily record that included a list of people working that day. It appeared as if there had been a crew of four servants working in the home six days a week. And the list of four remained the same at least as far back as the start of the ledger, nine months in the past. As such, each day's list included four names, always in the same order and written the same way:

B & G: Samuel "Stump" Aemich

S: Cornelia Ausmus

M: Veronica "Fanny" Wenner

B: Ludwig Yost

Two days before the coin appeared under Jennie Ownby's pillow, however, a substitution appeared in the list. The name "Mabel Schenker" replaced Veronica "Fanny" Wenner. Two days after that, Wenner's name was back in the daily list. He searched the ledger to see if Ownby's wife listed a reason for the change, and in fact she did. On the record of the day before Mabel Schenker's name appeared, Ownby's wife wrote that Wenner "fell ill." Kamp also saw that on the same day Wenner fell ill, Silas Ownby had left home for a business trip. "New York City–4 days." That meant that Silas Ownby may have never known that a person named Mabel Schenker had worked in his home. She'd arrived after he'd left, and she'd left by the time he returned home.

Kamp closed the ledger, put it in the sack and stood up. He struggled to get his balance and then got back on the trail. He figured he'd already walked a mile, and so far he hadn't seen any houses. He reached the base of a large hill and started climbing. As he worked himself up the trail, his mind started to clear, and he reflected on the fate of Silas Ownby. He knew the fire marshal would rule that the boiler accidentally exploded. In turn the coroner would rule the deaths of Ownby and his driver accidental as well. And once that happened, there could be no criminal investigation. Kamp realized that even if he were to investigate, there would be no way to prove that someone caused the boiler to explode. And if he were to interview the men who appeared immediately following the explosion, they would say they were just passing through and upon realizing they couldn't render assistance, vacated the property. He admitted to himself that he hadn't seen them commit any crime, apart from stealing the coin from Ownby's pocket.

Kamp kept marching the trail up the hill. He swung his arms at his sides and found they didn't hurt. He picked up the scent of burning wood on the breeze, and looking down through the trees, he caught sight of a small log cabin with wisps of smoke curling from the chimney. Two horses stood tied to a post next to the cabin. He began moving down the trail. When he'd gotten halfway down, Kamp removed the pistol from his belt and set the potato sack on the ground. He jogged the rest of the way down the trail, and when he reached the tree line that bordered the property, he crouched low and hustled to a window at the back of the building.

Kamp heard footsteps on the wood floor inside the cabin. He looked in through the window and saw the two men packing bags and tying up bedrolls. He studied their faces and didn't recognize either one. The shorter man wore eyeglasses with octagonal wire frames, and the larger man wore a scarf tied around his neck. Kamp also saw a bedsheet covering a large object inside the main room of the cabin. The shorter man doused the fire in the fireplace, and then both men went out the front door. Kamp knew that if he made a break for the woods, they'd see him. He sat with his back against the cabin and tried to slow his breathing. The men walked to their horses, and he heard one of the men climb into the saddle.

One of the men said, "I want to make sure the back door is locked."

"Hurry up."

Kamp didn't wait to be discovered. He sprang to his feet and pointed the pistol. When the man rounded the corner, Kamp saw it was the shorter of the two. The man saw Kamp and the gun and said, "Son of a bitch."

The man on horseback couldn't see them, as he was on the opposite side of the house. He called, "Something wrong?"

In a low voice Kamp said, "Tell him to leave. Tell him you'll be along in a minute."

The man yelled, "Help!"

As he said it, the man reached for the pistol at his waist. Kamp fired his last round, hitting the man square between the eyes. The man fell backward to the ground, clutching his face with both hands, blood pulsing be-

418 | Kurt B. Dowdle

tween his fingers. Kamp ran to the other side of the cabin and saw the man on horseback already at the road and disappearing at a full gallop. He went back to the first man and picked up the pistol lying next to him. He tucked it in his belt.

Kamp said, "What's your name?

"Can't speak."

"Tell me your name."

"I'm dying!"

He stared at the man and waited.

Between gasps the man said, "My name is Otto...Vor...dem...gent...schen...felde."

"Slow down. Breathe."

"I can't."

"Slow it down. You're going to pass out otherwise. Otto, who was that other guy? What's his name?"

"I don't know. They never tell me."

"Who's they?"

"I don't know that, either."

"Okay, who do you work for?"

"I'm a chemist." He gasped for breath. "At Native Iron."

"Who's your boss?"

"A manager."

"Stop lying. And sit up."

The man let out a loud wail and writhed on the ground. "They'll be back soon. For both of us."

"Listen, Otto, this is your last chance to die with a clear conscience. Who do you work for?" Kamp cocked the Pepperbox pistol.

"The man who runs Native Iron. Joseph Moore. But he takes orders from someone else."

"Moore ordered you to do the things you did."

"What?"

"You're the one who rigged the explosion in the mine in order to kill Roy Kunkle. And Silas Ownby's house. You're the chemist. You set it all up."

"I did." He let his head fall back on the ground.

Kamp could see that the man wasn't going to die. The bullet had struck the bridge of his eyeglasses, slowing it down so that the slug lodged in his face with part of it still showing. Apart from a broken nose and the bleeding, he was probably fine.

"Lie here, and don't move. I'll get bandages. Give me the key to the cabin."

The man fished in his pocket and handed him a skeleton key.

Kamp said, "No explosion this time."

The man shook his head, and Kamp went in through the front door. Once inside, he saw two one-pound gunpowder tins on the floor, both empty. He pulled the sheet off the object he'd seen through the window. It was made of wood with brass wheels and gears. Kamp had never seen such a contraption. He took a closer look

420 | KURT B. DOWDLE

and saw that it was a press of some kind, a coin press. He ran back out the door, and by the time he reached the backyard, the man had gotten to his feet and had started shambling toward the woods. Kamp pulled the pistol from his belt and fired into the air. The man stopped.

He said, "Here's the deal, Otto. You can come with me, or you can make a run for it, and I'll shoot you."

The man said, "You don't understand. We're dead either way."

"In that case start running."

28

The chemist decided not to run, choosing instead to let Kamp treat his wounds. Kamp removed the bullet with his thumb and forefinger. He tore the bedsheet into strips and packed one of them into the hole in the chemist's face. Since the wound was directly between the man's eyes, he had to wrap the dressing so that it blocked the chemist's vision.

Kamp said, "Let's go."

"Where?"

He guided the man back up the trail he'd followed to get there and found the sack he'd dropped on the ground. Together, they made their way to Silas Ownby's property. By the time they reached the wreckage of the mansion, only one fire wagon remained, with two firemen dousing the last of the embers. Kamp recognized them by face but not by name.

He approached the two men and gave a wave. "Evening, gentlemen."

The first fireman said, "Evening. *Wie gehts?*"

"Oh, it goes. Yourself?"

"Yah, it goes." The fireman tipped his helmet back on his forehead and gestured to the ruined house, "Jeezis crackers, what a *schlamassel.*"

The second fireman looked at the chemist and said, "Who's this?"

Kamp said, "Otto Vordemgentschenfelde."

"Hurt in the explosion?"

"Not exactly. Say, would you fellas mind giving us a lift back to town?"

"Why, sure."

Kamp helped the chemist climb into the wagon, and then he hauled himself in as well and lay down amidst the hoses with the gun barrel pointed at his fellow passenger. The fire wagon rocked to and fro along the rutted road up South Mountain. The firefighters talked about the day they'd had and how they wished for it to end, and the chemist crouched on his side, cradling his face. Kamp lay on his back and took in a long, cold breath and then exhaled a cloud of steam. He watched the starry host appear in the clear night sky, one tiny, silver emblem after the other. He felt the wagon crest the mountain, and he sat up so that he could look down at the glow of fires at Native Iron. A few more lines of the poem he'd been remembering when Daniel Knecht first flashed into view came back to him now. But most of it still wouldn't come to him, and he began to feel drowsy. The chemist had stopped moving, but Kamp made himself stay awake anyway.

When they reached the bottom of Wyandotte Hill, Kamp said, "Can you take us to the hospital?"

Half an hour later he unloaded the chemist from the wagon, tipped his hat to the firemen and rapped his knuckles on the front door of the hospital. The nurse who'd had him thrown out weeks before appeared at the window next to the door.

She slid the window open and said, "Who's there?"

"Evening."

She hissed, "Oh, for the love o' Pete. It's after midnight. Come back tomorrow."

"I have an injured man with me. See for yourself."

He heard the lock turning, and then the front door creaked open. The nurse held a candle, and Kamp walked the chemist into the light. Blood had seeped from the hole in his face and through the bandages giving him the look of a mummified Cyclops.

Kamp said, "Some men are going to come looking for him. You need to find a safe place for him, safer than the place you put Druckenmiller."

"Sir, you cannot come here making strange demands in the middle of—"

"Don't let anyone know where he is. Not even the police. And you probably want to have someone take a look at his face. He's been shot. I'll be back tomorrow to pick him up." And he stepped back into the darkness.

The early spring moonlight lit Kamp's way through the streets of the sleeping town, and he felt a profound calm settle over his world. He had passed through fatigue, the intensity of the day having long since drained out of him. His mind went quiet until all he could hear, all that existed, was the crunching of his boots on the road and the solemn notes of a great horned owl. He let his soul drift. He let it drift fathoms below the surface of the earth and then back to ground level and up and out into the sky. He traveled beyond calamities and collisions, explosions, broken bones, lost limbs, flashing gun barrels, beyond motives and malice, beyond the cosmos and beyond change itself. Along the way he saw all the phantoms he'd been chasing, the man irredeemable, the father unknown, the boy lost and gone. He saw each crime in sharp detail, the urge that incited it and the lust that led to its consummation. He saw Shaw's face as well as his daughter's, radiating, blazing out from their own light. He traveled to the beginning of the present and in it, the end. He intuited that this phenomenon could be attributed in part or entirely to the injuries to his head. He might not have been like this before. Kamp couldn't remember.

He let his soul float back into his body until he heard his footfalls on the earth and felt the breath in his chest. He began thinking about his investigation again, and he knew he could prove nearly everything. He had truth, physical evidence such as the coin. And he had documents outlining the business dealings among the conspirators. He had witnesses like Anton "Duny" Kunkle and Nyx Bauer as well as a confession from the chemist. He knew he lacked two pieces of information, the list of the members of the Order and the identity of the man who killed Jonas and Rachel Bauer. He believed he knew how to find each one.

But what he understood most clearly was that no matter how well he put it all together, neither the preponderance of the evidence nor the coherence of his fact patterns would make any of it mean anything. The powers that be would never use what he'd learned to hold the perpetrators to account. In that sense Daniel Knecht's death had merely been a sacrifice of sorts, an expiation for past, present and future sins. And since the sacrifice had been made and made in a most dramatic fashion, and the gods appeased thereby, no one else had to pay. At least for a while.

Not that it mattered to Kamp. He knew he would pursue all matters to their logical conclusion, in this case the completion of his investigation. He knew the forces arrayed against him would also seek his destruction. The slaughter would continue unabated, but in all their attempts to stop him, he knew they would fail.

He made it back before dawn to the place where his house had been. He went into the slaughterhouse and lay down so that his body blocked the door. Kamp felt a warm buzzing in his knees and fell asleep immediately. When he awoke, morning rays slanted in wherever they could, through knotholes in the boards and narrow gaps in the roof. He rolled over onto his side and saw his cache of county records in the spot where he'd left it. He opened the bag and began riffling through birth certificates, searching for the name Mabel Schenker. Not there. He switched to looking through marriage licenses and found a license from three years prior for a man named Rudolf Schenker and a woman named Mabel Arndt. Arndt. He switched back to birth certificates and discovered one for Mabel Arndt as well as one for her brother, Hugh Arndt. George Richter's hired man. The fact that a woman who worked in Silas Ownby's home was the sister of a man who participated in the hanging of Daniel Knecht proved nothing, but it seemed a vital link.

Kamp pulled his boots on, left the slaughterhouse and walked down the path and onto the road, going straight in the direction of George Richter's house. He carried the pistol he'd taken from the chemist, a Colt Pocket Revolver. He went to Richter's front door as he did the night Jonas and Rachel Bauer were murdered and started banging.

He said, "Richter! Richter!" He pounded on the door a few more times. A bleary-eyed George Richter swung the door open.

"Kamp?"

He pushed his way in and closed the door behind him.

"Sit down, George." Richter backed up slowly and took a seat in a chair in the front room. "Where's your man, Hugh Arndt?"

"Why, I don't know. What's the—"

"Where's he supposed to be right now? Where is he?"

The color rose in George Richter's face. "Ach, I don't *know* where he is. I let him go two weeks ago."

"Let him go?"

"Fired him."

"Why?"

Richter boomed, "None of your goddamned business! I sent him away, and he left." Richter's eyes went to the shotgun propped next to the entrance to the kitchen.

Kamp pulled the Colt from his pocket and pointed it at Richter.

Richter said, "Are you out of your goddamned *geisht?*"

"Show me where he lived, George. And don't go near that gun." Richter got to his feet and went back out the front door, grumbling.

Richter said, "You know I stood up for you after that rotten business with that fiend Knecht, after the way you acted so dumb. Well, not no more. Not no more."

"Where'd he stay, George?"

"Christ! I'm taking you there." Kamp followed Richter to the carriage house and walked up the stairs.

Richter said, "Now, don't get all *shnarrich.* I'm just going to open the door to this room. This is where Hugh lived."

Kamp pressed the barrel to the back of Richter's neck as Richter opened the door. Richter stepped into the room, and he followed. The room was empty.

Richter turned around and said, "Happy now?"

Kamp ran to the house of John and Charlotte Fogel and went straight for the back door. Through the kitchen window, he saw Charlotte Fogel cooking breakfast. One of the younger Bauer girls was helping her. He didn't see Nyx. Kamp rapped on the back door and waited until

Charlotte Fogel answered. When she saw him at the door, she stiffened and gave him a tense smile.

"Good morning," she said.

"Good morning, Mrs. Fogel. May I see Nyx, please?"

"Oh, well, I don't know. She's sleeping."

"Is John here?"

"Yes, well, no."

"Which?"

"He's working."

"Mrs. Fogel, I need to talk to Nyx immediately. Please wake her up. Hurry."

"Well, I just don't—"

Kamp rushed past Charlotte Fogel and bounded up the stairs to the second floor. He opened each bedroom door until he found Nyx. She was sleeping on her stomach, face turned to the side and obscured by her hair.

"Nyx! Nyx!"

She rolled slowly onto her back and rubbed her forehead. "Oh, you're back. I'll talk to you later."

"Nyx, I have to talk to you. Listen."

"Hang on. I'm naked."

Kamp stepped out of the room and closed the door. He heard someone come in the front door downstairs and then a man's voice. John Fogel. He could hear Charlotte Fogel talking excitedly and then John Fogel called up the stairs. "Kamp, I need you to come down once. Kamp!"

Nyx said, "All right, I'm dressed."

Kamp heard John Fogel's heavy boots on the stairs. Fogel said, "You *daresn't* talk to her!"

He went back in Nyx's room and locked the door behind him. He turned to look at Nyx, who had a bemused expression.

She said, "Boy, you just got here, an' you're already in trouble with old man Fogel."

"Nyx, I figured it all out. I figured out what they wanted from your father, what they were looking for in your house."

John Fogel banged on the bedroom door. "Open this door! Nadine, are you all right?"

"What?"

"A list of names. Where's the locket?"

"Locket?"

"Your mother's silver locket. The one she was wearing when it happened. I saw you wearing it one day. Did you ever look inside it?"

"No."

Fogel shouted, "Open this goddamned door!"

Nyx focused on him. "I didn't want to wear it anymore. I hid it in our old house."

"Let's go."

Nyx said, "Wait." She dove under the bed and pulled out the Sharps and a black canvas haversack. When she stood up and nodded at him, he opened the door and pushed past John Fogel with Nyx following immediately behind. They scrambled down the stairs and out of the house.

He knew George Richter would have had time by now to tell whoever he was going to tell that Kamp was in the neighborhood. Someone would soon be looking for him. Kamp and Nyx jogged the road to house where Jonas and Rachel Bauer had lived. As they reached the front yard, they heard hoof beats on the road.

Kamp said, "They're coming."

Nyx said, "Back door."

Kamp watched the road as he ran around the back of the house. A dray wagon stopped in front of the house. Three men jumped out running with pistols drawn. Nyx went in the back door of the house with Kamp following. Once inside, he looked for the lock on the door. It was gone.

Nyx said, "No lock here, either. And none on the cellar doors."

He looked for a way to block the door and found nothing. He said, "Where's the locket?"

"Down there." She motioned to the cellar.

"Show me."

Nyx ran for the cellar. Kamp walked backward, pistol pointed toward the back door. When he reached the top of the cellar stairs, he pulled the cellar door closed behind him and hustled down into the darkness. He heard footsteps on the kitchen floor, and then a man's voice.

"We don't want to hurt either one of you, 'specially not that girl!"

Another man said, "Yah, 'specially not her." Kamp heard the men searching the rooms upstairs.

He called to Nyx, "Did you find it?"

"Not yet. It's too dark."

Kamp felt along the floor for the punt gun and found it. Then he popped open a can of powder and poured a considerable amount down the barrel. He took Shaw's handkerchief from his pocket, tore it in two and stuffed one half of it in the muzzle, then he poured in two pounds of shot.

The man yelled again, "Why don't you send that girl out, and then we can talk."

Nyx screamed, "Why don't you shove it up your ass!"

Kamp stuffed the other half of the handkerchief in the muzzle and packed it as tight as it would go. The cellar door swung open, and sunlight spilled down the stairs. Kamp dragged the punt gun across the floor and realized he had no way to point the massive weapon up the stairs. He scrambled back across the floor and found the chest that held the personal effects of Jonas and Rachel Bauer. Kamp slid the chest next to the gun. He looked up the cellar stairs and saw a man looking back at him. It was the same man he'd seen with the chemist. Kamp ducked back into the darkness.

The man said, "You won't escape. And you don't need to. People just want this to stop. If you're reasonable, we won't hand you over to the mob."

Kamp propped the barrel of the punt gun on the chest. He felt Nyx crawl beside him.

She said, "I found it. The locket."

"Cover your ears, and watch the bulkhead."

Nyx pressed her palms tightly against her head. Kamp watched the stairs.

The man came running down the stairs, firing his pistol with the second man following right behind. At the same moment, the bulkhead doors swung open and the third man jumped down into the cellar.

Kamp waited until he could see both men on the stairs and then fired the punt gun, which erupted with a colossal *bang*. The blast took off the first man's legs, and the rest of him toppled to the bottom of the stairs, eyes staring straight up. The second man was hit in both shins and fell into the cellar as well. Kamp grabbed Nyx's wrist, and they stepped over the bodies. The second man grabbed Nyx by the ankle. She gave him a kick to the face, ran up the stairs and out the front door. The man who'd come in through the bulkhead doors did not emerge from the house. Nyx ran for the wagon.

Kamp called to her, "They'll be on the road," and he jumped down into the brambles. A train whistle sounded. "We'll catch out."

Nyx followed him, and they ran for the tracks. He looked back and saw the third man leaving in the wagon. Kamp and Nyx jogged alongside the tracks as the train reached them.

"Do it just like me." As he ran, Kamp waited for an open boxcar to appear. When it did, he leapt for the grab bar and caught it square with his left hand. His arm wailed with pain, but Kamp hung on, lifting his left foot onto the step. From there, he let himself glide into the car.

"Now you."

Nyx threw the Sharps and the haversack into the car and repeated his moves, albeit more gracefully than Kamp. She landed in the boxcar on her feet.

Nyx said, "Were those the guys?"

"Which guys?"

"The guys who killed my parents."

"No. Nyx, where is it?"

"What?"

"The locket. Open it."

"Right, right." Nyx took it from her pocket and opened it. It held a small, folded piece of paper. "Son of a bitch, so there it is." She unfolded it.

Kamp said, "Kunkle either wrote it and gave it to your father, or your father made his own copy. Read it."

Nyx squinted at the paper. "It says, 'FOR W.G.,O.V., J.M., J.S.'"

"Anything else?"

"At the bottom it says, 'Only 4' in quotation marks."

He stared up at the ceiling of the boxcar. "That could mean there's only four guys in the group, or he only got four of the names."

Nyx said, "Well, who are they?"

"Walker Gray, Joseph Moore and James Shelter. Those are the guys that run the companies. Iron, railroad, shipping."

"But not coal."

Kamp said, "Yah, why?"

"Well, you said these guys killed those miners. But they had nothing to do with coal mining."

"You're right. But Roy Kunkle knew who they were."

Nyx said, "Who's O.V.?"

"The chemist."

Kamp reflected on the implications of the list and whether it proved anything. It proved that someone wrote it and that the initials corresponded to what he already knew, or at least suspected. It was a credible link between what had happened to Roy Kunkle, then to Jonas and Rachel Bauer, and then to Daniel Knecht. The document itself provided no details, no context, no explanation of the meaning of the initials. But if one understood the components of the tale, the list was the central cohesive element, the linchpin. Given everything else Kamp knew, the list was evidence. As for "Only 4," he felt certain it meant that Kunkle was told only four of the names in the Order but probably the most important four. There were others. Perhaps there wasn't time to get the other names. Perhaps the informant, the rat squirrel, didn't know any others, though he knew there were more. The Judge, for example, wasn't on the list. Kamp felt a small measure of relief, but he knew the absence of the Judge's name meant nothing with respect to whether and to what extent the Judge was involved. For that matter, Kamp knew his understanding of the letters and their meaning was a story, too, one of several he could imagine.

Nyx handed the paper to him and said, "So *these* are the men who did it, the guys who killed my parents."

"They're responsible, but they didn't actually do it, no."

"Who *did*?"

"That guy Hugh Arndt. George Richter's man."

"Why aren't we going after him?"

"I looked for him. I couldn't find him. He left Richter's. He's gone."

The train click-clacked back and forth on the tracks, and Kamp lay down on his back, while Nyx watched the trees going by. They continued over the bridge and toward the Third Street Station.

He sat up and said, "When the train stops, jump off. Don't look around. Just run." They scanned the yard as the train eased to a halt. Nyx hopped from the boxcar, and Kamp clambered down after her. She took the rifle and the haversack, and he held the pistol.

He said, "Follow me." He cut down a series of alleys until he reached the back door at the shop of the druggist E. Wyles. He tried the doorknob and then banged on the door.

"Emma! Emma! Let us in!"

The door swung open, and there was E. Wyles herself, hair tied back and wearing her white blouse. She motioned for them to come in, and when they did, she embraced Nyx and said to Kamp, "Whatever you're doing, you better finish it."

"Yah, yah, I know. People are looking for me."

"You don't know the half of it."

"Emma, I need you to look out for Nyx for a while."

Nyx said, "As if I need anyone to—"

"She's safe here."

29

K amp shut the door behind him and ran down the alley. He hustled the few blocks between E. Wyles' shop and the impressive headquarters of Native Iron, a tall brick and glass building overlooking the ironworks. He walked in the front door, went straight for the stairwell and began climbing. He walked up the stairs until he reached the door at the top. Kamp emerged into a carpeted hallway that led to heavy oak double doors. He walked to the doors and tried one of the brass handles. Locked. He removed his hat, put the pistol in his belt and rapped lightly on the door.

A woman opened the door, smiled and said, "May I help you?"

Kamp said, "Yes, may I see Joseph Moore, please?"

"I'm sorry, Mr. Moore is busy right now."

She moved to close the door, but Kamp stopped it with his hand. "Mr. Moore wants to speak with me. He does."

"I'm sorry, Mr. Moore does not wish to speak with you."

"Please let him know I'm here. Police business."

The woman took in a sharp breath and stiffened her neck. "May I have your name, please?"

"Kamp."

"And your first name?"

"Please tell him I'm here."

The woman closed the door and locked it. A few moments later the door opened again, and Kamp stood face to face with Joseph Moore, outfitted smartly in a grey flannel three-piece suit and silk tie, minus the jacket.

Moore said, "Good afternoon. Pardon my informality. Warm weather. Follow me, please."

He turned on his heel and walked back into a large, wood paneled office that took up half the floor, including the corner that directly overlooked the iron-making operation. Kamp followed him in.

Moore said, "Thank you, Margaret. That will be all," and he took a seat on the edge of his massive wood desk and crossed his right leg over his left. He gestured for Kamp to sit down as well, then said, "I appreciate that you took the time to visit, though I admit I thought I'd see you sooner."

Kamp remained standing and said, "How's that?" He scanned the office, looking at the pictures on the walls. He took a long look at a large painting, depicting a battle.

Moore said, "Magnificent, isn't it? The British fighting the Indians in the Seven Years' War. Men talk about competition in business. That right there is real competition, the kind businessmen know nothing about. You've tasted war. You understand."

"Why did you think I'd be here sooner?"

Moore uncrossed his legs and put both feet solidly on the floor. "I'd heard you were diligent and tenacious. I also heard your theory about that situation with that poor fellow and his wife, what was his name, Boyer?"

"Bauer."

"Yes, Bauer. I heard you decided to investigate the matter as if it were part of a conspiracy. Very shrewd. That takes a certain kind of mind."

"You ought to know. It was part of your plan."

Moore held out his hands, palms up. "Why would I do such a thing? Why? I've already been blessed by the good lord far beyond what any man deserves. Why would I want to harm anyone?"

"Your man Otto told me he reported to you. He said that you ordered him to set off the explosion that killed those men in the mine. And that you ordered him to kill Silas Ownby."

Moore shook his head. "Such a shame. Though I did mean to thank you for the work you did there."

Kamp raised his eyebrows.

Moore continued, "Otto seemed like a good man and a loyal employee. A brilliant man, a genius, but as it turned out, a malicious one. I should have paid closer attention, but I chose to see the best in him. I'm grateful that you stopped him when you did, although I'm heartbroken that he destroyed so many lives before you apprehended him. As far as I'm concerned, you've done the community a great service. You're a hero. At least he won't be able to hurt anyone anymore."

"Why not?"

"I was informed that he perished from his injuries in the hospital. It was you who shot him, correct? Yes, well, in any case it's over and done with. And regardless of what he may have said and what you may believe, I have no quarrel with you. I hope we can go hunting, together. Someday."

Kamp said, "I'm compiling a report. I'll file it with the county and state attorneys. In it, I'll provide all the information I know. Every detail, outlining the existence of the Fraternal Order of the Raven and its members. Including this." He took the coin out of his pocket and held it up.

Moore smiled and said, "Ah, you found a coin, one of the first ones we made, I believe. Brilliant. We plan to make many, many more. We'll change the design, though. That one's just a first stab, really. We'll strike plenty for the celebration. They'll commemorate the creation of the most important enterprise this nation has ever seen, Black Feather Consolidated. As for your report, I admire the enthusiasm you've brought to your investigation, and I understand you must report everything, as you see fit. Thank you for your service to the community. Incidentally, I've spoken with my associate at the railroad, Walker Gray. You remember him. He is in complete agreement with me. We value and esteem your efforts."

Joseph Moore stood up and gestured politely to the door of his office, where two uniformed private security men stood waiting.

Moore said, "These gentlemen will help you find the exit. Good day, Kamp."

The men hurried Kamp down the stairs, through the lobby, and out the door. He walked down Third Street and took a left on Iroquois. He headed straight for the Monocacy and went in the front door. The lobby was empty, and the manager did not appear to block his path. Kamp climbed the stairs to the fourth floor and went down the hallway to the door where he'd seen Philander Crow dead on the floor. He knocked on the door, and the woman he'd met before, Elise, answered it.

She said, "What a surprise."

"How are you?"

"I'm fine, I'm fine." She looked at his clothes, tattered and bloodstained and said, "How are *you*?"

"May I speak with your husband?"

"My husband?"

"He's here, isn't he?"

"Why, yes, he's here. Please come in."

He followed her into the apartment.

She said, "Please wait," and she disappeared into a back room.

Kamp surveyed the front room. The twin babies were sleeping in their cribs. Spring sunlight slanted down through the window and onto the Persian rug in the center of the floor. When Elise returned, a man followed her, a man he'd had never seen before. But Kamp knew who we was.

The man said, "Kamp."

"James Shelter."

"It's good to meet you." James Shelter crossed the room and shook Kamp's hand. "Why don't we talk in my study?"

He turned and walked down the hall with Kamp following. James Shelter sat down in a leather chair in front of the desk in his study.

Shelter said, "Sit down. Please, please," and he motioned for Kamp to sit in an identical chair across from him. He produced two pipes and a tin of tobacco. "May I offer you a smoke?"

"No, thanks."

"Well, I hope you don't mind if have one."

James Shelter packed the bowl and struck a match. He took a few short puffs to get it burning and then he slid open the window next to him and sat back down. "She hates the smoke. Says it's unhealthy. Imagine. Now, what would you like to talk about?"

Kamp studied James Shelter. To say that his features were nondescript would have been an overstatement. He possessed an exceedingly regular face and regular build. He had no distinguishing features of any kind, except, Kamp noticed, that when Shelter spoke, a shimmering intellect radiated.

"Mr. Shelter, I've been investigat—"

"James."

"I've been investigating a series of crimes, beginning with the murders of Jonas and Rachel Bauer. "

"Among other things."

"What do you mean?"

"You've done other things besides investigate crimes."

"That's not my point."

James Shelter settled into his chair and took a long, contemplative pull on the pipe. "Of course it's not."

"During the course of my investigation, I've learned that the Jonas and Rachel Bauer were murdered for the sole purpose of covering up another crime, namely an intentional explosion in a coal mine that killed six men. The purpose of the explosion was to eliminate a man named Roy Kunkle, a highly vocal critic of the management of the mine."

"You're saying, let me understand, are you saying this Kunkle was killed for being a troublemaker?"

"No. Another man, Daniel Knecht, was summarily hanged for the murders of Jonas and Rachel Bauer, and while he was complicit in the plot, he did not carry out the crime and so was wrongly executed. The explosion in the mine was carried out by a chemist, an employee of Native Iron, Otto Vordemgentschenfelde. The chemist was responsible for at least one other explosion, the one that destroyed the home of Silas Ownby. The chemist also had a hand in the creation of silver coins that were delivered to Roy Kunkle and Silas Ownby with the intention of striking fear not only into them but also into the general populace who became aware of what happened to people who received such a coin."

James Shelter leaned forward in his chair. His eyes twinkled with revelation. "Go on."

"Kunkle was murdered because he stumbled onto the existence of a secret society. He'd been given a list of names that made up the partial membership of an organization called the Fraternal Order of the Raven. Since Kunkle knew that he would likely be killed, he gave the list to Jonas Bauer, and both men were murdered because they'd seen the list. In the course of my investigation, attempts were made on my life and on the life of my family. All of these attempts were unsuccessful."

Shelter sat in rapt attention. He said, "I love it."

"The Fraternal Order of the Raven is really just a shadow organization that exists for the purpose of carrying out criminal acts in order to expedite business dealings among seemingly legitimate business enterprises, namely Native Iron, Lehigh Railroad and your shipping company, Castor and Pollux. The three companies are being combined to form Black Feather Consolidated, a single entity that will effectively monopolize these industries in the region."

"Bravo."

"And I've learned, James, that you're at the center of all of it. You're in charge. The Fraternal Order of the Raven is, in essence, your creation, and ultimately the responsibility is yours."

James Shelter sat back in his chair and let out a long breath. He said, "Anything else?"

"That's it."

Shelter squinted and looked at the ceiling. "Breathtaking, Kamp, just breathtaking."

"Did I get it all?"

"You missed a few details here and there. For instance, I didn't create the Order. And there were plans you couldn't have known about. If Ownby hadn't been killed in the explosion, for instance, we planned to burn him alive during the upcoming Black Feather celebration. We were going to set the viewing stand on fire by making it look like a mishap with the fireworks and then handcuff him to the stand. By the time investigators got to the scene, the handcuffs would have been gone. It would have appeared as if he'd tripped and been knocked unconscious and then, alas, consumed by the inferno. That type of thing. Exploding his house was just as good, albeit not quite as dramatic. Or satisfying. No one really remembers anything, though, not even the catastrophes. Everything changes too quickly these days."

"He was a good man. And none of the other people you had killed deserved what happened to them."

"I don't disagree. But I gave you the opportunity to kill some people, too, and truth be told, you probably didn't mind. All in all, I give you credit. You comported yourself with great vigor. And you solved almost all of the riddles. The gist, the machinery, the moving parts.

You figured it out. I told them you would. I put my money on you. And I won."

Kamp said, "I can prove everything, too. I have evidence. Witnesses. I'm writing a report for the county and the commonwealth."

"That's fine. I only have one question."

"Shoot."

"Why bother telling me?"

"Because I want you to leave me alone."

Shelter said, "You want to make peace."

"Tell Moore and Gray and all the assholes chasing me to stop."

"I already did, believe it or not. No one will bother you or your family, at least no one who works for me. And as for the bodies you've left strewn around the greater Bethlehem area, I can assure you that the police and probably everyone else has already forgotten about them."

Kamp said, "Why?"

"Why what?"

"Why did you call them off?"

"The Judge made a deal with me. You can ask him about it."

"What about Hugh Arndt, the man who killed Jonas and Rachel Bauer?"

Shelter said, "Yes, well, you're on your own with that one. Bit of a loose cannon, isn't he?" Kamp stood up to leave. Shelter took a puff on his pipe and said, "I know it all seems personal. It isn't."

Kamp passed Elise Shelter on his way out. He tipped his hat to her, said, "Goodbye," and shut the door behind him.

EPILOGUE

In the days following his conversation with James Shelter, it became obvious to Kamp that he was, in fact, no longer being opposed by the forces that had previously been arrayed against him. A week after the talk, and a year to the day after he officially became the detective for the Bethlehem City Police Department, Kamp tendered his resignation. He handed a letter to Sam Druckenmiller, who had been promoted to Assistant Chief. Druckenmiller said he would deliver the letter to the Chief of Police and said nothing else. Kamp noticed a brass plaque on the wall of the station that read, "Dedicated to the fallen Markus Lenz, Deputy Chief of Police. May the light of his integrity be a beacon to all."

From there, he visited the Judge one last time. Kamp asked the Judge about the nature of the deal that resulted in the cessation of hostilities against him. The Judge told him that he'd had to give Shelter three of his favorite properties and that all things considered, it was "a small price to pay" for Kamp's well-being. The Judge did not say why he bartered for Kamp's life in the end, or why Shelter took the deal.

Rather than thanking the Judge, Kamp asked for the deed to the property as well as the Judge's tobacco pouch. The Judge handed over both, willingly. He also presented Kamp with a check from the City of Bethlehem in the amount of one thousand dollars. The Judge said it was a bonus for "service far above and beyond the call of duty." Knowing that he would try to refuse it, the Judge added that the bonus could not be considered "hush money," as everyone knew that Kamp would freely share what he'd learned with anyone who cared to ask, as well as anyone who didn't. Along those lines, Kamp wrote a lengthy and detailed report, including all the names, dates, and other relevant facts he'd amassed in the course of his investigation. In the finished report Kamp delivered to the commonwealth, he included the coin. He expected no response of any kind, and he received none. He tied up all the other loose ends he could think of as well, including the return of the unloaded Pepperbox pistol to Anton "Duny" Kunkle, who did not say thank you.

On the day he returned to his property from delivering his reports, Kamp found Joe waiting for him next to the slaughterhouse. Joe extended his hand, and Kamp took it. He showed Joe the tobacco pouch, and the two men buried it at the base of a tree in the backyard. In the following weeks, He and Joe hauled away what remained of the house where he and Shaw had lived. They tore down the slaughterhouse as well. The hen house they left standing. Once everything had been cleared away, they chose another site on the property, back from the road and closer to the creek, for a new house. One by one, all of his neighbors appeared and began to help. Within days, the foundation had been dug, and Kamp used the money from the bonus to pay for all the materials. Over the course of the summer, they built the house.

On the day they finished the front steps, Joe said, "Look who it is."

Kamp stood up, wiped the sweat from his brow with the back of his hand and turned around. Shaw was there with the baby strapped to her back. Tears rolled down both cheeks. He ran to her and hugged her and kissed the baby.

"You're here."

Shaw said, "We're here."

The next morning Joe told him he'd had a dream, and in the dream he'd been given the baby's true name. As such, they could proceed with the traditional naming ceremony, which Joe would lead. Kamp, Shaw and Joe found a suitable place, a clearing on top of the mountain on the property for the ceremony, and on the afternoon of the day Joe chose, the four of them gathered there for the sacred ceremony.

What they didn't know was that a hunter was stalking them. Ever since he vacated George Richter's home, Hugh Arndt had been waiting, waiting for everyone to forget that he'd gone missing. And waiting for Kamp to let his guard down. He hadn't traveled far from Bethlehem, no farther than Easton. And during the two weeks prior to the day of the ceremony, he'd been living in a tent just beyond the border of the property. Each day he'd watched them from the woods at the tree line. He blamed Kamp for everything that had gone wrong for him since the day Daniel Knecht died. He'd watched with a loaded rifle at his side, waiting for the right moment to exact his revenge on Kamp as well as his family. In his opinion the whole lot of them deserved to go.

When he saw the family walking the trail up the mountain, Hugh Arndt realized the moment had arrived. He waited until they'd walked a safe distance ahead, then started to follow, knowing that with each step, they'd walk farther and farther from where anyone could see what was about to happen. The family reached the clearing. Joe started a fire and smudged Kamp's and Shaw's faces with the sacred smoke. He invited the Seven Directions, and then he asked Shaw to let him hold the baby.

When he'd come within a hundred feet of Kamp and his family, Hugh Arndt circled around behind them, searching for a place with a clear line of sight. He kept his eye on them as he moved, stepping lightly and watching the ceremony from a distance. He noticed their full attention was on each other. Their guard was down for sure. When he'd found the right spot, Arndt leaned against a tree to steady himself and he sighted the first of his targets, that son of a bitch Kamp.

Shaw handed the baby to Joe, who lovingly cradled her and whispered in her ear. He then held her up with both hands. Arndt saw him do this and thought it would be fitting to shoot the baby first, and then Kamp. He shifted his aim. What Arndt didn't know was that another hunter was in the woods that day and that a different rifle barrel was pointed at him.

Nyx Bauer had woken up that morning, knowing that the day for Hugh Arndt to pay for his sins had come. She dressed carefully and wove her hair into a tight braid so that it wouldn't blow across her face at an inopportune moment. Kamp had invited her the previous day to the naming ceremony, and she had declined, sensing that she might need to protect him and his family. Since she knew where the ceremony would take place, she'd scouted the area early that morning, looking for the place where a sniper would most likely set up. She'd watched from a distance when Kamp and his family started up the trail, and she wasn't surprised to see Hugh Arndt stalking them. So focused was he on them that she had no trouble following him up the trail without him noticing. And when he selected the place she knew he'd fire from, she was already in her own spot.

At a distance of fifty yards from Arndt, Nyx sat cross-legged on a flat rock. She found this position to be the most relaxing for shooting. Nyx had cleaned and loaded the Sharps earlier that morning, and now she raised it to her shoulder. Nyx felt her breathing slow as she looked down the barrel at her parents' killer. She didn't want to disturb the ceremony any more than necessary, and so in spite of her urge to make the man suffer, Nyx resolved to finish him with a single shot. Besides, if she fired a second time, Kamp would know where to find her. As Arndt raised his own rifle and quieted his body, Nyx squeezed her trigger gently. The Sharps erupted, and the bullet struck Hugh Arndt in the left temple. He crumpled silently to the soft ground beneath him.

Kamp and Shaw were startled by the gunshot, and Joe held the baby close to his chest. They all waited a minute and then assumed that it was just a hunter passing through the woods. Joe lifted the baby to the heavens, and in a voice choked with emotion, he spoke her true name. After that, Joe passed the ceremonial pipe.

They sang and danced and celebrated the child, and their ceremony was complete.

That night, Kamp sat in a chair on the front porch, watching the day going down to dusk. Both Shaw and Joe noticed that although his work was finished and his family intact, Kamp had a troubled expression on his face. They stood on either side of him, and each put a hand on his shoulder.

Shaw said, "It's over."

Joe said, "Their world is no longer your world. Let them go."

That night in bed, Kamp lay close to Shaw with his sleeping daughter on his chest. He felt a powerful and all-encompassing fatigue overtake his body. Shaw heard him murmuring.

"I got it," Kamp said, "I remember it."

"Remember what?"

"That poem. I remember the whole thing."

Then Kamp went silent, and Shaw thought he was asleep.

He opened his eyes one more time and said, "When I was in the war, we walked everywhere."

Made in the USA
Middletown, DE
10 January 2016